Another Kind Of Light

A Biographical Novel

Gretta Curran Browne

SPI

Seanelle Publications Inc.

To My Beloved Ellena

Prologue

Italy
December 1816

In her father's house at Filetto in Northern Italy, seventeen-year-old Teresa Gamba, escorted by her maid, slowly made her way down the long staircase of her father's house dressed in a simple gown of white silk to indicate her purity.

She was the second of Count Ruggero Gamba's five pretty daughters, and the most attractive. Like many Italians from the northern parts of the country, Teresa's colouring was light; her hair fair. She possessed a kind of classic grace, for she had been well-tutored in all matters lady-like, so necessary to the daughter of a Count.

Yet she was not happy, for she had just left behind her sixteenth year, and had come home from school, having spent most of her life in education at Santa Chiara's Convent at Faenza, returning to her family only for a few short weeks during the summer holidays and at Christmas.

And now, she had thought, she would have all the time in the world to spend at home in the company of her brother and sisters; and the nuns and the strictness of their education would belong to the past.

Reaching the dark oak door of her father's study, her maid swiftly inspected Teresa's appearance one last time, and then knocked on the door, waiting for the call to enter.

A moment later Count Gamba called *"Entra,"* and the maid opened the door for Teresa to enter.

Teresa took a step inside the room, and suddenly came to a halt, incapable of moving any further, her face white with shock.

Standing next to her father was a young man of twenty-years old – her brother Pietro – and next to Pietro stood a tall elderly man with greying red hair and whiskers.

Her father came and took hold of her arm, walking her into the room. "Teresa, this is L'Conte Alessandro Guiccioli. He has asked to meet you."

Almost without thought, so well had she been trained, Teresa curtseyed silently to Count Guiccioli, and then lowered her eyes to hide her disappointment.

It was evening; the room was well lit, yet Count Guiccioli lifted a candle and began to walk in a circle around her, inspecting her from head to shoe. Not that he needed to, for he had seen Teresa Gamba on one occasion before, although she had not noticed him. He had studied her then, and liked what he saw. Most of all he liked the fact that she was the daughter of a Count, and as such, was a Countess in her own right, and so a worthy choice for him.

"Teresa," her father said, "has been educated to a degree of excellence. The Abbess of Santa Chiara's has claimed her as a prize pupil of the school. She can talk to you of Dante and Petrarch and has studied all the classics of our literature."

Count Guiccioli was not impressed. "The Church does not approve of Santa Chiara's methods of educating girls as if they were boys. The Church believes that too much learning is damaging to women."

"And yet Teresa is not damaged," answered her father with a proud smile. "To me, she is a perfect daughter."

Count Guiccioli passed a finger over one eyebrow. He was a clever man, skilled at making bargains, always ensuring that he got the best of it. He never allowed himself to appear eager, just mildly interested.

"I have conditions, to which she must agree," he said quietly, and then beckoned to his manservant who was standing like a mute in the corner of the room.

"Read, Paolo."

Paolo unfolded a square of paper and began to read aloud: — "Let her always determine to be a solace to me, and never a trouble. She should therefore always be cheerful with me, annoy no one in the house, ask politely for anything she wishes, but accept in silence any refusal."

Teresa glanced at her father who merely shrugged, saying to the Count: "That is no more than any husband would ask."

Paolo continued reading: — "Let her be true and frank, so that she will have no secrets from me, but let her be prudent in handing on my confidences to others.

"Let her be docile and ready to execute all my directions. And let her be faithful and beware of any appearances to the contrary."

Teresa waited for Paolo to read out the conditions for Count Guiccioli's side of the contract, but nothing further was said.

"Teresa, you may leave us now," her father said, and Teresa obediently curtseyed again and left the study, closing the door behind her.

"*Così?*" her maid inquired anxiously and Teresa collapsed into her arms. "Rosa, he is *old*! Older than my papa!"

Moments later she was surrounded by her clamouring sisters who dragged her into the sala where her mother sat smiling, ready to congratulate her.

"You should be happy, my child. You have been chosen by one of the richest men in Ravenna."

"But Mama, he is *old!*" Teresa protested. "At least eighty years old!"

"He is younger, barely sixty. A man of experience, so he will know how to look after you. L'Conte Alessandro Guiccioli is held in great respect in Ravenna."

"Si-ixty?" Teresa stammered. "More than forty years of life between us!"

"So he will die a long time before you do, and then

you will inherit his great fortune. You must do so, Teresa, for your family. We have four more daughters to secure, but with L'Conte Guiccioli as your husband, we will know your financial future is safe."

"I don't know," Teresa was still stammering. "I – am *afraid* – to marry – such a man."

Countess Gamba glanced around at Teresa's sisters with a commanding look in her eyes, and they all immediately obeyed, exclaiming how lucky Teresa was to have caught the eyes of such a wealthy man.

"You will have so many servants, Teresa, and all dressed in fine livery!"

"You will have your own box at the Opera!"

"A fine house all your own to rule as mistress!"

"And a carriage with *six* horses!"

Her mother interrupted. "Teresa, what special qualities did the nuns teach you at Santa Chiara's?"

"To be noble and self-sacrificing – but Mama, they teach that because they are *nuns* – and have sacrificed all to become a bride of *Cristo* – not the old Count Guiccioli!"

All protests were futile. It was the Italian way. The parents arranged the marriage and the daughter obeyed.

The two men remained in the study debating and wrangling over all the details, until the arrangement was finally agreed and concluded. The marriage would take place in three months. The contract was signed.

Count Guiccioli had driven a hard bargain. In return for her care and shelter, and the huge fortune that Teresa Gamba would one day inherit as his wife, her father, Count Ruggero Gamba, had agreed that Teresa's dowry on marriage would be the amount of scudi 45,000.

A large amount; and one which Count Alessandro Guiccioli needed quickly, to pay off his increasing debts.

~~~
~~~

By the time Teresa had returned to her bedroom she had worked herself into a rage, tears streaming from her eyes. Despite all the efforts of the nuns at Santa Chiara's, she was not noble nor self-sacrificing, she was proud and vain and had imagined that her husband in the future would be young and handsome.

"I cannot endure it, Rosa! To be married to a man more than forty years older than I! And twenty years older than my Papa! Even to think of it is more than I can bear!"

"Cara, *cara* ..." Rosa gathered the girl into her arms and soothingly hushed comforting words to her; but even as she did so, she was afraid for her master Count Gamba if the marriage did not proceed as agreed.

Rosa knew a lot about L'Conte Alessandro Guiccioli of Ravenna, more than she liked to know; but all of it was whispered gossip, and she had often wondered how much of it was true?

All the whispered gossip had been confided to her by Fanny Sylvestrini, her aunt, who lived in the household of the Count at the Palazzo Guiccioli in Ravenna, and had served as a maid to the Count's first and second wife.

Rosa glanced at Teresa now sitting alone at the window of her bedroom, staring out at the darkening evening and weeping silently, her hand constantly wiping at her face.

Had she been told that she would be Count Guiccioli's *third* wife?

Just the thought made Rosa shiver, for although they did not know it here in Filetto — in Ravenna there had been many whispers and rumours about the sudden deaths of both those wives.

Count Alessandro Guiccioli's first wife had been the Contessa Placidia Zinanni —"an ugly woman" — according to Fanny Sylvestrini, who was thirty years Guiccioli's elder, but she made up for her age by bringing him a large dowry, which made Guiccioli as rich as the highest ranking families in Ravenna.

During this time there were rumours of mysterious assassinations of any man who stood in his way, usually by dagger in a dark street at night. Not to be proved – no finger could point – but many had their suspicions.

"The sudden death by dagger one night of Domenico Manzoni," Fanny had said, "a rich landowner from whom the Count had bought a lot of land, and then had not paid, still caused rumours in the salas of Venice to this day."

The Gamba family, here in Filetto, would know nothing of this, and Fanny had bound Rosa to an oath of secrecy on the Gospels that would lead to Hell and Damnation if she ever broke her sworn oath.

"During his first marriage," Fanny had said, "Guiccioli seduced many of the maids and then dismissed and replaced them with others. Only to one maid did he stay true, Angelica Galliani, and she stayed true to him also, providing him with six illegitimate children before his wife found out and complained. So he sent his wife to a lonely country house, and did not allow her to return to her rightful place in the Palazzo, until she had made a will in his favour, leaving all she possessed to him. Soon after her return to the Palazzo, came her death.

"Oh, so many whispers of 'murder' and 'poison' from his enemies," said Fanny, "but he met all of them with a high head and spoke with honey on his lips about the sad loss of his wife, until all were silenced.

"Soon after," Fanny had said, "he married Angelica Galliani, legitimised his six children with her, although many scorned him for marrying a servant – and now Angelica has suddenly died!"

Again Rosa glanced at Teresa sitting at the window, her heart throbbing with fear, because now Count Guiccioli was already seeking a new wife – a young lady of wealth and rank this time – but why oh *why* did he have to choose one so young and innocent as her beloved Terasina?

Rosa began to weep, and then wail, until Teresa

rushed to her with love and tried to comfort her.

"Don't cry, Rosa. I know I cannot disobey Papa, but I have thought, and L'Conte Guiccioli is very old, so I will be good and kind and will regard him like I do my grandfather, until he dies, which Mama thinks will be soon."

Rosa stared at the girl in utter pity. Had she been taught *nothing* useful to woman by those nuns at Santa Chiara's? *Mio Dio* – what use would books and Italian literature be to the girl when she found herself locked inside a bedroom with an old murderer? No use at all.

Venice

December, 1816

Some two hundred miles north of Filetto, at Fusina, having left their carriages and horses stabled at the inn, two young men, Lord Byron and John Cam Hobhouse, walked down to the waterfront to hire a gondola to take them over to the island of Venice.

It was raining, so they selected one of the larger and more expensive gondolas, a *battello*, five-foot wide, and thirty-five feet long, which could accommodate six to eight people, and had a large black-wooden cabin built onto the mid-section of it. Because of its size it also had two gondoliers, one at the prow and one at the stern.

Curious, Byron spoke in Italian to one of the gondoliers about the cabin, and learned it was called a *felze*.

"The *felze?*" said the gondolier. "Out here, and on the sea, it is good for protection from the weather. In Venice, in the city, it is good for privacy from onlookers."

Byron smiled. "And do you sing as you row?"

The gondolier also smiled, but impatiently. "Signore, we sing only for the lovers, when asked to sing. But even when asked, we do *not* sing for anyone in this rain. Now please, Signore ..." He waved a hand for Byron to move under cover.

"*Grazie,*" said Byron, and stepped inside the *felze,* which was more comfortable than it looked from the outside – and very much like sitting down in a small floating drawing-room. The brocade upholstery of the sofa-like seat was red and soft and luxurious to sit on.

"This seat is almost as comfortable as the one in your carriage," Hobhouse said, and was even more gratified by the small window on either side of the cabin, draped in curtains of black lace. He pulled aside the curtain on his side and peered through the window. "I can't see Venice, not yet, not through this rain."

"How long," Byron asked, "did the gondolier you spoke with say it would take to get across the lagoon?"

"I didn't ask how long, but I know it is about five miles across."

"Oh well then, if there's nothing to see but sea ..." Byron settled himself in his seat, leaning back against the cushions and closing his eyes, enjoying the gentle swaying motion of the gondola as it glided over the water.

The front of the *felze* was open, and yet the only sound in the silence on the sea was the splashing of the oars and the gentle swishing of water against the sides of the gondola.

Tired out from all the travelling down from Milan and Verona, Hobhouse also settled himself back in the seat and closed his eyes, drifting into a gentle doze, until some time later the echo of the oars became louder and Byron opened his eyes, saying: "We must be under a bridge."

The gondolier, who was standing at the back of the boat behind the felze, on a raised deck, banged on the roof and shouted, "*Rialto!*"

Shortly afterwards they were landed under the canopy of the *Hotel della Gran Bretagne* on the Grand Canal – the Hotel of Great Britain – which lived up to its name when the hotel's manager greeted them in perfect English.

"Oh, thank God for that," Hobhouse murmured to Byron. "Unlike you, *I* don't speak Italian."

"And I speak it more fluently than accurately," Byron said. "But no matter. I'm told the Venetians use their hands a lot when speaking, so we can do the same."

"At first sight," Hobhouse said, "Venice to me looks like Cadiz or some handsome town – flooded."

Byron smiled. "You knew it would be so."

"Yes, but one has to actually *see* it, to believe it."

As soon as the manager of the hotel inspected the two passports, and saw the name of the youngest of the two Englishmen – Lord Byron – he waved away the Bellboys and personally escorted the two men up a magnificent staircase to their rooms of gold gildings and painted silks.

"My lord ...?" he said; and once again John Hobhouse noticed that Byron was given the best room, the largest and most opulent – and yet this very fact caused a stirring of uneasiness in Byron.

Years before, as an unknown student at Cambridge, he had loved going down to London just to stay in the hotels; but since his fame as a poet, and his recent experience in the Hotel d'Anglettere in Geneva when he had been watched and followed and spied upon at every moment during his stay there, he now had a horror of all hotels.

"I shan't stay here long," he said later to Hobhouse. "My main reason for coming to Venice, this out of the way place where few English tourists come now, was to enjoy some privacy for a change, to become anonymous and be able to enjoy life again."

"We have to stay here." Hobhouse was disturbed. "Have you forgotten that my brother and his wife will be joining us here in a few days, in *this* hotel, and by *my* arrangement. I can't just wander off now to somewhere else. Besides, that manager was not kow-towing to a famous poet, because I daresay no one in Venice has ever heard of you. He was merely being obsequious to your rank and title, nothing more."

"Are you sure?"

"I am certain."

"Oh, well then ..." Byron smiled and relaxed; until half an hour later when there was a knock on his door. He opened it to a stranger ... a white-haired Englishman with a delighted smile on his face and holding out a card.

"Ah, pray forgive my calling, but I was so excited when the manager gave me your room number. My name is Lansdowne, and I have come to introduce myself to the first poet of England."

After a pause, Byron looked cynically over his shoulder at Hobhouse who had been busily writing a letter. "Lord Byron, it seems you *are* known in Venice, because you have a visitor."

"What?" Hobhouse stared in confusion, and then, realising what prank Byron was playing, blurted out the first thing that came into his head – "Can't you see that I am *writing!*"

Byron looked at the stranger with an expression of true sympathy. "His lordship is very temperamental, and hates to be disturbed."

"I merely wished to see ... if I could be useful to him in any way," stammered the Englishman, and after two or three silent fits, took his leave.

Byron closed the door.

"You do no favours to your reputation, Byron, not with pranks like that," Hobhouse said irritably. "And it was rather cruel of you, because now he will be following *me* around the hotel, thinking I am you."

"Ah, not so certain and blasé now, are you?" Byron grinned. "Not now the shoe is on the other foot."

~~~
~~~

London

December 1816

In the dull murkiness of England's winter, Percy Bysshe Shelley was looking back on that long tranquil summer in Geneva with Byron as if it had been a dream, now over.

Now there was no tranquillity, no careless days boating on the lake, only misery. England was in a terrible state, the poor and starving were increasing by the day, and young people everywhere were committing suicide. The ruling Tory Government, as usual, cared nothing and did nothing to alleviate the situation.

Mary's sister, Fanny, had committed suicide by overdosing with opium, leaving behind her a sad suicide note – although her death and burial had been hushed up with the explanation that she had gone to Ireland. Later it would be announced that she had died in Ireland from a severe chill.

Her stepfather, William Godwin, had been outraged at Fanny's rash act, and fearing people might attribute the cause of her deadly depression to life in his household, had insisted upon silence.

And Shelley, being the son of a Baronet, had behaved like the perfect gentleman throughout, following all instructions and never speaking of the matter. Fanny was in Ireland, that was all he knew.

Fanny's death had brought one benefit, as tragedies often do, because now William Godwin was prepared to reconcile with his daughter Mary, whom he had coldly disowned for running away at sixteen to live unlawfully with Shelley, a married man.

Yet now, needing Shelley's help and the public support of his daughter, Godwin had offered to welcome Mary back into his good graces.

Not that Mary had moved back into her former home on Skinner Street in London, forced as she was to stay in the lodgings they had rented over a hundred miles away in Bath, in order to hide and care for Mary's stepsister, Claire Clairmont, who was now heavily pregnant – a state that would lead to more outrage, not only from Godwin, her stepfather – but all decent society.

Shelley hated all these domestic disputes, and was now in London for only one reason, to try and get a publisher for his poetry.

John Murray, of John Murray Publishers, to whom he had personally delivered the new manuscripts of poetry which Byron had written in Geneva, had agreed to read Shelley's new poetry also, and after doing so, expressed praise for it, but made no offer to publish.

He had then sent his latest poem *Hymn To Intellectual Beauty* to Leigh Hunt, one of the two brothers who published a liberal monthly magazine, *The Examiner*.

Leigh Hunt had now replied by return of post, stating his admiration for the work, and his desire to publish it, but first he begged a possible favour of help from the author – "a loan, not a gift"– to be repaid with interest; to help a cause in aid of prison reform that he was organising.

Shelley did not even pause to wonder if the loan requested was actually a bribe, so delighted was he at the news that his work would be published and reviewed favourably in a liberal journal – so much *better* than the gossipy newspapers that preferred to publish nothing more than trivial gossip, unfounded lies, and the latest lauded activities of the vile Prince Regent.

Shelley immediately wrote a cheque made out to Leigh Hunt for fifty pounds – an amazingly large sum, considering the rent on Shelley's house in Bath was that amount – fifty pounds a year.

The fact that his contribution to a worthy cause might also be seen as a bribe on his part, did not occur to Shelley.

Nor was he given time to consider it, for the very next

day another crushing blow fell – this time not on the Godwin family, but on Shelley himself – when his friend, Thomas Hookham, informed Shelley that his twenty-one-year old wife, Harriet Shelley, had committed suicide by drowning herself in the Serpentine River in Hyde Park.

"Everybody will blame you as the cause, for deserting her," Hookham said. "So if I were you I would go back to Bath and stay there. At least for a while."

Shelley had no intention of doing such a cowardly thing. He had left his marriage and Harriet two years earlier, so why the suicide now?

He went immediately to the Westbrook's house in Grosvenor Square, where a maid told him Mr Westbrook was too grieved to receive anyone; but Harriet's older sister, Eliza Westbrook, was quick on the scene – a spinster of thirty-three, and a virago of a woman, whom Shelley had always blamed for her continual interference which led to the eventual collapse of his marriage.

"I don't know how you have the *nerve* to show your face here today!"

Shelley was distraught. "What of my children?"

"What of your children, pray?"

"I have never failed to financially support them, and now that they have no mother, I must be allowed to take care of them."

"No – No! You abandoned them along with your wife, so you should be rejoicing, Mr Shelley – because now you are free to marry your atheist whore! Get away from this door!"

The door slammed in his face.

Normally, it would have been Shelley's way to turn and walk away, but today he felt a violent need to fight for something precious to him.

He banged on the door furiously, his shouts becoming shrill ... but no matter how long he stood there banging, the door was firmly locked against him. And now he knew that it would never be opened to him again.

Eventually he turned and walked away, now convinced that Harriet had *not* committed suicide; or, if she had, then she must have been *driven* to self-murder by her hateful sister.

The following day Shelley visited Thomas Hookham in his bookshop and questioned him about Harriet.

"She was only twenty-one," Shelley said, "with two small children, and most of her life still before her – so why should she want to commit suicide?"

Hookham thought Shelley somewhat disingenuous. After all, he had left Harriet and the two children for another woman, but then – "*Judge not, lest ye also be judged.*"

"I believe she *was* sent out of her house by her sister, solely to hide her advancing pregnancy from the wrath of her parents, due to her attachment to a groom named Smith. She left her children in the care of her sister and took lodgings in Chelsea, near the barracks, under the name of Harriet Smith. And now, according to her landlady, who spoke to the police about Harriet's solitary depression, she went out one night over a month ago, and was not seen again until her body was eventually found floating in the deepest reaches of the Serpentine.

"Harriet was pregnant?"

Hookham's face was red with embarrassment. "Some say by you, others say by Smith."

"Not by me – how *could* it be me? – I left England nigh on eight months ago!"

"That's what *I* said, but Eliza has her suspicions. She said you visited Harriet before you left."

Eliza – Harriet's sister! Now Shelley was not only traumatised, but incandescent with rage.

He left Hookham and went straight to Mr Longdill his solicitor, who greeted him with sympathetic condolences.

"Poor Harriet! Her body must have been in the water

for almost a month. Strange that no one went looking for her, especially when she had disappeared for so long a time. No one at all. And, of course, *you* were abroad. So how could you know?"

"I need to recover the custody of my children from that house – from the Westbrooks," said Shelley, and I need you to do it for me, legally."

Mr Longdill was not so confident. "Are you still associated with Miss Godwin?"

"Yes. And we have a child, a boy."

"In that case, Mr Shelley," said Longdill, "if you were to legalize your union with Miss Godwin, in marriage, making her the lawful stepmother of your children, then your legal custody of the children would almost certainly be a matter of general routine."

For the first time in days, Shelley managed to smile.

Arriving back at his lodgings, he wrote a letter to Mary:

It seems that Harriet, the most innocent of her abhorred and unnatural family, was driven from her father's house in order to hide her illegitimate pregnancy by a man named Smith.

There can be no question that the beastly viper her sister Eliza, unable to gain profit from her connection with me – has secured to herself the fortune of the old man – who is dying – by the murder of this poor creature.

Shelley was beyond the capability of allowing himself to believe, even for a moment, the possibility that Harriet had killed herself willingly. She had been a gentle creature, and yet this was not only an act of violence against herself, but also her two children. He *had* to get them back into his care, and so he would marry Mary.

They had been living together like a married couple for more than two years, so it would make no difference to their daily life.

I told Longdill that I was under contract of marriage to you; and he said that in such an event, all their pretences to detain the children from me would cease."

A week later, distressed and anxious, his assurance destroyed, he wrote another confidential letter, this time to his friend, Lord Byron; knowing he would sympathise. Of all the poets, Byron was truly the most political, and he was famous for those beliefs, which were the same as his own – libertarian, anti-monarchical, and free-thinking. Byron also knew all about hateful in-laws.

I write to you, my dear Lord Byron, after a series of the most unexpected and overwhelming sorrows. My late wife is dead. The circumstances which attended this event are of a nature of such awful and appalling horror, that I dare hardly to avert to them in thought. The sister of whom you have heard me speak , may be truly said (though not in law, yet in fact) to have murdered her for the sake of her father's money.

The sister has now instituted a Chancery Court process against me, the intended effect of which is to deprive me of my unfortunate children, now more than ever dear to me; and to throw me into prison, and expose me on the pillory, on the grounds of my being a REVOLUTIONIST and an ATHEIST. It seems whilst she lived in my house she possessed herself of such papers as to establish these allegations.

The opinion of Counsel is that she will certainly succeed to a considerable extent; though I am given to understand that I could purchase victory by recantation of my sympathies and beliefs; this I will not do before their tribunals of tyranny.

So here is an imperfect account of my misfortunes. I have no other news to tell you, but I often talk, and oftener think of you. In poetry I still feel the burden of my own insignificance and impotence.

Faithfully yours, P. B. Shelley.

~ ~ ~

Venice
December 1816

Still in the *Hotel della Gran Bretagne*, Byron passed through the spacious main hall into the foyer, and came face to face with Lady Francis Shelley, a nice-looking woman in her early thirties, and a friend of his sister Augusta. She was accompanied by her husband, Sir John Shelley, and both appeared very surprised to see him.

"Lord Byron. we were told you were here, but we thought it was just gossip."

"Lady Shelley." Byron bowed and warmly shook Sir John's hand. "You have just arrived?"

"No, we are just leaving," said Lady Frances. "We have been here a full week. You do not use the dining room?"

"No, but my friend Mr Hobhouse and his relatives do. Have you not seen them?"

Lady Frances looked at her husband. "I don't think we know a Mr Hobhouse, do we?"

Byron smiled. "You would certainly know if you did. He and his tribe have just left for Rome. I intend to join them in a few weeks."

During the polite conversation that followed, Byron was anxious to know any news of his sister from Lady Frances, and agreed to take tea with the Shelleys in the tea-room, which was quite empty. They sat in a secluded corner where Lady Frances shook her head negatively.

"We have been touring all over the place. I believe we missed you at Geneva. So no, I have heard nothing at all from England."

"Which reminds me," said Sir John, "Madame de Staël begged us, if we met you in Venice, to give you her *amour,* and to remind you that she intends to join you and your friend in Italy very soon."

Byron smiled, but did not respond, knowing Madame de Staël would never arrive in Italy; and disappointed that Lady Frances could tell him nothing of his sister.

Still, she made up for it by telling him all that she knew about the mode of life of the society in Venice.

"You have not yet been to the Salon of Madame Albrizzi?"

Byron smiled a supercilious negative. "They say she is the Italian Madame de Staël, but I doubt there could ever be a fair copy anywhere else in the world."

Sir John seemed to agree, but Lady Frances felt bound to say, "Although Madame Albrizzi is very *nice,* very welcoming, and I'm sure you would also find her so. Two nights ago, we left her salon at half past ten, intending to return to our beds to sleep, but then our friend the Marquis of Cigognera took us on to the salon of Madame Benzoni, where we *also* met a really very agreeable society of Venetians and strangers from all nations. All the Venetian ladies were escorted by their *cavalier serventes* but two or three actually brought their husbands."

Byron was puzzled. "*Cavalier servente?*"

"Their lover," said Sir John. "They are really quite open about it, and very different to all the bam and hypocrisy in England where that kind of thing is every bit as bad."

Lady Frances voiced her objection, and Sir John glibly apologised. "Yes, Frances, it was wrong and rude of me to say such a thing about our countrymen and women in London society – and the more so for it being true."

Byron smiled. "Truth is a strange thing, isn't it? Very few people seem to like it. I once escaped a duel for writing the truth about a very bad and stupid actor, who had ruined an entire production and yet did not seem to realise he had done so. I wrote two lines, only, a couplet, but the truth – for which I was furiously called out to a duel to the death."

"My goodness," said Lady Frances, "what was the offending couplet?"

> *"Not to be hissed delights the dunce,*
> *But who can groan and hiss at once?"*

Sir John laughed. "And who won the duel?"

"No one. He did not show up at the appointed time or place."

Lady Frances was smiling. "So he was not so stupid after all."

"What *is* stupid though," said Sir John, "are the damnable late hours they keep here in Venice. Truly exhausting. The theatre does not begin until nine o'clock and the casinos open at midnight. The salons and the *converszationes* can go on until all hours, and many of the coffee houses stay open all night. Very few go to bed before three in the morning."

"And staying up with them is exhausting," said Lady Frances. "But this I have learned about the life here from Madame Benzoni. A Venetian lady's day is thus passed – she rises about twelve o'clock, and accompanied by her *cavalier servente,* attends daily Mass. She then takes a few walking turns on the Piazza San Marco for her health. She lunches between three and four, and then undresses and goes to bed completely. At about eight o'clock she arises, and then spends until three or four o'clock in the morning at the theatre and casino, or, in the summer, in the cafes on the Piazza."

"So no different to the English ladies in London then?" Byron grinned. "At least the ones *I* knew."

Lady Frances looked at him judiciously. "You have read Lady Caroline Lamb's novel, based on you – *Glenarvon*?"

Byron shrugged. "If it's supposed to be me, then it can't be a very accurate portrait, because I did not sit long enough for the painter."

Lady Frances nodded. "She is quite mad of course. And just as vindictive as Lady ..." her face began to redden as she realised what she was about to say, and to whom.

Byron spared her blushes by asking Sir John about Shelley. "My friend in Geneva, Percy Bysshe Shelley – is he a relative of yours?"

"A very *distant* relative," Sir John replied quietly. "I'm afraid the Shelley family don't talk about Percy Bysshe any more. Not since he was sent down in disgrace from Oxford, and then ran off with the daughter of a wine-merchant to marry her in Scotland. Even his own father, Sir Timothy Shelley, has disowned him for being a radical and an atheist."

"Is he still in Geneva?" asked Lady Frances.

"No, he has returned to England."

"And so, regrettably, must we," said Sir John, looking at his fob-watch. "Still, it has been a pleasure, Lord Byron, a pleasure."

Byron escorted them out to the steps of the hotel and their gondola, which was packed with their luggage and waiting.

As she was about to step down into the gondola, he said quietly to Lady Frances: "When you see her, you will give my love to my sister Augusta, and tell her that I am well."

She nodded. "I will – and it will be the *truth* – because to my eyes you look better than I have ever seen you look. Your time in the peaceful Swiss Alps must have done you great good."

"And you will tell her so? You know how she fusses and worries."

Again she nodded, and added, "Truly, if this gondola did not await us, I'm sure we would be happy to stay another day or two, if only to introduce you to the society of the Countesses Albrizzi and Benzoni."

Byron answered good-naturedly. "I have already received invitation cards from both of them. I shall go, but in my own good time."

"Pray may I ask," said Sir John, "why you did not go to Rome with your friends?"

"Because I hate hotels, and Rome will still be there in the future, but as I intend to stay in Venice for a while I need the time to find myself a good private apartment."

"Well, good luck to you then, Lord Byron," said Sir John, and then added warningly. "And you mind yourself in this beggary place. Venice may be beautiful in its way, but it's also full of starving beggars that would not hesitate to kill a decent-looking man to get a few *soldi* to buy food."

Byron considered that to be a typical English exaggeration. He had seen the beggars, and they had held out their hand, and he usually dropped in a few coins, but none looked as if they would kill. Or maybe he was just being naive? He would give it some thought.

He watched as they boarded the gondola, and as it began to glide off down the Grand Canal, both waved back to him, with Sir John calling out – "Cheerio, Lord Byron! Cheerio!"

Cheerio, indeed. The meeting had unsettled him, for it reminded him too much of his former life in England. But, dammit, the world was bigger than England – that tight little island, with all its hypocrisy and its cold climate and chilly artificial women – so why the deuce was he feeling homesick?

A sensation of the moment. Nothing more. It would soon pass.

~~~

Italy
January 1817

Inside the Palazzo Gamba at Filetto, Teresa Gamba had always enjoyed Christmas with the delight of a child, and then looked forward to the coming new year, wondering what unexpected miracle or what new happy times it might bring.

But this new year held no wonder for her, nor any of the years after that. The long road of her future on this earth was to be filled with unhappiness and the servile meekness of a wife complying with all orders from her husband ... *Let her determine to always be a solace to me and never a trouble. Let her be docile and ready to execute all my directions.*

Yet she could not speak out, could not complain, nor defy, for now she understood that her father was not only asking her to do her duty to her family, but also to her country.

"God first, the family second, Italy third. The three sacred duties for all Italians," her Papa had said. "And
~~~

that applies to you, Teresa, as well as to Pietro, and I know I can trust you to do your duty to all three."

She had felt very honoured and very grown up when her father had explained to her the realities of Italy outside the world of Santa Chiara's convent.

"After the defeat of Bonaparte," he had said, "the British handed Italy over to the Austrians – as a gift. Now we are ruled by the Austrians, and they rule us hard. And now our hearts and minds are determined on only one acceptable destiny – the freedom of Italy."

Teresa had trembled when she heard her father say the word *"Carbonari"* – the secret army of men pledged to rise and reward the Austrians in blood for their theft of Italy.

"But not until the time is right. Not until we are big enough and ready," her Papa had said. "And so you, Teresa, must be a good daughter, by being a good wife, and then come and tell your Papa everything that you see, everything that you hear, in the house of your husband, L'Conte Alessandro Guiccioli."

"Why? Is he a bad Italian?"

Her father had shrugged. "He was a friend to the French, and now he is a friend to the Austrians. He goes wherever the smell is sweetest. We in the Carbonari know that, but Guiccioli is not aware that *we* know."

Her father then stood up from his desk and presented her with the Family Bible, reached down and placed her hand on it. "Now, Teresa Gamba, in the name of God, and in the name of the Gamba family, swear your oath that you will never breathe a word of what I have said to you this day."

Teresa obediently swore her oath, and knew she would never break it.

Later that afternoon, Teresa's maid, Rosa, found her alone in her bedroom, sitting in an armchair and silently weeping.

"Terasina, why are you crying?"

Teresa lifted the book she had been reading and

showed it to Rosa – the story of Paolo and Francesca, by Dante.

"It is so beautiful," Teresa said, "and in the past, when I have read the part where the love between Paolo and Francesca grows as they read a book together about Lancelot and Guinevere, my heart used to beat with excitement ... but now it makes me sad."

And Rosa knew why, and felt like crying herself. She still could not understand why Signor Gamba had agreed to such a marriage. How bad it was, and how hard it would be for a pure young maiden in her teens to be married to a hoary old sinner.

Yet she said encouragingly, "L'Conte Guiccioli is still a handsome man, stands tall, a man of power and respect, even to the Austrians."

Teresa nodded. "I know. And I also know that he is twenty years older than my papa."

Which reminded Rosa of why she had entered the room: Teresa had been summoned again to her father's study.

Teresa laid down her book. "Do you know why?"

Rosa shook her head. "How would I know? Your mother is in there with him, so it must be important."

"Then I must go quickly."

Teresa rushed downstairs and entered her father's study with increasing uneasiness. She curtsied before her parents, and then looked at her father with dread.

Ten minutes later she came out of the study and found Rosa waiting for her as usual.

"*Che cosa?*"

Teresa's face was flushed, her eyes glowing. "A miracle!" she whispered; and then beckoned for Rosa to come up to her room.

Once inside, she told Rosa the good news. "The priests of the Church have stood against him. They say it is not good Catholic practice to marry so soon, and he must wait for a year after the death of his last wife before he can be married again by the Church."

Rosa clapped her hands. "So, it is not to be?"

"It is still to be. The contract is signed," Teresa said quietly, and then she smiled again. "But not for almost a year, and perhaps another miracle will come to me before then?"

"*Per favore Dio!*" Rosa prayed

The Man ... The Poet ... The Legend

PART ONE

"Italians marry for their parents; and love for themselves."

Lord Byron

Chapter One

~ ~ ~

In London, on this morning in March 1817, John Murray was feeling quite sad, not only for the lady, but also for the health of his publishing business.

In January he had heard from her brother Henry, that Miss Jane Austen was ill, causing weakness and mental fatigue, which explained the reason why no completed manuscript had been forthcoming from her since the publication of *Emma* in 1815.

And now, in the same post, he had received a letter from Madame Germaine de Staël in Geneva, full of apologies and begging pardons for being *'indisposè'*, so that her book on the French Revolution would not be completed this year after all, due to her being unwell and unable to write more than a few lines in a letter.

This was all rather disconcerting and disagreeable. He had a business to run, an income to earn, a reputation to maintain, and his two best female authors were indisposed.

And now, here also, was a letter from Lord Byron in Venice. He always left Byron's letters to be read last, because they were usually so careless and amusing. But he had not heard a word from him in months, and now ... now he hesitated to open the letter, fearing that Byron was also writing to say that he too was now dangerously ill, or on the verge of dying from the contagion of some malicious fever in that foreign place.

It was certainly possible; although being a young male of no greater age than twenty-eight or twenty-nine made it unlikely to be anything so serious as dying or on the verge of it.

Yet no one knew better than he just how much this firm's reputation was powered by Lord Byron. He was the flame that drew all other writers in. Five years ago the establishment and fame of John Murray Publishing had started with Byron and *Childe Harold's Pilgrimage* in Greece, and now was still continuing with Byron's third episode of Childe Harold's life in the Swiss Alps, which had been another major publishing success last December, along with his *Prisoner of Chillon,* and *The Dream.*

Despite all the scandal of the breakdown of his marriage, the English were still hopelessly infatuated with Byron, and still rushed to buy any work that had his name on it. He could do no right and he could do no wrong – either way he outsold every other writer living, and usually on the first day of publication.

Murray shrugged; annoyed that he should be fretting. He had always prized himself as being a man of calmness, common sense, and a master of control in all circumstances. It was the only sensible way to live.

But then ... there were days like today, with such sad and bad news ... and they *did* say that these things often happened in threes ...

He slowly opened the packet from Byron and took out the letter, which was as thick as thirty or more foolscap pages – a new work of poetry – *Manfred* – a drama in Three Acts

He eagerly began to read, for no person on earth appreciated Byron's poetry more than he did. He rapidly devoured line after line, thinking *Manfred* to be strange beyond all strangeness, yet smiling with relief at the masculine and youthful *energy* of it all –

I am the Rider of the wind,

The Stirrer of the storm;

The hurricane I left behind

Is yet with lightning warm;

To speed to thee o'er shore and sea

I swept upon the blast –

In Venice, Byron was sweeping through the water of the Grand Canal with lightning strokes, cheered on by all the watching gondoliers who had bet their money on the young Englishman in the swimming race. He had covered a stretch of over two miles, leaving the weakening *Di Zorzi* far behind him.

When the news shouted out from one gondolier to the next that Di Zorzi had given up and climbed into a gondola, the cheering of the Venetian gondoliers was like an excited roar all along the Canal, and who could blame them? They lived daily lives of great monotony, and so welcomed any excitement that came their way, and they loved to gamble.

But the greatest gain of all was not just the money they had now won, that was just a part of the fun. The true joy was the defeat and humiliation of Signor Tommaso Di Zorzi who was the meanest miser of a man, as well a being a boasting loud-mouthed *spaccone,* and they all despised him.

Tita Falcieri, who was not only one of Byron's gondoliers, but also his bodyguard, was cheering the loudest.

"Bravo!" Tita smiled as he bent over to help Byron to climb back into the gondola. *"Molto bene!"*

Byron was laughing. There was nothing he enjoyed more than a good long swim, the one sport he excelled in and had never known defeat. Nor did he feel exhausted now, but completely refreshed.

"I did tell him," Byron said, "that I was the only man on earth who had ever succeeded in swimming across the Hellespont in Greece – but Di Zorzi would *not* be told, would he?"

"You swim like a fish and he like a horse," Tita said contemptuously, throwing a huge velvet cloak around Byron. "Now his fat purse of ducats will be empty when he pays all the gondoliers their winnings."

"Did *you* make a wager with him?" Byron asked.

Tita nodded. "Not for money – I wagered only in words – that you would win."

Byron nodded, and sat back against the felze of the gondola, his eyes on Tita as he moved towards the back of the boat to take up his long oar and row them home.

Tita – huge and black-bearded and ferocious in appearance, had been sent to him by his old friend Mathew "Monk" Lewis, who had now gone to Jamaica, and had sent a letter recommending his manservant with these quickly-written scrawled words, so typical of Lewis.

"Byron — I recommend to your service my former valet, Giovanni Battista Falcieri, a native of Venice, known as Tita. He is a son of the Falcieris who follow the trade of gondoliers. For this man I have great respect, because he is reliable, trustworthy, and loyal. In his time with me he has stabbed and killed two or three men without hesitation – all banditti who posed a murderous threat to his employer – so he would make an excellent bodyguard. He is now also a trained valet, for which he has great skill, due to his love of wearing fine clothes.

Byron already had his own reliable and trustworthy valet in William Fletcher, who had looked after him since he had been a boy, and over the years had travelled everywhere with him; so he had employed Falcieri as his personal bodyguard and gondolier.

Fletcher, initially, had not taken kindly to the employment of Tita Falcieri, but now the two were great friends, because despite his forbidding demeanour Tita was usually the gentlest of men, with an amiable face, a happy laugh, and a good-natured heart.

As the splashing oar pushed the gondola homewards, Byron sat gazing at the golden glow over Venice, shining its rays down on the Rialto bridge. He loved this city of water, loved the noisy life of the Grand Canal and the peaceful silence of the narrow canals down every side street.

Everyone he knew who had ever visited Venice spoke mostly of its famous inhabitants of the past, Titian, Canaletto, Casanova – but upon his own arrival and his exploration of the place, in his mind he had seen only the art of one great man – Shakespeare.

In those first few weeks when he had glided around Venice in a gondola, in his imagination he saw Shylock, that miserly and proud Jewish moneylender in *The Merchant of Venice,* and had even imagined he heard his voice – *"Hath not a Jew eyes? Hath not a Jew hands ... "*

And then, at night, in the darkness, when all the palaces along the grand Canal were lit only by the torches on the passing gondolas, he saw again that brooding and jealous Moor, *Othello,* and heard again the voice of Iago – *"Beware, my lord, of jealousy. It is the green-eyed monster which doth mock the meat it feeds on ..."*

And poor Desdemona was innocent ... Othello got it wrong ...

"Scusaci!" Tita called out to a passing gondola, and the other gondolier cheerfully replied, – *"Grazie!"*

Even now, Byron was still amazed at the unimagined speed with which the gondolas slid along, and the expert dexterity of the gondoliers in cutting round the corners of the lanes and narrower canals.

"Siamo qui," sad Tita, and the gondola gently bumped against the steps of the high-topped house where Byron had rented private apartments in the Frezzeria, a small street just off the Piazza San Marco.

Five minutes later, as he crossed the scagliola floor of the lower level to reach the stairs to his rooms, his landlord's wife appeared in a rush to greet him – *"Mio*

Byron!" – throwing up her hands to his face and kissing his mouth passionately.

After three months in Venice, he was now convinced that it was due to the years of being held in sacred seclusion and away from males, that made young Italian women so *wild* after a marriage arranged without her consent. Not all, of course, but some. And one of the "some" was twenty-two-year Marianne Segati, his mistress and master.

He had now learned that what Marianne wanted, Marianne got, and she was so pretty and charming, with her black braids and dark eyes alight with romantic glances – how could one ignore or refuse her? Not he – he was too much of a coward when it came to the Italian feminine temperament.

Later that day, he wondered if his publisher, John Murray, had received his manuscript of *Manfred*, and if he had also read the letter enclosed at the back of it?

The thought of John Murray reading the letter amused him, for he knew what happened at Murray's *"four o'clock afternoons"*. And so, out of defiance, and also for the fun of it – and despite the fact that what he wrote was true – he made his letters to Murray as *scandalous* as possible.

Then he wrote a long and sympathetic letter to his friend Shelley. Poor Shelley ... it sounded like his dead wife's sister was every bit as vindictive as the cold and calculating Miss Milbanke.

~ ~ ~

In the first-floor drawing-room of his publishing house in Mayfair, John Murray held a regular four-o'clock open house, when his male authors, friends, and the occasional literary-minded politician or two, dropped in for afternoon tea, an hour of chat, and all the latest news.

"Any news from our noble exile?" asked Thomas Campbell, a poet in his forties who had once been an acquaintance of Byron. "Tom Moore gets the occasional letter from him, but Moore never shares."

"Well, yes, a new manuscript," said Murray, "which I was not expecting so soon after the success of those published at Christmas time, but it seems the air and altitude of the Alps must have had a very beneficial effect on his lordship's creativity. This latest tale, *Manfred*, is set solely in the Alps, and is somewhat metaphysical and rather strange. Other than that, I will say no more until it is officially published."

Campbell asked: "Has Gifford read it?"

"Oh yes. He reads every Byron manuscript immediately after I have done so, and he says *Manfred* is Byron's best so far – although he says the same after reading every new manuscript from his lordship."

Campbell frowned with envy; unlike Samuel Taylor Coleridge who was beaming with delight.

Coleridge adored the young lord, because Byron's personal kindness had helped him out of severe financial difficulties; and also due to Byron's recommendation, his long unpublished poem *Christabel*, as well as *Kubla Khan*, had now been published by the eminent John Murray. But aside from all that –

"Byron's face," said Coleridge, "is so beautiful, he has a countenance I scarcely ever saw, and his eyes are like the open portals of the sun – things of light, and for light."

John Murray looked discerningly at Coleridge, wondering if he had been chewing one of his opium pellets again. He had that dreamy look in his eyes.

"However," Murray said, addressing the group, "it was not until I had read the new manuscript that I discovered his lordship's letter, which I *can* share with you all. Some of it is, of course, about Venice; but as for the rest, gentlemen – prepare to be shocked.

"Shocked?" said Rogers; and immediately all sat alert as Murray read aloud:

My dear Mr Murray,

In the first place, I think you a very impolite person

for not answering my letters from Milan, Verona

and Venice ...

Murray looked up – "I *did* answer all his letters from Switzerland – all of them! But I received none from Milan or Verona – none! And besides, at that time I was so busy rushing out his new poetry in time for Christmas. Do you know, as soon as the work came from the printers – in one evening during a pre-Christmas dinner for booksellers, I sold seven thousand copies of Canto Three of *Childe Harold's Pilgrimage,* and an even larger number of *The Prisoner Of Chillon* – all in one evening!"

"Marvellous!" said Sir Francis Burdett, a Whig politician. "That young man could knock blocks off a mountain with his words."

"The letter, Mr Murray, the letter?" urged Coleridge.

"Oh, yes ..." said Murray, and continued reading:

"In the next place, – I forget what was next – but in

the third place, I hear nothing from England and

know nothing of anything or anybody. I have but one

correspondent, – except for Mr Kinnaird on Business

now and then, and that –"

"Is that the Kinnaird of the Drury Lane Theatre Committee?" asked Sir Francis Burdett.

Murray nodded. "Yes, but Kinnaird is also his lordship's banker. Kinnaird's father and family own Moreland's Bank."

"Do they indeed? I did not know that. I thought Kinnaird was merely a *theatre* man."

"... and that other correspondent," Murray continued reading, "*is my sister; and her letters are so full of mysteries and misery, and such a quantity of the trivial and conjectural, and lack of any useful information, that I know no more of your island or city than the Italian version of the French papers choose to tell me.*

Hobhouse has gone to Rome and on to Florence with his brother and sister, but I intend to stay in Venice for a time. Venice pleases me as much as I expected, and I expected much. It has not disappointed me. It is one of those places which I know before I see them, and has always haunted me most, after the East. I like the gaiety of their gondolas and the silence of their smaller canals. Yet one may be rowed all day without knowing there are any solid streets in Venice – and one may walk about through their large squares and narrow alleys of shops of green-grocers, butchers, and all sorts, like the courts between the London squares, without knowing there are any canals.

Besides, although Venice is perforated on all sides by canals, there are pathways all along the shores of the canals, by which the whole city may be traversed on foot. The communication between different quarters is further aided by upwards of 400 small bridges, although there are only three bridges over the whole stretch of the Grand Canal.

It is a magical world, a theatrical setting for life, and its melancholy history inspires an emotion of sympathy in me. Besides, I have fallen in love, which, next to falling into the canal, (which would be useless as I can swim) is the best or worst thing I could do.

I have got some extremely good apartments in the house of a "Merchant of Venice", who is a good deal occupied with business, and has a wife in her twenty-second year – Marianne. She has the large, black, oriental eyes, with that peculiar expression in them, which is rarely seen among Europeans – even the Italians – and which many of the Turkish women give themselves by tingeing the eyelid – an art not known out of that country, I believe. This expression she has naturally. I cannot describe the effect of this kind of eye – at least upon me. Her figure is light and pretty, and her hair is of the dark gloss, curl, and colour of Lady Jersey's. Her voice is very sweet; and the naïveté of the Venetian dialect is always pleasing in the mouth of a woman.

You will perceive that my description of her has the minuteness of a passport!

As to her spouse, he is about five years older than me, and is an exceedingly good kind of man, who occupies himself elsewhere, and so the world goes on here as it does everywhere. My attachment to my Venetian has already lasted one lunar month, and I am more in love than ever, and so is the lady – at least she says so. She does not plague me, and I believe we are one of the happiest – unlawful couples –on this side of the Alps."

Coleridge was laughing; while Thomas Campbell was close to outrage. "Does he not consider what Lady Byron would say, if she were to hear about this affair?"

John Murray looked at Campbell with eyes of shrewd intelligence. "I would suppose that his lordship no longer cares or feels obligated, as they are legally separated. Indeed, on the contrary, he probably expects someone rather like you, Mr Campbell, who knows her, to tell her."

"Me?" Campbell sat back. "No, not me. Why on earth would I? I was *Byron's* friend."

Coleridge grunted. "Lord Byron had many friends, until his wife turned all the world and *some* of his friends against him."

"We could do with Byron back in England now, that's for sure," said Sir Francis Burdett. "Back in the House of Lords to fire some more of his eloquent rage against those damned Tories and what they are doing to this country."

Murray, who was a Tory, inquired politely, "Shall I continue, gentlemen, or have you heard enough?"

"Oh, continue, continue ..." they all insisted, even Thomas Campbell.

So Murray continued:

"I meant to have given up gallivanting on leaving your country, where I was tolerably sickened of that

and everything else; but I know not how it is, my health growing better, and my spirits also, the "need to love" came back upon my heart again, and, after all, there is nothing like it.

Although you may suppose (and rightly) that I do not shine in the courtship department, so little so that a few nights ago – instead of handing the lady as duty-bound into the gondola, I nearly conveyed her into the canal, and this at midnight. To be sure it was as dark as possible – but if you could have seen with what gravity I was committing her to the waves, my mind miles away, thinking of something or other not to the purpose. I always forget that the streets are canals and was going to walk her over the water if the gondoliers had not awakened me. So much for love and all that.

There is, to my mind, a big difference between French women and their Italian sisters. The French consider love ridiculous, and their exalted admiration of love is mostly literary; but the Italians reverence love, and refuse to ignore it.

Here in Venice though, especially amongst the upper class, the morals are somewhat lax; so much so, that a lady with only "one" lover is not reckoned to have overstepped the modesty of marriage. Some of the ladies have two or three lovers, but those who

*have more than one are considered a little "wild".
The husbands of course belong to anybody's wives –
but their own.*

*I know a woman of fifty who never had but one
lover, who dying early, she became devout,
renouncing all but her husband. She piques herself
upon this miraculous fidelity, talking of it
occasionally with a species of misplaced morality,
which is rather amusing.*

*I have not been out a great deal, but quite as much
as I like. I am going out this evening in my "cloak"
and "gondola" – there are two nice words from Mrs
Radcliffe's gothic novels for you.*

*P. S – I forgot to tell you that my dog – Mutz by
name and Swiss by nation – shuts a door behind him
when he is told."*

After a silence, Coleridge said sadly: "Do you think he
knows, Murray, how much we all miss him?"

"And damnably so," agreed Sir Francis Burdett.
"Especially in politics and Parliament. Only there did I
ever witness how Byron will say anything to anybody
when he is angry, and not give a damn."

"I would say the Tories," Coleridge smiled, "would be
terrified to have him back."

"There was one occasion in the House," Sir Francis
continued, "when Lord Byron was giving it hot and
furious to the Tories on the other side, until all their
faces were as red as a matador's rag, especially Lord
Eldon's face, but Lord Holland and the rest of us Whigs
were laughing, hugely entertained by his boldness."

"At least," said John Murray, turning the subject away from divisive politics, "we are not to be deprived of his poetry, because now his writing has become even more prolific than ever."

Chapter Two

~~~

Fletcher could not help wondering if it was the letter that came from his lawyer in London at the end of March, which had caused Lord Byron such anguish, that had eventually caused him to take to his bed for almost a week now with a slow fever.

What was in that letter? Fletcher wished he knew; and the desire to know obsessed him, although he dared not ask. Whatever it was, it was too awful to be confided to a servant – not even one so close and long-serving as he.

A few nights later, when his lordship was sound asleep due to the help of a large dose of laudanum, Fletcher took his chance and crept into his bedroom, his breath trembling with fear, for if his lordship awoke and he was caught, there was a good chance he might find himself being hurtled through the window.

He did not have to search for the letter, for there it was on his desk with the lawyers bright red seal on it. It was not there earlier in the day, so his lordship must have been reading it again.

Fletcher slowly and very quietly picked up the letter and slipped out onto the landing to read it under the light of a candle in one of he sconces on the wall.

As Fletcher read the letter, his hand went to his mouth, for this was more than awful, this was a tragedy, at least for his lordship.

His lawyer reported that Lord Eldon had already heard and agreed to the legal application of Lady Byron for her daughter to be made a Ward of the Court of Chancery, with herself and her father Sir Ralph Milbanke as sole guardians. The case was over, signed and settled in his lordship's absence, and there was nothing that John Hanson could do – it was too late.
~~~

Lord Byron's shared custody of his daughter Ada was now in the past. All the rumours of his behaviour with the atheist Shelley and the two immoral sisters in Geneva had contributed to the decision. An appeal was possible, but unlikely to succeed, due to his lordship's long absence abroad. His financial support for his wife and daughter of £3000 a year, of course, would still be liable, as per the Separation Agreement.

Oh, that vixen, that horrible woman, why the deuce had he married her? His first and favourite great love had always been Mary Ann Chaworth, his boyhood sweetheart – and, aye, the sweet of his heart long after that, and he of hers. Why, only the other day he had told Fletcher that his initial softness towards his landlord's wife was because her name was Marianne, the Italian version of Mary Ann.

Oh, that vixen, that Miss Milbanke – from the day she had become Lady Byron, Fletcher had hated living in the same house as her. Begad! – when he thought back to her conduct and high-nosed coldness during that time, he wondered how any man could live a twelve-month with her.

Fletcher crept back into the bedroom and replaced the letter just as he had found it; and very glad he had read it. Now he would know in the days ahead to tread carefully and not say the wrong thing. Thank God Mr Hobhouse was on his way back to Venice. *He* always knew how to advise his lordship in the right way. A rock of common sense was Mr Hobhouse.

~ ~ ~

John Cam Hobhouse did not arrive back in Venice from his extended tour of Italy, until three weeks later, and was immediately perturbed by the change in Byron. All his flippancy and laughter had gone, and now he was doing what he had done in Greece when he wanted to retire into himself – he went every day to a monastery, and spent most of the day there.

"But why?" Hobhouse asked.

"I am learning the Armenian language."

"But why?" Hobhouse asked again. "For what purpose? In Athens you retired to a monastery to study the Romaic language, and what use has *that* ever been to you?"

Byron could not be dissuaded, taking off early every morning in his gondola for a day of isolation and study at the Armenian Monastery of St. Lazarus on the island of San Lazzaro, near the Lido.

His tutor was Father Paschal Aucher, who was slowly coming to the conclusion that the young Englishman was a saint in disguise; for not only did he study their language long and hard, but now he also agreed with Father Paschal that a dictionary of Armenian and English Grammar should be published to the world, and the printing of which, Lord Byron would bear the expense.

"*Mio Dio!*" It was a prayer answered, a dream come true, and time the English-speaking world began to understand the language of Armenia and returned her to her rightful place in the world.

And true to his word, Byron wrote to John Murray seeking his help.

I go every morning to the Armenian Monastery to study the language. I mean the "Armenian" language, (for as you know – I am versed in the Italian) and if you ask my reason for studying this out of the way language – I can only answer that it is Eastern and difficult and employs me – which are reasons sufficient.

Padre Paschal, with some help from me as a translator of his Italian into English, is also proceeding with a manuscript grammar for the translation of Armenian into English – We want to know if there are any "Armenian types" or letterpress in England – at Oxford – Cambridge or elsewhere. Pray enquire among your learned acquaintance. When this Grammar is done, will you have any objection – say yes or no as you like –

John Murray put down the letter with irritation. Byron must be mad to think he would involve himself with a subject so unprofitable! And who would be interested in learning such an "out of the way" language?

He picked up the letter again, and saw that Byron had anticipated his question, by enclosing his own 'Preface' to be published in the finished book, which would answer all ... and which he had not written in his own free and rapid handwriting, but had carefully *printed* out neatly.

On my arrival at Venice, in the year 1816, I found my mind in a state which required study, and study of a nature which would leave little scope for the imagination, and furnish some difficulty in the pursuit.

At this period I was much struck – in common, I believe, with every other traveller – with the society of friars at the Covent of St. Lazarus, which appears to unite all the advantages of the monastic institution, without any of its vices.

The neatness, the comfort, the gentleness, the unaffected devotion, the accomplishments, and the virtues of the brethren of the order, are well fitted to strike the man of the world with the conviction that

"there is another and a better" even in this life.

These men are the priesthood of an oppressed and noble nation, which has partaken of the same proscription of bondage as the Jews and the Greeks, without the sullenness of the former or the servility of the latter. This people has attained riches without the usury of lending or borrowing money, and all the honours that can be awarded to slavery without intrigue. But they have long occupied, nevertheless, a part of the House of Bondage, who has lately multiplied her many mansions.

It would be difficult, perhaps, to find the history of a nation less stained with crimes than those of the Armenians. But whatever may have been their destiny – and it has been bitter – whatever it may be in future, their country must ever be one of the most interesting on the globe; and perhaps their language only requires to be more studied to become attractive.

If the Scriptures are rightly understood, it was in Armenia that Paradise was placed – Armenia, which has paid as dearly as the descendants of Adam for that fleeting participation of its soil in the happiness of him who was created from its dust. It was in Armenia that the flood first abated, and the dove alighted. But with the disappearance of Paradise itself may be dated almost the unhappiness of the country; for though long a powerful kingdom, it was scarcely ever an independent one, and the satraps of

neighbouring Persia and the pashas of Turkey have alike desolated the region where God created man in his own image.

John Murray was floundering in utter confusion, as happened always and only with Byron. One never knew what to expect next.

Demon or angel – what was he? In his last letter he was making love to his landlord's wife, and in this letter he was daily helping Armenian monks ... Perhaps Madame de Staël was right when she had once described him as a "fallen angel".

Murray removed his spectacles and sat for a time in thought ... finally supposing that, well, he *could* make some tentative inquiries to Oxford and Cambridge about printers of antique lettering. To his knowledge, the Armenian language was not very different to the Greek, or was it? One would need a Dictionary of Armenian and English grammar to know.

Chapter Three

~ ~ ~

Like a man with a firm purpose; Byron left his lodgings early the following morning to sail over to the monastery on the island of San Lazzaro, stepping outside to be detained by a strange gondolier on the steps, holding out a note.

"I was asked to give this to the English Mylord."

"By whom?"

"By a very reverent person."

They were speaking in Venetian and Byron was not sure if he had understood correctly. He glanced at Tita standing in his gondola, who shrugged. "He has just arrived. His gondola is blocking mine."

Byron read the note, intimating a wish on the part of the writer to meet with the English Mylord, either in a gondola, or on the island of San Lazzaro, or a third place which Byron did not know. There was no signature.

A third gondola was turning into the narrow canal and Tita let out a shout for it to hold back.

Byron said quickly to the gondolier: "Neither of these places suit me, but I will be at home alone at ten tonight, or at the ridotto at midnight. Those are the only times I have free."

He stepped down into the gondola; and after Tita had assured himself that Mylord was seated comfortably, he took up his oar and pushed off down the canal.

Arriving at San Lazzaro and walking into the monastery, Byron suddenly looked at Tita, perplexed. "Tell me, Tita, when I am with Padre Paschal all day, what do you do with your time?"

Tita shrugged. "I sit with the friars in the kitchen. We talk of God." He looked gravely at Byron. "I am very devout."

"No, you're not!" Byron laughed. "You're as much a sinner as anyone else."

"Of course," agreed Tita. "How is a man to learn if he does not do wrong and sin now and then. How is he to be a *human?*"

"The friars here never sin."

"And I don't judge them for being so good," replied Tita, "but I do spend many hours *helping* them. I carry buckets of water in and out, and whatever other work they need me to do – as long as it is not dirty and soils my clothes."

"Oh yes, your clothes ..." Byron glanced over the clothes Tita was wearing today – a dark blue Fez hat with a plume of black feathers hanging down one side. A red waistcoat over a white shirt with huge voluminous sleeves. Black pantaloons. Hessian boots, with tassels down the outsides; and a dark blue sash around his waist holding a knife in a scabbard and a large pistol, revealing his status as a bodyguard. He was a fearsome looking man, but a fine one.

"And that's what you do all day – help the friars?"

"No." Tita shrugged. "Some of the time I sit in my gondola and smoke."

Ah, that sounded more Venetian.

Byron grinned and headed towards Padre Paschal's library while Tita headed towards the kitchens.

~~~

That evening Byron was relaxing in his apartment, and glad of the peace. His mind was tired and all he wanted now was some solitude.

Hobhouse, after dropping in for a quick chat that had lasted two hours, had at last gone off, dressed in his best, to the salon of Madame Albrizzi where he had arranged to meet some German professor who personally knew the great Goethe.

Byron preferred to stay at home with the great Voltaire, having brought 25 volumes of Voltaire's works with him to Venice. Marianne was gone with her husband to a conversazione.

Lying back on the sofa in his drawing-room he began
~~~

to read Voltaire's *Letters On The English*, which, surprisingly, was full of praise for the English system of government, and very critical of the French.

How the deuce could Voltaire think the English system was the fairest, when the country was ruled by a privileged few who ensured they reaped all the benefits and taxes for themselves and their monarch, while the ordinary man got nothing he had not worked for.

He had been reading for some time when he heard the door quietly click open, and turned his eyes to look, expecting to see Fletcher – not a girl of about nineteen or so. He was furious. Was he not deprived of living in hotels just to avoid intrusions like this?

"Who are you?" he said, sitting up. "How did you get past my servants?"

"Mylord," she said in Venetian, "you said I could come, tonight, at ten, when you are alone."

"Did I? When?"

"This morning. In reply to my note."

"The note was from you?"

"Yes."

She was quite pretty, but there was a sauciness in her eyes.

He stood and said: "May I ask again, who are you?"

She curtseyed to him, and then told him she was married to the brother of Marianne.

"Oh, so you are one of the family?"

"Yes, but I come to ask, Mylord, if you speak Romaic?"

Already he felt tired. The Armenian language all day, and now Romaic.

"Yes. I studied Romaic in Greece."

"Will you speak it to me?"

"Why, pray?"

She then explained that her mother was a Greek of Corfu, and she missed her mother so badly; but if she could speak to someone in Romaic again, she would feel closer to home, closer to Greece.

The word Greece revived him. He acquiesced with a

gesture for her to sit in one of the armchairs.

She chose instead to sit beside him on the sofa.

They had been speaking politely in Romaic for only a few minutes, when lo! – to his astonishment – in walked Marianne, and after making a polite curtsey to him, she greeted her sister-in-law by seizing her by the hair and bestowing upon her face some sixteen hard slaps which made his ears ache from the echo, and his face sting from two of the slaps he had received himself while trying to stop the assault.

The screaming which ensued was deafening, until the sister-in-law took flight. He grabbed Marianne who, after several furious attempts to get away in pursuit of her enemy, finally relaxed in her efforts.

"Why did you leave the conversazione?" he asked. "How did you know she was here?"

"I saw her gondolier on the steps this morning, and I knew then – I *knew* she wanted *my* amoroso!"

And then she fairly went into fainting fits in his arms; and in spite of reasoning, eau de Cologne, vinegar, half a pint of water, and God know what other waters, continued in her wailing and fainting fits until almost midnight.

All the screaming had brought Fletcher and the other servants running, and he damned them all furiously for letting someone in without apprising him beforehand.

Marianne had collapsed into another fit of fainting on the sofa. He had seen dramatic fits before, but this was incredible.

And then, lo! who walks in but her husband, Signor Segati, who had undoubtedly been deserted at the conversazione.

He looked at Mylord, and then at his wife lying in a faint on the sofa, and then at all the apparatus of confusion, dishevelled hair, hats, handkerchiefs, salts, smelling bottles – and his wife as pale as ashes, without sense or motion.

He said, "What is all this?"

Byron could see that he was quite calm, and so

answered calmly, "Signore, the explanation for this is the easiest thing in the world, but in the meantime, I think it more imperative for you to recover your wife – at least to her senses."

Signor Segati walked over to his wife, and talked to her quietly, without any tone of admonishment, "Marianne, you must come to your bed. Here is not the place to be ill."

Byron knew he was being diplomatic.

His voice seemed to bring her back to consciousness very quickly. Without a word she stood, and picked up her hat, and her sister-in-law's hat, and then handed the hated sister-in-law's hat to her husband, by way of explanation, and then both left the room in silence.

Byron was so disturbed by it all, he did not go to San Lazzaro the next day, and instead called in on Hobhouse at the *Hotel Gran Bretagne* to tell him what had happened.

Hobhouse's first response was to suggest that they get out of Venice, and quick.

"You need not be alarmed, Hobby, jealousy is not the order of the day in Venice, and daggers are out of fashion. And calls for a duel on love matters are unknown – at least, from the husbands."

"Then why are *you* alarmed?"

"I am not alarmed, I am disturbed, because Signor Segati is such a *good* kind of man, and I know he was merely being very dignified and diplomatic about it all."

Hobhouse stared, confused. "So it's the *husband* you feel sorry for – the same man you cuckolded?"

"There's no such word in Venice. You would know that if you had not spent so long in Rome and Florence."

Byron sighed. "I have no patience for hypocrisy, but despite all that, it was an awkward affair. He must have known I had made love to Marianne, yet now I believe he was not fully aware of it until last night. It is well known that almost all the married women have a lover, as do the men – but it *is* usual to keep up the forms as in other nations, so I didn't know what the devil to say to him. I could not out with the truth, out of regard to her, and I did not choose to lie for my sake. Besides, the thing told itself. So I thought the best thing to do was to let her explain it to him as she chose – a woman never being at a loss – and the devil always sticks by them."

"True. And did she explain? Have you seen either of them today?"

"Yes, both of them, this morning. I know not how they settled it, but settle it they did, and Signor Segati seemed very concerned that the women's regrettable *combattimento* of the night before should not cause me to leave."

"Ah, so yes, he is a *good* man," Hobby said. "Good at taking care of all the money you pay him in rent. I reckon he earns more in a month from you, than he does in his draper's business."

"No!" Byron laughed. "The truth and the evidence is here before our eyes in Venice every day. Here, nobody minds such trifles, except to be amused by them."

"If you say so."

"Still, I never saw a woman in such a fit of fainting, and the screams! I thought she was determined to kill her sister-in-law. But the *worst* thing she did – was to sneeringly call the girl 'a Greek' – I found that rather unforgivable."

Hobhouse rolled his eyes. "You and Greece. I sometimes think you must be Plato or Aristotle reincarnated."

"We are halfway there, you know? To Greece. Shall we go?"

"No, Byron." Hobhouse was moving his head from side to side. "Greece is to be the *last* stop on our tour. I think we should go to Rome."

"Rome?" Byron was baffled. "You have already been to Rome."

"Indeed." Hobhouse folded his arms. "And who would ever say no to going back to Rome? It's magnificent, Byron, truly magnificent."

"Is it? – that good – truly magnificent?"

"Indeed. Every person should see Rome at least once in their life. And while we are there, we could also go on to see Naples."

Byron sat back. "Next you will be trying to persuade me to go back to England with you. And no – that will *not* happen. Not now I have lost all rights to my daughter until she is grown and able to decide for herself. England for me, Hobby, is a continual sore, but I have supped enough from the cup of sorrows and can take no more. So I intend to enjoy the last of my youth as best I can, and bedamned to the consequences."

Hobhouse was silent. The love and friendship he had long felt for Byron was immeasurable; and he, too, had been very hurt by the shameful way the English gossips and newspapers had treated him.

"Did I mention England? I merely suggested Rome. If nothing else, it would take your mind off hurtful things."

"I'm tempted, Hobby, but I wish to reside in *Venice*. I like the free and easy atmosphere here, and I do have my servants to consider."

Hobhouse blinked. He had never believed in being so free and familiar with servants as Byron was. "What the devil have your servants got to do with it?"

"Well, one servant in particular – Mr Berger. He travelled all the way from Switzerland with me to Venice, and now he is in love. How do I know? It would be hard *not* to know! He spends most of his time leaning out of his window shouting and cooing to a woman in a house on the opposite side of our narrow canal. And she leans out of her window shouting and cooing back to him. Love in middle-age. Who could ruin it? No, I must stay in Venice."

"And we will *return* to Venice," Hobby assured him. "I have not yet explored a *tenth* of the place for my new Travel Book. But now – think on *this,* my friend – our removal to the mainland for six weeks or so will give you the perfect *excuse* to leave your lodgings in the troubled Segati house. And Berger knows where the woman in the window lives, doesn't he? So he can always go back to that canal in the evenings and serenade her from a gondola. The Swiss love to sing and yodel, don't they? Is she married?"

"No. Fletcher says she's the widowed aunt of the married couple who live there."

"The widowed aunt? Oh Lord help him! – Berger will be cooked and peppered before she finally devours him."

They walked to the square of San Marco where Byron was still hesitating about leaving the Segati house.

"I can't just *desert* Marianne, not now that her husband appears to have forgiven us both. And apart from being lovers, she and I are also good *friends*."

"There is talk at the hotel that you have been seen out walking with her."

"Yes, because I like her company, so why not?"

"A *tradesman's* wife? A man of your rank and title openly mixing with such people is causing a fuss at the hotel."

"Then let them mind their own business."

"What they *don't* like, is that you show so little interest in them, and yet you are so amenable to the traders and merchants and even the beggars. It's not on, Byron, and it's causing a dreadful fuss amongst the English who will carry it all back home."

Something in a jeweller's shop window caught Byron's eye and he walked over to look more closely at whatever it was; while Hobhouse fretted and wondered if Byron realised the scandal he was stirring. All this would go back to England wrapped up in plenty of embellished embroidery.

"What is it?" he asked, and walked over to the window where Byron pointed to a black box containing a set of diamonds – two earrings and a necklace.

"Are they not beautiful diamonds, Hobby?"

"Exquisite, yes, and costing a small fortune no doubt." Hobby stared at him. "Surely you are not thinking of –"

"Buying them for Marianne? Do you not think they would set off her dark hair and eyes beautifully?"

"They would certainly enhance the looks of any woman, but –"

"*Not* Marianne," Byron said irately, and entered the jewellers shop.

Hobhouse sighed hopelessly when the window was unlocked and the box of diamonds were lifted out, which meant Byron was buying them.

Was there ever a more kind-hearted and generous *fool*? What would a tradesman's wife want with diamonds? A lady or a duchess, yes, but the wife of a draper?

Hobhouse stood alert when the box of diamonds were placed back in the window – not bought – and then Byron came back outside.

Relieved, Hobby grinned. "I'm glad you were not foolish enough to waste your money on such useless feminine adornments. If a woman needs such –"

"*Don't lecture me,* because I won't bear it and will turn savage!" Byron warned.

Shocked, Hobhouse stared. "Why such anger? Were they too expensive?"

"No, they were the same price as they were two weeks ago when I bought them for Marianne."

"What?"

Byron looked deeply hurt. "First, I had to make sure they were the same ones, which they were; and then I was hoping it was possibly her husband who had brought them back, but no ... the proprietor said it was the Signora Segati herself who had brought them to him, and she had fought a hard bargain to get the highest price she could – which was *half* of what I paid for them."

"Did he say when?"

"Yes, only a day after *she* pointed to the diamonds in the window and told me how lucky and *fortunate* the woman would be who received them ... I can't believe ...

she said she would treasure them forever ... her only valuable heirloom ... and all that."

"Well, I could lecture you on your foolishness, but I would hate you to turn savage. So, what are you going to do now?"

"The only thing I can do – the only thing I *want* to do now – quit the Segati house as soon as possible and go with you to Rome."

"Oh well done! There are no fakes in Rome! But are you not going to say anything to her – tell her you found her out?"

"Certainly not." Byron looked at Hobhouse with half-shut eyes. "She may be a money-grasping minx, but I remain a gentlemen."

~

Four weeks later, in Mayfair, John Murray received another letter from Lord Byron, from Rome, which he thought to be a wonderful place – *"Beats even Greece!"*

PART TWO

~

What then, will be the right way to live? A Man should spend his whole life "at play". And not withstanding that human affairs are not worth our earnest effort, necessity counsels us to be in earnest, and that is our misfortune.

Plato, The Laws VII 803

Chapter Four

~ ~ ~

John Cam Hobhouse was very disappointed that Byron had declined to go with him to Naples, preferring instead to return to Venice where, he insisted, he felt more anonymous.

Hobhouse could not blame him, not after some of the incidents in Rome which had been rather vexing to both of them.

Rome itself was awe-inspiring in so many aspects; but some of the English tourists sought to spoil it all by recognising Lord Byron and following him everywhere – even up to the roof of St Peter's to which it had taken three hundred and twenty steps to reach, and where they had paused in the gallery inside the dome looking down into the basilica – absorbing the astonishing beauty of the cupola from within, the breathtaking mosaics, and then dizzily looking down on the main altar.

"To realise that Michelangelo himself designed this dome," said Hobhouse.

"*After* he saw Greece," Byron murmured. "That's why he did not build this dome as wide across as it could have been."

"How do you know that?"

"I read it – in an Italian book. Michelangelo said at the time, 'I could build one bigger, but not more beautiful than that of the Pantheon'."

Hobhouse sighed as he gazed around. "No wonder they called him 'the Divine One' ... his work is certainly divine."

Byron was gazing down into the basilica. "Imagine it, Peter the apostle, who walked beside Jesus for all that time, is buried here, right beneath us."

"Is he though?" Hobhouse said cynically. "Or does the

Vatican just say that to their faithful?"

"Yes, they say it, and as Saint Peter was crucified by the Romans right here in Rome, I would say it is more than likely to be true."

"There he is, Lord Byron, there he is!" cried a girl's voice, making them turn and look to see a matron with three teenage girls who were obviously her daughters or nieces, heading towards them.

"Avert your eyes," the matron warned loudly. *"Whatever you do don't look into his eyes or you will be lost!"*

Like a shot – Byron was gone – through a door and up the remaining two hundred steps to the top of the dome, hopping as fast as he could on his good foot to aid his speed, which was quite a task, as the stairs and passageway were narrow.

Following behind, Hobhouse arrived on the roof out of breath and gasping, "You were always stronger than me, despite that lame foot of yours."

"Because I regularly swim and have boxing sessions with that mastiff Fletcher. You should try a sport, Hobby, instead of all those useless politics. It's a rigged game, so why play it?"

"I want to *un-rig* politics if I can, that's why."

"Oh, look ..." from the roof of the Sistine Chapel they now had a 360 degree panoramic view of Rome, and made the most of it, walking around the railed-roof slowly, and taking in every detail in silence as the sun was beginning to descend over the red stone ruins of the Roman forum.

Hobhouse continually kept pausing with his pencil and pad to make notes on the spot, while Byron was content to stand and stare at every view of the Holy City, delighting in its ancient beauty; and yet remembering that Rome was not *quite* so holy in the days of yore —

Alas! the lofty city! and alas!

The trebly-hundred triumphs ! and the day

> *When Brutus made the dagger's edge surpass*
>
> *The conqueror's sword in bearing fame away!*

"There he is! *Lord Byron!*" a girl's voice – *"He can't move away from us now!"*

But he could – through a second door on the roof and upon which stairs he practically slid down to a door to the gallery; and from there down more stairs where he came out at the rear of St Peter's Nave in the middle of Mass, dropping down onto one knee and piously making the sign of the Cross over himself.

Coming up behind him a few minutes later, Hobhouse bent and whispered – "Byron, what are you *doing?* You are not a Catholic."

"When in Rome, Hobby, when in Rome," Byron whispered. "Pray show some respect and do you the same."

Hobhouse had no intention of doing what the Romans do, and crept out – fuming when he was left waiting for almost half an hour before Byron also slipped out.

"What think you of this Catholicism, Byron?" Hobhouse asked seriously. "Surely you are not sympathetic to their beliefs? Especially their belief in the infallibility of the Pope?"

Byron shrugged. "I like that, the *infallibility* of the Pope, so his word must always be obeyed. Yes, I like his Holiness very much, particularly since he has lately decreed that *no more miracles* shall be performed."

Hobhouse sighed hopelessly. "I was a fool to even ask."

From then on their days were spent on horseback, riding around the city, until walking inside Rome's great Coliseum. Hobhouse marvelled aloud at the great circular terraces of ancient stone, one circular terrace on top of the other where the crowded audience had sat and enjoyed the revelry or the bloodshed.

Byron was moodily silent, gazing down at the stone floor of the arena, his mind drifting back into those barbarous days of Rome's long-ago past:

I see before me the Gladiator lie,

He leans upon his hand – his manly brow

Consents to death, but conquers agony,

And his drooped head sinks gradually low –

And through his side the last drops, ebbing slow

From the red gash, fall heavy, one by one,

Like the first of a thunder-shower; and now

The arena swims around him – he is gone.

They rode on, to the Alban hills over the Campagne and everywhere else of interest.

And then on to Florence, where, after only one day and one night in Florence, seeing only those sights he wished to see, Byron decided he had done enough touring for a while, and prepared to return to Venice.

Hobhouse was sorry to see him go, and promised to join him later back in Venice.

"You must understand, Byron, that I must go to Naples and Pisa because, unlike you, I have a *serious* book to research before I return to England."

"Your *travel* book."

"About Italy, yes. I'm hoping it will be a fine handbook for Englanders coming to Italy next year."

Inside the carriage on the journey back to Venice, pencil and notebook in hand, Byron was writing his own *serious* book, with some new stanzas on Rome for Book 4 of 'Childe Harold's Pilgrimage':

But lo! the dome — the vast and wondrous dome,

Christ's mighty shrine above his martyr's tomb!

Chapter Five

~ ~ ~

When Hobhouse finally arrived back in Venice five weeks later, Byron was not there.

Even his servants were gone, and none of the servants at the Segati house knew where the English Mylord had gone. Signor Segati was at his business, and the Signora was not at home.

"Typical!" Hobby muttered, furious with Byron. "As unreliable as a woman and fickle as the wind."

He returned to the *Gran Bretagne* sour-faced and irritable, even with the desk-clerk who gave him his key.

Turning to make his way towards the grand staircase and his room, he was stalled by the voice of the hotel's manager who came rushing behind the desk. "Oh, Mr Hobhouse, my apologies, sir, my *sincere* apologies."

Hobhouse glared at him disagreeably. "For what?"

"I regret my oversight, but yesterday, you see, was my day off, I was not here, and so I could not give you this."

In his hand the manager held a folded piece of paper which was sealed. "I was entrusted by Lord Byron to give this note to no person but you, sir."

In such a bad mood, Hobhouse was not prepared to be forgiving. "Oh, so he at least had the goodness to do that – leave me a note."

"Indeed, sir, but of course, like myself, he could hardly know the precise day of your arrival."

Hobhouse opened the note to read that Byron had fled *'the choking summer heat of the city'* and had taken a house, the *'Villa Foscarini'*, in the countryside, approximately ten miles outside the city of Venice, at La Mira.

Already feeling the summer heat himself, Hobhouse was relieved and pleased. "This place, La Mira," he asked the manager, "can you advise me how to get there?"

"Ah yes, La Mira is in Veneto, about sixteen kilometres from here. I will write it down for you. One of our gondolas will take you over. So do you wish to vacate your room here at *Gran Bretagne?*"

"No, at least, not yet. Not until I see how the land lies, so to speak."

"Very good, sir. We shall keep the room for you, and ensure it is dusted daily, until your return."

"Thank you. However, I will use it now, to take a bath. Pray have some hot water delivered to my bathing closet as soon as possible."

"Certainly."

Hobhouse walked towards the staircase and the manager thoughtfully watched him go. Usually Mr Hobhouse was a nice enough man, who carried himself with dignity and politeness, but there was a stiffness in his bearing and manner, which contrasted so sharply with Lord Byron's easy elegance.

~~~

Arriving at La Mira, Hobhouse was delighted to find that the Villa Foscarini, a large and handsome house, was pleasantly situated on the banks of the River Brenta, from which it was separated by an avenue of trees. Its windows overlooked the river, lively and charming with little passing boats, and gave a view of the opposite bank, all dotted with the villas and summer residences of the Venetian nobility who, Byron said, came here in the summer to breathe the cleaner and cooler air of the mainland.

Hobhouse loved it, most especially because the ground floor led to a long covered walk where coolness and shade could be found on the very hottest days. A garden luxuriant with flowers shed its fragrance all around; and then Hobby's eyes were also captivated by a second garden – an *English* garden – in which small lakes, and bridges were tastefully scattered in miniature.
~~~

"Well, Byron, this is a very graceful retreat, I must say!"

Over dinner they caught up on all their news.

Naples, Hobhouse said, was really not worth the time it took to travel there – nothing exceptional worth seeing – except of course the Roman ruins of Pompeii, the paintings of Caravaggio, Mount Vesuvias, and at least ten more sights which took him at least an hour to describe.

So, with so little to see in Naples, he had gone yet again to Florence, simply because it had been the home of Michelangelo – *'Il Divino!'*

"That's how they all refer to him in Florence, *'the Divine one'*. And how could I *not* go there again, to his home in Caprese, after seeing the Sistine Chapel in Rome and his stupendous painting of the *Creation of Adam* on the ceiling and *The Last Judgement* on the wall."

Byron agreed. "A man who *must* have been touched by God or the gods to produce such art. What is strange though, is he had the talent of *three* men in one – how else can you explain it? A sculptor, painter, architect, and magnificent in all three."

"In Florence – I will tell the readers of my new travel book – is where they will find one of the most magnificent examples of Il Divino's genius in his marble statue of *David*. The perfection of it is sheer breathtaking. Even his hands, Byron, his right hand in particular, tensed in readiness for battle with Goliath, and you can see that tenseness in the slightly-protruding veins of his hand – so life-like, yet all done in stone – a work of absolute *perfection*."

Hobhouse knocked back his wine. "And now *your* news?"

Byron's news was not so good. He told Hobhouse about the latest letter he had received from Shelley relating to his battle for the custody of his children in the Chancery Court.

"He failed. And even though he is now married to

Mary, he was judged as no fit custodian. They even produced his old pamphlet on *The Necessity of Atheism* to prove he was not fit. The Westbrooks were given full custody, and poor Shelley was denied even visiting rights. He sounds quite broken by it all."

"Poor man. I was an atheist once," Hobby said. "Perhaps I still am. I don't know anymore. Not after seeing the art of Michelangelo. That divine stream of genius came from no earthly spring."

"However, a new child has come into Shelley's life, who apparently he delights in. My daughter."

"Ada?"

"No. Claire Clairmont's daughter. According to Shelley the child is beautiful, with black hair and blue eyes, and Claire has temporarily named her Alba, but says she prefers for *me* to choose the name."

"And will you?"

"Alba is a ridiculous name. In Italian it means 'dawn' but in other languages it means hill or mountain. I wrote back saying if I *must* make the final choice, then my choice would be the name Allegra."

"Why so?"

"So as not to confuse the child entirely with a totally different name. Also, apart from it being an Italian name, meaning '*happy*' it also reminds me of the harbour and place where they all lived when in Switzerland – Montalegre."

Hobhouse sat back. "So what will you do now? About the child?"

"My duty. Financially I am fully supporting it, but I am still not fully certain that she *is* my child. There is a strange bond between Claire and Shelley that even Mary cannot seem to break. And it causes her great unhappiness, *that* I do know. One only has to see all three together to know it."

"But ... surely you don't think –"

"Anything bad of Shelley? I would find it difficult. But he is merely a man, and you would have to *know* Claire to understand. She is a very clever seducer. Although, on balance, I suppose the child must be mine."

Hobhouse did not like this subject and was anxious to change it. Byron had suffered enough with his little legitimate, Ada, and now this new child ... Hobhouse could only see more suffering ahead."

"So?" he said. "How did matters go when you left your apartments in the Segati house?"

"Oh yes, the *Segatis*!" Byron said laughing. "And after all my guilt about *him!* It turns out he has had his own Venetian mistress for the past two years."

"No! How do you know?"

"He told me so, and quite casually too. He said a married man having a mistress was 'standard' in Italy, and even more so in Venice. The wives are the same. The only thing they consider wrong, is trying to *hide* the fact. That they consider to be the worst kind of deceit."

After a thoughtful silence, Hobhouse said, "Of course, I could not put facts like that in my new Italian travel book." He looked questioningly at Byron. "Or could I?"

Byron laughed at the very thought. "Not if you don't want the English to *hit* you with it!"

Later that evening, strolling through the cool garden lit with torches, the conversation returned to Shelley.

"Lord Eldon adjudicated his case, as he did mine – and so we both lost. If I ever go back to England, I know at least three men I will call out in a duel to the death. One will be Sir Samuel Romilly, who acted for Miss Milbanke against me. Mind, I have called on Nemesis to exact a speedy vengeance against *him*."

"Was he not originally *your* lawyer?"

"Yes, but the Milbankes must have offered him a bigger fee to represent them instead. A bigger fee – how cheap of him! And the second man I intend to shoot into Hell or Purgatory is her attorney, Stephen Lushington, who so readily believed everything Miss Milbanke said. And the third will be Eldon – and there will be *two* bullets for him – one from me, and one from Shelley."

"I don't know why you expected any better from Lord

Eldon in your own case, not after you gave him so many hard times in the House of Lords."

"The damned brute deserved it."

"And gossip has it that Lord Eldon has never forgiven you for arriving at the last minute to hand your vote to the Whigs in favour of Catholic Emancipation for the Irish. Your vote tipped the scales by one vote – *one* vote – no wonder Lord Eldon and the Tories hate you and are glad you are gone."

Byron looked at him archly. "Oh, but I am not gone. I still have my vote from anywhere in the world – by *proxy*. And damnit, I shall use it – *every time* – against them. Do they care about all the suicides in England? No, they don't give a damn. I wish I could be there to tell them so."

"The worst of them all though, is Lord Castlereagh, that damned blaggard. He and Lord Liverpool together have got to be the worst demons on this earth."

"Castlereagh will be assassinated. You can depend on it. The poor and starving can endure only so much at his hands. Fletcher tells me from his latest letters from England that the Luddites in Nottinghamshire are planning an uprising."

"I detest any kind of bloodshed," Hobby said, now feeling extremely happy that the conversation had turned to politics, his own favourite subject. It gave him the same rush of excitement which he had often thought Scrope Davies must get from gambling.

Yet Byron was beginning to irritate him, due to his strange new habit of continually halting in his walk to step aside a fraction, and then walk on.

"Why do you keep doing that?" Hobby asked irritably. "Stopping, stepping aside a pace, and then walking on. Anyone would think you were practising a dance step."

Byron pointed to some ants and other insects wandering here and there on the stone path. "I would hate to hurt or kill any of them by treading on them."

"Oho!" said Hobhouse sneeringly. "Ten minutes ago you were threatening to shoot dead three men in duels, and now you are fearing to step on a few insects. Is that not hypocrisy?"

"No, not at all," Byron replied seriously. "Those insects are innocent of all harm, and are merely getting on with their own lives. The three men are guilty, for doing their utmost to harm and ruin mine."

"Well ..." Hobhouse could not disagree. The attacks on his dear friend had been brutal, and at the time no one had fought harder in Byron's corner than he had ... And yes, there were times when *he* also would have liked to kill all three men, and a few dozen more besides. But Byron was recovering, the hurt lessening, so what good would it do him if they were to prolong that topic now?

"So, as I was *saying*, about politics, before your dance steps interrupted me – When I go back to England, as soon as a Borough seat becomes free, I intend to put my name forward for election into Parliament."

"When you go back to England?" Byron looked at him curiously. "So when *are* you going back, Hobby? You've been away from England now for how long ... ten, eleven months?"

Hobhouse shrugged. "There's no rush, is there? Not unless a Borough seat comes up. And I hate to think of you here in Venice all on your own. Besides, we have not been over to Greece yet. And I still need to visit Pisa and Bologna."

"More for your *serious* travel book?"

"Indeed. Some of us have to earn a living. We can't all live like a lord as you do."

Byron laughed. "So says the son of one of the richest men in England, a son who has never yet done a day's work in his life. And you accuse me of hypocrisy? They should bury you in *Bologna*."

~~~

Now that he was on the mainland, and had retrieved his horses from the stables at Fusina, Byron enjoyed nothing more than horse-riding every evening along the
~~~

banks of the Brenta; usually with Tita, but now with Hobhouse.

"Not that you would be any use as a bodyguard, Hobby, but fortunately, here in La Mira, I don't need one."

"And yet you do in Venice, in the city?"

"Tita thinks so; but so far in Venice I have always been treated with the greatest kindness and respect. Signor Segati said it was because I appear to be very fond of Venice, when so many other Englanders complain about the *decay* of the place. The *decay*, indeed. What did they expect? Of course some of the major buildings are decayed, but that's because the city is over a thousand years old, as old as the Roman Empire."

"Older than Britain?"

Byron shrugged. "No, not even *God* is older than Britain."

Hobhouse loved these summer evening rides, strolling about on horseback with Byron until the snowy peaks of the distant Alps were flushed red with sunset. Occasionally they came across various groups of peasant women who sat around idly talking, and after the usual polite salute or nod, they rode on.

Yet tonight, as they rode by the village of Dolo, their progress was halted when one of the younger women stepped forward in front of Byron's horse and boldly put her palm up for him to halt.

"You are very well known in the city, Mylord," she said in Italian, "for your generosity in giving relief to the beggars and your peasant neighbours."

Byron shrugged dismissively and said to Hobhouse in English. "Generosity at very little cost to me when it is given in Venetian livres."

"And yet it is a lot to Venetians," Hobby replied, and then lowered his head and his voice as he leaned closer to Byron's horse, saying – "Peasants they may be, but are these not two of the prettiest Italian girls you have ever seen?"

Byron nodded; indeed, he had noticed that most of Italy's beauty and attractiveness was to be found in the lower class, whereas the features of most of the upper class and nobility were hardly worth a longer look.

The bold one, who had spoken, had been joined by another girl, who nodded in agreement when the bold one spoke again. "If you help them, why do you not help us?"

Byron smiled, thinking her audacity and effrontery to be amazing ... like the rest of her. She was about five foot ten inches tall, black-haired, black-eyed, and about twenty years old ... slim and lithe in her movements, and yet she looked strong enough and tall enough to breed gladiators.

"Cara," he said, *"tui se troppo bella e giovane par aver'bisogno del' soccorso mio."*

She flourished a hand and tutted at the suggestion that she was too young and beautiful to need his help. "If you saw my house, and the food I eat, you would not think so."

Byron was surprised, for the village was clean, the people looked happy, with smiling faces, and there were no beggars.

And the girl, although she was blatantly asking for help, she did not appear to be in much need, looking healthy and clean and neatly clothed in a light summer dress and ornaments of coral and Venetian chains around her neck. As haughty as a princess. Instinctively he suspected she would be insulted if he were to hand her money. So what the deuce *did* she want?

Hobhouse was now talking down to the other girl, who was smaller than her friend, and a lot shyer than she had at first appeared, her face flushing crimson when she realised he was flirting romantically with her, although clearly not understanding a word of his poor Italian.

"I know you, Mylord," said the haughty one to Byron. "I have seen you riding on your horse. Would you like to know me?"

"Know you? In what way?"

She smiled daringly. "I could be your *donna*, and you my *amoroso*."

Hobhouse, although a little shocked to hear the words '*donna*' and '*amoroso*', looked hopefully at the second girl, who blushed again, and then spoke up to him quickly in Italian.

Hobhouse listened, and then looked eagerly at Byron. "What did she say to me?"

"She said for herself, she would not hesitate , but she is unmarried, and although married women will do it, in Italy no single girl will do anything before marriage."

"Do it? I was merely seeking some romance," Hobby said huffily. "Talk about jumping from A to Z without anything else in between!"

Byron looked at the haughty one, who, the more he looked at her, the more magnificent she appeared to him.

"May I know your name?"

"Margarita Cogni. You may name me as Margarita."

"Well, Margarita, supposing that you are in genuine want," he told her, "I will offer to help you – without any conditions."

"No." She shook her head stubbornly. "I take nothing for nothing. I want the condition of being your donna."

"Are you married?"

She nodded. "To a baker. A ferocious brute."

"Then how can you dare to ask to be my mistress?"

"He will kill me, but I don't care. I saw Mylord on his horse three evenings ago and I felt love for the first time. If you do not make me your donna, I will kill *myself!*"

"Good grief!" Hobhouse heard the word "*uccisione*" and knew it meant 'kill' or 'murder' and frantically reached for the small gun in his pocket, until he saw that Byron was smiling.

"What?"

"She has no wish to harm me, Hobby, but she is shameless and brazen and beautiful and I know it would be folly to have anything to do with her."

After some more conversation, more in half-jest than anything else, they said their farewells to the girls, and then rode back to the Villa Foscarini – Hobhouse to rest and read as usual, and Byron to work; for night was his favourite time to write his poetry, when the world was asleep, and he was wide awake.

On entering the villa, to Hobhouse's shock, who was sitting in the drawing-room, relaxing in an armchair as if he lived there, but Signor Segati.

Hobhouse's hand immediately went to the pocket holding his gun to threaten and order out – yet Byron at once greeted the man with a smile and a warm handshake and a number of sentences in Italian.

Segati laughed, chattered out some Italian sentences of his own, and then handed Byron two letters, before taking his leave.

"Well I'll be damned," said Hobhouse when the man had gone. "So did he come over here from Venice just to deliver you some letters?"

"No, he was merely passing ."

"Merely passing ... all the way over from Venice?"

"Not to visit me." Byron grinned. "His Venetian mistress, the one I told you about? She lives in a village quite near here."

"Not in the village of Dolo?"

"No, not Dolo. While you were away in Naples and Florence, Segati dropped in here a few times."

"To bring you letters delivered to his house?"

"No, sometimes just to say *Ciao* as he was passing. He and Fletcher are great chums. And sometimes he drops in to deliver notes from the widowed aunt to Mr Berger. Now *there* is a romance for you!"

"Not for me! I'm too young for a widowed aunt. I'd much prefer one of those lovely girls at Dolo. They *all* looked beautiful to me."

Byron chuckled and lifted the letters to take up to his bedroom to read in private, knowing from the handwriting that one of the letters came from his sister

Augusta.

Hobhouse secured for himself a glass of brandy and took it up to his bedroom, where he finished the day by making his usual notes in his journal:

"Ride along the Brenta with Byron. Return over the other side of the river from Dolo. He remarked on the moon reigning on the right of us, and the Alps still blushing with the blaze of the sunset. The Brenta came down on us all purple – a delightful scene, which Byron intends to put into his new "Childe Harold."

Here at La Mira – a strange life; very tranquil and comfortable."

In his own bedroom, Byron was feeling neither tranquil nor comfortable, but utterly exasperated as he rapidly wrote a reply to his sister:

Dearest Augusta – I have received your letter, which is full of woes, as usual, megrims and mysteries; but my sympathies remain in suspense, because, for the life of me, I can't make out whether your disorder is a broken heart or the earache – or whether it has been you that has been ill or the children – or what your melancholy or mysterious apprehensions tend to, or refer to – whether to Lady Caroline Lamb's novel – Lady Byron's magnanimity – or some other piece of imposture. I know nothing of what you are in the doldrums about.

> *And as for me – leave me to take care of myself. I may be ill or well, in high or low spirits, in quick or obtuse state of feelings, like anybody else – but I can battle my way through.*

The following day he complained to Hobhouse about Augusta's *"damned crinkum-crankum"* way of talking to him in her letters.

"They read as if she has written half a paragraph, then is called away by one of the children or her hapless husband, and then returns to the letter and continues writing the paragraph – but on a completely different subject. Not to mention all the *unfinished* sentences! How she expects me to make sense of it all, I don't know."

Hobhouse could only listen, unable to say anything that might help to clarify poor Augusta's distressed situation. He knew things that Byron did not know, but in the carriage on their way to Switzerland, he had sworn his promise to Scrope Davies that he would not say a word to their mutual friend about it.

Living part of the year in nearby Cambridge, as well as his visits to the racecourse, Scrope occasionally dropped in on Augusta at her home in Newmarket to ensure she was well. A timid and sweet person, Augusta was one of those inoffensive women that was easily bossed around, by her children, her servants, and her husband. None gave her any consideration, and the only one who truly cared for Augusta was her half-brother, Byron, and also Byron's friends.

But now poor Augusta was in the hard grip of one of the worst bullies ever born – Miss Milbanke, now called Lady Byron – a woman so cold and calculating that Hobhouse hoped he would never have to set eyes on her again.

Shocking it was, and if the world only knew – Lady Byron was now forcing the timid Augusta to show or send to her every letter she received from Byron, and even dictated Augusta's reply to him.

Scrope had been enraged; but he, too, had been sworn to secrecy by Augusta, who, in her usual timid way, believed that the easiest path was to placate her brother's wife and do what she was told, on the grounds that she "had nothing to hide".

Yet no wonder poor Augusta's letter were full of mysterious hints to Byron, trying to warn him to say nothing of his affairs and life abroad in his letters to her; hints that he still as yet did not understand.

Nor could he or Scrope Davies tell him, because God knows what catastrophe that would lead to. Byron would be fit for murder – yet he had to be warned in some way.

"You must remember," he said to Byron, "that your sister not only has a large family and husband to care for, but she is occasionally called in to be a lady-in-waiting to the Queen down at James's Palace, so her life is lived in a constant state of flurry and rush."

Byron agreed. "I know it. That is why I have invited her and the children to come and stay for a few months here at La Mira – away from it all."

Hobhouse was alarmed. "When did you do that?"

"A few weeks ago, but she made no reference to my invitation in her reply; just a catalogue of megrims and mysteries and all the aches and pains of the day."

"It was a silly invitation, when you think about it," said Hobhouse, "and hardly a holiday for her – having to lug a gaggle of children all over the Continent to get here."

"I hadn't thought of it in that way."

"No, and nor should you be expecting long and newsy letters from her about life in England. I wonder how she finds the time to write to you at all. Would *you* have much time to write long letters – if you had four or five children and a husband and Queen to look after? And as you know, *all* of them can be very demanding."

Byron pondered for some moments, and agreed

again. "Demanding, yes — especially that dim-witted, horse-mad, bullying husband of hers."

Chapter Six

~ ~ ~

The following day, while revising the third act of *Manfred* on the advice of John Murray's editor, William Gifford, Lord Byron received a visit from a man who introduced himself to Fletcher as Richard Belgrave Hoppner.

"Never heard of him. Can't you say I am out – not at home."

Fletcher looked doubtful. "I don't think so, my lord."

"Why not?"

"He says he is from the British Consulate in Venice."

"Oh I detest those people! Remember how we were deceived by the British Consul at Malta? Sending us on a wild goose chase into the most dangerous parts of Albania?"

"So what shall I say to him, to Mr Hoppner?"

Byron hesitated, and then shrugged. "Tell him I will be with him in five or ten minutes. I have no intention of *jumping up* just because some British bureaucrat decides to call on me."

Fifteen minutes later, Byron did not even trouble to put on a coat to meet the man, deciding it was too hot anyway for such torture; entering the drawing-room in his shirt and open green waistcoat.

Mr Hoppner appeared slightly startled when he saw his lordship in such casual dress, making Byron wonder if the bureaucrat had expected him to enter the room wearing his lord's coronet on his head.

"How may I help you, sir?"

Mr Hoppner appeared even more surprised. "Oh no, my lord, I came here to ask you the same question."

Within minutes, Byron was feeling remorse that he had left the man to sit waiting for so long, because Richard Hoppner, who was no more thirty, turned out to be very likeable man; and it also transpired that they had a lot in common. Hoppner had passionate literary interests, and politically he was a Whig.

Byron apologised. "I regret keeping you waiting for so long, but I had a task to complete for my 'literary father' in London, Mr Gifford."

Hoppner smiled. "Mr William Gifford?"

"Yes. Why, do you know him?"

"I am his godson."

Byron stared. "Are you indeed? Then pray don't reveal to him that I admire him so much, or he might start sending me even *more* revisions."

Hoppner grinned. "I believe he admires you very much too, my lord."

As they talked, Byron was impressed by Hoppner's gracious friendliness, and his eagerness to be of as much service as possible to him.

"As your Consul, it is my duty, and my pleasure."

Hobhouse walked in, and was introduced: "Mr Hoppner is not only our Consul here, Hobby, he is also a firm supporter of your Whigs in Parliament."

Not even a political supporter of the Whigs, could persuade Hobhouse to lose his stiff yet polite manner with a stranger.

Nevertheless, Byron left him to it while he sought out Fletcher and ordered him to bring in refreshments.

"There is one thing you may be able to help me with," Byron said later to Mr Hoppner. "My bankers in Venice are supposed to be Messrs Siri and Wilhams, but for the life of me I have not yet been able to find them."

"That is because the bankers here do not have their buildings lined up along the Grand Canal, or on the squares like San Marco, as they do in London. No, like all the merchants of Venice, one has to venture down the smaller canals to find their establishments."

"Then tell us where," said Hobhouse who was now running out of money. "Siri and Wilhams are my bankers also."

"I can do more than tell you," said Hoppner good-naturedly. "If you wish to come back to Venice with me now in my gondola, I can take you to their door."

"Oh jolly good," said Hobhouse eagerly. "What say you, Byron?"

"I am down to a few *sequins*, so yes, a cooling cruise across the water would be very refreshing, and hopefully profitable as well."

"Do you have circular notes with you?"

"I do," said Byron. "Mr Kinnaird, my banker in London, provided me with a number of circular notes worth five hundred pounds each."

"Oh goodness – then pray cash no more than one circular note at a time. It would be unwise to carry such a large amount of money around the city of Venice."

The Consul looked at Hobhouse. "And you, Mr Hobhouse?"

"The same amount, five hundred pounds a note."

"Then pray bring your bodyguard with you, Lord Byron. Five hundred pounds can be lost in a night at the gaming tables in London, but here in Venice it could buy three houses."

"Well, if I don't cash some money soon, I will be asking the beggars for help, so let us go. Thank you, Mr Hoppner, your visit here has been most opportune for us."

Richard Hoppner smiled. "That is precisely what Consuls are for. To help their nationals."

In the gondola over to Venice, under the shade of the felze, Byron and Hobhouse learned a lot more about their Consul. He was not happy with his posting to Venice, and was hoping for one in Milan.

"Do you not like Venice?"

"Oh, I do. I like Venice well enough. But my wife, you see, is Swiss and pregnant, and so a posting to Milan would bring us nearer to the Swiss frontier, and nearer to her family and friends."

"Can you not apply to be moved?"

"I can. I have. But in the Diplomatic Service, it has

always been the rule that one goes where one is sent."

Arriving in Venice, the rest of the afternoon was spent on business, with Mr Hoppner making all the introductions, and ensuring that all transactions were correct.

"Now," he said when they were ready to leave, "here is my card, and my address in Venice, and whenever you need help, Lord Byron, pray do not hesitate to call or send for me."

"A nice man," said Byron as the gondola glided away from the city. "And I would say a *good* man."

Hobhouse was not so sure. "I would not trust any man from the Diplomatic Service. Remember how that British Consul in Malta completely fooled us – sending us into Turkey as decoys to divert Ali Pasha while the British brigades were taking over the Ionian Islands behind Ali's back."

Byron laughed. "Will we *ever* forget that? We thought we were being sent as British envoys – not *decoys*."

"It's not funny, Byron! We could have been brutally *murdered* – and would have been – if Ali Pasha had found out their scheme before we had luckily left his palace in Tepelina. We went to him as representatives of *Britain*, as friends – and all the time the British were taking over the Greek islands behind his back."

Byron sighed. "It was a long time ago, Hobby, seven long years ago. It's over and forgotten by everyone but us."

"Is it though? Is it forgotten? I doubt anyone there would remember *my* name, but I'm sure the name of Lord Byron is remembered well and grimly by the Turks."

"I doubt it. They are too busy enslaving the Greeks to remember or care about one solitary Englishman. Now I suggest we get out from under this felze and enjoy the sea breeze."

"No, you go. I'm happy to stay here in the shade and close my eyes."

"To sleep?"

"No, to think about Venice."

"Venice? To think *what* about Venice? You've seen it all before."

"Yes, but it may surprise you to know, that while we were walking from here to there and everywhere, and you and your diplomat were looking around and chattering like woodpeckers, I saw *nothing* in Venice today, nothing except the white veils and dark eyes and fine skins of the women. Such beauty! Let me now dream of them for a while."

Byron laughed, and moved out from under the felze to sit nearer the front of the boat and enjoy the cooling breeze, relaxing in the silence, and hearing no sounds now but the rhythmic splashing of the oars and the swishing of the water.

He loved Venice, loved Italy, and loved its warm climate – too hot today – but generally the sunshine every morning was a wonderful mood enhancer, and a daily delight. Where else could one sit in their garden and smell in the air the delicious aromas of lemons and limes and the fruit of the fig trees? In Greece, yes ... but then Greece had so many other problems.

As Fusina came into sight in the distance, he was unaware of it; his eyes transfixed on the glow of the setting sun, orange and green in the sky, which he had never seen before, as if Heaven itself was throwing down another kind of light on Italy. The reflecting water of the sea spread out in front of him was now one glowing orange flame.

Chapter Seven

~~~

A few evenings later they rode along the Brenta again until they reached the village of Dolo where, this time, it was Hobhouse who was hailed by one of the young peasant girls.

She moved up to his horse and spoke flirtatiously up to him in Italian; while Hobhouse, instantly infatuated by her prettiness, nodded agreement to everything she said; and then asked Byron to translate.

"She was told you were an English lord who had won many battles in the war against the French."

"Tell her, yes, I won them all."

"And do I confirm you to be a lord?"

"No, a duke."

During the back and forth of the translating, Byron glanced around for Margarita Cogni, and saw her standing with her shoulder leaning against a wall. She remained silent, and made no move to step forward.

"Now ask her, Byron, if she is married?"

Byron asked, and then told Hobhouse – "She is, but says she was forced to marry her husband whom she has never liked ... and has always dreamed of meeting a duke ... *un duca.*"

During the translating, Byron often glanced at Margarita Cogni, who remained silent, but her dark eyes were doing a lot of talking to him.

A whispered assignation had just been made for the duke's hopeful *amica* to meet him privately the following evening, when a smiling little man, aged somewhere in his forties, came upon the scene, asking to know who were the two gentlemen on such fine horses?

Byron looked at the man who had burst upon the scene in such a inquisitive way.
~~~

"*Et tu sei?*" – (And you are?)

"Signor Cogni."

"Cogni?" Byron looked incredulously at Margarita, his expression asking her if this smiling little man truly was the 'ferocious brute' of a husband she had spoken of?

She nodded. "My husband, the baker."

"You know these gentlemen, Margarita?"

"No."

"Who are they?"

"A lord and a duke," answered Margarita, betraying that even from her distant stance at the wall, she had been listening keenly to every word.

"*Un signor e un duca?*" For a moment the man seemed shocked, then moved forward in a series of grovelling bows exclaiming, "*Eccellenze!*"

Byron then heard him asking the girl standing by Hobhouse's horse which one of the Excellencies was "*un duca*", and when she pointed up to Hobhouse, the baker asked the duke if his household needed a regular supply of bread – the finest Italian bread ever baked.

"Just tell him 'No, *nessuna!'*" Byron said, and Hobhouse did so, but the baker was not to be put off so easily and begged on; leaving Byron free to look at Margarita and respond to the talking in her eyes with an answering message of his own.

She smiled in response, and then she stepped forward and haughtily ordered her husband to stop making a beggar of himself, slapped him on the head, and escorted him home.

Byron was still quietly laughing on the ride home. "A ferocious brute ? How women do exaggerate!"

John Hobhouse was not listening, lagging behind on his horse and reflecting on the wisdom of his assignation with the Italian girl. He had enjoyed the flirting, but the appearance of a husband had killed all the fun. After all, *she* was married, and *he* was not really a duke, and not even a *bad* actor – so how would he be able to act like one and keep up the pretence?

Also, it *was* rather immoral, especially for a single man who had no ties and therefore could honourably avail himself of the choice of one of all those beautiful high-class courtesans in Venice.

In England, high-class courtesans were the norm for all young gentlemen. What else was he to do when every respectable young English lady interpreted a kiss on the cheek as a marriage proposal — and worse — her parents expected it too. A lifetime of marriage in return for a kiss on the cheek!

The only solution was to keep as far away from them as possible, not stand too close in conversation, and then seek all the delights of love and romance with the courtesans.

During their student days at Cambridge he and Byron and Scrope Davies had often gone down to London just to visit the courtesans – *"for some clean feminine fun"* as Scrope Davies used to say. The courtesans charged a fortune but half of them were aristocrats, or the daughters of aristocrats, with the highest standards, and the only ones they would regularly visit. Not for them the low street prostitutes whom they would not touch with a barge-pole.

Those were the days! Young and free in London, and then back to the serious world of study in Cambridge.

The evening was still bright, and he decided to discuss the wisdom of his assignation now with Byron, explain his sudden unwillingness — until he saw that Byron was a good way ahead of him, his head turned to look at all the various houses on the hills overlooking the Brenta on this side of the river.

Grasping the reins, Hobhouse was about to move forward at a quicker pace when a carriage suddenly came alongside him with a burly Englishman leaning out of the open window, calling up to his driver: "That's Lord Byron ahead! I'd know him anywhere! Go faster! Push the scoundrel off the road!"

Before Hobhouse could even blink, the whip in the driver's hand lashed down and the two carriage-horses bolted forward, squeezing Byron to the side of the road while his horse reared up in whinnying fright – coming down again in the path of the two horses – forcing the driver to quickly halt or deposit the carriage and its occupant into the river.

Still on his horse, Byron wheeled round in fury and called out to the driver, asking him what in damnation he was doing?

The driver shook his head, pointing down to the carriage.

"You were told to drive at such speed?"

The driver nodded.

Byron immediately dismounted and walked up to open window of the carriage and spoke to the man inside.

Hobhouse could not hear the low reply, but whatever it was – it was enough to make Byron suddenly reach inside the open window and angrily slap the Englishman's face.

"Oh good grief!" said Hobhouse, dismounting also, but Byron had already opened the carriage door and invited the Englishman to step out.

"For what purpose?"

"So that I may pave the road with your remains!"

"Good God!" Hobhouse was now in a hot sweat knowing from experience that Byron was capable of saying or doing anything in a rage.

The Englishman suddenly leaned out and yanked the door of the carriage shut, quickly locking it from the inside, and then shouted some menacing blasphemies at Byron while banging his cane on the roof for his driver to go!

The carriage lurched forward, almost knocking Byron over and leaving him standing furious with exasperation as he looked around at Hobhouse. "Did you see that damned coward!"

"Disgraceful, and certainly not a man of honour!" Hobhouse agreed. "Remaining in his seat after you had slapped his face. What did he say to make you do that?"

Byron remained silent for a moment, and then shrugged huffily. "He insulted my horse."

"Oh," Hobhouse nodded, "so you are not going to tell me?"

"It's not worthy of repeating. But he *could* have injured my poor horse!"

He moved over to his horse, inspecting him from head to shoe, patting him all the while to reassure the poor animal who kept twisting his neck around and neighing complaints to him in horse-talk.

They remounted and rode on. "Nevertheless," Hobby said after a while, "it was an outrageous way for the man to behave in the first place. I heard him say your name up to his driver, so he must have recognised you."

"And I recognised *him,*" Byron replied. "As soon as I saw him. He is a nephew or some kind of relative to my former father-in-law, Sir Ralph Milbanke."

Hobhouse sighed, wondering if there was *no* escape from those troublesome Milbankes and their cohorts?

Returning home and entering the Villa Foscarini, Fletcher said to Byron: "Signor Segati was here again. He brought you over another letter."

Byron grinned. "I do believe he is now using my letters as the perfect excuse to come over here to see his *donna.*"

"You will have to inform people of your new address," advised Hobhouse, "or just direct all to *Venice, post restante.*"

"I will, yes, I will ..." Byron had opened the letter and was reading it, his mood now sombre and his expression sad.

Hobhouse was alarmed. "What is it?"

"It's from John Rocca in Geneva ... he writes to inform us that our dear friend at Coppet, Madame de Staël, has died, so she will not be joining us in Italy."

Chapter Eight

~ ~ ~

In his publishing offices in Mayfair, John Murray was also reading the same sad news – not in a letter – but in an article which *The Times* had picked up from one of the French newspapers. The great French novelist, Madame de Staël, had died at the age of fifty-one.

Murray sat back in dismay.

This was turning out to be a very bad year for the health of his female authors. First, Miss Jane Austen dies, and now Madame de Staël dies, and both in July. And neither of them had reached a great age. Miss Austen had been only forty-one.

Forty-one? Only two years older than he was now – a damnably early age for a good writer to die. And he could not even express his regret and respects by posting a notice of sorrow for the loss of one of his authors in a newspaper, as was the custom, because no one had ever heard of the lady. Miss Austen was totally unknown to the world. She had been determined to remain anonymous, and so all her books had been written and published by 'A Lady'.

At least in Miss Austen's case, her brother Henry had now brought him two new manuscripts for publication, *Persuasion,* which was just as delightful as her other works; and *Susan* – a terrible title, which he had now changed to *Northanger Abbey*. Although the latter was not a *new* manuscript at all, but one which had been written over a decade ago and sold to Crosby's for ten pounds.

When Henry Austen had told him this, Murray had been surprised, curious to know why Crosby's had not published it.

"They simply could not be bothered," Henry Austen had replied. "They resold it back to me after her death for the return of their piddling ten pounds."

Murray sighed ... well, at least *he* could console himself with the knowledge that he had treated Miss Austen better than that. All her previous books, self-published at her own cost and printed by Egertons, had sold no more than 350 copies; yet he had immediately ordered a first print-run of 2000 copies of *Emma,* and had sold them all, and into a second print-run, much to Miss Austen's delight.

Why did she have to die? It was such a shame. With more and more of her wonderful books, they could have made a fortune together.

And now, with the forthcoming publication of *Persuasion* and *Northanger Abbey,* Henry Austen had decided to make one particular change to his sister's books, of which John Murray approved – Henry Austen was now determined that England should know his sister's *name.*

"Because Jane *deserves* to be known," Henry had said. "She was not just *'a lady'*. She also longed to be recognised as a good writer, but was always too modest to say so."

Unlike many of the *male* authors who were now circulating London in their abundance and not modest in any way, Murray reflected cynically. Minor novelists who wrote one mediocre book and then walked around London with an air of the 'author' about them; and usually carrying their book like a social adornment; and if not carrying the book, then constantly talking about it, making sure everyone knew they were *'a writer, an intellectual, a man of consequence."* At how many literary parties had he been bored to sleep by such impostors?

And yet, the *real* writers, some of the greats, also disappointed him. Take Coleridge – his talent was now being slowly eroded by his addiction to opium.

And then there was Thomas Moore – his latest epic poem, *Lalla Rookh,* was fair enough – but it was all Byron.

How did Moore, an Irishman who had never travelled farther than England, think that he could copy Byron simply by setting his tale in the East? Library books were not good enough. *Maps* were not good enough – not to hike oneself onto the same level as the man who had *been* to the East, and *lived* there.

And more than that. Byron was a poet of natural *genius*, a man apart, in every way. Even if he had not been predestined to be ranked a 'Lord' he would not have been very much dissimilar to the man he was now, and that was a man who truly was *different* to the crowd. Not only for his good looks or his great mental powers, but *who,* pray, could even successfully *imitate* his tender passion or his biting irony?

Not Thomas Moore nor fifty other hopeless copycats, that's for sure.

What these others did not understand, was that Byron's originality was deeply rooted in himself. *He* was his own poem. Everything he wrote was based on his own actual experience, or the people he came across in his life. Byron was the opposite to a fiction writer or an actor – nothing was made up.

Murray reached across the desk and lifted the first pages of the new Canto of *Childe Harold's Pilgrimage* which had arrived in yesterday's post. And now, reading again the first beautiful stanzas, he saw the truth of his words that Byron's life had always been his main poem; using nothing but his own eyes, and his own mind and emotions, to convey his poetry.

I stood in Venice, on the Bridge of Sighs;

A palace and a prison on each hand:

I saw from out the wave her structures rise

As from the stroke of an enchanter's wand:

A thousand years their cloudy wings expand

Around me, and a dying Glory smiles

O'er the far times, when many a subject land

Looked to the winged Lion's marble piles

Where Venice sate in State, on her hundred isles!

In Venice, Tasso's echoes are no more,

And silent rows the songless gondolier;

Her palaces are crumbling to the shore,

And music meets not always now the ear:

Those days are gone — but Beauty is still here.

States fall, arts fade —but Nature doth not die,

Nor yet forget how Venice once was dear,

The pleasant face of all festivity,

The revel of the earth, the masque of Italy!

Sitting back in his chair, John Murray wondered if and when Lord Byron would come back to England.

He sat gazing back in nostalgia to that wonderful time when Byron was all the rage, and he the envy of all other publishers.

A time when Byron had hated being recognised, and yet was always watched. But how could he not be, when his natural elegance carried with it an air of royalty, which quickly turned to embarrassment when he saw he was being stared at by the crowd. He was different, and they knew it. He was not one of them. He was a beautiful genius, and even more interesting when rumour said that he was mad, bad, and dangerous to know.

John Murray had to smile. He had known Lord Byron long and well, and was very certain that he was as sane as himself, even though Byron's wife had tried to prove that he *was* in fact mad when she realised that he no longer loved her. Even when she had got her doctors to slyly examine him on some pretext about his health, and they had pronounced him sane, had she refused to accept it. And now the poor woman was driving *herself* mad by continually trying to persecute him.

No, Byron was sane, but the one person that Murray thought might truly be a slight mad, was Byron's atheist friend, Mr Shelley.

~~~

Since his return to England, Shelley had suffered enough to make any man, if not mad, at least distracted and unfocused, and all in all totally miserable. He could not concentrate on his poetry, and neither Claire nor Mary was making his life any easier – Mary because she wanted Claire gone – and Claire because she desperately wanted Byron back.

It was still a puzzle to him why women believed the practice of constant nagging would eventually make a man do something he did not want to do.

Yet, contrary to that, he eventually gave in and did what Claire had been nagging him to do, and wrote a letter to Byron:

My dear Lord Byron,

I called on Rogers the other day and heard some news of you, viz. that you had been to Rome, and that you had returned to Venice. How is it that I have not heard from you? At first I drew from your silence a favourable augury of your early return. This is in a degree confirmed by the circumstance of Newstead Abbey being advertised for sale. I shall be among the first to greet you on your return.

At present I write only to inquire what are your
~~~

plans with regard to little Alba. She continues to reside with us under a feigned name. But we are somewhat embarrassed about her. We are exposed to what remarks her existence is calculated to excite. At least a period approaches when it will be impossible to temporise with our servants and visitors.

There are two very respectable young ladies in this town, who would undertake the charge of her, if you consent to this arrangement. Claire would then be able to superintend her; and I cannot but recommend this measure to you as a provisional one, if any other is at present inconvenient to you. If you return to England in the autumn, or even in the winter, we should experience no inconvenience from deferring the question until that period.

I ought to tell you that your little girl is in excellent health and spirits. She improves very much, and although small for her age, she has an extraordinary degree of animation and intelligence. Our Genevese nurse walks about with her and William all the day in the garden; and she is bathed like him, in cold water.

I suppose you know that the tyranny, civil and religious, under which this country groans, has visited me somewhat severely. I neither like it the worse nor the better for this. It was always the object of my unbounded abhorrence. But it may become necessary that I should quit the country. It is possible that the interference exercised by the Chancery Court in the instance of my two other children might be attempted to extend to William. Should this be the case, I shall depart. And in this case, what shall I do with Alba?

I have read "Manfred" with the greatest admiration. The same freedom from common rules that marked the 3rd Canto of "Childe Harold" and "Chillon" is visible here; and it was that which all your earlier productions, except "Lara" wanted. But it made me dreadfully melancholy, and I fear your other friends in England too. Why do you indulge in this despondency? "Manfred" as far as I learn, is immensely popular; it is characterised as a very daring production.

Leigh Hunt has been with me here, and we often speak about you. Hunt is an excellent man, and has a great regard for you. How is your health, and the resolutions on which it depends?

I have lately had a relapse of my constitution, and if the Chancellor should threaten to invade my domestic circle, I shall seek Italy, as a refuge at once from the stupid tyranny of these laws, and my disorder.

I suppose Claire will write to you herself. Mary desires her kind remembrances to you, and I am,

Ever sincerely yours, P. B. Shelley.

P.S: Alba has blue eyes and dark hair, which has now fallen off. William and she are very good friends.

Byron said to Hobhouse after reading the letter, "Is it not strange, that Shelley insists on referring to the child as *'your little girl'*, and never once as 'Claire's child'?"

Hobhouse read the letter, frowning at the part where Shelley says he might have to depart England ... "*And in this case, what shall I do with Alba?*"

He looked curiously at Byron. "It is almost as if the mother has left all responsibility for the child to Shelley and you – to sort out between you – and *that* is very strange. Most mothers can't bear to part with their babes."

"It's a trick, I'm sure of it. I write only to Shelley, never to her, so she is clearly dictating to Shelley what to write to me. And poor Shelley has enough of his own problems. Well, if the child is such an embarrassment, and Claire does not want to, or is not capable, of looking after her, then I *would* be prepared to take the child and bring her up myself, but only – *only* – if it was guaranteed that I would never again have to set eyes on her selfish mother."

"Then write back and tell him so, and then the choice of one or the other would be hers. Although I doubt she will be willing to give up the child on those conditions, so call her bluff."

PART THREE

Margarita Cogni

"Mad, Bad, and Dangerous to Know."

Chapter Nine

~ ~ ~

Fletcher was terrified of her. Hobhouse had quickly moved back into the *Hotel Gran Bretagne*. Yet Byron liked her – because she made him laugh.

To his eyes, as well as admiring her beauty, he was amused and fascinated by her leonine fierceness and her passionate nature, and finally he wrote in a hopelessly lamentable tone to his friend and publisher, John Murray, about his new *amica*, Margarita Cogni.

I know not how, but she has gained an ascendancy over me. The reasons for this are, firstly, her person – very dark, tall, the Venetian face, fine black eyes. She is a thorough Venetian in her dialect, in her thoughts, in everything, with all their naiveté and humour.

Besides, she can neither read nor write, so cannot plague me with letters. In other respects she is somewhat fierce, and likes to walk in whenever it suits her, with no great regard to time, place, nor persons, and if she finds any female in her way, she knocks them down.

She has inordinate pride and self-love, and will not tolerate any other women near me, and so for the most innocent of female visitors there is great confusion and demolition of head-dresses and handkerchiefs, and sometimes my servants in "redding the fray" between her and other feminine persons, receive more knocks than acknowledgements for their attempts at peaceful endeavours.

Yet even when I have started in a rage, she always finishes by making me laugh with some Venetian saying or foolery or another, and the Gypsy knows this well enough, as well as her other powers of persuasion, and she exerts them with the usual tact and success of all She-things — and "may the gods give us joy!"

John Hobhouse was horrified when Byron laughingly told him about the letter to John Murray.

"You know Murray will not approve — not of you mixing so freely with the lower classes."

Byron shrugged. "Well, if he dares to say so, I shall remind him that he was nothing more than a bookseller in a shabby shop in London's Paternoster Row before I made him rich and moved him to offices in Mayfair. Is that not true?"

"It is true, yes, but it would be very rude of you to say so."

"Then I won't, because I like him."

"But *why* do you do it, Byron — send letters like that? You know he will read it aloud or pass the letter around his four o'clock cronies to read for themselves, and they will tell others until it is general gossip and then another scandal against you. So why?"

In one beat Byron's expression changed from warm amusement to defiance.

"At the time of the Separation and during my time in Switzerland, the disgraceful behaviour of English society outraged me — and now I intend to *outrage*

English society." He grinned wickedly. "I'll give them enough scandalous gossip to make their teeth fall out."

They were on the island of Lido, about to mount two horses to ride along the stretch of the beach.

"And as for the lower class here in Venice," Byron said as he mounted his horse, "let me tell you, Hobby, I would prefer to spend one day with my tigress from Dolo, than a whole month with that humourless and artificial woman who bears and disgraces my name."

Hobhouse sought to end the subject. "Well, we've got the horses, so let's make use of them."

Byron looked at him with half-shut eyes. "As long as you never question my reasons again."

"Oh good grief – the half-shut eyes – but you don't frighten me!" Hobby laughed, and rode off at a gallop, with Byron riding as fast and chasing him.

The island of *Lido* was a strip of land of seven miles long that separated the central part of the Venetian lagoon from the Adriatic sea. A calm and serene island with a beautiful beach of cool breezes and blue waves under a golden sun.

Byron now had two of his saddle-horses stabled on Lido permanently, so that he and Hobhouse could ride there regularly during the summer. The sea was always calm and the crystal clear waters were fun to swim in.

After the noisy hubbub of Venice and the Hotel Gran Bretagne, Hobhouse loved the beauty and tranquillity of the island. He knew he should have returned to England months ago, but he was loathed to leave Venice. England was so boring nowadays. No Byron, no Beau Brummell, no conversation except politics and poverty of the masses, and the indolence of the Prince Regent.

Later that evening, after enjoying a lovely dinner at Byron's hospitable mansion at La Mira, Tita rowed Hobby back to the *Gran Bretagne* where, once he had changed into his dressing-gown, he wrote in his daily journal:

Went with Byron to Lido. Lovely day. A light breeze.

Can still recollect the glee inspired by galloping along the beach.

~~~

At the same time, Margarita was sitting under the moonlight beside Byron on a bench in the rear garden at La Mira, the air heavy with the perfume of flowers and fruits.

Byron had been contemplating the sky: it was a night of a thousand stars and she had slipped into the garden like a ghost; and she was very quiet tonight.

He looked at her. "What is wrong?"

She pressed her palms together against her breast as if in devout prayer. "I pray to the Virgin that one day I can marry you."

"I may be separated, Margarita, but I am still legally married, and from what I know of my virtuous wife, I always will be."

She then proposed that he should now seek a divorce from his wife. "*Un divorzio, sì?*"

"In England, we are not allowed to divorce, except for *female* infidelity."

"So how do you know," said she, "what *she* has been doing while you are here in Venice?"

Byron smiled. "I could not know what she is doing, other than she will never give me grounds for a divorce."

"Why not?"

"Because she is who she is, cold as ice, and vengeful. And because the married women in England are not the same as they are here."

"Can't you do something to get rid of her?"

"No more than has been done already. Why, what else would you have me do ... poison her?"

Margarita pondered silently, as if seeming to think the solution of poison was worth considering.

Which made him laugh. Even though she was twenty-two she had a childlike ruthlessness and temper, as well
~~~

as a childlike innocence about her. And even if she refused to tolerate any female rivals, she was incapable of causing any real harm, apart from ripping off hats, and threatening to kill everybody.

To him though, she was beautiful, and funny, and always very gentle and loving to his dumb animals, and that told him a lot more about her than all her threats.

"Your vengeful wife – make her come to Venice, and let me kill her for you."

He laughed at her nonsense, but she was passionately serious. "*Mio amore,* for you I would go into the midst of a hundred knives!"

"Margarita, if you don't stop talking like this, I will have to send you away and never see you again."

"No! I will be good, very good, *lo prometto!* I will let her live alone and cold in *Inghilterra.* Tell me how the women in your country are not the same as here?"

"Well, they do not display such violent jealousy as the Italians."

"Jealousy means love."

"And they do not know how to *kiss* as good as the Italians."

"No?" She smiled. "Not so good? Let me kiss you now!"

And she did, until the night of a thousand stars eventually vanished into the dawn.

Hobhouse arrived promptly the next morning at ten, only to be told by Fletcher that his lordship was still in bed, and so was his *amica.*

"What? She is here – even in the day?"

"Oh, she comes and goes whenever she pleases, and his lordship allows it."

"Should you not say something to him?"

"Me?" Fletcher shuddered. "I wouldn't dare. *He* is the only one who can keep her in order, but he will never allow anyone else to interfere with her."

Hobhouse dared, as soon as Byron appeared washed and dressed and ready to go over to Venice.

"Byron, this Italian girl, do you know what you are doing?"

"Yes, I know exactly what I am doing, Hobby. I am confining myself to the strictest adultery, because that is the only choice my wife has left to me. What would you have me do with the rest of my life – join the Armenian monks?"

"No, at least not yet; not while you are still in your twenties."

"Twenty-nine. And as a matter of fact, even when I had relations with Claire I was legally separated, and the marriage vows to my wife were rescinded in law. So I did not commit adultery even then, nor am I now."

Hobhouse shrugged. "Technically, no. But –"

"But don't you start your superior *skimbling-skambling* with me, Hobby. You and Scrope Davies are every bit as carnal as me, and you know it."

Hobhouse stared. "Skimbling-skambling? Where do you get these words from – or do you just make them up?"

"They come out of the blue, when people like you annoy me."

Hobhouse grinned. "Well, we have an appointment in Venice, so let us declare a truce, and go."

~~~

Before leaving to go to Venice, Byron was delayed by the arrival of another letter from Percy Shelley.

My dear Lord Byron, — since I received your letter, my own destination has been so uncertain, that I have taken no steps about the little girl. I shall, if possible, spend this winter at Pisa, and in that case I shall myself be the lion in charge of the little one. If I am compelled to remain in England, I shall commit her to the charge of some person on whom I can
~~~

entirely depend.

Once again Byron was astounded as he read out the paragraph to Hobhouse. "You were right – to read this it seems as if the welfare of the child is nothing to do with Claire, and all consideration of her welfare is being left to Shelley and I."

"Still, it is very good of Shelley to take on the business of it all. Any other man would say the child was not his responsibility."

Byron nodded. "Shelley has a good heart, but he is foolish to allow Claire to use him in this way."

To save repeating it, and because he had always valued Hobby's judgement on these matters, he read the rest of the letter aloud:

My health is in a miserable state, so some care will be required to prevent it speedily terminating in death. They recommend Italy as a certain remedy for my disease

I told you what I thought of "Manfred" – and the impression of the public seems to be the same. Your "Lament of Tasso" I do not think so perfect a composition."

"Your Lament of Tasso?" Hobby said curiously. "What is he talking about?"

"Oh, something I wrote one night and sent it to Murray with the manuscript of Manfred. He must have now published *Tasso* too."

"Indeed? It makes one wonder how your dear publisher would thrive without you," Hobby said sarcastically; and then waved a hand. "Well, read on, read on ... "

"Although there are passages indeed, most wonderfully impressive; and those lines in which you describe the youthful feelings of Tasso, in his solitude, have a profound and thrilling pathos, which I confess to you that whenever I read them, make my head wild with tears. Since I wrote to you last, Mary has presented me with a little girl. We call her Clara —"

"*Why?* Byron exclaimed incredulously. "Why give his child *that* name? I'm certain Mary did not choose that name for her child, — not the name of her insufferable stepsister! But do you see now – do you see how Claire has got Shelley tied to her little finger?"

"It all sounds somewhat incestuous to me. Certainly not right in some way or another. And Shelley sounds as if he's at death's door. I feel quite sorry for him."

"At this moment," Byron said, "I feel more sorry for Mary Shelley, his wife. Imagine living in the same house as Claire? You have no idea how slyly *manipulative* she can be."

"As can I." Hobhouse stood up. "Allow me now to manipulate you over to Venice, otherwise we will be rudely late for our appointment with Mr Hoppner."

<p style="text-align:center">~~~</p>

In Venice, the British Consul, Mr Richard Hopper, had been eagerly awaiting the arrival of Lord Byron, with the hopes of also manipulating him to his own ends. Not that it was a crime in any way, as his lordship was obviously very rich, and if he was not so rich as one suspected, then he was certainly richer than a poor diplomat on a British Government wage.

As soon as the two men arrived, Mr Hoppner was all friendly heartiness in his greetings to his lordship, full of solicitude, tenderly inviting his lordship to sit down, while ignoring Hobhouse entirely.

Instantly Hobby was alert, choosing to remain standing by Byron's chair like a suspicious bulldog or bodyguard. Diplomats were full of lies and chicanery, and Hoppner was a fine specimen of the type.

Byron leaned forward in his chair. "You letter said it was very important, Mr Hoppner?"

Hoppner huffed and bluffed. "Well, to me it is, yes, but I am also hoping it will be of some interest to you."

"How so?"

Hoppner looked at Hobhouse. "Will you not sit down also, Mr Hobhouse?"

"No thank you, I've been sitting long enough in the gondola."

"Oh, quite so, quite so. Now gentlemen, brandy, wine, coffee?"

Both men declined the offer of any refreshment, so Mr Hoppner got straight to the point. "Your summer house at La Mira, Lord Byron, do you find it suitable?"

"Suitable enough. It is very spacious."

"Yes, but far too large for comfort, I would say, and outrageously expensive. Do you find it expensive?"

Byron looked at Hobby – he was not used to talking to acquaintances about money, nor answering this kind of question.

"It is expensive to *run*," Hobby said, "due to his lordship's need of so many servants whom he has to feed and fee."

"Indeed? So many servants? How many?"

"Four when he left Switzerland, but now the total is fourteen –the last ten all Italian, and all in need of work, so his lordship takes them in like lost puppies. Why do you ask?"

"But they are all *good* workers," Byron insisted. "Have you ever known such a good and loyal worker as Tita?"

"Fourteen servants is far too many," Hoppner said, "but with a villa that big, I suppose there is a need, and the cost must be enormous."

"Why do you ask?" Hobhouse repeated.

Mr Hoppner addressed the rest of his conversation to his lordship. "I hope and trust you will not consider it a liberty on my part, my lord, but you told me you were looking for an alternative house?"

"Yes, in Venice, for the winter. Preferably on the Grand Canal."

"Oh, not in the countryside?"

"And miss out on the Carnival and all the other amusing festivities in the city?" Byron smiled. "Besides, the countryside is as dead as death in winter."

"Why do ask, sir?" Hobhouse repeated again.

Hoppner flashed Hobhouse a quick look of dislike, and then smiled at his lordship and produced a few sheets of paper.

"I must have misunderstood you, my lord, because I have here a fine house which I thought would suit you much more comfortably than the one at La Mira. This house consists of three large bedrooms, and a number of smaller bedrooms for four or five servants. There are also sitting rooms, five or six in number, and all completely furnished. It also has the rare advantage of being well supplied with water, and there is a coach house and a three-stall stable."

"Where is this house?"

"In Este. It stands in about four acres of ground well stocked with all kinds of vines and fruit trees, almost at the foot of the Euganean Hills, and the house overlooks the town of Este. The neighbourhood is very quiet, and abounds with pretty rides. If your lordship should think it worth your while to ride over there and look at the house, I shall have great pleasure in showing it to you."

"There's no point, is there?" Hobhouse said to Byron. "Not if it's a house in the city you want."

"No, no, I am interested in this house. It sounds an ideal family home." He looked at Hoppner. "Is it for sale or to rent?"

"To rent. The lease extends to another three years."

"And who rents it now, do you know?"

"Yes ... I do know ... and well, the present resident is,"

Hoppner gave a little laugh, "myself."

"You? You are living there now?"

"No, no, I am back in Venice now. Duty calls and all that."

"Is it *your* lease that goes on for another three years?" asked Hobhouse.

"Yes, but I can sign it on to another tenant if need be."

"But if the house is so wonderful, why would you?" asked Hobhouse.

Hoppner flashed him another look of dislike. "Mr Hobhouse, as you intend on going back to England, this really is a matter only for his lordship to consider."

"Do you have drawings I may look at?" Byron asked. "With room sizes and measurements?"

"Certainly." Hoppner pushed the papers across the desk. "Right here before you."

While Byron looked at the drawings, Hobhouse looked at Hoppner, wondering what his smarmy game was? Damned diplomats! You couldn't trust one of them.

"So why do you wish to offload it? The house?" Hobhouse persisted.

"No, my own wish would be to *keep* it, for as long as I possibly could, but circumstances may require my return to England, if not this winter, then perhaps in the Spring. However, my recall is certainly due sometime soon, and I do hate to arrange things in a rush."

Byron put down the drawings. "The house does indeed look very pretty, and I thank you for your kindness in considering me for the property, sir, but I would like to walk over the premises before I reach any decision."

"Why, of course, of course. And it will always be my great honour and pleasure to escort you there whenever it is convenient for you, Lord Byron. But, pray, do not leave it too long. I could be recalled at any moment."

Once they were outside and out of earshot, Hobhouse said cynically: "I don't believe he is being recalled at all.

In fact, I will wager you that he will still be here in five years time. Why did you allow him to waste your time like that?"

"It was not time wasted, because I am interested in the house."

"Why? Your house at La Mira is far superior." Hobhouse was baffled by Byron's gullibility in this instance. "Can't you see what Hoppner is up to? He does not want to pay the rent during the winter months when he can't be there, so he is trying to palm the house off onto you, so that *you* will have to pay it, and he saves himself a few shekels."

"I don't believe forty-eight golden louis in rent every month could be termed as 'a few shekels'."

"Exactly, and that's why he doesn't want to pay it. You weren't seriously interested, were you?"

Byron nodded. "I seriously was, and I still am seriously interested in the house – the *Villa Cappuccini*, as it is named. It appears to be a nice family home, not too big and not too small, and just the type of establishment I will need."

"For what?"

"For when Shelley arrives with my little girl, if he ever does arrive. She is only a baby, so she will need a quiet and comfortable home for herself and her nursemaids, and like Mr Hoppner, *I* don't like to arrange things in a rush either."

Hobhouse was astounded. "So you were not being gullible after all."

"Was I ever? Am I ever? Did I ever? No, I never!" Byron laughed. "Do you remember when we used to say that at Cambridge?"

Hobhouse heaved a sigh of nostalgia. "Those were the days. The great days of our careless youth. If only we could go back and live those days again."

Byron agreed. "If only."

While the two Cambridge friends were spending the day in Venice, Margarita Cogni was showing off her acquisition of a young chestnut mare to the other women at Dolo.

The women were looking in adoration at the lovely small horse. "Where do you get her, Margarita?"

"From the Mylord's stables."

"You *stole* it?"

"No, I did *not* steal it! Do I look like a thief? Do I look like a sinner?"

"The Mylord *gave* it to you?"

"No, not gave," Margarita shrugged, "but he said for me to use it. He does not like me to walk to the Villa Foscarini in the dark."

"Sit on her, Margarita, let us see if you can ride her better than on your tyrant's mule."

Margarita's dark eyes flashed. "A tyrant, *si!* The little baker hit me with a stick last night because I would not let him ride my new horse. Then he took her and rode her all the way to Padua and back!"

"*Tch! Tch! Bastardo!*" All the women agreed. "Did you hit him also, Margarita?"

"No, the Mylord said I must be good and not hit anyone."

"*Ah, l'inglese!*" The women laughed. "Sit on the horse, Margarita, let us see you ride her!"

Margarita mounted the horse, and then pulled down her *fazziolo* head-veil over her face, and sat looking as haughty and as proud as princess. "Do I look good?"

"*Si! Si!* The jewel of Dolo!"

"When I ride with my veil, will I look *incognito?*"

A loud angry shout prevented the women from answering – all heads turned to the approach of three angry young women marching towards them. The one marching in front was Marianne Segati, who had relatives living near here.

"Why do you shout, Marianne? What is wrong, eh?"

Marianne Segati spoke only to Margarita, shaking her fist up to her and warning her to stay away from the Mylord. "He was *my amoroso* until you took him."

Margarita threw back her veil and said in very

emphatic Venetian:

"*You* are not his *wife*. I am *not* his *wife*. You were his *Donna*, and *I* am now his *Donna*. Your husband is a cuckold, and *mine* is another. For the rest, what right have you to reproach *me*? If he now prefers me to you, is it my fault?"

The truth of her words hit Marianne like a stick, and she was left standing red-faced and speechless as Margarita pulled down her veil and rode off slowly on her small chestnut mare as if Marianne no longer existed.

The women all laughed and clapped with glee. The Dolo village girl had won magnificently over the arrogant city woman – the puffed-up *merchant's* wife.

By the end of the following month, John Murray in London received another letter from Lord Byron, which carried a final few paragraphs about his *amica*, Margarita Cogni, which made Murray laugh –

"In her fazziolo, the dress of the lower orders, she looked beautiful; but, alas! she longed for her own hat and feathers, and all I could say or do (and I said much) could not prevent this travesty. I put the hats into the fire; but I got tired of burning them, before she did of buying them, until she has made herself a figure – for they do not at all become her.

Then she said she would like her gowns with "a tail" – like a lady, forsooth : nothing would satisfy her but "l'abito colla coua" or "cua" (that is the Venetian for the Italian "la coda" the tail or train of a dress) and as her cursed pronunciation of the word made me laugh, that was the end of the controversy.

And so now she wears her hats and drags this diabolical train after her everywhere."

Yrs most truly - B

P.S: I read of my death in the papers – which was not true.

Chapter Ten

~ ~ ~

A change of circumstances caused Byron to spend much of his time in Venice, leaving Margarita bereft and heartbroken in Dolo.

Occasionally she consoled herself by going down to the Villa Foscarini at La Mira to boss the servants about, but it gave her little joy.

Finally she stopped wearing her hats and dresses with tails, and returned to wearing her normal style of the fazziolo.

"We told you, Margarita, we told you," the women said; but Margarita would not believe them. The Mylord, she said, adored her, and soon he would come back.

Byron was back in his former apartment at the *Gran Bretagne* because some of his favourite friends had arrived in Venice – Douglas Kinnaird, his friend and banker; together with his brother, Lord Kinnaird, and his wife. The Duke of Devonshire had also arrived, after a voyage to Russia.

The duke was delighted with Russia, telling them the emperor had as much pride in his capital and empire as a private gentleman in his house and park, but the citizens are not allowed to whitewash a house in Petersburgh without his permission.

All the friends had news to tell, and the conversations went on long into the night.

Byron and Hobhouse were more than happy to join the visitors in all their sightseeing. First to the Grimani Palace, and then to the gardens.

Then a night at the arena, sitting in the open air under the delightful starry climate, with only the stage lighted. The Great Devil was the hero of the piece, and the audience entered into all his distinctions about robbing.

The British Consul, Richard Hoppner, also called, into the *Gran Bretagne* and told the visitors that he felt no sympathy for the Italians who lost their liberties to the French before the Austrians came.

He then went on to say that the education of the higher classes was, before the French came, almost nothing. The women could positively hardly ever write, or play, or dance, or do anything but embroider, and perhaps sing the psalter – accomplishments which they learned in the convents, where they were kept until they were taken out to be married at sixteen.

"And the *men* were nearly as ignorant: could scarcely write, or even dance, and were ashamed to be thought fond of reading."

Hobhouse was furious, muttering to Byron behind Hoppner's back: "You see now, *this* is the way these diplomatic scoundrels talk and write home to their Governments, who in turn call their nonsense *'good information'.*"

Byron said to Hoppner. "Were *you* here in Venice, all those years ago, when the situation was so?"

"No, but I was told it."

Hobhouse scoffed. "By yet *another* diplomat no doubt!"

Hoppner diplomatically decided to take no offence, still too delighted and relieved by Lord Byron taking over the lease for the *Villa Cappuccini* at Este that morning. Yet, strange to say, he still intended to keep his country residence at La Mira.

When Hoppner had asked him why, Byron had replied that the villa at Este was to be the main home for his child and her carers.

The socialising in Venice continued. Some evenings they dined at *Pellegrino's,* and then went on to a play at St Benedetto, which Byron always thought ludicrous – "There is too much of an exaggerated nature of the Italians in all their acting."

Douglas Kinnaird agreed. "In Drury Lane we would consider that type of performance to be almost *pantomime*."

Hobhouse agreed. "There are none so fine as our own sons of Shakespeare."

One a November afternoon, after the Kinnairds had left Venice that morning, Tita arrived with a letter for Byron. Once again the letter was from Shelley.

Mr dear Lord Byron, – Since I last wrote to you, I have lived in weekly expectation of leaving England, in which case I should have, in person, brought you your little girl. But my affairs have been so uncertain that after this constant and gradual delay, it is decided that I must abide in England. As soon as this became evident, I looked about for some suitable person to whom I could confide the little Alba. You know my secluded mode of life. These circumstances have prevented me from finding any person fit for this purpose. I write therefore to ask – have you any friend, or person of trust, who is leaving England for Italy?"

Annoyed and somewhat disgusted, Byron said to Hobhouse. "I truly find it astonishing that Claire is so willing to give up the child to *anyone* who may take her abroad. And if Shelley refers to her as *'your little girl'* one more time –

"I'm sure that *she* is the one who is instructing Shelley to continually use those words."

"Then the child will certainly be better off well away from her. Do we know anyone who could safely bring her?"

"No, but Douglas Kinnaird probably does. A pity he left Venice this morning."

"Then I will write to him immediately and the letter should reach him as soon as he arrives in England."

Dear Douglas, – Inferring that, by the time you receive this, you are in England – Shelley has written to me about my daughter, (the little illegitimate) and wants to know what he is to do about sending her. I think she had better remain until the spring; but will you think of some plan for conveying her here, or placing her in England. I shall bring her up myself, and mean to christen her Allegra.

If you see Augusta give my love to her, and tell her that I do not write because I really and truly do not understand one word of her letters. To answer them is out of the question. I don't say it out of ill-nature, but whatever the subject, there is so much paraphrase, parenthesis, initials, dashes, hints – and so much damned crinkum-crankum that if I don't know what the meaning or no meaning is, I am obliged to study Armenian as a relief.

Leaving Venice and returning across the water to La Mira, Byron and Hobhouse were rowed in an open gondola, without a felze, by two smiling gondoliers – at least, the two gondoliers had *appeared* to be cheerful and happy on the Grand Canal; but as soon as they reached the open sea, a strange kind of torture began.

One gondolier was at the prow, the other at the stern, and both began to sing, and continued singing – shrill and monotonous – the same two songs over and over; *"The Death of Clorinda"* and *"The Palace of Armida"* and they did not even sing in Venetian, but Tuscan. The one at the front kept forgetting the words, and had to be prompted by the gondolier at the stern.

Halfway across the sea a wind blew up, and the gondoliers' appalling singing turned into a shrill screaming as they strived to defy the wind and make their singing heard.

The gondolier at the stern desperately attempted to assist the loudness of his voice by constantly putting one hand to the side of his mouth to improve the echo.

"Oh good grief!" said Hobhouse, unable to bear any more. "Pray will you stop SINGING!"

The gondoliers were instantly silenced, staring at each other, and then at their passengers, until the one at the front said to Byron, who had earlier spoken to them in Italian: "We must sing, Signore. We earn more money if we sing."

Hobhouse understood enough to say: "No, stop! stop! Just row!"

The gondolier at the front was close to tears – at least Byron thought so, but it could have been the wind that was watering his eyes.

"Look at us," he cried. "Look at our clothes – can't you see we are *starving!"*

Byron turned and looked at the gondolier at the stern, who nodded. "That is why we came from Tuscany to Venice, to row and sing and earn our living."

Byron was deeply affected by this, and translated for Hobby, who also became somewhat shamefaced by his outburst.

"Then sing on, sing on, pray do," Hobby said. "Your singing was delightful."

"No." Byron waved a hand. "Silence, until we get to Fusina."

The gondoliers rowed on glumly in silence, and Byron said quietly to Hobhouse, "I am expecting you to place the entire contents of your wallet in their hands when we reach Fusina."

"What about you?"

"I did not shout and bawl about their singing. I suffered it in respectable silence."

"You were wincing."

Stepping ashore at Fusina, they left the two Tuscan gondoliers laughing with joy at their large tip, bowing up and down non-stop to the two signores until the door of the hired carriage had closed and rolled off towards La Mira.

"Poor fellows," Hobhouse said. "But if they intend to keep rowing in Venice, they really should get some singing lessons."

~~~

In the first week of December Byron received a letter from his lawyer in London, John Hanson, informing him that his country estate of Newstead Abbey in Nottinghamshire had been sold for almost £100,000.

"How much?" Hobhouse asked in amazement. "One *hundred thousand* pounds?"

Byron looked at the letter. "The exact amount is ninety-five thousand."

"That's an absolute fortune! And your property in Rochdale *still* has to be sold. That must be worth at least sixty thousand."

Byron continued reading Hanson's very detailed letter, until two more pieces of information delighted him.

"Guess who the buyer of Newstead is? – Tom Wildman!"

"And he is, pray?"

"One of my school friends at Harrow. You must remember him – he was at my twenty-first birthday party at Newstead."

"I don't remember much from that party. My eyes were too boggled from all the champagne. So, he must have been very taken with Newstead Abbey, even back
~~~

then, if he is buying it now."

"And the other good thing is that Tom Wildman – dear Tom Wildman – has agreed to my request for old Joe Murray and Nanny Smith to be kept in employment there."

"Old Joe? Is he still working there? I thought you gave him a pension."

"I did, but it would kill Joe to leave Newstead Abbey, his pride and joy. And I'll wager Joe is *still* cleaning the silverware every week."

"So, what are you going to do with all that money?"

"Nothing, yet. It will take months to reach me. Papers have to be signed and exchanged and all that kind of thing, which Hanson will take care of. But my immediate need now is to find a suitable residence in Venice for the winter. And for that, I will need the help of our local diplomat.

Byron arrived at the Consul's office to be greeted warmly by Mr Hoppner. "Now you did say in your note that you prefer somewhere *spacious*, my lord, and I believe that I have found for you a most suitable place, most suitable. I am certain you will like it."

"Where is it?"

"Oh, on the very steps of the Grand Canal." Hoppner handed Byron the drawings. "I thought it the perfect place for an aristocrat with a lot of servants – the Palace Mocenigo."

"A palace?"

"Or as they say here – a *palazzo*."

Byron looked at the drawings, read the measurements, and then looked at Mr Hoppner. "I like the look of it, and the size of it, but I would want to –"

"Walk over the premises, before you decide. Yes I do understand. We can go there now if you wish. Is Mr Hobhouse not with you today?"

Byron nodded. "Yes, he is. He's sitting outside in the gondola."

Hoppner immediately lost his cheerfulness. "How

very convenient. I'm sure he will wish to give you his own opinion."

"He usually does."

John Hobhouse thought the Palazzo Mocenigo far too large a residence for one man, but said to Hoppner: "All told, though, it is still less than *half* the size of Newstead Abbey where his lordship lived from a boy."

"Indeed? Is that why he has a liking for such large houses?"

"I believe so. But he also likes to have plenty of space for his animals."

"His animals? My goodness, does he have *many* animals?"

"Oh, yes, a whole zoo of them; but only the dogs are allowed inside his private apartments. The dogs and Jade the cat ... oh, and occasionally the monkey, and sometimes the parakeet ... the rest are all usually animals he has rescued on the road and are injured in some way. But those he keeps in his hospital, which is usually a large room or a part of the garden designated for that purpose."

"And does he attend to these injured animals himself?"

"Of course not. He calls in a vet."

~ ~ ~

The letter, which came from his father in Whitton Park in Surrey, had given John Cam Hobhouse a jolt, and awakened him to the reality of the world outside Venice.

His father reminded him that he would soon be thirty-two years old and had a political career to pursue, a career in England.

Sadly, Hobhouse saw the sense of it. It was time for him to leave Byron's life and return to his own.

He had been away from England for a year and a half; and as personal matters, including the possible arrival of his child, had forced Byron to defer their journey to Greece, there was no further excuse to stay.

And now that he knew he must leave and return to his own country, every moment of his last week in Venice struck Hobhouse with a brilliant clarity and awareness that left him sad and drenched in melancholy.

"Went in gondola: found Byron well and merry and happy, more charming every day."

Byron took the news of Hobby's departure with a show of little feeling, nothing more than a shrug; and yet he was quiet and uncommunicative for the rest of the day.

"I think we should get to work," Hobhouse said, and Byron nodded his agreement; passing him page after page of his final edited version the Fourth Canto of *Childe Harold's Pilgrimage* for which Hobby studiously spent the next few days writing all the explanatory 'Notes' for the reader.

'The Bridge of Sighs' (il Ponte dei Sospiri) divides the Doge's Palace from the State prison. It is roofed and divided by a wall into two passages' – By the one, the prisoner was conveyed to judgment – by the other he returned to death, sighing sadly as he took his last glimpse of Venice from the windows while crossing the Bridge.

Annotating Byron's work was something Hobby had done for years, ever since their days at Cambridge, and now he was happy to find himself doing it once again. He was Byron's harshest critic, and his closest friend.

January 7th, 1818 – Passed the evening with Byron, who put the last hand to his "Childe Harold" and then

I took leave of my dear friend, for so I think of him, at twelve o'clock. A little before going he told me that he was originally a man of a great deal of feeling, but that it had all been absorbed. I believe the first part of what he said literally. God bless him !

Chapter Eleven

~ ~ ~

February 2nd — Arrived at Dover and landed back in England.

February 4th — I gave "Childe Harold" to Murray. He was in raptures.

John Murray was indeed in raptures as he glanced through the pages of the poem, reading a verse here and there, with the intention of reading and enjoying it in its entirety as soon as Mr Hobhouse had left his office.

He then lifted a sealed letter at the back of the manuscript, opening it to find that it was not a letter to him at all, but a carefully printed long *'Dedication'* to be placed at the beginning of the work.

Hobhouse was about to leave when Murray called him back. "Mr Hobhouse, I think you should see this."

Hobhouse turned back. "A problem with the notes?"

"No, and not a problem at all."

Hobhouse took the two pages from Murray's hand and began to read:

Venice, January 2nd 1818

**TO JOHN HOBHOUSE ESQ., A.M., F.R.S
etc. etc. etc.**

My dear Hobhouse,

After an interval of eight years between the composition of the first and last cantos of Childe Harold, the conclusion of the poem is about to be submitted to the pubic. In parting with so old a friend it is not

extraordinary that I should recur to one still older and better — to one whom I am far *more indebted for* the social advantages of an enlightened friendship, than I can or could ever be to Childe Harold for any public favour reflected through the poem on the poet – to one, whom I have known long and accompanied far, whom I have found wakeful over my sickness and kind in my sorrow, glad in my prosperity and firm in my adversity, true in counsel and trusty in peril – to a friend often tried and never found wanting; – to yourself.

Wishing you, my dear Hobhouse, a safe and agreeable return to that country whose real welfare can be dearer to none than yourself, I dedicate to you this poem in its completed state; and repeat once more how truly I am ever

**Your obliged
And affectionate friend,
BYRON**.

Hobhouse put the pages down on Murray's desk as if there was a slight heaviness in his hand. Rain had begun to splash against the windows.

"Thank you for showing it to me," he said quietly, and then turned and left the room.

John Murray knew that Hobhouse had been deeply affected by the dedication, but he was not a man to show his personal feelings – a true Englishman.

And yet, like Byron, Murray had never underestimated John Hobhouse's intellect and true capacities, and knew that if he ever got into Parliament, he would be a political force to be reckoned with.

Treating himself to a glass of brandy and lighting a cigar, John Murray sat down languorously to read every word of the 133 stanzas of the last episode of Childe Harold's Pilgrimage.

Some time later, when he had finished reading, he immediately took up his pen and wrote a letter to Byron, full of praise, and, in such a good mood, he even took the time to fill his letter with gossipy news of this person and that person; finally concluding with an inquiry about his lordship's own news? Was he still in love, or out? And what had happened to the Italian girl who demolished all rivals and liked to wear hats?

He had to wait a few months for a reply from Lord Byron, but when his letter eventually arrived, it was as candid and amusing as always.

Dear Mr Murray — Since you desire the story of Margarita Cogni, you shall be told it, but it may be lengthy.

When I left La Mira and came to Venice for the winter, she followed, and brought with her a thousand of her fooleries. At the "Cavalchina", the masked ball on the last night of the Carnival, where all the world goes, she slipped inside and then snatched off the masque of Madame Contarini, a lady noble by birth, and decent in conduct, and for no other reason than she happened to be leaning on my arm. You may suppose what a cursed noise this made; but this is only one of her pranks.

She then quarrelled with her husband, and ran away again to my house on the Grand Canal. I told her this would not do: she said she would lie in the street, but would not go back to him; that he beat her (the gentle tigress), spent her money, and scandalously neglected his Oven.

As it was Midnight I let her stay and the next day there was no moving her at all. Her husband came, roaring and crying, and entreating her to come back — but lo! – <u>not</u> she!

He then applied to the Police, and they applied to me: I told them and her husband to <u>take</u> her; that she had come to my house and I could not fling her out the window; but they might conduct her out through the door if they chose it. She then went before the Commissary, but was obliged, she said, to return with that "becco ettico" (consumptive cuckold) as she called the poor man, her husband. In a few days she ran away again, and fixed herself in my house, really and truly without my consent.

Madame Benzoni also took her under her protection, and then her head turned. She was always in extremes, either crying or laughing; and so fierce when angered, that she was the terror of men, women, and children — for she had the strength of an Amazon, with the temper of Medea. She was quite untameable. I was the only person who could calm her, and when she saw me really angry (which they tell me is rather a savage sight), she subsided.

In the meantime, she beat the women of the

household and stopped my letters. I found her one day pondering over one: she used to try and find out by their shape whether they were feminine or no; and she used to lament her ignorance, and actually studied her Alphabet, on purpose (as she declared) to open all letters addressed to me and read their contents.

She then made herself our housekeeper. I must not omit to do justice to her housekeeping qualities: after she placed herself in my house as "donna di governo" the expenses were reduced to less than half, and everybody did their duties better − the apartments were kept in order, and every thing and everybody else, except herself.

That she had a sufficient regard for me, in her wild way, I had many reasons to believe. I will mention one. One day, going to the Lido with my Gondoliers, we were overtaken by a heavy Squall, and the Gondola put in peril − hats blown away, boat filling, oar lost, tumbling sea, thunder, rain in torrents, night coming, and wind increasing.

On our return, after a tight struggle, I found her on the open steps of the Mocenigo palace, on the Grand Canal, with her great black eyes flashing through her tears, and the long dark hair, which was streaming drenched with rain over her brows and breast. She was perfectly exposed to the storm; and the wind blowing her hair and dress about her tall thin figure, and the lightning flashing around her, with the waves rolling at her feet, made her look like Medea – and she was the only living thing within hail at that moment except ourselves.

On seeing me safe, she did not wait to greet me, as might be expected, but called out to me in Venetian – "Ah! Dog of the Virgin, is this a time to go swimming at the Lido?"– and then scolded the boatmen for not foreseeing the tempest.

I was told by the servants that she had only been prevented from coming in a boat to look for me, by the refusal of all the Gondoliers of the Canal to put out from the harbour at such a moment: and then she sat down on the steps in all the thickest of the Squall, and would neither be removed nor comforted. Her joy at seeing me again was moderately mixed with ferocity, and gave me the idea of a tigress over her recovered cubs.

But her reign drew near a close. She became quite ungovernable after that; and a concurrence of complaints against her, some true, many false – "a favourite has no friend" determined me to part with her. I told her quietly that she must return home (she had acquired a sufficient provision for herself and her mother in my service). She refused to quit the house. I was firm, and so she went, threatening knives and revenge.

The next day, while I was at dinner, she walked in (having broken open a glass door that led from the hall below to the staircase) and, advancing straight up to the table, snatched the knife from my hand, cutting me slightly in the thumb in the operation. Whether she meant to use this against herself or me, I know not — probably against neither — but Fletcher seized her by the arms and disarmed her. I then called my boatmen, and told them to get the Gondola ready, and conduct her to her own house again, seeing carefully that she did no mischief to herself on the way. She seemed quiet, and walked downstairs.

We heard a great noise: I went out, and met them on the staircase, carrying her upstairs. She had thrown herself into the Canal. That she intended to destroy herself, I do not believe; but when we consider the fear that men and women who can't swim have of deep and even shallow water (and the Venetians in particular, though they live on the waves) and that it was also night, and dark, and very cold, it shows that she had a devilish spirit of some sort within her. They had got her out without much difficulty or damage, excepting the salt water she had swallowed.

I foresaw her intention to refix herself in the house,

and sent for a doctor, inquiring how many hours it would take to restore her; and he named the time. I then said, "I give you that time, and more if you require it; but at the expiration of the prescribed period, if <u>she</u> does not leave the house, <u>I</u> will."

All my people were consternated — they had always been frightened of her, and were now paralysed; they wanted me to apply to the police, to guard myself, etc., I did nothing of the kind.

I sent her home quietly after her recovery. She made attempts to return, but no more violent ones. She has considerable beauty and energy, with many good and several amusing qualities, but wild as a witch and fierce as a demon. True it was, they all tried to get her away from me, and no one succeeded until her own absurdity helped them. And this is the story of Margarita Cogni, as far as it belongs to me.

Yours very truly — B.

What? Was the letter finished? Murray still had eight or ten pages in his hand.

He turned over a page and scanned the next one, smiling with absolute delight to see that Byron had included a new poem — another *new* poem to increase the firm's bank balance – entitled "*Beppo*".

A poem on the Venetians and their regular life in Venice.

Oh, this would be so *very interesting* to all the ladies here in England who rarely saw or knew much of the world beyond their own village or town ... although, as he commenced to read through the verses, Murray began to realise that Byron had written this one more for the *men* than the ladies.

John Murray loved *Beppo* so much that, at his next *'four o'clock afternoon gathering'* with some of his authors and friends, he insisted on reading out to the group some of his favourite verses on Venice.

'Tis known, at least it should be, that throughout,

All countries of the Catholic persuasion,

Some weeks before Shrove Tuesday comes about,

The people take their fill of recreation,

And buy repentance, before they grow devout,

However high their rank, or low their station,

With fiddling, fasting, dancing, drinking, masquing,

And other things which may be had for asking.

With all its sinful doings, I must say,

That Italy's a pleasant place to me,

Who love to see the Sun shine every day,

And vines (not nailed to walls) from tree to tree

Festooned, much like the back scene of a play,

Or melodrama, which people flock to see,

When the first act is ended by a dance

In vineyards copied from the south of France.

I love the language, that soft bastard Latin,

Which melts like kisses from a female mouth,

And sounds as if it should be writ on satin,

With syllables, which breathe of the sweet South,

And gentle liquids gliding all so pat in,

That not a single accent seems uncouth,

Like our harsh northern, whistling, grunting gutteral,

Which we're obliged to hiss, and spit, and sputter all.

I like the women too (forgive my folly)

From the rich peasant cheek of glowing bronze,

And large black eyes that flash on you a volley

Of rays that say a thousand things at once,

To the high dama's brow, more melancholy,

But clear, and with a wild and liquid glance,

Heart on her lips, and soul within her eyes,

Soft as her clime, and sunny as her skies.

Into the story entered a young Venetian Miss named Laura, who fell in love with a Turk!

By the end of the poem everyone was smiling and chuckling. "Well, this shows," said John Murray, "that Byron is not at all the gloomy fellow the public think he is. Indeed, I know that he is usually a facetious and laughing companion amongst those with whom he is intimate."

Coleridge said: "But Lord Byron can be strange, you know? One day he said to me – `Why must our poets always write like poets?'

"Why, says I, how else should a poet write?

"`Like *real* men,' says he. `Men of the world who speak the language of the world. Normal, simple language, in verse.'

"Oh, well, says I, that would hardly be poetry then, would it?"

"And what if they are *not* men of the world," said Thomas Campbell, "but men who live solely for the glory of literature?"

John Murray was smiling to himself, for *he* understood Byron's gripe; and had understood it ever since the day Byron had said so glumly and quietly to him during a literary party – "One hates an author who is all author. One doesn't know what to say to them ... unless to puff them up even more ..."

'Not that Coleridge could be accused of being anything like that,' thought Murray. 'But Thomas Campbell ... ?

And now Coleridge was arguing with Thomas Campbell in *defence* of Byron.

"You're talking rot, Man, But there you go! Like so many in this country – always ready to judge Byron guilty until proven innocent."

Coleridge looked at Murray. "They do the same to me, you know? Say all kinds of rot. Why, some devils have even accused me of opium addiction."

PART FOUR

"The English Mylord "

"I found nothing in him of the arrogance of a man who had become famous so young; nothing of the English pride; nothing of the contempt which he is said to show to some people."

Pietro Giordani

Chapter Twelve

~ ~ ~

The *Palazzo Mocenigo* was a massive building on the Grand Canal, within sight of the Rialto Bridge and only a few hundred yards from the Piazza San Marco. It was only two centuries old, so it still had an air of Venetian youth about it.

The front door opened onto the steps of the gondola's landing platform; but, like most of the houses on the Grand Canal, the back of the building could be entered by land; and the back of the building was the prettiest, with a small quiet courtyard and stone staircases covered in greenery and flowers.

The ground floor, with its marble floor and wide hall and many rooms, became the residence of Byron's family of animals. He had now acquired another small "unwanted" bear, and a limping fox. The three monkeys were given their own dormitory.

Above the ground floor were another three storeys of dozens of rooms, allowing his family of servants plenty of spacious accommodation for themselves, and room for more if needed.

Byron's floor was the first floor, containing his drawing-room, library, dining-room, study and four bedrooms; one of which was Fletcher's bedroom, not only because he was head of the household, but also because Byron liked Fletcher to be near-by, in case he needed help removing the special shoe he wore on his right foot.

My dear Hobhouse – I miss you damnably. There is no fun at the Ridottos. I have lately (as a resource to supply your loss) taken again to the natives. Hoppner has got a son, a fine child. The Carnival was very merry.

Fletcher has been "bursten" with an indigestion, screaming for me to get the "pottecary" and I was obliged to root out an apothecary at three in the morning to attend upon him.

Is Scrope facetious? What does he? What says he? Where dines he? What wins he? How is he?

"Ah, Coquin, vare is my shild?" You must see and speak to Shelley about sending out my child with a nurse.

I had fifty gossips of my own to tell you, but am in haste, and have forgotten them.

Go on and prosper, and believe me ever yrs. truly. B.

When Hobhouse had left him on his own in Venice, "without friend or foe" – he had decided to take up Richard Hoppner's invitation to allow him to be introduced to some of the leading figures in Venetian society.

The first place they had attended was Madame Albrizzi's *Conversazione*. This was the lady who prized herself on being the Venetian Madame de Staël.

Having known Madame de Staël so well and for so long, Byron did not understand the comparison, for Albrizzi had written nothing great; but she was a Greek immigrant, and pleasant to look at, and that alone made her interesting to him — that and the divinely beautiful bust of Helen of Troy, sculpted by Canova, which she displayed in her Sala.

As for the majority of people who frequented her *salotti*, he found most of them to be pompously literary and artificial — *"Except Giordani, and Buratti – and – and – I really can't name any other."*

He was about to slip out of the crowded *sala* when Madame Albrizzi caught his arm and begged a favour.

"Mylord Byron, the Count Guiccioli from Ravenna is here and wishes to speak in private to my husband, Giuseppe. While he is doing so, his new bride, a very young girl, has voiced her wish to see Canova's bust of Helen, so would you be kind enough to give the Countess Guiccioli your arm and escort her over to the display?"

"Of course."

The young *bride* to whom he gave his arm, could have been the devil in disguise, for she was draped in veils, her face hidden, as was the custom in public during the first year of marriage. She also kept her head bowed low, as if she was desperately shy, even though no one could actually *see* her.

Byron stood in silent patience while she stared through her veil at the bust of Helen of Troy, but then his attention was caught by the loud voice of a young man, named Piazza, a prig who sniffed snuff, and who had just returned from his first visit to England and Bond Street and now considered himself to be a dandy.

It seemed that the fuss of his complaint was because the Venetian poet, Buratti, had reputedly written a satire on him while he was away. Piazza was now insisting that Buratti read the thing aloud, saying, "If there is anything in it ungentlemanlike, you shall fight me."

Now everyone's attention was caught by such a threat, and poor Buratti had no alterative but to take out the paper, stand up, and read his words aloud.

At the end, Piazza, hesitating a little, said, "I don't know, but I believe it will do."

Everyone relaxed. And only then did Byron realise that the veiled bride whose hand had been on his arm, had gone.

"She never once lifted her head," said Madame Albrizzi later, "not even to me, a woman!" She then slyly fluttered her fan over her mouth and said in a gossipy way – "Guiccioli's *third* wife, straight out of a Convent, married only three days, and no more than sixteen or seventeen."

"How old is he?"

She smiled satirically. "He *admits* to fifty-eight, but Giuseppe says he is sixty."

Byron saw the prig Piazza walking towards him, and bid his hostess a hasty goodnight. "You will forgive me, but I must away. My valet is extremely ill."

"Your valet? You must go to attend upon a *servant?*"

"Yes, a good man, goodnight."

~~~

In her bedroom at Count Guiccioli's house in Venice, Teresa Guiccioli Gamba was almost weeping with exhaustion as Fanny Sylvestrini helped her to undress.

After two days of travelling and three of married life, she had climbed into the carriage bound for Venice from the very door of the Ravenna church where the ceremony had taken place; and on entering Madame Albrizzi's sala, she had been too tired even to look at the sculptured bust of Canova's Helen while holding onto the gentleman's arm. Who he was, she did not know, nor did she look at him, for her eyes were closing in sleep under her veil, until she jerked awake with a small start, and quickly rushed away to sit in an adjoining room.

What else could she do? If she had collapsed into a faint in the room, her husband would have severely reprimanded her for causing a scene.

She looked tearfully at Fanny, a woman in her early forties, who was now her maid and only companion. She still missed dear Rosa who had been passed on to her younger sister when Teresa had left her home in Filetto to marry Count Guiccioli.

No more miracles had come to save her.

"Do not speak to anyone! Do not smile! Do not look! Keep your head bowed!" she said vehemently to Fanny.
~~~

"Is that how the Guiccioli expects me to live my life from now on? And those vile *veils* I am forced to wear! Why does he not just lock me in a cage and throw food inside the bars to me?"

"He is an old man with old ways," Fanny said. "He does not remember that we are now living in the nineteenth century, and have been for eighteen years. That is why he has so many rules – he thinks you are his *servant*. He was the same with his other wives."

"And they are both dead. Now I know why," said Teresa, slipping into the white nightdress laid out on the bed.

"No, you don't know why," Fanny muttered ominously, and then caught herself with caution. "And you won't know if you listen to gossip at Ravenna," she added. "The two wives, they died peacefully in their sleep, like all good souls should."

Teresa was not listening, because she had heard a sound at the door, and saw the handle turning.

"Did you lock it?"

Fanny nodded. "I always lock the door until you are in your nightgown."

"Teresa?" said the Count's voice. "Teresa, open this door."

Teresa looked desperately at Fanny. "No, not again. I can't bear it! Tell him I am sick and you are nursing me."

"*Oh, Madre di Dio!*" Fanny exclaimed. "Can I dare?"

"You must! I am too tired to suffer an old man fondling me! It is *ripugnante!*"

"*Si, si ...*" said Fanny, and made her way hesitantly to the door. "*l'Conte,*" she said through the door. "*Signora has been sick, oh so sick, and is almost asleep now.*"

Teresa waited for him to shout and bang in rage on the door, as he had done on the first night, but moments later she heard his footsteps walking away.

Fanny turned her head and smiled with relief. "He must be tired also."

"Then why did he come?"

Fanny shrugged. "Duty," she said, unable to think of any other answer to give to such a young girl. Teresa may be eighteen now, but she was as innocent of the world as a newborn lamb.

"Will he come *every* night?" Teresa asked.

Fanny was not sure, so she gave the only answer her intuition fed her. "I think he will soon tire of the novelty of you. He is too old now, and too impatient to keep banging on doors. Soon, I think, he will go back to the pleasure of counting his money."

"So why did he seek to get another wife – *me?*"

"To get your *money*. The dowry from your father. *l'Conte* is always in debt, and always in need of money. All his riches came from his first wife, the Contessa Zinanni. She was a good woman, but very old, much older than he – old enough to be his mother!"

The word "mother" caused Teresa to feel extremely homesick and lonely.

"Will you sleep with me tonight, Fanny?"

Fanny was taken aback. "Sleep with you ... in *your* bed? Servants do not do such things, Signora."

"But you are now *my* servant. So if I command you?"

Fanny shrugged. "Then I must agree."

Later, snuggled up in bed together, Fanny was happy to answer all of Teresa's questions about that rigid, eccentric old man with the polished and formal manners, to whom she was now married.

"He is greedy. He has always been greedy – for *land*. The more land he owns, the more *power* he feels. But he is strange – as soon as he owns land, he will never then go to see it himself, but leaves it to his steward to rule under his orders."

"Why does he not go and see?"

"They say he does not go and see, because he cannot bear to see where the boundaries of his land end, and the land owned by another begins."

Teresa was puzzled. "How do you know all of this?"

Fanny shrugged, "I am a servant, and servants know everything."

In the Palazzo Mocenigo, Byron was writing again to John Murray, telling him of the only woman of note he had met that evening.

The Contessa Isabella Albrizzi – not young, but a good-natured woman, unaffected, and very polite to strangers. She has written on the works of Canova. She is of Corfu, but married a dead Venetian – that is, dead since he married.

~~~

The following morning Count Guiccioli sent a maid to bring his wife to his study.

Teresa entered, extremely pensive, and saw that Alessandro's expression was stiff and grave.

"Sit," he commanded.

She sat.

"During our journey here to Venice," he said, "I thought I had explained to you very carefully, and that you had understood, my requirements of you as my wife and consort."

"Alessandro I was so tired after such a journey, I could not help it. A faintness came over me so strongly that I had to leave the salon for another room."

"I will forgive, because you are still very young." The Count smiled mockingly. "You think all your schooling ended at Santa Chiara's, but that was just child's play and not fit to prepare you for the real world. Now, as my wife, it is time for your real schooling to begin."

In the silence, the Count took his time lighting a cigar.

"As you get older, and live longer, Teresa, you will learn that there are only two truly important things in life. Money and business. All great men know that. And as a great man I chose you as a wife for one particular
~~~

reason."

"Alessandro, last night I was so tired I could not help falling asleep so quickly."

"No, not that ..." he wiped away some of the cigar-smoke gathering between them, "I have others, more experienced, who can provide me with that whenever I wish, right here in my own house. But we must follow the rules, and *your* behaviour must be pure at all times. I *insist* upon it."

Teresa remained silent, her head lowered.

"I chose you, not because of your beauty, but because of your youth and innocence. A very powerful attraction to older men. Not to me, I find youth and innocence irritating. But to others ... and in business ... your youth will be a great asset to me."

Teresa stared in astonishment as he told her what he required of her ... she must be his consort in all matters of business, but only when he requested.

"Any man with whom I am seeking to do business, *you* must make him feel special. You must smile and look at him with admiration, so that he will believe the closer he gets to me in business, the greater will be his chance of heaven awaiting for him with you."

Teresa was so shocked she stood up in protest. "No man will touch you! I will not allow it," Alessandro assured her. "All I require of you is pleasing and youthful allurement, nothing more. And only with those men I mention to you. I do not require you to *do* anything, in fact, I forbid it, but there is no harm in letting a man wonder. In all other situations you must be very remote in your manner, and not too friendly with anyone."

"And if I tell my Papa what you request? If I refuse?"

"I will go straight to the Cardinal and priests and tell them I was duped and found you not to be a virgin bride. How will your father cope with the shame of that? How will you? Your father's position in Filetto will not be so honoured as it is now"

He paused, and looked at her, deadly serious. "So you

see, Teresa, this must be our little secret, our own little business arrangement. You must speak of it to no one. Fulfil your duties as my consort, and at all other times you will not be troubled by me."

Teresa returned to her own quarters with tears spilling from her eyes, alarming Fanny.

"Cara, *cara* ... what happened? Why did he send for you?"

"To instruct me."

"In matters of the bedroom?"

"No, in using me for his avarice."

Fanny did not understand, but closed her arms around the girl and comforted her anyway. "Ah, my Terasina, so the locked bedroom door angered him?"

Teresa was now thinking of her beloved father, and Guiccioli's threat to disgrace them both.

"Yes, the bedroom door ... we must not lock it again."

Chapter Thirteen

~ ~ ~

During the following weeks, Byron regularly attended Madame Albrizzi's sala; until he discovered that she had started writing a book about him, with the intention of publication; which was ridiculous, for what could she know of him after a few evenings of his attendance at her *Converzationes* when he had often listened a lot, but said very little in return.

Disappointed, and disillusioned, he called on Madame Albrizzi, only to be told that she had left Venice to spend the summer in Paris.

His only immediate option was to write to her daughter, Guiseppina Albrizzi, still in Venice, forbidding such a book about himself after so short an acquaintance.

I have not the least idea of its contents – nor have any reason to suppose them unfavourable – but I have no ambition of appearing personally in print so publicly now, or at any future period. You will therefore oblige me by respectfully requesting the Countess your Mother to deliver such pages to the flames, as the publication or circulation of which would be painful to me – at the same time assuring her that I am honoured by her intention, although I feel it my duty to decline, and beg that the pages so far be destroyed.

After that, he declined all invitations to *Conversaziones* or parties, until Richard Hoppner persuaded him to attend the sala of Madame Albrizzi's rival, the Countess Marina Benzoni, who had been pleading with Hoppner to get the English Mylord to attend.

"You will find she has far more discretion than Albrizzi," Hoppner assured him. "And, more importantly, she is not a gossip, nor has she any ambitions to be a published writer."

Byron was reluctant, but eventually agreed. He still missed the more relaxed company of Hobhouse; and, apart from his household of servants, he was beginning to feel rather *alone* in Venice.

On the arranged evening of the visit, it was not Richard Hoppner who called for him, but his Diplomatic Secretary, a young Scotsman appropriately named Alexander Scott.

As soon as Alexander Scott had arrived at the Palazzo Mocenigo and addressed him as *"Laird Byron"* the mountains and streets of Aberdeenshire, the Scottish home of his childhood, came back to Byron in a wave of nostalgia and he grasped Scott's hand with warmth and smiles.

"My mother was a Scot," he told the Secretary.

"So was mine," Scott replied, and both men laughed, instantly becoming friends.

In the gondola Byron asked Scott, "Madame Benzoni'? How is she so very different to Madame Albrizzi?"

Scott smiled. "Here in Venice, the Contessa Marina Benzoni is very much beloved by all. Firstly, she is a *true* Venetian, and a true believer in the ideals of liberty and hopes one day that Venice will return to being a Republic."

"So she is political?"

"I know only what the Venetians tell me, and to them she is famous. She is sixty now, but when she was young she had tremendous beauty. During Napoleon's time, when the French came to Venice – before the rule of the Austrians – she danced with Ugo Foscolo in the square of St Mark's around the Tree of Liberty, dressed only in an Athenian tunic, which revealed her fine legs and thighs. To this day the gondoliers still row up and down the canals singing the love song that she inspired, *La biondina in gondoleta.*"

"I have heard them sing it! La biondina ... and is she blonde."

"Yes, very blonde, and still is, but as hair thins with age, now I suppose it is a wig she wears."

As soon as they entered the Countess Benzoni's grand salon, Byron liked Marina Benzoni on sight. Even at sixty she still possessed some beauty, to a degree, and she was so kind, so charming; but what he liked most was her vivacity, and the free and easy way she made her guests relax.

Upon first arriving there, she had unashamedly introduced her *cavalier servente* to him, Count Giuseppe Rangone, a man of seventy who had been her best friend and lover for almost thirty years, ever since her husband had died.

Byron smiled. "Thirty years?" he said to Count Rangone. "And you are still in love?"

Rangone nodded happily, insisting that he still considered Marina to be "a divinity."

The Countess interrupted by calling those men whom she wished to introduce to Mylord Byron, calling them cheerfully by their name aloud, often from the other end of the room, and gave a description of each one before they had even approached. Thus, one was a *savant* and had published such and such a book; another had *des qualités des malheurs,* and so on. Byron thought it a very agreeable custom, as it instantly gave one a topic for conversation.

Although he felt bound to ask Madame, "Why do you speak in French?"

She stared at him. "Because you are English. It is the only other language the English know, yes?"

"I can *read* French with pleasure and facility, though I neither speak nor write it. But Italian I *can* speak with some fluency."

"You speak Italian?" She laughed and clapped her hands. "Now we won't have to *think* before we speak! So more natural for us all, eh?"

In the following weeks Byron often attended her sala, and always accompanied by Alexander Scott who was glad to have another Scot – or even a half-Scot – to talk with, apart from his boss Richard Hoppner and Hoppner's Swiss wife – and such a relief to be able to gabble away in *English* with Byron.

Pietro Giordani was also at Madame Benzoni's one evening, and begged Byron to have a private talk with him.

"Only if our talk is not about poetry or my works," Byron warned. "And worst of all – not about the *Romantics,* a term which I think ridiculous."

Giordani laughed. "Some say you are the *leader* of the Romantic movement."

"Some say? Who say? Not I say."

"Then we must talk of other things, as I intended," Giordani said, after which their conversation was so long, so private and so intimate, that the numerous assembly was surprised and amused.

When the time came to leave, Alexander Scott was curious. "For a conversation that lasted hours, you and Giordani must have been debating an interesting subject.

"Yes, immensely interesting," Byron agreed. "We talked about Italy, Greece, and politics."

"Politics?" Scott groaned. "As a diplomat I try to spend my evenings as far away from politics as possible."

Madame Benzoni and Count Rangone were also curious about the long private conversation, asking Giordani about it.

"To speak in private with him is pleasure," said Giordani. "When he talks, just one to another in private, his mind is strong and masculine with sound reasoning and great intelligence; but when another person comes and interrupts, he instantly changes and becomes funny and flippant with them, and the private magic is gone."

Giordani then lowered his voice conspiratorially. "He is sympathetic to Italy. He has already met with our friends in Milan."

The Austrian police also knew that Lord Byron had met with subversive Italians in Milan. His lordship was a famed political dissident who had not hidden his hostility to his own king and government in England. His fame and his politics could be a danger to the stability of the Papal States. As soon as he had entered Italy, regular reports had been written about him and sent to Rome.

From Geneva, – it was reported – Lord Byron had sent his spy on ahead of him into Lombardy; a Doctor Polidori, who claimed he had *walked* all the way from Geneva to Milan with the intention of waiting there to meet up again with his employer, Lord Byron. This Polidori was seen to call on Monsignore Ludovico di Brême, a suspected member of the secret Carbonari. One night at the theatre, this Dr Polidori displayed an arrogant attitude to a member of the Austrian police. He was arrested and deported out of the country within twenty-four hours.

Upon his own arrival from Switzerland into Milan, Lord Byron and his companion, a Mr John Hobhouse, spent three weeks in the company of Ludovico di Brême and his fellow subversives. These two Englishmen had been known supporters of Bonaparte and made no secret of their wish for Britain to become a Democracy or a Republic. Many of their evenings were spent with other suspected Carbonari at Di Brême's house. More meetings were held in Di Brême's private box at the Opera. These included other Liberal intellectuals, Pellegrino Rossi, Sylvio Pellico, Vincenzo Monti, as well as other enemies of the Austrian rulers of Italy.

Chapter Fourteen

~ ~ ~

No less than in Switzerland, where the English visitors had spied on his home with binoculars and telescopes, Byron was now being watched with great interest by the Venetians.

No *Conversazione* was successful unless someone had some news or a fresh story to tell about *l'Anglico Mylord.* He was rich, he was handsome, and he was famous all over Europe. So why should they not be glad that he had come to live in Venice?

And yet, like most of the *Inglese,* he was an eccentric with some *strange* habits. His midnight swims in the Grand Canal was one of them. His peculiar tribe of animals – monkeys and foxes and parrots and dogs and horses. There were only four horses in the whole of Venice, and all four belonged to the English Mylord, stabled on the island of Lido. His daily rides on the sands there. His regular visits to the Armenian Monastery at San Lazzaro. His kindness to the poor and his generosity to the beggars. His hatred of people knocking on his door without invitation. His love of women. Oh! – not since the days of Casanova had a man been so pursued by the women of Venice ... *"Vergognoso!"*

His looks and personal charisma also appealed to men, and one of these was Cavaliere Angelo Mengaldo, a stout and serious little man who had served under Napoleon and had distinguished himself with valour in the Moscow campaign. He had met Byron in person only once, and briefly, before managing to get an Italian edition of *The Corsair* which moved him so strongly he wrote in the flyleaf –

My fantasy is very agitated by this reading. I fear that Anglomania has entered my body. Every man of genius flames and transports me.

Mengaldo also wrote poetic verses, and now his fantasy was that he should become to Mylord Byron like Boswell was to Johnson – a friend, a guide, a diarist. He would then write a great book and become very rich and famous.

First he must make and cement the friendship, and to this end he visited every *conversazione* where he might see the English poet – and finally met him at the Contessa Benzoni's.

Mengaldo immediately manoeuvred himself into a seat on the sofa beside Byron and praised his poetry, and then informed Mylord that they had so much in common. Yes, so much! Were they not both poets and writers? Both Liberals? In one way *only* did they differ – and here, the Venetian Boswell began to lecture and advise –

"The rumours of your *casualness* in love affairs is truly shocking, Mylord, and it is not good. Not good for your reputation. I, too, pass from one love-affair to another, but I do so like a good Catholic. I know it is a sin, and so I confess it in Confession. Women should not be treated so casually. They say you have a good heart, Mylord, so why are you not good in body? With me at your side, as your closest friend, I can help you to be a good citizen, and help you to conduct your passions and love-affairs with order and method."

Byron was listening with eyes wide, thinking the man must be some kind of lunatic.

"And as a former soldier, I can ride a horse like a hussar. I rode all over Russia with Napoleon. So I can go horse-riding with you on the sands of Lido if you would like?"

The mention of Napoleon was interesting, but – "No, I usually go to Lido to get a swim in the Adriatic."

"You swim? That is good to know. Why? Because there is no better swimmer in the whole world than myself, Angelo Mengaldo."

Alexander Scott could no longer restrain his laughter. "You are surely not claiming to be a better swimmer than Lord Byron?"

Mengaldo nodded emphatically, "Better than any man alive."

Now Byron was also laughing. "I have swam the Hellespont in Greece – from Europe to Asia – and still recorded officially as the first and only man to do it."

Mengaldo tutted, as if that was nothing. "I have swam, *under fire,* across the Danube and the Berezina."

"And I," said Byron, "have swam, *against the current,* from the North bank to the South bank of the River Tagus in Lisbon. One of the most *dangerous* swimming feats there is."

Mengaldo was not impressed. "When I swam *under fire* across the Berezina, I was also saving the life of a fellow officer from drowning, because be could not swim."

"All that is true," said the Count Rangone, who had been listening. "Saving the life of that officer was the reason Signor Mengaldo received distinction for valour."

"Then let us put it to the test," suggested Byron. "If you beat me, Signore, then I will know, and concede to you, that I am no longer the best."

"A swimming test?" Mengaldo was surprised and delighted. Now the friendship would begin. "From where to where?"

"From the island of Lido, through the length of the Grand Canal."

"So, to swim more than four miles of water?" said Mengaldo. "Yes, I think that will be easy for me."

"You don't just have to swim it," said Byron. "You have to prove yourself the strongest and the fastest – even when swimming in and out amongst the gondolas."

Alexander Scott was still laughing. "May I join you? I am a fair swimmer myself, and I wouldn't mind the chance of possibly beating the pair of you."

Mengaldo shot a jealous look at Scott. "It is better it should be only two."

"Why? The Grand Canal is plenty wide enough?"

"No, more than two will be confusing. And the test should be only between Mylord Byron and myself."

"The more the merrier!" said Byron. "Bring along a regiment and I will try my strength against the lot of them." He smiled at Mengaldo. "It will be *fun*."

~~~

My dear Hobhouse,– Pray tell Master Murray to pay in "money," and not in bills. I insist on ready money, as I am sure I have always given him ready poetry.

Since my last I have been swimming against Scott and the Chevalier Mengaldo (a noted Italian swimmer who traversed the Danube in Napoleon's campaigns), and, I flatter myself, I gave them enough of it.

Mengaldo, whom both Scott and I beat hollow, leaving him five hundred yards behind us before we even got from Lido to the entrance of the Grand Canal.

Scott went from Lido as far as the Rialto, and was then taken into his gondola. I swam from Lido right to the end of the Grand Canal, including its whole length, besides that space from Lido to the canal's entrance (or exit) by the statue of Fortune, and coming out finally near the end opposite Fusina, which is computed by the Venetians to be four and a half of Italian miles.
~~~

I was in the sea from half past four till a quarter past eight without touching or resting. Scott swam well, with Mengaldo miles behind and knocked up, hallooing for his boat.

Yours very truly and affectionately, B. P.S. The wind and tide were both with me.

~~~

The letter containing the news that Percy and Mary Shelley had reached Italy with his daughter Allegra, and at present were lodged in the *Hotel Reale* in Milan, pleased Byron – until he read on through the letter and discovered that Claire Clairmont had also brought *herself* along with the child.

What game was this? From England they had persecuted him with letters saying that Claire was unable to take care of "*your little girl*" and now she had come along with her.

And now, as much as he liked Shelley, Byron was losing patience with his constant parroting of the words Claire Clairmont dictated to him.

Claire will write to you herself a detail of her motives. Her interference as the mother of course supersedes mine, which was never undertaken but from the deep interest I have ever felt for all parties concerned.

You write as if from the instant of departure all future intercourse were to cease between Claire and her child. This I cannot think you ought to have
~~~

expected, or even to have desired. What should we think of a woman who should resign her infant child without ever seeing it again, even to a father whose tenderness she entirely confides.

If she forces herself to such a sacrifice for the sake of her child's welfare, there is something heroically great in trampling upon her own strongest of affections, but the world would not think so. She would be despised as an unnatural mother, even by those who would see little to condemn in her becoming a mother without the formalities of marriage. She would thus resign her only good, and take to herself in its stead, contempt on every hand.

Besides, she might say, "What assurance have I of the tenderness of the father for his child, if he treats the mother with so little consideration?"

Furious, Byron vented his anger to Fletcher. "Is this not a trick on her part? When they kept persecuting me with letters to take responsibility for the welfare and upbringing of the child, there was no mention of *her* constantly being on the scene as well. Why, she was even ready to hand the child over to a stranger to be conveyed to Italy!

Fletcher thought it was indeed a trick of some kind. "In my humble opinion, my lord, if I may say so, that's like a man who keeps persecuting you to buy his horse from him, and when you do, he insists that he be allowed to keep sitting on it."

Byron read some more of Shelley's letter:

I am a third person in this painful controversy, who, in the invidious office of mediator, can have no interest, but in the interests of those concerned. I am now deprived of the power to act; but I would willingly persuade

You know my motives, and therefore I do not fear to ask you to come and see me at Como; and for the sake of your child's welfare, to soothe Claire's wounded feelings by some reassurances in the meanwhile.

He threw the letter down without reading any more, saying to Fletcher: "If Claire Clairmont does not wish to give up her child, then why doesn't she keep her and look after her? Why keep plaguing me to take the child, even though she receives my financial support? Does she think I am a fool? And even more disappointing – does *Shelley* think I am so easily duped?"

He wrote back to Shelley saying more or less the same words he had said to Fletcher, and making it clear that, in any event, a child was usually better off in the care of the mother, and was pleased that Claire had come to realise that.

~~~

Calling in on Byron at the Mocenigo Palazzo a few evenings later, Alexander Scott laughingly asked: "Did we, or did we not, beat Mengaldo in the swimming race?"

"We did. We beat the bubbles out of him. Why?"

"He is telling everyone that I was left stranded a far way behind him, and you beat him only by an unfortunate accident."
~~~

"The unfortunate accident of me being three miles ahead of him?"

"And all the gondoliers along the Canal saw it!" Scott was shaking his head. "Why does the man have to keep boasting so ridiculously? What purpose does it serve, other than making him look foolish?"

Byron was thoughtful ... most boasters were plagued with sensations of unimportance, urging them to try and fool others by boasting non-stop. Yet, in Mengaldo's case, that was unfair. As annoying as he was, and as idiotic as he seemed – somewhere in France there was a former French officer still living his life because Mengaldo had kept swimming with him, *under fire,* and brought him to safety and clear of the enemy.

"Is it a fact, then? The reports of him swimming the Berezina with a fellow comrade in tow? Rangone says it's true."

"Yes, it is true. So he may not be a fast swimmer, but he must have been strong and courageous then, and not the fool he has now become."

"Indeed."

They were about to set off for the Contessa Benzoni's sala, but Byron hesitated; holding up his hand, and then disappeared for some long minutes, returning with a smile and ready to go.

"Would you prefer to dine at Pellegrino's?"

"No, no, the Contessa's *conversazione* will do fine. Besides, I am not a big eater at the best of times."

"No? And you a half-Scot! I love nothing more than a good feast."

Upon entering Madame Benzoni's sala, Angelo Mengaldo's face turned a deep red when he saw the two men entering. Now the disagreements and arguments would begin. Now he would be disgraced in front of all these high-class people of Venice.

As soon as they were given wine and were seated, Count Rangone said loudly and cheerfully "We hear from the gondoliers, Mylord, that you were victorious in the swimming race?"

Byron imitated Mengaldo with a dismissive wave of his hand, as if that was nothing. "The Canal is easy to swim, with no obstacles but an occasional gondola. Unlike Signor Mengaldo, who swam through the strong currents of the Berezina with a floundering comrade, and under fire."

Mengaldo was staring white-faced at him, along with all the others who were staring also, as if this was completely unexpected.

Yet Byron *was* interested, especially in the actual details of the swim and escape.

"I have not heard the details, Signor Mengaldo, so would you be kind enough to tell me ... if you wish?"

Mengaldo looked around him, wondering if this was some kind of trick to humiliate him, but seeing the same surprise on many faces, he realised it was no trick. He looked at Byron. "You truly want to know?"

Byron nodded. "I do, sir. I wish I could know everything about Napoleon."

Others agreed, and although Mengaldo was still in the shock of surprise, it was not hard for him to look back at that terrible Russian campaign which had nearly killed him, and had damaged his lungs.

"It was only six years ago ... less ... in the November of 1812. We had been driven back from Moscow by the armies of Mikhail Kutuzov and Admiral Chichagov, but we were not defeated by the Cossacks, but by the freezing cold. Our soldiers had never experienced such cold as the one we found in Russia. Some of our men were dropping lifeless onto the snow and dying soon afterwards – all from the bitter and biting cold. And so we in the Grand Army, and Napoleon's Imperial Guard, were driven back into a retreat.

Napoleon's plan was to cross the Berezina and head for Poland, but our Russian enemies wanted to trap and destroy him. But fortunately, and to our good, the French commander of the engineers and the bridging equipment, General Eblé, succeeded in constructing a bridge wide and solid enough for Napoleon and the

Imperial Guard to get across. The Cavalry quickly followed, and some of the infantry, but most of us had no choice but to try and swim across in the freezing water while our rear-guard, the Swiss Infantry, bravely fought off the Cossacks."

Mengaldo put a hand to his eye, because the memory of the battle at Berezina was such a tragic disaster.

"Many of the brave Swiss were butchered by the Cossacks, and more than ten thousand Frenchmen were butchered also. We lost many more thousands in the icy water. I was lucky, because I would not give up and kept going, even though I thought a bullet or cannon-ball would hit my head before I reached the other side. I remember how my lungs felt as if they were going to burst if I swam one stroke more, but what else could I do? I had an unconscious comrade in tow, and if I went down, he went down too. I could not allow that to happen. Like me, he was an Italian."

"An Italian?"

Everyone in the silent room was looking at Mengaldo with new eyes, new respect. For almost an hour the conversation and questions were about no other subject but the terrible battle of Berezina.

"When Napoleon got to the other side of the bridge," said Mengaldo, "his horse was not able to stand on the ice, so he had to get off and walk. Someone gave me a dish of hot coffee. I shared it with my comrade who was now half conscious and half a fool, not knowing what had happened to him. That dish of hot coffee made all the difference between life and death for two men that day. Now I love hot coffee, it is my favourite drink."

More questions were asked about Napoleon.

"He was standing on the far bank of the river," said Mengaldo, "waiting and watching, and every time word came that another of his generals had got through safely, Napoleon would jump high in the air with joy. He loved his generals, and they loved him."

When the evening's *conversazione* had come near to its end, and people were standing to leave, Byron approached Angelo Mengaldo, and took out of his pocket the thing he had delayed to collect before leaving the Mocenigo Palace with Alexander Scott.

It was a medal, once dirty and tarnished, but now clean and perfect, and the ribbon spotless.

"May I?" he said to Mengaldo, and then pinned the medal on the lapel of the Italian's coat. "I think this would be better served if worn by you, a survivor of Berezina, than left to sit in my memento box."

Mengaldo raised his hand to lift the medal by its red ribbon and then stared down in astonishment at the small gold crown hanging from it, and underneath a green and gold wreath around a gold medal.

"What is it?" asked the Contessa Benzoni. "A medal? What kind of medal?" She moved closer and peered at the words inscribed within the circle around the gold medal ... *Napoleon. Emp. Des Francais*

Mengaldo had known what it was as soon as he had seen it. "It is a medal of the *Légion d'Honneur,* and given only by Napoleon himself."

He looked at Byron with tears in his eyes. "Where did you get it?"

"I found it in a ditch."

Mengaldo stared. "A ditch?"

"Yes, I found it lying dirty in a ditch ... on the battlefield of Waterloo."

"Waterloo? The battlefield of *Waterloo?* You have been there?"

"Yes, in the springtime of 1816, less than one year after the battle. I walked over every inch of it. It was the yellow daffodils growing by the ditch that caught my attention, before I saw the red ribbon in the dirt, and then the medal."

"From one of the fallen ..." Mengaldo placed his hand over the medal on his breast as if it was sacred; and Byron nodded, "I knew it would mean more to you, than to me. And it sits better on you, an actual soldier in Napoleon's army."

Tears were slipping down Mengaldo's face, and

suddenly everyone began clapping loudly and calling out *"Bravo! Bravo!"*

Mengaldo looked around in more astonishment as he saw they were all applauding him, not Mylord Byron, but *him*, Angelo Mengaldo, who had indeed served with Napoleon's Legions of Honour in that long and freezing Russian campaign.

Count Rangone handed Mengaldo a glass of wine. "We will all now drink to you and your bravery at Berezina, Signore, when you saved the life of another Italian."

Mengaldo shook his head and handed back the wine. "No, pray forgive, I am too affected, too emotional, so please, if I may – a dish of hot coffee?"

Chapter Fifteen

~ ~ ~

Eight days had passed since his reply to Shelley, and now another letter had arrived.

My Dear Lord Byron, — It certainly gave me much pleasure to be able to bring your little girl to Italy, as indeed I was puzzled as to find a person I could trust her with; but the purpose of my journey was, I lament to say, in no manner connected with it.

My health, which has always been declining, had assumed such symptoms that the physicians advised me to proceed without delay to a warmer climate.

Allow me too repeat my assertion that Claire's late conduct with respect to the child was wholly unconnected with, and uninfluenced by me. The correspondence from which these misinterpretations have arisen was undertaken on my part solely because you refused to correspond with Claire. I am sorry that I misunderstood your letter; I hope that on both sides there is here an end to misunderstandings.

You will find your little Allegra quite well. I think she is the most lovely and engaging child I ever beheld. Tell us what you think of her, and whether or no, she equals your expectations. Her attendant is the Swiss maid, Elise, who has attended my own children, in whom Mrs Shelley entirely confides, and whom Mary parts with solely that Claire and yourself may be assured that Allegra will be attended almost with a mother's care.

Claire, as you may imagine, is dreadfully unhappy. As you have not written to her, it has been a kind of custom that she should see your letters to me. I have not seen any of those which she has written to you; nor even have I often known when they were sent.

I am commissioned by an old friend of yours to convey to you the book "Frankenstein" and to request that if you conjecture the name of the author that you will regard it as a secret. It is of course Mrs Shelley's. It has met with considerable success in England; but she bids me to say, "That she would regard your approbation as a more flattering testimony of its merit."

Address your next letter "Poste Restante, Pisa," as we leave Milan for that city tomorrow. We have been disappointed in our house at Como; and indeed, I shall attempt to divert Claire's melancholy by availing myself of some introductions at Pisa. I ought to say that we shall be at Pisa long before the return of post — when we expect (pray don't disappoint us) a letter from you to assure us of the safe arrival of our little favourite. Elise's wages with us were 20 louis.

My dear Lord Byron, yours always sincerely,

P. B. Shelley.

It took some time for the news that the child, still only a baby, was already on her way to him, and the responsibility for her life and welfare from now on, was to be his alone.

The thought terrified him, until Fletcher reminded him of how easily he had taken to, and been able to care for his legitimate daughter, Ada.

"Why, the poor nursemaids always had a hard job of getting you away from her!" Fletcher declared.

The memory of his baby daughter Ada brought a pain to his heart and tears to his eyes, but he wiped them away.

Now was not the time to be melancholy, now was the time to be *practical* and to make arrangements for the care of this new child.

Months before, he had leased a country house from Richard Hoppner in Este, quiet and peaceful in beautiful scenic surroundings, solely for the purpose of providing a quiet home for Allegra.

Even so, he was not stupid, and he knew Claire Clairmont too well not to be certain that she would try and foist herself upon him at some time in the future, using her need to see the child as an excuse.

For that reason, and that reason alone, had he leased the house at Este, solely as a place where the mother, if she so wished, could visit her child without his presence.

The following day he received a letter from Claire herself. Usually he discarded her letters without opening them; but as this one was undoubtedly relating to the child, he opened it.

"I have one favour to beg of you. Send me the

smallest quantity of your own dearest hair so that I may put it with some of Allegra's inside a locket. My dearest Lord Byron, best of human beings, you are the father of my little girl and I cannot forget you."

Her letter served only to dismay and annoy him. If she had shown that she was only interested in the welfare of her child, and now felt indifferent towards him, he would have been ready to treat her with much courtesy and regard her with more kindness.

But no – he was now certain that she was still using the child to force herself into his life again – making it truly impossible to ever see her in any environment, or under any conditions whatsoever. And the very fact that she was still *using* the child – even to actually giving her away – only served to make Claire Clairmont truly repulsive to him.

His only fear now was that he would allow himself, in the future, to transfer that repulsion to the innocent child.

Later that day, confused by his own thoughts, he asked Fletcher to read all of Shelley's letters to him.

"You are always bragging about what a man of *learning* you are, Fletcher, so pray read the letters, and then tell me if there is anything rather odd in them that strikes you."

Fletcher was puzzled. "Why should I do that?"

"Because I'm the employer who pays your wage and I ask you."

"You've never let me read your letters before."

"And I probably never will again. So Fletcher, will you just *do* as I say or – by the heavens – I will fling you into the canal."

"Oh, well, in that case ..." Fletcher sat down and slowly and seriously read through Shelley's letters, raising an eyebrow occasionally, and slightly frowning now and again, until he finally set the letters down, declaring that there was nothing odd in them at all.

"No?"

"Not to my mind, at any rate ... excepting that I did think it odd that he should refer to her as *'the most lovely child I ever beheld'* .. also here, in this one ..." Fletcher lifted the letter, "where he calls her *'our little favourite'*... Doesn't Mr Shelley and his wife have a child of their own – a little boy?"

Byron nodded. "William, and also a girl who was born about six or seven months ago."

"Then it's strange, that, because most parents usually think no other child in the world can compare to their own."

"Perhaps he was merely being polite," Byron said. "Or exaggerating in order to encourage me to take her."

"I suppose so ... and that would explain why in the letters he always calls her *'your little girl'*."

"You particularly noticed that too?"

"Aye, – as if she had come down out of the sky and you were her only kin. No mention of the mother having any responsibility for her at all."

After a long silence, Fletcher said in the blunt way of his own people of Nottinghamshire, "Poor little mite, seems to me that no one really wants her, not for keeps, anyway."

Byron looked at him in startled realization, and Fletcher knew he had hit home.

"Legitimate or no, if she's your child then what's the difference between her and Ada? Is one copper and the other gold?"

After another long silence, Byron said, "Well, I don't know if the child will be happier here with us in Venice, but as soon as she arrives, I know that she will be fussed over and spoiled to vanity by all the attentions of our Italian servants."

Fletcher smiled. "Aye, to these Italians, all children are blessings from Heaven."

PART FIVE

1818

The Shelley Ménage

"A house with a lawn a river or lake – noble trees and divine mountains that should be our little mousehole to retire to. But never mind this – give me a garden and *absentia Clariae* and I will thank my love for many favours."

Letter from Mary to Shelley.

Chapter Sixteen

~~~

Mary was in a state of silent depression, not only because her book *Frankenstein* had received bad reviews – *The Quarterly Review* had called it "*a tissue of horrible and disgusting absurdity,*" while others condemned it as "unrealistic" and "undoubtedly the work of an atheist." Thank goodness she had not put her name to the book and had published it anonymously.

All that she could cope with, because she knew she had chosen a divisive subject for a novel; consoling herself with the thought that, perhaps, with some amendments, she could try and make the story better, more acceptable.

But there was no consolation, no relief from the daily irritation of her nerves due to her suffering from the same old problem – the constant presence of Claire in her marriage.

Yet now, as much as she loved Shelley, and she loved him much, she felt great resentment towards Shelley also, for he always somehow managed to make things worse.

Back in England, when they had been living in Bath, with Claire having a child to care for, and still mooning around hoping that Byron would relent and return her affections, Mary had felt safe – *safe* in her own relationship with Shelley.

But then, as the spring progressed into summer, Claire seemed to have come to the realisation that Byron would never change, and once again she turned her attentions back to Shelley.

How easy it had been then for Claire, when she herself had been pregnant again, to latch onto Shelley and join him in his long walks and talks, becoming his sole *confidante* again, so that when Shelley returned from his walks he had few anxious worries to confide in
~~~

his wife, or any need to seek her advice – because he had confided and talked them all out with Claire.

Mary had wished she could scream at Claire, or throw tantrums with Shelley, but it was not her way, not her temperament; and as it had always been, the more unhappy she felt, the quieter she became.

Shelley had not liked Bath, deciding to go and look for a new house nearer to London, in Marlow, near to where his friend Thomas Peacock lived.

She had agreed, for she did not like Bath either; but then she had been struck into dumb silence when Shelley decided to take Claire and little Alba with him – *"To make life easier and more peaceful for you in your pregnancy,"* he had told her. *"You just rest while we find a nice house for you."*

And she had been left alone, pregnant as she was, with only one young maid to help her to look after William – a young girl named Milly Shields whom they had brought with them from England – but not the older and more capable Elise – because Claire had decided to take Elise along with her to look after little Alba – or Allegra as she was now called.

It was then she had written to Shelley, letting him know that she would truly prefer a house and a home which would contain "Claire's absence."

Shelley had made no mention of her request in his reply, staying away for over two months *"due to business with Leigh Hunt in London"* before he had returned to collect her and William and move them to a house in Marlow, where she later gave birth to their baby daughter, a delightful child, whom Claire had begged Shelley to name Clara.

It was then that she had asked Shelley to try and persuade Byron to legally adopt his daughter Allegra, if only to allow Claire to stride out and make a life of her own, without always being so dependent on them.

When Shelley had balked at this, she had quietly but firmly made the situation plain to Shelley – it was her or Claire – the decision was his.

He had covered her with love and insisted that of course it was *her* – and it would *always* be her, his Mary, his *divine* Mary – but they had to be kind to poor Claire, if only for a short time longer.

And now, here they were – in Italy! And nothing had changed – except Elise had now taken dear little Alba down to Byron in Venice – but Claire was *still* here, *still* living with them, and showing no inclinations to leave; packing up her stuff and getting ready to move with them to Pisa, instead of returning to England as she had once promised.

Now her excuse was that she needed to stay in Italy for a while longer, to know how the child was settling into her new life in Venice. And Mary knew, only too well, that later on it would be some other excuse.

Was there *no* way of getting rid of Claire to find a life and husband of her own? No way at all?"

Claire had no intention of returning to England, not while Byron was here in Italy. As fond as she was of Shelley, Byron was still the one she loved, the only one. Just thinking of him was like a drug to her – "*A drug, sir, a drug!*"

Now she was hoping that once he had met Allegra, and fallen in love with her, he would begin to think more kindly of Allegra's mother, and wish to see her again.

She had given strict instructions to Elise – that stupid girl – to write often and tell her *everything;* and, in particular, *anything* that would necessitate her presence in Venice; any little thing at all that might call for a mother's presence.

And knowing Byron, there would be something. With Byron there was *always* something to get people talking.

After leaving Como they had spent a whole month in Livorno, in the West of Tuscany, with Maria Gisborne, a woman of forty-eight who was a painter and writer and had been living in Italy for twenty years. And who, as a girl, had once been a close friend of Mary's mother, Mary Wollstonecraft.

Maria and her husband had welcomed the trio warmly, but all of Maria's attention and fuss was for Mary Wollstonecraft's daughter. "Dear Mary," she kept saying. "Dear Mary," until none knew which Mary she was speaking of, the mother or the daughter.

Maria agreed with Shelley that Britain was no longer a good place to live, because it had become "too Conservative". All the good liberals had left, and now there was only tyranny and oppression of speech and ideas.

"And that monster, Castlereagh," Maria said.

Shelley visibly shuddered at the mention of Lord Castlereagh's hated name. "You know what torture and torment he caused when he ruled Ireland?"

Maria nodded. "Nemesis will get him one day."

"Nemesis?" Shelley smiled; and Maria asked why?

"You remind of me of Lord Byron," Shelley replied. "He is a firm believer in *Nemesis*, the Greek Goddess of Retribution. He is certain that she will make all his enemies pay one day, and pay hard."

"Lord Byron?" Maria asked in astonishment "The poet?"

Shelley nodded. "He is a friend of ours."

"*Mio Dio!*" said Maria, like an Italian in shock, and then rushed to find and bring back to the table a stack of Byron's books, saying she had read them all many times over.

"What a man, what a voice! When he speaks I feel I *know* him, like a friend."

Claire was startled and confused. "You know him? Lord Byron?"

Maria nodded. "Yes, I know him well, in his books I know him."

"In his books? You have not met him in person?"

"No, but they say he is somewhere here in Italy." She looked at Shelley. "Is that true?"

Shelley decide to err on the side of caution, knowing

how cold and distantly unfriendly Byron could be with strangers.

"I'm not sure where he is. We have not actually *seen* him since we left Switzerland eighteen months ago. *Is he here in Italy?*"

"They say so. My English neighbour rushed to see him in Rome when she was told he was there, but, alas, he had gone on to somewhere else."

Claire was no longer listening – Shelley's words still ringing in her ears and making her feel ill – "*We have not actually seen him since we left Switzerland ...*"

She excused herself and went up to her room, desperately trying to formulate a plan that would allow her to *see* Byron again, and for him to *see* her ... She was slimmer now than she had been in Geneva, in the early stages of Allegra's pregnancy; and quicker and lighter on her feet ... in fact all her movements were now quicker and lighter – Heaven forfend that she would ever get pregnant again. In future, she would be more than happy to leave all the child-bearing to Mary.

~~~

After a month living with the Gisbornes, Shelley finally found a house that he liked in Bagni di Lucca, in Northern Tuscany – the Villa Bertini – a three-storey house on a hill looking down into the green valley – and less than a day's ride away from Livorno.

Mary loved her new home from the first moment they reached the secluded dusty path leading to the house, overhung with the richest foliage of green trees; and then the lovely peaceful Villa Bertini with its secluded garden, sitting just above the pretty collection of villages that made up the town of Bagni di Lucca. The city of Pisa was only a few hours ride away.

Before leaving Livorno, Maria Gisborne had also found them a new servant, a strong young man named Paolo Foggi, who helped them to move into the villa and show them what produce to buy in the villages, while he negotiated in Italian with the locals.
~~~

Paolo also managed, at a very reasonable rate, to hire a woman to come in daily to clean, do the laundry, and cook. And – to Mary's surprise – the woman seemed to think that the agreed payment to her was a fortune for doing the normal things that all Italian women do every day for nothing. The woman beamed as she rejoiced in her good fortune. "*Grazie*," she kept saying. "*Grazie*."

The trio soon settled into the villa, all their books and belongings unpacked. Shelley found a secluded woodland stream where he would go every day to read and then bathe naked, until he was cool and refreshed.

The heat was having the opposite effect on his baby daughter Clara, who became sickly and whingey with signs of a fever; but she was still teething, and the heat had become oppressively humid. Nevertheless Mary worried and did everything she could to cool her little girl, sitting up at night to wave a fan over her while she slept.

Claire, meanwhile, was anxiously waiting for a letter from Elise in Venice for some *news* of Byron. Did he like Allegra? Did he love her? Were his thoughts straying to her mother?

She found out a few days later, when Paolo returned from Pisa with two letters, one of which was for Claire from Elise, telling her that Lord Byron had made her move out with Allegra into the house of the British Consul's wife, Madame Hoppner. She must come and take Allegra back, because Lord Byron's house was full of noisy Italian servants – whose language she did not understand, and even worse – Lord Byron had said that when Allegra grew up he intended to marry her.

Claire appeared to believe every word, but Shelley and Mary did not.

"If he has moved them, there must be some good reason," Mary insisted; while Shelley laughed at the most ridiculous part of Elise's letter –

"Marry her? That's a regular jest of Byron's. When we did our eight-day tour around Lake Geneva, and children of the villages would run up to talk to us strangers, if there was a shy little girl amongst them, Byron would always bend down and say to her – 'When you grow up will you marry me?' making her and all the other children laugh."

Claire was having none of it. No, they must go to Venice *immediately* to find out what was going on.

Mary looked at her, askance. "We cannot pack up and leave this house to go to Venice! Most likely Byron is not too happy with Elise, and shows it. But I will *not* believe that he is capable of being anything but good to any child. And are you forgetting, Claire, that our little Clara is sick?"

"*Teething*, that's all!" Claire then reduced herself to such a tantrum, Shelley was forced to take her outside for a long walk to calm her down.

When they returned, Mary could not quite believe what Shelley was saying to her: "Claire is not to be consoled, so I suppose we should go to Venice just to assure her that all is well with Allegra."

"We?"

"Claire insists that I go with her. She is too nervous of Byron's reaction to appear there alone."

"And what of I, here alone?"

"You will not be alone, my love. You have Milly and Paolo to help you, and we will make a speedy return, I promise you."

"You will go with her, even though our little Clara is sick?"

"As Claire says, it is just her teeth cutting through, as well as discomfort from all this infernal heat."

Once again Mary was left struck into dumb silence when, at Claire's insistence, she and Shelley left immediately for Venice.

Now Mary had only Milly for company in the Villa Bertini, and two children to care for. Paolo was not much company as he usually spent most of the time running errands, or out in the garden fixing things or trimming the hedges.

Young Milly did her best to distract and play with

William, but only two-and-a-half-years old, and his daddy suddenly gone, William became whingey too and would not leave his mother's lap.

Mary was close to tears. Once again Claire had got her own way. Oh, how she now *hated* her selfish stepsister!

~~~

As their journey to Venice progressed, Shelley became increasingly anxious about Byron's reaction to the sight of Claire.

Byron had made it very clear – unfairly in Shelley's opinion – that he never wanted to see or have anything to do with Claire again. His sudden detestation of Claire in Switzerland, was something which Shelley still could not understand; especially as his strange aversion to her had began even before he had known Claire was pregnant.

Shelley certainly had no wish to damage his friendship with Byron, and nor did he believe that anything terrible had happened to Allegra or Elise.

And was it not a little strange, now he had time to think about it, that Claire, who had often complained of Elise being so stupid, was now willing to believe every word Elise had said in her letter?

An involuntarily smile crossed his face as he remembered Elise's actual words in her letter ... *"He's only growing her up so he can later make her his mistress or marry her."*

Poor Byron, he had to be the most unfairly maligned man in the history of England ... which did not excuse him being so unfair to Claire ... yet Byron could instantly wither a man's pride with just a look or a sentence, and Shelley was not prepared to risk one of those looks or satirical sentences directed at himself.

If he did, it would cause an end to his friendship with Byron, and Shelley was not willing to risk that, not even for Claire.

It took them four days to reach Padua, travelling
~~~

sometimes at fifty to sixty miles a day, during which time Claire had softened Shelley's doubts with explanations of a mother's tenderness and terrible fears, and her heart's everlasting love for Allegra.

Shelley of course understood, and the rest of the journey was exhilarating and exciting, especially their first sight of Florence, where they ate figs and peaches and sumptuous fruits that tasted as if they had grown in Paradise.

By the time they reached Padua, Shelley had decided that it would be more prudent if Claire was to wait for him at the inn at Padua, while he went on to Fusina and Venice alone, when he would either return with good tidings, or have Allegra with him.

Claire would not even consider it – Padua was twenty-five miles from Venice – so no, she could *not* be left here on her own. "I *must* go into Venice. I *must* see my darling Allegra and know if she is well or not."

Claire began to cry, and Shelley finally came up with a solution.

"Elise said Byron had moved them out to live in the house of the British Consul. So if we were to go directly there, to the Consul's house, you would be able to see Allegra without Byron seeing you, or knowing you are in Venice."

Claire agreed. It was certainly better than the ridiculous suggestion of leaving her on her own in Padua.

Before leaving Padua, Shelley sent a letter to Mary, telling her, untruthfully, that Claire would now be staying alone at the inn at Padua, while he travelled on to Venice alone.

From then onwards the journey was a true delight, full of the joys of new and novel sights, especially the sight of the gondolas at Fusina. It was night and dark, but torch-lanterns were burning all along the waterfront, and it had started to rain.

"Rain!" Oh, such cooling bliss!

They giggled like children at the novelty of sailing in

one of Venice's famous black gondolas, huddling together in the cabin on the soft sofa, cosy and comfortable, while the rain poured down outside. Then Shelley was distracted by his fascination with the gondola's windows, pulling at the string of the small blinds that went up and down.

"These must be what they call *Venetian* blinds," he told Claire. "And look here," he added, showing her the window behind the blind which had small flowers stained into the glass. "Is that not delightful?"

But Claire was not interested in the window-blinds, whispering him that she was feeling very frightened of the way the waves were lashing against the sides of the gondola.

"These boats are very safe and sturdy," he assured her, "because they are *flat*-bottomed boats, not curved like canoes," and then he did his best to comfort her fears.

Venice finally came into view, its lights twinkling like stars in the rain.

Shelley had told the gondolier they did not want to stay at an expensive hotel, so he dropped them off at a small inn on a side-street, down one of the small canals.

It was Saturday night, and midnight. Too late to do anything now but go to bed. But tomorrow was Sunday – *Sunday* – the perfect day to call on the British Consul at his home. And surely everyone in Venice, at least the managers in the hotels, would know exactly *where* the British Consul lived.

~~~

In the Villa Bertini, Mary was still awake, in the darkness of the nursery with little Clara, who was still not quite better.

When the child finally drifted off to sleep, Mary gently laid her down in her cot, and then returned to the bright lights of the kitchen where Maria Gisborne sat waiting for her.

Dear Maria, how quickly she had come when Mary
~~~

had written to her, saying she was "*at my wits' end*" pleading for Maria's help.

Maria Gisborne had come as fast as she could, by carriage, and found Mary crying over her sick little girl.

"I could not bear to lose my little girl again," Mary wept, and then told Maria about her daughter Ianthe, her first adorable child, who had suddenly died in her sleep after only a few weeks.

"I found it hard to bear then, and I was only sixteen at the time. But now I am twenty, I know I would find it even harder to endure if it were to happen again."

Maria assured her that such a thing would not be allowed to happen. She inspected the child and was certain that the fever had spiked and was now cooling down. "See, put your hand here, and see how cool she feels, almost normal."

Mary had placed her palm on Clara's brow and, yes, she did feel the coolness. Her palm moved slowly down to Clara's little chest, and that too felt a lot cooler.

She looked at Maria and smiled apologetically. "I think I called you too soon, but I was so worried here on my own. It was so good of you to take the trouble to come."

"It was no trouble." Maria waved a hand dismissively. "For the daughter and granddaughter of my dear friend, Mary Wollstonecraft, I would go anywhere to help. But I think the child is still dehydrated, so you must give her plenty of water, and lots of quiet and rest."

Mary almost laughed, ironically. "It has been so quiet here on my own. Even William has turned into a quiet little Wilmouse. We all miss Shelley terribly."

Maria Gisborne's expression became slightly stern. "My dear, you are the daughter of the woman who wrote the book *The Rights Of Women!* So why did you not stand up for your own rights? Why did you allow him to go?"

Mary shrugged. "I could not *forbid* him to go. No, that would be very difficult for me. I am so used to doing whatever Shelley says."

"Why?"

Mary wondered why also. "I suppose," she said, "it's because I have been in Shelley's care since I was barely sixteen, and he being older than me, I always did what he said we should do. I have always trusted his judgement more than my own."

"How old is he?"

"It was his birthday two weeks ago, so now he is twenty-six."

"Still young," Maria said, and smiled pityingly. "You are both so young, and already you have had two children."

"Three children," Mary said. "Don't forget my little Ianthe. She may be dead in body, but she still lives in my heart and dreams."

~~~

Late on Sunday morning, Shelley and Claire set off in a gondola to the house of the British Consul, Mr Richard Hoppner.

The previous night they had spent a long time discussing how they would go about it. Claire's preferred way was to first go to the Palazzo Mocenigo and confront Byron about Allegra, before speaking to any strangers; but Shelley was against any kind of confrontation.

"I'm not prepared to confront anyone or jump to conclusions based solely on what Elise has written. She has confused Mary and myself about William a few times in the past, all due to a misunderstanding of our English."

Claire agreed, and sniped. "Even her own French is not that good."

Shelley was also worried about how it would look to Byron if he knew that he and Claire had travelled all the way from Tuscany, and had lodged at inns alone, without Mary.

"I think we should first find out how things lie with
~~~

the Consul and his wife, and if Allegra is there. If so, if you say you are her mother, they may be able to tell you what has been going on."

"Very well," Claire agreed. "But if what I am told is not good or unsatisfactory, then I *must* be allowed to visit Byron."

At the Consul's house, Claire went in alone, while Shelley remained in the gondola's cabin, insisting his presence would only lead to curious speculation.

He lay back, preparing himself for a long wait, knowing how Claire could quiz and question.

Yet, much to his surprise, after only a few minutes a servant came down to the mooring steps asking for "Signor Shelley?"

Shelley sheepishly emerged from the gondola and followed the servant into the house, where he found Mr and Madame Hoppner to be very pleasant indeed.

"I have heard of you, Mr Shelley, from Lord Byron."

Madame Hoppner nodded, saying in her Swiss accent, "Yes, he has told us all about your time in my country. It was good, yes?"

"The scenery was beautiful," Shelley replied, looking around him and admiring the rich comfort of the Consul's home.

Madame Hoppner spoke to Claire. "Now, you wish to see the child? I will send for her."

While they waited, Claire asked Madame Hoppner why the child was no longer living with Lord Byron. "Does he not want her?"

"Oh, my goodness," exclaimed Madame Hoppner, shocked at the question. "Why would that be so?"

Richard Hoppner then explained that the roof of the Palace Mocenigo had endured a big leak with the rain running down one wall, and so his lordship had placed the child in their care – "just temporarily, you understand, to get her away from all the banging and hammering. But I believe all the repair work has now been completed."

Shelley emitted a sigh of relief, and then smiled when

Elise carried the child into the room. Allegra looked sleepy, having been awoken from her nap, but she looked as healthy as ever.

Claire immediately took the child into her arms and Madame Hoppner smiled sympathetically. "You miss her, yes? I understand. I have my own little boy."

While the women were conversing, Richard Hoppner took Shelley into his study, where his attitude underwent a complete change. "I must be frank with you, Mr Shelley, because this visit is most unexpected."

"Yes, sir, and I apologise, but you see –"

"Lord Byron will not like it. Miss Clairmont being here. He has occasionally confessed to me his extreme horror at her possible arrival in the city, and the necessity of which it would impose on him of instantly quitting Venice."

Shelley said he was aware of Lord Byron's sentiments. "I'm afraid the letter from Elise confused us, and no doubt you understand the alarm a mother feels when she believes all is not going well with her child."

Hoppner looked at him blankly. "Then why did she give the child away?"

Shelley stumbled over his answer. "I have two children of my own, and we are not rich, and –"

"Lord Byron is financially supporting the mother and child is he not? He tells me he is. But if he is not, then I wonder why she passed the child to him? It's a very uncommon thing for a mother to do, especially with a girl child. Men are more inclined to take over the rearing of their sons, understandably. Is that the reason for the handover? No financial support?"

"I believe," said Shelley, "that Claire's motives are selfless and honourable, in that she is convinced Allegra would enjoy a better and more comfortable life with Lord Byron than she herself could ever provide."

"Well, yes, there is that ... an unmarried mother with a child has few opportunities open to her; and of course I do understand. But I must say, her manner when she first arrived ... I do hope, Mr Shelley, that she did not for a moment believe that Lord Byron is not giving the child the best of care? Why, it was only to spare the child the nuisance of all the noise that he requested us to temporarily take her."

Shelley was silent, wishing he could throttle Elise.

"And Allegra's nurse, Elise?" he asked.

"Ah, Miss Duvillard does not like Venice. All the water everywhere. She is certain all the houses are about to sink."

Madame Hoppner popped her head round the door. "You will stay for luncheon, Mr Shelley? The mother has agreed to stay."

Shelley suddenly realised he was starving. They had not eaten since they had left the inn at Padua.

"Thank you, I am most obliged."

Elise, being a servant, was not present at the dining table, so all of Claire's questions were about Lord Byron.

Madame Hoppner, a devout Swiss Calvinist, looked as if she did not approve of Lord Byron in some ways.

"He is very popular here with some, but others disapprove of his behaviour. He is inclined, on occasions, to be a little *wild.*"

Richard Hoppner chuckled. "Only he could get away with it, being a lord."

"Why?" asked Claire avidly. "How? In what way is he wild?"

Madame Hoppner laid down her knife and fork. "Well, he is known to be quite wild during the Carnivals, but then all Venetians go wild during the Carnivals – their *excuse* is that they must enjoy themselves and have a good time before they settle down to all the fasting and prayers during the seven weeks of Lent."

"I think," said Richard Hoppner to his wife, "that many of the tales we hear about Lord Byron contain a lot of exaggeration."

His wife ignored him. "Also, for a man of his rank, a noble and an aristocrat, I would expect him to display more propriety in whom he mixes with – but there have been times when he has freely mixed with merchants and people of trade – drapers and bakers and their wives. The only thing that people like us do with traders and their sort, is *trade."*

When Shelley and Claire remained silent, she gave a small titter and added, "Of course, we are all very fond of him, nevertheless."

Shelley broke the silence by asking Madame Hoppner. "You must know Lord Byron very well, for him to trust you enough to leave Allegra with you."

She nodded. "Quite well. He is always very polite and most respectful to me, but his friendship is mainly with my husband."

Richard Hoppner smiled cynically. "As their Consul, most English people eventually call on me for one reason or another; but of late they usually only call for one purpose – to find out how or where they might see Lord Byron. It seems, that after Saint Marks, he is now one of the main attractions of Venice. I believe he endured something similar with you in Geneva."

Shelley nodded. "When we were in Geneva, the English people behaved very badly towards us. They accused us of living the life of the most unbridled libertines. I won't go into details, but there were things, sometimes terrible, sometimes ridiculous, that were imputed to us. Yet none would leave Byron alone. The inhabitants on the banks of the lake opposite his house used telescopes to spy on his movements."

Hoppner lifted his wine glass. "Of course he is fascinating, and his poetry is so different to other poets, but I am constantly amazed by the curiosity expressed by travellers of all classes who wish to see him. Also their sheer eagerness to pick up any anecdotes about his life is hardly to be credited. And if they fail to get any information from me, then it's the gondoliers they question – and *they* are usually very happy to tell them the most extravagant and unfounded stories in return for a sizable tip. Not all, of course, but some gondoliers, for an even bigger tip, will go so far as to point out the house where he lives, and to give hints of his movements which might allow them an opportunity of seeing him."

"Poor Byron," said Claire. "It must be horrible to be so famous."

"Yes, horrible, that is what I say," agreed Madame Hoppner.

"The worst of all, though, are some of the English visitors," continued Mr Hoppner. "Under pretext of knowing him, some have even contrived to gain entrance into his house with the most bare-faced impudence. Hence his understandable bitterness towards them."

Shelley was frowning. "Do his servants not protect him from such intrusions?"

"Indeed they do," Hoppner replied, "His family of servants are all very attached to him, especially the Italians who will endure anything on his account. But it is impossible for him to win, because when the visitors are not allowed entry, they go away and make up the most incredible stories about his hatred of society and all mankind. And that is not his natural feeling at all, for I am certain that I have never witnessed greater kindness than in Lord Byron."

Madame Hoppner's face made a little moue of disapproval. "A big fault, when he behaves so with his servants."

Her husband shrugged. "Well, yes, I agree, Lord Byron *is* culpably lenient with his servants. Even in instances of their neglecting their duty, or taking an undue advantage of his good nature, he prefers to banter than speak seriously to them about it. And even when he does, he cannot bring himself to discharge them, even when he has threatened to do so."

Claire put her hands to her brow. It was all becoming too much for her to endure, to know that Byron could be so warm to others, and yet so cold to her.

"I need to lay down," she said tiredly. "All the travelling has left me quite weary."

"Oh, my dear," said Madame Hoppner, "we have worn you out with all our talking. I will bring Allegra to you."

"Just to kiss," Claire said. "One last kiss for my angel."

Before leaving, Shelley said quietly to Hoppner. "You will not tell Lord Byron that Miss Clairmont has been here in Venice."

"No, I will not tell him," Hoppner assured him. "And as one Englishman to another, you have my word on that."

Shelley believed him. "And your wife?"

"I will instruct her likewise."

Back at their inn, Shelley was consumed by a sudden compulsion to go and *see* Byron, but knew he could not take Claire, not even for a minute – not after Hoppner's warning.

"I really *should* go and see him," he told Claire. "If he was ever to find out that I was in Venice, he would wonder why I had slipped in and out so sneakily without calling on him."

Claire was too downcast to argue, surprising Shelley with her agreement. "Ask him when he intends to take Allegra back into his care. I gave her to *him*, not the Hoppners. And ask him if I am ever going to be allowed to see my child, at *his* home, in *his* care, not the Hoppners."

Shelley could see that Claire had lapsed into one of her dark moods. "I will stay if you wish."

"No, go."

"What will you do while I am gone?"

"I will go to bed and sleep. I sorely missed my afternoon sleeps on the road. Tomorrow morning, do you think we can take the time to walk around Venice and see some of the sights. It would be a shame not to do so, as we are here."

Shelley hesitated, thinking of Mary, but Claire interrupted his thoughts. "At least let us go and see the famous Piazzo San Marco?"

"Very well, but only to San Marco, and then we must leave Venice."

Claire walked over to the window and looked down at the narrow canal beneath. "Are you *sure* this Venice is not sinking?"

Shelley grinned. "If it is, then it has been sinking for over a thousand years, and yet here Venice still stands. Of course it is *not* sinking!"

"And if you come back to find this building and I have vanished underwater?"

"Impossible. Even if the building were to sink, you would still be quite dry and squalling at the window."

"Why so?"

"Because even the Grand Canal is no more than sixteen feet deep, at the most."

"How do you know that?"

"The gondolier told me."

~~~

On the Grand Canal, in the gondola taking him to the Palazzo Mocenigo, Shelley's anxiety returned. He knew Byron hated unexpected callers, and what reason could he give for being in Venice?

By the time the gondola had stopped at the water steps outside the Palazzo, Shelley had quickly devised a plausible reason.

After yanking the bell-pulley a number of times, instead of coming down to open the door, a man popped his head out from an upper window and peered down. Shelley instantly recognised him.

"Hello, Fletcher!"

"Why – by the heavens – is that you, Mr Shelley! Hang on a tick, sir, and Tita will come down and let you in."

The door was eventually opened by a handsome but fearsome-looking man with shoulder-length black hair, a black beard, and wearing a gun and large knife at his waist.

"Signor Shelley?" Tita was smiling. "Mylord is most
~~~

happy to see you."

And so Byron looked, smiling and genuinely delighted to see Shelley again.

"You know, I kept having this premonition last night that *someone I actually know* from England, was going to call on me today. But you are not from England, merely Tuscany. Still, my premonition was close enough."

Servants were called to wait upon Mr Shelley with drink and refreshment. "And yes," Byron laughed at Shelley, "we do have *green* tea."

Byron took Shelley into his library: a huge room full of book-cases and cream carpets, a large ornate desk and beautiful red velvet Italian chairs and a long French sofa.

"Come in here and we will allow Voltaire and Rousseau and all our literary predecessors to listen in while we talk. Now, what brings you to Venice? Is all well?"

"Oh, very well." Shelley then explained that, while it was summer, they had all decided to tour as far as Verona to see Juliet's tomb; and now Mary and Claire were lodged at Padua.

"Padua? There is little in Padua to see, so why lodge there?"

"Well, being so close to Venice, Claire was anxious to see Allegra again. She misses her terribly, and wondered if now would be a convenient time to take the opportunity to see her child sometime soon?"

"Of course, although Allegra is presently not here, but at the British Consul's house."

Shelley was taken aback. "You agree?"

"Why not? After all, I have no legal right over the child. Claire is the mother who gave birth to her. So if Claire wishes to take her back into her own custody, then let her take her. It has never been my wish to deprive the mother of her child, or the child of her mother."

Shelley was at a loss for a response.

"And I don't say, as most people would in this situation, that I would then refuse to provide for Allegra or abandon her. But Claire must now make up her mind, one way or another – does she want to keep the child, or does she not?"

Shelley hesitated. "All she wants is to be allowed to see the child periodically."

"Is that all?"

"Yes, that's all. She has no wish to take Allegra back, only to be able to see her when time and distance permits."

"Then there must be conditions. I am not prepared to be used merely as a baby-sitter."

Byron sighed, his expression cynical. "You know, I *knew* this would happen. I knew it would not be long before Claire began sending letters wanting to visit the child. I foresaw the problem. And that is the sole reason why I leased Hoppner's country house at Este, as a maternal residence where the mother could spend some time with the child if she wished. I have only been to that house once, to see it, and I doubt I shall ever go there again. I have my own summer villa at La Mira."

"Do you?"

"Yes, and if it wasn't for this damned roof, Allegra and I would be there now."

Both looked upwards, and it was only then that Shelley noticed the ceiling was decorated with baroque gilded carvings in white and gold.

"This actually *is* a palace, isn't it?"

Byron nodded. "It once belonged to a Venetian prince, or so they say. I have leased it from the Mocenigo family, former nobles of Venice. You are welcome to stay here any time you wish. As you can see, it's big enough."

Byron suddenly stood. "Come, the day is still young, so let us go in my gondola to Lido where we can ride horses along the edge of the Adriatic sea. You are looking pale, Shiloh, so it will do you a power of good."

Shelley laughed at hearing the sly nickname Byron

had given to him in Switzerland

"Just out of interest, why *did* you name me Shiloh?"

"What else? – when all you talked about was wanting to save the world and mankind from itself."

"From *religion*. I still believe mankind should be saved from the lunacy of all religions."

"Then don't tempt the gods, Shiloh, or they may turn *you* into a lunatic in retribution."

Shelley laughed derisively at the notion; but not as much as he laughed while riding at speed along the sands of the island of Lido, his face flushed and all his cares dissipated by the fun and the freshness of the sea air.

They slowed into a canter, and then to a leisurely stroll as they talked and caught up on their news.

"We will come again tomorrow," Byron suggested. "You are looking better already."

Shelley was surprised. "Why, did I look unwell to you?"

"No, just a shade pale."

In truth, Byron had been slightly disturbed by the change in Shelley's appearance. He was thinner, his eyes were slightly bloodshot, and now there were fine streaks of grey in his hair.

"Are you still dosing on the laudanum?"

Shelley shrugged. "Now and again, but not as much as I did in England when Lord Eldon and the Chancery Court ruled me down as an atheist and unfit to have my children. Harriet's sister has legally got them now, that old spinster."

"You know if I had been in England, I would have moved Heaven and Earth to try and prevent such a decision. Lord Eldon and I are old foes."

"Which reminds me; before I left England, Leigh Hunt and many others all asked me to give you their good wishes. They say the House of Lords needs someone like you in there again, fighting the good fight on behalf of the ordinary people."

"No, there are too many reasons why I will not go

back to England, not until my daughter Ada is old enough to recognise me, and old enough to be told who I am when I visit her."

Once again, as he had occasionally done in Switzerland, Shelley expressed his wonderment at their situations being so similar.

"Still, let us not get dejected," Byron smiled. "Not here on Lido where the sun always shines."

The narrow island was seven miles long on which they galloped and cantered along the seashore for another hour. The enjoyment and strenuous exercise in riding and controlling his horse seemed to lift all the weight from Shelley's shoulders and bring a lightening to his mind.

Turning to ride back at a leisurely pace, Shelley said, "I know I worry too much and take life too seriously. I shall be more aware, and try and counter that in future."

"And less of the laudanum," Byron advised. "In my opinion, the best medicine of all is laughter, and it's cheaper than any drug."

And then, with a flow of humour and hilarity, Byron began recounting events with Dr Polidori in Switzerland; and then poor Hobhouse too shy to play the duke here in Venice with a village-girl from Dolo; not to mention Mr Berger in his gondola cooing up to a Venetian widow at her window, and she cooing down to him, until Shelley found himself in a state of uninterrupted merriment and laughter.

Byron suddenly fell silent and pointed to the sun, now on the descent and beginning to set, covering the whole length of the narrow island in a magnificent coppery glow.

Shelley stared in awe at the orange light shimmering over the orange sea, not wanting the day to end. The cares and troubles of his life had truly felt so much heavier of late, and it was a long time since he had enjoyed such freedom, or such careless enjoyment.

All at once, without a word or warning, Byron set his heels to his horse and started off at a full gallop, riding with the greatest haste to get to his gondola.

Shelley could not comprehend what fit had seized him, looking around to see if he could discover the cause of Byron's sudden flight ... and then he saw, at some distance, three or four young gentlemen who were running along the opposite side of the island nearest to the lagoon, running parallel with Byron towards his gondola.

Shelley suddenly realised that a race was actually taking place between Byron and the running men, and Byron endeavouring to outstrip them. In this he succeeded, throwing himself quickly off his horse, leaping into his gondola and cabin, and hastily closed the blinds on the window.

Shelley reached the place of embarkation at the same time as the young men, witnessing and hearing their disappointment at having done their run for nothing.

Tita and the two stable-hands barred their attempts to get past the barrier and closer to the gondola.

"For one minute pray, or for only a few seconds, ask Lord Byron to come out and speak to us!"

One of them held out a book. *"Or pray ask him to personally sign this for me!"*

Tita replied with a storm of Italian abuse, while Shelley entered the cabin to find Byron sitting in the corner, away from the windows, and exulting in glee at his success in outstripping them.

"They were English," Shelley said with astonishment. "Some of our own countrymen, carrying on like that."

"I don't care what nationality they were. I'll not be hounded or chased down by impertinent strangers. If they catch me I'm forced to be polite, but if I can avoid them I will."

Shelley could not help but smile at his impatience, and described the mortification of the unfortunate pedestrians who had failed in their eagerness to see him.

"Most poets would find it highly flattering."

"To be gawked at? Due to idle curiosity? You would

find that flattering?"

"Idle curiosity? They were running almost as fast as your galloping horse."

"Oh, here we go – back to the floating city." Byron grinned as the gondola moved off. "At least no one can run after me there, not along the canals – not without sinking."

Shelley suddenly thought of Claire, and the reason why he had come here to Venice in the first place. And *worse*, how terrible he would feel if Byron found out that he had colluded in sneaking Claire into Venice and the Hoppners house.

"The house at Este?" Shelley asked. "How soon could Claire go there and spend some time with Allegra?"

"As soon as she likes, but only for a month or so, before the summer ends. You say she and Mary are at Padua with the children?"

"Yes."

"Then it would be nice for Allegra to play with William again. Your letters describing your happy home made me feel quite melancholy about my own cold and lonely life."

"With a tribe of servants to look after you?" Shelley smiled. "You're being facetious again. And I dare not ask you about your women."

"My women?" Byron laughed. "All delightful, I assure you. Although I have not bothered much with them of late. Venetian women can be frighteningly dangerous in the heat of their passions. The last one – from Dolo – seemed to think there was nothing unreasonable about her wishing to get rid of my wife with a knife or poison."

Byron opened the blind on the window. "Talking of wives, how is Mary?"

"Tired. The heat of Tuscany was having an adverse effect on little Clara, and Mary often stayed up half the night with her, trying to cool her down."

"Then don't go back to Tuscany until the weather cools down. Instead, why don't you all go across from Padua to the house at Este for the rest of the summer?

It's in a cool country setting, masses of shady trees and small rivers, and all surrounded by the Euganean Hills."

"It sounds wonderful."

Shelley flushed guiltily, hating the deceit, and furious with Elise for causing it – and all because, it now seemed, *she* did not like Venice.

They had reached the mooring steps of the Palazzo Mocenigo and Byron moved to get out. "You will take dinner with me?"

"No ..." Shelley could not bear the thought of more lies and evasions, more deceit. "I have to get back to Padua."

"So soon?" Byron looked disappointed, sitting back in his seat again. "Then let us arrange it. I will give you the address at Este, there are some regular servants already there, and if you all go across I will send Allegra to you in four or five days."

Shelley managed to nod his agreement. "I'm sure that would make Claire very happy."

"Yes, and about Claire," Byron added, his tone becoming matter-of-fact. "When you return to Padua, would you be kind enough to convey my future conditions to her about Allegra."

Shelley remained silent.

"As I said to you earlier, it is a house which I leased solely as a place for the mother to visit the child – but only on the condition that enough prior warning is given to me by post, so that I may arrange to be absent during her presence there. Also, the time arranged for Claire to be resident at the villa at Este must be agreed beforehand, and never exceeded."

Shelley could make no dispute. "That sounds very fair."

"But you must also tell Claire, that if these conditions do not suit her, she has her time at Este with Allegra to decide if she wants to take the child back into her own care. And if so, she should take her, and let that be the end of it."

The end of it?" Shelley said, confused, "What do you

mean?"

"I mean that if Claire sends Allegra back to me again at the end of summer, I intend to legally adopt her, and name her Miss Byron. And if that happens, and if Claire then wishes to see her in the future, she will only do so at *my* convenience, not hers."

I have told you, Claire has no intentions of taking the child back."

"And I told *you* that I am not prepared to be merely a baby-sitter for Allegra, and then to have Claire walking in and out of my life whenever she wishes. She has already forced the child on me, but now I am giving her a chance for her to change her mind, once and no more."

Shelley did not know how to answer, except to say in a stuttering way, "Of course women sometimes *do* change their minds."

"And is that fair to the child? I confess I have been reluctant to get too fond of Allegra, because I knew it would not be long before Claire started to pester me in letters or in person. If she misses the child so terribly, then let her take it."

"I will tell her."

"And you will all go across to the house at Este for the rest of the summer?"

"Yes, thank you."

"My pleasure." Byron moved to get out of the gondola. "Oh, and I pray a favour? When I send Allegra to Este, will you retrieve her incompetent nurse back into your employment; and I will seek out a new nurse in the meantime."

"Elise?"

"Who should never have lifted her feet off terra firma. A sweet girl she may be, but she is neither use nor ornament to us, and she is driving poor Fletcher out of his mind with her continual fears about living on water."

Shelley readily agreed. "I believe Mary would be very happy to have Elise back to help her with the children. Elise was always very good with our children."

"On solid ground," Byron said, and grinned as he moved to get out of the gondola. "Lord preserve poor Venice from the land-lubbers!"

Chapter Seventeen

~ ~ ~

The sticky summer heat continued, but baby Clara was slowly recovering.

Relieved and grateful, Mary knew she would not have coped so well without the help and company of Maria Gisborne.

"You are so kind," she said to Maria, and she knew it sounded a weak way of expressing her enormous gratitude, but Maria was not listening to her.

She was looking at a letter which had just been handed to her in the garden by Paolo Foggi. "This has been sent by *poste-express*, from Padua."

"From Shelley!" Mary practically snapped the letter from Maria's hand, fumbling as she hastened to open it. "If he sent this from Padua, then he should be home soon."

Maria saw the delight on Mary's face change to confusion as she read the letter, and then redden slightly with anger.

"He is not coming home," she said. "He wants me to go immediately to Venice."

"What? Is he crazy? Does he know the child has been sick and you with no rest?"

Mary tried to take in the details of the letter, which were very precise. They had seen Allegra, and could now say that Elise's claims were false. He had seen Byron, who could not have been more agreeable nor kinder. He had offered to send Allegra to spend time with them at his country house at Este, in the Euganean Hills.

Shelley's predicament was that he had lied to Byron, leading him to believe that it was Mary and Claire and the entire family who were at Padua. He was certain it was because Byron believed that Allegra would also be in the care of Mary and also have William to play with, that he had agreed to release Allegra without any worry.

So she must come, and come at once. He and Claire would delay in Padua and its environs, as he did not want the servants at the Villa Este to inform Byron at a later date that he and Claire had arrived there alone.

Byron believed Mary was already at Padua, and did not know about Claire's presence in Venice, so in order to make his story to Byron appear true – speed was essential; and for that purpose, and to make it easier for her, he had itemised the itinerary which she should follow:

"Pray come instantly to Este, where I shall be waiting with Claire and Elise with the utmost anxiety for your arrival. You can pack up directly you get this letter and employ the next day in that. The day after get up at four o'clock, & go by post-chaise to Lucca where you will arrive at 6. Then take Vetturino for Florence to arrive the same evening. From Florence to Este is three days. I shall count 4 days for this letter, 1 for packing, 4 for coming here – on the ninth or tenth day we shall meet."

Maria Gisborne was astounded when she read the letter Mary handed to her. "Rise before dawn, and then so many days hard travelling with children in this August heat? What is he thinking?"

"Of Claire's happiness, as usual," Mary replied resentfully. "It has always been so. Everything must be fitted to Claire's convenience.

"Don't go," Maria said.

"I must," Mary replied. "I'm sure Shelley's intentions are all for good, they usually are. For Claire to be able to see her child for a few weeks, when we can see ours every minute of every day ... it will be something good and kind like that he is thinking, I'm sure."

After a pause she slammed her fist down angrily on the table. "And yet it is all bunkum on Claire's part – all this worry about her child. If she cared so much about Allegra, then why did she keep trying to have her sent away to Italy from when she was an infant of only a few months old? It's *Byron* she wants, not Allegra."

"Don't go," Maria said again. "Write back and tell him you can't go."

"I must go, because Shelley says I must."

Maria sighed. "You know, your mother used to say, 'I *don't wish women to have power over men, but over themselves'*. You are not his slave. You don't have to do this."

"Yes I do!" Mary snapped irritably. "I love Shelley, and I don't want to lose him to Claire. I know her too well – if she can't have Byron, she will do her utmost to try and take Shelly from me. She has tried it before. And if I ruin things by allowing Byron to find out that Shelley lied to him ... so I must go."

Maria was silent. She now knew all about their involvement with Lord Byron, and thought Shelley was taking a big risk in trying to deceive him. If the man was anything like the poet in the books, he was no fool.

"I know Shelley now," Maria said, "and I do not believe he would ever abandon you."

"Why not?" Mary said anxiously. "He abandoned his first wife and children for me. So why would he not ever abandon me for Claire? I'm sure *she* would be very happy if I did not go."

Maria was shocked by this revelation of toxic jealousy between the two stepsisters. "Why do you allow it? Why do you allow her to keep living with you?"

"Because Shelley insists. *'We must look after Claire, poor Claire."*

After a silence, Mary pushed the hair back from her face and said quietly, "You don't know Shelley as I do Maria, and the fact that he has written his instructions in such strict detail, means he really needs me to go."

Maria rose from her chair. "Then all I can do now is to help you."

And help Maria did, packing clothes for the children; playing with them while Mary was doing her own packing, and then rising at three to wake Mary with tea, and dress the children, before they left the Villa Bertini at dawn, accompanied by the servant, Paulo Foggi.

Maria was sad as she embraced Mary in farewell. "One day, you must try to find your own power," she said. "You are the daughter of Mary Wollstonecraft, an advocate of women's rights, and you should never forget that."

Mary kissed her. "I will write to you at Livorno. Thank you for coming, Maria, dearest Maria ..."

And then she was gone, into the carriage with a child in her arms and another at her side.

Maria was shaking her head with worry as the carriage moved off. All those days travelling with a two-year-old child and a ten-month baby was going to be very hard for her.

It was harder than Mary could have possibly imagined, it was gruelling. If the weather had not been so hot, so humid, it all might have been easier.

Little Clara was slightly feverish again, with no interest in food, and Mary became extremely worried about her. William never stopped whinging, hating the daily confinement of the carriage.

The day after leaving Florence, little Clara was showing signs of a stomach upset and crying constantly, until Mary was near to crying herself.

Six days after leaving Bagni di Lucca, Mary arrived, a wreck, at Byron's house at Este, where she was greeted by Claire, Allegra and Shelley, all looking healthy from their days in the sun.

"We have been here three days," Claire said. "The house is beautiful! And let me show you the summerhouse at the end of the garden."

"I'm too exhausted to see anything," Mary said flatly.

"And Clara is becoming increasingly ill."

She looked woefully at Shelley. "Some of the inns we stayed at were awful. And now I think Clara has dysentery as well as a fever."

"Dysentery?" Shelley was immediately alarmed. "Dysentery can be serious."

"*All* sickness can be serious to a baby," Mary snapped. "She was unwell when you left us, Shelley, and then you make us come here. Now she is very weak."

"Perhaps she is weak from the travelling and also the aggravation of her teething," Claire suggested.

"Yes, that will be it," Shelley agreed, and then busied himself fussing over Mary and Clara and William, making sure they were settled in and feeling more happy.

The house really was lovely, and Mary spent her days in the shaded summerhouse with Clara, while Shelley played with Allegra and William in the garden, watched over by Claire.

"*It's so peaceful here, and I am feeling much rested,*" Mary wrote to Maria Gisborne a week later; which was not quite true, for Clara was not improving, and seemed to be getting weaker by the day, causing Mary to stay up half the night cooling her face with a damp sponge, and endeavouring to get to her to sip some water.

Shelley rushed off to find a doctor, returning to say there was only one *medico* in the village, and he was away on his summer holiday.

"So I sent a letter poste-haste to Byron in Venice. He is sure to know of a good doctor."

Byron replied by return, saying the only good doctor he knew was his own, Professor Francesco Aglietti; but he was unable at present to travel out of Venice. However, if Mary was to bring the child into the city, he could promise that Aglietti would immediately be at her disposal and give the child all his attention. He provided the doctor's address."

Mary and Shelley left Este at dawn the next morning. Clara was sleeping peacefully, but Mary was still anxious; constantly kissing her cheek and wiping back her curls back from her face, and willing some of her own strength into her.

At Venice, Mary insisted she did not wish to impose on Byron by turning up at his door with a sick child. Shelley agreed, and so they checked into an inn, where little Clara suddenly started convulsing.

Shelley rushed to the address which Byron had provided; and came back with Professor Aglietti, who carefully inspected the child under their eyes, and then paused, informing the parents that there was no hope.

Mary and Shelley simply stared at the doctor in shock.

"I'm so very sorry," he said in English

He then carefully lifted the unconscious child and gently placed her into her mother's arms, where Mary watched her little daughter pass out of life some short minutes later.

All Mary knew in that moment was that she would never forgive Shelley. She would never forgive him for making her risk her sick daughter's life just so his precious Claire could spend a few weeks playing with *her* child – the same child that Claire had previously and deliberately given away.

~~~

Even in Italy, as it was also the custom in England, women were not allowed to attend funerals. In consequence, Shelley had only one friend in Italy to whom he could turn to for help.

Byron was prepared and ready to do whatever Shelley asked, and had already made inquiries as to where the child could be buried.

Yet even now, Shelley remained staunch in his atheism, pushing away Byron's list of churches. He had already decided where he wanted his daughter to lay in peace – "Some lovely place, where she would be happy to be if she were alive
~~~

The following morning, Lido's long beach was empty, as it usually was, apart from a few locals in the afternoon, but the golden rays of the sun were beaming along the seashore and soft sand as usual.

Shelley finally chose a secluded spot in a corner of Lido's small cemetery for foreigners, burying his daughter without a stone or marker, covering the small grave with only his tears.

~~~

Mary had retreated into an ice-cold silence, freezing Shelley out of her conversation and thoughts. She no longer cared about Claire nor anyone else. Her heartbreak had left her numb. She had no wish to go back to the house at Este and try to resume a normal life again, not yet. She wished to stay a while longer in Venice, near to where her baby daughter would remain for ever.

Kind Italian people tried to help her, tried to distract her. One of them was Lord Byron's friend, Signor Angelo Mengaldo, a strange little man who knew how she felt, because he too was still lamenting the loss of Napoleon.

"Exiled to live on barren rocks, is that not a death?" Mengaldo said woefully; and Mary found herself wishing that she, too, could find some barren rocks to live on.

But Signor Mengaldo was very kind, escorting Mary out to the opera; and even to some comedies which he hoped would make her smile, but which she thought to be "*stupid beyond measure*" although she did not say so. forcing a smile onto her face, which seemed to please Mengaldo.

"I read your good book," he told her. "Mylord Byron he allowed me to read his copy. *Frankenstein*. I lay awake all night reading. You have much talent for a lady writer."

Mary stared at him. "You liked it?"
~~~

"Si! *Eccellente!* I did not sleep until the end came."

He then related to her from start to finish the entire story of Doctor Frankenstein and his man-made human that turned into a monster; and she knew his reading of it was genuine.

"The reviewers did not like it," she said.

Mengaldo shrugged. "Most reviewers are mean. What we say of them here in Venice – *cattivo e cattivo.*"

Mary was not sure what that meant, but she liked the sound of it.

The fact that some other person besides Shelley and Byron liked *Frankenstein* cheered her; but only for a few moments.

After that, the deadness returned to her mind and soul, and all that she was capable of in the days that followed was to lie in her bed in silent misery.

"I don't know how to reach her," Shelley said. "She has no interest in anything or anyone, lost and alone in a silent trance of her own misery. She says nothing, eats nothing, and drinks only water."

Byron felt disturbed enough to ask Professor Aglietti to visit Mrs Shelley again.

Professor Aglietti did; and when he called on Byron after his visit, his prognosis was not good. "What her husband does not seem to realise, is that his wife is on the verge of a nervous breakdown."

"Did you tell him so?"

"No, the poor man is too confused and heartbroken himself. I gave Madame Shelley some medication, and suggested they leave Venice and try to start their life again in some other place – some *new* place, where all will be of interest. She is still very young, and new sights and novelty always revives the young."

Byron was cynical, certain that sorrow was not so easy to dispel, although moving abroad had certainly helped him.

"And she, Madame Shelley," asked Aglietti, "do you know what things interest her?"

"All I know of her, is from our summer in Geneva. And there she liked ... green tea, our evening cruises on the lake, reading books, and writing them."

"Reading is very good for the mind," said Aglietti. "It takes the mind to another place, and gives it a rest from all the worries."

It also gave Byron an idea; a foolish one, perhaps, but worth a try.

His idea was supported by Shelley, who arranged a time to call when he would be absent.

Shelley was out at the Hoppners when Byron called on Mary.

Even though it was mid-afternoon, Professor Aglietti's nurse said Madame Shelley was still in bed.

"She will not see you," said the nurse. "She will not see anyone."

"Will you at least ask her?"

The nurse curtsied. "Of course."

"Although, don't say my name," he added quickly, "not as you know it."

The nurse was a little confused when she entered the bedroom. "Madame," she said, "Madame Shelley? There is a gentleman who would very much like to see you."

Mary slowly turned her head and looked at her. "The doctor again?"

"No, it is the *Inglese* Mylord. He said to tell you his name is Albé."

"Albé?" It was the nickname they had given to Byron in Geneva due to his many tales of his adventures in Albania.

Mary's mind drifted back to the Villa Diodati, that lovely house perched on the hill above the blue Lake Leman. "I have not seen dear Albé since we were all in Switzerland."

No, she and Albé had not met since then.

In the small parlour, Byron felt instant pity when she came out to see him in her dressing-gown, her face white and her hair loose around her shoulders. She looked no older than a girl of sixteen.

He did not ask about her health or how she was, nor appeared concerned about her in any way; adapting the same manner had had often used with her in the Villa Diodati in Geneva.

"Mary, I'm in a pickle, can you help me?"

"Help you?"

"Yes, I find myself in dire need and despairing of finding someone competent – and then I thought of *you.*"

In his hands he held some short manuscripts. "These need to go off to Murray as soon as possible, but no one here in Venice can read my scrawl. Could *you* possibly transcribe them into fair copies for me, as you did with all the stuff I wrote in Geneva.?"

Mary put a hand to her head. "No, I couldn't possibly, not at all ..." Her eyes then went to the manuscripts with a flicker of interest, "Is it some new work?"

"No, well *one* is not. Do you remember in Diodati when you wrote your *Frankenstein* and I wrote my *vampyre* story, and we said we might publish them together?"

Mary remembered. "That very strange story ... set in Greece?"

"Yes. I think I will take your advice and publish it."

Mary sank into a chair. "I think you should. I liked it very much."

"But would you be so kind as to transcribe it into your neat and tidy hand for me?"

Her eyes were on the manuscripts again. "What are the others?"

"Only two, both new, but quite short." He handed her the manuscripts and she slowly read the title of the one on top ... "*Ode To Venice...* by George Gordon Byron."

A tear slipped down her cheek. "Venice will always be very special to me now," she said quietly. "I think it deserves an Ode."

"So do I."

She looked at the title of the second manuscript and

saw it was his story set in Greece ... *"The Burial, A Fragment"*

"You have not changed the title to 'The Vampyre?'"

"As I told you in Switzerland, that title gives the end away."

"Is it finished? Did you write the part where he returns to London alive and well again?"

"No, I thought I would leave what happened next to the reader's imagination. Hence my reason for not calling it *'The Vampyre'*.

Mary half-smiled. "That night, after you had read the story to us all, I was so frightened I could not sleep."

She looked at the title of the third manuscript: *Mazeppa.*

"Is it an Italian story?"

"No, it's a narrative poem about Ivan Mazeppa, a young Ukrainian gentleman who, in his life learned how to cope and endure suffering, and all for love of a woman."

Mary's brow puckered in puzzlement. "How on earth do you come up with all your varied ideas?"

"It is not an idea, it's a true story. Later he became known as *Hetman of Ukraine'.*"

"How? What did he do?"

"Read it and see."

Shelley came in – genuinely surprised to see Mary out of her bed.

"Mary?"

She looked at Shelley, and finally spoke to him. "Albé has brought some copy-writing for me to do. Should I refuse him?"

"That is up to you, ... But now that you are up, will you drink some tea?"

"I don't know," Mary said hesitantly, and looked at Byron.

"No, no tea for me," Byron said quickly. "I must be off."

During the following days, while Mary was neatly

writing out Byron's poetry she was also reading them, learning more about the history of Venice; and giving her mind some respite from her agony.

And when occasionally commenting on the work to Shelley, she was also communicating with him again, and noticing *his* agony also. He too had lost his child.

From the moment of the Shelley's tragic loss, Mr and Mrs Hoppner had been ready to help them in any way they could; inviting the Shelleys to stay with them; come and eat with them; anything at all that might help.

Mary, at last, decided it would be rude to keep declining, and agreed to go to the Hoppners for dinner, where she found Mrs Hoppner to be very kind.

Shelley was more interested in hearing the British Consul's views on the occupation of Venice by Austrian troops; disgusted at the sights he had seen of their soldiers swaggering through the streets, bullying the inhabitants.

"And that is not the worst of it," said Hoppner. "They have levied a rate of sixty-per-cent taxes on the Venetians, which means their hard work is more for the Austrians than for themselves. No wonder so many of them are poor."

Now that the men's conversation had turned to politics, Mrs Hoppner saw her opportunity to take Mary into another room to drink tea and talk quietly about Switzerland.

"I miss my own country so much," sighed Isabelle Hoppner. "Will you tell me about your time there, Mrs Shelley?"

"Switzerland ... my time there was truly one of the happiest times of my whole life," Mary said; and then found herself talking at length about that wonderful summer in Geneva with Shelley and Byron, and she even remembered the hapless Dr Polidori with some kindness.

Madame Hoppner smiled with secret satisfaction, knowing this talking would prove to be a great help to the sadly bereaved young woman. But there was more still to be done, more memories to evoke, to bring this young mother's mind back to its rightful place.

She excused herself for "one moment" and left the room; leaving Mary to drift back into thoughts of her baby daughter, conceived in Switzerland ... that wonderful summer with Shelley, when Claire had been too busy chasing Byron to distract them. ... And now, so soon after that summer, little Clara had been born and now was gone again ... If only there was some magical way to bring Clara back from death ... Ianthe too ... her two baby daughters back in her arms again.

Mrs Hoppner returned, holding the hand of her toddling little boy. "Come, *mon petite fils,* come and meet Madame Shelley."

Mary stared at the little boy, stared and stared until the boy started to cry. Yet Mary could not stop staring at him.

It was like a bang on the head, knocking her vision and memory back into place, for now she was remembering her own little boy, William, the only child she had left.

It brought her back to her full senses, thinking of poor little Wilmouse, who must be wondering where his mama and papa had gone, and why they had left him behind. It was time to get back to the Este and William as quickly as possible.

Mrs Hoppner took her boy away, and when she returned Mary was already in the hall, putting on her bonnet.

"We must go," Mary said hastily. "We must leave very early in the morning, as early as we can, and return to Este."

When the young couple had gone, and the door was closed, Richard Hoppner looked in astonishment at his wife. "What did you say to her, to galvanise her in such a way?"

Mrs Hoppner flicked her hand, as if it was no matter. Men did not understand the minds and hearts of women, so why try to explain?

Instead she shrugged, "As we say in Switzerland – the earth must keep spinning, the clocks must keep ticking, and life must go on."

~~~

At the end of October, now that the autumn had arrived, Shelley and Mary decided not to remain in the northern climes of Italy, but to leave Este and head south to spend the winter in warmer Naples.

Insisting it was to Allegra's advantage to be under the care of her father, Claire sent her child back to Byron in Venice, and then prepared to go to Naples.

"With us – to Naples – not back to England?" Mary asked Shelley in a dolorous voice of dismay. "I thought the purpose of her giving up Allegra was to allow her to stride out on her own and make a new life for herself?"

Shelley was more compassionate. "You know she has been feeling rather ill of late."

"I know she went to see a doctor in Padua with a stomach upset."

"From which she has not fully recovered. She insists she is not yet well enough to leave Italy and travel back to England on her own."

Mary lifted her hand in protest, and then slowly lowered it again as her stare faltered. She abruptly turned and walked away, realising there was no point in disputing it any further with Shelley. Claire had insisted, and when Claire insists ...
~~~

PART SIX

1819

Teresa.

"Round her she made an atmosphere of life,
The very air seemed lighter from her eyes ..."

BYRON

Chapter Eighteen

~~~

Springtime had come to Northern Italy under the disguise of summer. Although usually mild and pleasant, the first week in April was extremely hot with long days of sunshine, relieved in the evenings by a mild breeze that was as welcome as it was sweet.

Upon her arrival in Venice, her body aching and tired from the long journey which had began at Ravenna, Teresa objected when her husband insisted they go to the theatre that night.

"Alessandro, we have been travelling for three long days," she pleaded. "I am too tired to go to the theatre tonight."

"No, we must go," he said. "For me the theatre is a necessity. It helps me to relax."

His tone was final, indicating there was no point in arguing with him, and Teresa knew it; reluctantly resigning herself to an early hot bath and complaining to Fanny Sylvestrini as she assisted her to dress and then arranged her hair.

"It is true, he must always have the theatre when he is not pleased with life," Fanny said. "As he must also have the theatre when he is happy and wishes to congratulate himself. But you know all this, so why do you complain?"

"In my present circumstances," Teresa said with quietness, "I think I should be allowed to complain. In the theatre he laughs so loudly, and I have no heart to laugh at anything."

"Ah, *mia cara*, Fanny is a fool!" exclaimed the maid, full of remorse for momentarily forgetting that Teresa was still in deep mourning because her mother had recently died from illness; and very soon after her mother's death, Teresa's eighteen-year-old sister,
~~~

Faustina, had died during childbirth – the tragic loss of both women causing such unexpected and devastating sorrow to the Gamba family at Filetto.

"When the theatre is over, my Terasina, you must come back to bed and rest," Fanny said. "Let him have his night at the theatre. It will put him in a good mood and make him kind to you. Such are the wise ways of wives in marriage."

"But why does it always have to be the *theatre?*" asked Teresa impatiently. "Most of the plays he has seen many times over."

"I don't know," said Fanny, who usually knew everything. "I know he shocked the whole of Ravenna when his second wife Angelica died, and that same night he arrived at the theatre and took his seat in his box to enjoy the play as usual. He seems to have no sympathy for the death of anyone."

After a silence, Teresa said, "Perhaps it is because he knows, at his age, that his own death is drawing closer, and he does not like to be reminded that it is so."

"Perhaps," answered Fanny, removing the small hot poker from the last ringlet she had curled into Teresa's long hair. "A few more hours of patience, and then you can come home to rest."

But it was not to be. The night at the theatre progressed from bad to worse when Alessandro insisted they must take supper and dine at Pellegrino's restaurant, stretching the evening out even longer; but the night-life in Venice was not like Ravenna – it lasted until the small hours, until the Venetians were tired – and because of this, the coffee houses in the squares stayed open all night.

Finally they were in the gondola on their way home, until Count Guiccioli suddenly decided that now he wanted to see Count Giuseppe Rangone on business.

"Alessandro, it is now midnight, *too late* for business," Teresa remonstrated. "And this man's place of business will be closed."

"No, it is not too late," he replied. "Count Rangone is

the *cavalier servente* of the Contessa Marina Benzoni, and her *Conversazione* does not begin until after the theatre, at eleven, and usually goes on until after three. We will go there to see him."

Teresa argued with him, but he would not tolerate it, reminding her sternly of her marriage vow of *"obedience"* which did not impress Teresa at all, for the marriage itself had been a business arrangement and nothing else.

She finally gave way when he told her they would stay at the salon for only a few minutes, and she made him promise, "Only a few minutes and no more? You promise?"

He smiled and promised and indulged her in her silliness, knowing that once they were inside, he would stay for as long as he wished.

In the lobby of the salon, he bade Teresa to sit on one of the chairs and wait for him, while Madame Benzoni took him off to another room, telling him she would bring Count Rangone to him. "Business" was not allowed during her *conversazione,* only sociable converse.

The lobby was dreadfully hot. Teresa removed her wrap and then sat to wait.

An elderly lady came out of the salon, smiled at her, and passed on, leaving the salon door wide open behind her, allowing Teresa to see inside, expecting to see only a collection of old people. Alessandro had told her that Madame Benzoni was sixty, and so she had concluded that all of her friends would be around that age too.

Yet what she saw surprised her, for the sala was not very busy, and some of the men she could see were fairly young. One young man, in particular, the youngest of the men, sitting on the sofa opposite the door, caught her eyes, and she sat staring at him as at an apparition.

He was sitting sideways on the sofa, carelessly leaning his elbow against the back of the sofa, with his head resting on his hand as he listened to the man sitting near him. His elegant, entirely black clothes only stood out against the dark purple of the sofa due to the pure whiteness of his shirt between the coat-lapels at his breast, and at the end of his sleeves. His hair was as dark as night, and his eyes as light and blue as the morning sky.

She suddenly realised that she no longer felt as tired as she did on entering the palazzo. The sudden and mysterious attraction she felt was trembling her to her soul and making her afraid.

The arrival of Madame Benzoni blocked her view. She looked up at the woman's kind and smiling face.

"Contessa Guiccioli, it is not good for you to sit here alone. Would you not like to come inside the sala and be introduced to some of my guests? There are other ladies inside to whom you may speak."

Teresa nervously declined, lowering her head, and then quickly looked up again. "The young man on the sofa, in black attire ... he is not Italian is he?"

Marina Benzoni smiled, knowing exactly who she was speaking of. "No, *Inglese,* but he speaks good Italian. Do you wish to be introduced to him, Contessa?"

Teresa first shook her head, and then nodded. "Yes, I have not met any person from Inghilterra."

"No? Then you must come to Venice more often."

Marina stretched out a motherly hand and urged Teresa to her feet, leading her like a consort inside the open door of the sala, about to walk her down the length of the long room when Teresa tugged back on her hand, her face turned towards an empty sofa just inside the door. "Please, Signora, may I sit there?"

Marina could feel the girl's nerves trembling through her fingers.

"*Certo!*" Marina agreed, leaving the girl to take her seat and continuing on down to where the young Northern prince sat talking to Signor Scott.

"Mylord Byron, I wish to introduce you to a young lady from Ravenna."

Byron politely declined. "You know that I don't want to be introduced to any more young ladies. No, not to be kind to them because they are ugly, or to be happy if they are pretty, and not while Scott is telling me all about all the changes in Aberdeen and Edinburgh. I am half-Scottish, you know?"

"I know that she is very young and her husband is a cold and eccentric man, forty years older than her. She is a Contessa is in her own right, the daughter of Count Gamba of Filetto; and yet, tonight, he has forced upon her the indignity of sitting to wait outside my sala for his return, as if she is his servant or his *schiavo*. So, Mylord, as a courtesy to me – "

"*Certo,*" Byron said glibly, standing and walking beside Marina as she escorted him down the room.

"And as a courtesy to *me*, Madame, you will come and rescue me in five minutes?"

Marina nodded. "If her husband does not come and rescue her first."

As they approached the sofa the young lady's head was bowed, and Byron was surprised to see that she was a *bionda*. It was not usual to meet a blonde Italian.

Marina said, "Contessa Guiccioli, here is Lord Byron to meet you."

Teresa looked up, and Byron saw her eyes were very blue.

She stood to formally offer him her hand, and he took it in his own and bowed.

Marina left them to it, gliding off to converse with some of the other ladies who were sitting in a circle of chairs and speaking only to each other, causing her to sigh with disapproval at this very *old-fashioned* manner of behaviour.

She humorously chid the ladies about it, and they did not like it; making it clear to her that they had come out tonight *not* to speak to their husbands or other men, but to chat to each other and catch up on everyone's *news*.

Marina shrugged and left them to it, rejoining the men whose varied and witty conversation was more to her taste. What did she care if so-and-so's daughter had given birth to her sixth child? Hers was a sala for *intellectuals,* not domestic gossip.

Glancing up the room to see how Lord Byron and the young Contessa were getting on, she saw that he had sat down beside her and they were talking.

About Venice and Ravenna – until Teresa's curiosity overcame her and she asked, "What do you do?"

A smile of surprised delight moved on Byron's face. "What do I do? Very little. I ride most days, swim most nights, and scribble a little poetry now and then."

"Poetry?" Teresa was enchanted by such a revelation, and spoke of her love for the great Dante, and the Renaissance poet, Petrarch. "You have read Dante's *La Divina Comedia?*"

Byron knew every word of Dante's Divine Comedy, especially the most famous part, the *Inferno,* but he affected vagueness about the work; so with reverential enthusiasm for the great Italian writer, Teresa gave him a short but very knowledgeable synopsis of Dante's epic poem – "He is buried in Ravenna."

Byron did not know that. "Is he? In Ravenna, where you live?"

Teresa nodded. "In the Basilica of San Francesco."

An hour later, Marina Benzoni was very surprised to see the two were still seated together, still conversing, and still her husband had not returned.

In that first hour they had fallen in love with each other, and neither had expected or wanted to be in love.

Byron was the most surprised of all, but his attraction and delight in Teresa was undeniable, even to himself. Not since those halcyon days of his youth, and his first and only true love, Mary Chaworth, had he felt the force and flame of heady *romance* and all the enchantments that surrounded it.

Their conversation had become secondary, for now they were only interested in each other, unconscious of everyone else in the room.

Count Guiccioli arrived and spoke to Teresa, but she did not hear him. Byron did, and looked at him.

"Teresa, I am very tired, so we must leave now," the

man said; and Byron then realised who he was, and stood.

Teresa stood also, knowing it was useless to protest or beg for more time; and after a small regretful smile to Byron, she obediently turned and left the room, followed by Count Guiccioli.

Byron watched her go, wondering if he would ever see her again.

Some minutes later, when he was about to take his own leave, Madame Benzoni approached and cheered him.

"It seems, Mylord, that we are to see more of the Guiccioli and his young wife. The Count has told Beppe that he intends to call in here every night after the theatre or dinner – every night – until they return to Ravenna in three weeks. He no longer has any interest in the salon of Madame Albrizzi."

Inside the *felze* of the gondola taking them back to the Count's Venetian house, Teresa sat as if in a dream, not speaking at all.

The Count did not notice, assuming she was too tired, and he, too, was now feeling very tired. Nor did he ask her about the young man she had been speaking with, for he had not even looked at him. His only concern now was that Count Rangone would consider the business proposition he had put to him ... a proposition that could be very profitable to himself in the future. Regrettably, Teresa would be no asset to him in this piece of business. Count Rangone was still too adoring of Marina Benzoni.

As soon as they had disembarked from the gondola entered the house, Teresa curtsied quickly to her husband and hurried up to her bedroom, where Fanny was sitting by the empty fireplace smoking a thin long-stemmed pipe.

Fanny quickly attempted to hide the pipe, but Teresa was oblivious to everything but her own excitement, telling Fanny all about the young *Inglese* gentleman she had met at the Contessa Benzoni's – his beautiful face, the tone of his voice, his manners, the indescribable magic of his smile, and a list of other wonderful things that she considered to be so different, and so superior to anyone else she had ever met.

"I did not know he was a lord, not until Contessa Benzoni introduced him."

"*A lord?*" Fanny was now so excited herself, she unconsciously stuck her thumb down into the white bowl of her pipe, and quickly put a taper to a nearby candle and relit the tobacco. "Did he come from Rome? The Vatican?"

No, he is not a *holy* lord. He is an *Inglese* lord. A Noble."

"A Noble?" Fanny sucked in some smoke and blew it out again. "*Santa Madre!* – a Noble? That is higher than a common Count! It is, eh?"

Teresa was not sure, nor did she care. "He writes poetry, a little, and he told me he would like to know more about our great *Dante.*"

"Dante Aligheiri? The Inglese have never heard of him? Not even the Nobles? Do they not know he is buried in *my own* Ravenna?"

Teresa's shoulders dropped. She did not want to think of Ravenna and returning there, for that would mean leaving Venice.

In the Palazzo Mocenigo, Byron was standing on the balcony outside his drawing-room, his arms leaning on the stone balustrade as he gazed down at the dark waters of the Grand Canal.

Now that the night air had cooled him, he was able to think more rationally about the girl.

For some time now, ever since Shelley had brought his poor little unwanted daughter back to him, he had turned over a new leaf in his life, determined that he would rise above any further inclinations towards women, and spurn even the possibility of developing an attachment to any of them. He had vowed to fly from all attachments and emotional involvement of the heart. He would bring up his little daughter, and educate her, and live the quiet and peaceful life of a poet and stoic intellectual.

He looked up at the night sky teeming with gleaming silver stars ... Were there more of them out tonight? Why did each star seem so bright in its silvery brilliance?

As he stared up in wonderment, it was not the poetry of Shakespeare, as it so often was, but the words of Dante Aligheiri himself that strayed into his mind.

Yet my wings were not meant for such a flight –

Except that then my mind was struck by lightning,

Through which my longing was at last fulfilled.

By the Love that moves the sun and the other stars.

He shook himself. *Love?* How foolish. The usual idiocy that affects the human mind under the glow of starlight and the beauty of Venice by night.

He turned and slowly walked back into the drawing-room, followed by the two dogs who had been sitting patiently at his feet.

He paused by the cold fireplace where Mutz, always a curious dog, barked up at him sharply, three times, as if demanding to know what he had been thinking. So why not oblige and answer him?

"All the major sufferings of my life," he told Mutz. "were inflicted upon me by women. First my ranting mother, then my first love Mary Chaworth, who never could make up her mind. Then the mad and bad Lady Caroline Lamb, who was determined to follow me everywhere and persecute me to Hades. And not to leave out the mad one who followed her, my wife – mine own dear wife – whose displays of religious righteousness would surely bore and embarrass even God."

He sighed. "And then ... well, it's pointless to go on, because being Swiss, you met none of those women did you?"

Mutz growled and took a step back, as if conveying that he was very glad he had not met them, because if he had – another growl.

"Oh, stop – your displays of savagery don't impress me. I *know* what an abysmal coward you are, Mutz. See poor old Leander here on the floor, already asleep, even he has more guts than you. I wonder why? Is it because you have no tail?"

Mutz gave a short bark and lifted his snout high, as if disgusted by such sarcasm.

Byron grinned. "But don't fear, my little Swiss yodeller, from now on we shall live a quiet life with no insane women like Margarita Cogni banging our doors and threatening us with knives. Troth! I have suffered so much in my life from women, I am firmly and irrevocably resolved to never again expose myself or my life to their capricious consequences."

Yet his resolve did not prevent him from going to Contessa Benzoni's salon the next night, nor from looking round every time the door opened, to see who entered. It was more of the normal crowd tonight. All the usual faces, some new; but not one belonged to the girl from Ravenna. And amidst all the conversation of the arriving ladies, not one seemed to speak in the soft tones of her voice.

When the man who was her husband arrived on his own, he pretended not to be listening while Madame Benzoni asked the husband about his young wife?

"No, not coming," Guiccioli said. "The drama of the opera was too alarming for her, so she chose to go home and retire early to her bed."

"The opera, which one was it?" asked Marina.

"Rossini's *Otello.*"

"Otello – the jealous husband who murdered his wife?"

"All melodramatic nonsense," Guiccioli chuckled; and

moved off to join Count Rangone.

Teresa had entered the theatre still in a dream-like state of fascinated romance, but watching Rossini's *Otello,* a story she did not know, the jealousy of the Moor when he thought his wife was unfaithful to him, was frightening to witness; and when he strangled her in her bed, amidst all the thunder of Rossini's music, she became so terrified she could barely breathe.

She had left the theatre in a state of turmoil, knowing that could be her own fate too if she was ever unfaithful to Alessandro – was it not rumoured that he had murdered his first two wives? And not for infidelity, but for being no longer useful to him.

She could not believe it, no matter how many times Fanny Sylvestrini insisted it was true. Alessandro went to Mass every Sunday and upheld all his religious duties, so how could he be capable of a such a terrible and mortal sin as murder?"

Nor could Alessandro ever be so passionately jealous about her as *Otello* was about *his* wife, because – apart from his occasional banging on her door at night – a rare thing now, thank God – Alessandro showed no real interest in her at all.

Even here in Venice, he hardly ever went out in the daytime, except on business. He was not at all jealous, and paid little heed to her, and gave no thought at all to her entertainment. Due to the difference in their ages, they had not a single like or idea in common.

Only one concession he had made to her before leaving Ravenna, and that was his permission for her to take Fanny to Venice with them, so that she would not be lonely; and also for Fanny to act as a chaperone for her in the daytime if she went out.

His daily routine rarely varied. He took dinner at five, and always dined alone; after which he took an hour's rest in his bed.

Not until the time when the theatre started, at nine o'clock, was she to be ready to accompany him out.

So how could he ever become jealous enough to murder her in her bed?

"All melodramatic nonsense," Alessandro kept saying during the opera. Yet, on her returning home and telling all to Fanny Sylvestrini – Fanny had placed one finger against the side of her nose and closed one eye, saying, "He laughs and calls it nonsense because he knows it is true, and also to throw off all suspicions that he has done the same murdering of wives himself - twice – with poison."

And being late at night and dark; the bedroom dim with flickering candles, and the drama of *Otello* and the music of Rossini still in her ears, Teresa became frightened again, hoping that number of "*twice*" would never increase to *thrice*, due to some fault of her own. She was only nineteen, too young to be choked to death by hands or poison.

Chapter Nineteen

~ ~ ~

The next evening, after attending the theatre alone, Count Guiccioli was not prepared to arrive at Contessa Benzoni's *conversazione* on his own.

"Not again. *Non da solo.* What will you have people think of your absence? They will think you are a wife who is careless of her duties."

Despite her protests, and without any more ado, Teresa was dragged back to Contessa Benzoni's by the Count.

As soon as they entered the palazzo, once again Alessandro went off to another room to wait for Count Rangone, leaving Teresa to amuse herself on her own.

As soon as she entered the salon, her eyes met those of Lord Byron.

She sat down on the nearest sofa, and he came to sit beside her, asking her why she had not come the previous evening.

She refused to tell him, but her excitement at seeing him again, her embarrassment and silence, was of the kind that made her heart beat so strongly, she was sure he could hear its pulsations.

Their conversation became more intimate and more inexhaustible.

But they were being widely watched; and some were watching with jealousy. The preference Lord Byron was showing to a young lady, and only to her, which was so unlike his usual habits, was already causing gossip in the feminine circles; and was also particularly annoying to some of his male friends, such as Angelo Mengaldo and Alexander Scott.

The young ladies, though, appeared to be the most annoyed as they passed back and forth, leading Byron to remark, "We're really being forced to talk like two old philosophers, under fire from all those spiteful looks."

"What are we to do?" Teresa whispered.

"I will think of something."

She told him that she went out every afternoon in her gondola, accompanied by her chaperone, Fanny Sylvestrini.

"Chaperone?"

"Chaperone and *confidante.*"

"And the Count?"

"He does not look for me until the evening."

"Sometime tomorrow," he said, gazing casually around the room, "you will hear from me. Is that acceptable to you?"

She smiled, giving him one of her silent answers.

Returning home in the gondola, she sat silent in her dream-like state again, until the Count began talking, asking her what did she know of the Inglese?

"What do I know of him? Nothing, save that he is an Englishman and a lord, and he likes to talk of Dante."

"Dante?" The Count shrugged. "Yes, That is understandable."

She then learned from him, to her utter amazement, that the Inglese Lord Byron was reputed to be a man of genius, and was famed in France, Germany and America as England's greatest living poet, second only to Shakespeare.

"In England, they say he has caused some scandal with his wife, but that is gone now; and even though he too is gone from England, they say his poetry is even more successful there than ever. They also say he is extremely rich."

"Who told you so?"

"Count Rangone."

Teresa's face was reddening with embarrassment. To pretend he knew so little about poetry, and he a great poet himself. Did he know more about Dante than she did? Did he know all of Dante's works – and yet let her tell him all over again what he already knew?

Well, she decided, if she *did* see Lord Byron tomorrow, the first thing she would do was *accuse* him. But accuse him of what? Of being modest, or being dishonest?

And then another strange thought came to her mind. "Alessandro, why do you ask me about him?"

"I ask, Teresa, because if he is rich, as they say, he sounds interesting. All rich men are interesting. So I think, perhaps, before we return to Ravenna, I would like to be introduced to Mylord Byron."

Teresa stared. "Introduced? By me?"

"Of course not. When I need that service provided, I will ask a man of the rank of Count Rangone.

The following morning a sealed note was brought to the Guiccioli house by Tita Falcieri, addressed to Teresa. He had been instructed to place the note in Teresa's hand, and no other.

Teresa read the note and her fair skin blushed a bright pink. She had to think quickly; his gondolier was waiting downstairs for a reply.

She hastily wrote her reply. "*I will come, but I make the condition that you respect my honour.*"

Teresa watched the gondolier row off and wondered how trustworthy he was. The two notes were in the language which she and Lord Byron spoke to each other, in Italian, for she knew no other.

She showed her own note from Lord Byron to Fanny and asked, "Can I dare?"

Fanny smiled and closed one eye. "Who will know?"

"You must come also."

"Of course, as always. It would cause a scandal if you went alone and were seen."

"Is our gondolier to be trusted?"

"He hates the Count. Does that answer?"

The appointment was for the two gondolas to meet at a certain point near the entrance to the lagoon.

When the time came to leave, and before they left the house, Fanny packed for herself a small box of smoking *polenta,* for she had been a lover a few times herself in her younger days, and she knew how long these assignations could take.

At the appointed time and place, when the two gondolas drew alongside, Tita spoke to Teresa's gondolier, telling him to hold the sides of the two boats together, and when this was done, Tita Falceiri stepped from one gondola to the other, lifted Teresa in his arms, and carried her into Byron's gondola, before rowing off, leaving Fanny and her gondolier to sit staring after them.

"Now all we must do is wait," said Fanny, laughing as both servants lit their pipes and sat to chat. "Who is he, Ippo? Mylord's gondolier? He's big and handsome, eh?"

"Too young for you, Fanny. Under that beard and mustachios and that long hair, Falceiri is still in his twenties, maybe thirty."

"How do you know?"

"I am of Venice so I know him well. All his family and brothers are gondoliers, but only he, the youngest, is a bodyguard. He has protected more than one Inglese, and he will kill before allowing his master to be harmed by robbers or banditti."

"So my Terasina is safe. That is good. Now I must rest in the shade."

The gondolier sat at the brow of the gondola smoking in the sunshine, while Fanny pulled herself inside the cabin, closed the door, and opened her bag and her box of tasty *polenta,* sitting back on the cushioned bench and nibbling quickly on the still-warm tasty grits which delighted her taste-buds.

Finishing, she smacked her lips. Could she do this in the presence of her mistress? No, because Terasina did not like the strong garlic smell of polenta, and if she ever got the smell of garlic in her bedroom – *tantrums!*

She moved forward and pushed wide open the door of the felze to let out the smell, sitting back down again. Now she could relax. Now she could think. And did she not have so much to think about these days, eh?

Cruising over the lagoon, Byron and Teresa talked like two old friends, but now they were less formal, less guarded, for now they knew they were not being watched. They had the privacy of the felze, although the door was wide open, and so they were both more relaxed.

She learned more about him, and he about her. She told him about Santa Chiara's Convent, and how her marriage had been arranged soon after.

"Could you not object?"

"No, that would be an unforgivable insult to my Papa, and to the Covent. All the girls in Santa Chiara's spend their days and nights wishing to be married."

"Why?"

"Because if they do not have a marriage arranged before they leave, they must stay in the Covent, even for all of their lives. Those that are forced to stay for a long time, usually give up hope and become nuns."

"Were *you* forced to stay there?"

"No, because my father is Count Gamba of Filetto, a rich man, and the daughters of rich fathers may come and go at their father's pleasing. It is only the daughters of poor fathers who must stay, until a husband can be found to give her a good home and secure her future."

"But not you. Those rules did not apply to you?"

"No, I was sent there for the same purpose as many others with rich fathers, to be educated. And the Convents educate very well."

"In Dante."

She smiled. "No, not just in Dante, but Petrarch and almost all Italian literature. We also learned some of your Shakespeare."

"Shakespeare?"

"Only one, *Hamlet*, The Prince of Denmark. I loved that play. I read it over and over again. We performed it three times in two years, and now I can say every line off by heart."

Byron laughed. "I don't believe you. There are over four thousand lines in *Hamlet!*"

She nodded. "And I can speak ... well, nearly *all* of them."

"Prove it."

She closed her eyes and began to recite, while he lowered his head and listened to the words of Hamlet being spoken in Italian, and by God, although his own Italian was not perfect, she seemed to have it near enough in a good translation.

He finally stopped her, telling her she was a show-off, and she laughed. "You are jealous?"

"I am more fascinated by the colour of your *bionda* hair. It reminds me of when I was in Milan."

"Milano?"

"Yes. Have you been there?"

"No."

He then told her that after he had crossed the Alps from Switzerland, he had spent three weeks in Milan where he had attempted to see everything – churches, theatres, libraries.

"The Cathedral is noble, the theatre is grand, and the Ambrosian Library is excellent. What delighted me most was the manuscript collection preserved there, of the original love-letters of Lucretia Borgia and Cardinal Bembo; and a lock of her hair – so long – and fair and beautiful – and the letters so pretty and so loving, it made me feel wretched not to have been born sooner to have at least *seen* her. The hair and the letters were so beautiful, I did nothing but pore over them, and made the librarian promise me a copy of some of the letters."

"And did he?"

"No, the next day he told me it was prohibited, and so I managed to learn some of them by heart. They are all quite short, but the prettiest love-letters in the world. I went there every day, when the librarian always wanted to enlighten me with sundry other valuable manuscripts, classical, philosophical, and pious, but I told him I was sticking to the Pope's daughter and wishing myself to be a cardinal."

Teresa smiled.

"And then, finally," he said, "on the day before I left Milan, when the librarian was off in some other part of the library, I managed to carefully pull and steal two single strands of her hair as a relic."

Teresa was smiling. "Lucrezia was very beautiful, and not as bad as the slanders say. She was kind and gentle and did not poison anyone."

"If she was anything in life as she is in her letters, then she was indeed very sweet and good-natured. How come she had such a father?"

"You know about him too?"

"The whole world knows about Alexander Borgia and his evil deeds as Pope. I have read everything that has been written about him, leaving me always with the same conundrum – how a girl like her could have such a father?"

"Not *all* the slanders about the Borgia Pope are true. His enemies created many of them, and they even spread the rumour that he was secretly a Jew who had come to destroy the Christian Church."

Byron laughed. "I haven't heard that one. But he was certainly a cruel and devious man under a front of smiles and a charming manner."

Teresa sat silent for a moment, enjoying her happiness. For her to speak with him, and for him to speak with her, so naturally, to be seated side by side, to breathe the same air, and to give proof of their mutual attraction by their wish to meet again.

"Do go to the opera at night," he persuaded her, "and I will too. At least that way we can *see* each other, even if we do not speak. And then when it is over, we can meet and talk at the Contessa Benzoni's."

She was hesitant. "The opera? Will it be *Otello* again?"

"No, it changes every night. Othello will not be on again until Thursday."

"And our gondolas, will they not meet on the water again?"

"Of course, if you wish, tomorrow. Our gondolas can

meet at ... noon?"

Teresa nodded, knowing she would be awake from as early as six just to count the hours.

As soon as she returned to her own waiting gondola, and was lifted from one vessel to the other, before Tita rowed off, Fanny almost jumped on top of her as she demanded to know – "Did he respect your honour?"

"More than you," Teresa replied, pushing Fanny off her. "We are to meet again tomorrow."

"Again tomorrow?" This caused Fanny to pause and ponder. "I think," she said, "that you will have to give our gondolier some money, a big tip, for sitting around for hours when he could be out earning some scudi for himself."

Teresa stared. "I have no money."

"Then Mylord will have to pay. He is rich. I am sure he pays his own gondolier a handsome sum."

"No!" Teresa was horrified. "To ask for money in return for meeting? I will not be shamed in such a way!"

"But what about our poor Ippolito, eh? He has to earn too, same as Mylord's gondolier. The Count pays Ippo very little, barely enough to feed his pipe."

Teresa was becoming distressed. "What will I do? Will I give you something of mine to sell?"

"No." Fanny had a better idea. An idea that she could not let Terasina know, so she would have to be very careful.

"I will arrange something for Ippolito. You now leave the problem to Fanny. Doesn't she always know how, eh?"

Teresa smiled with relief. "How would I cope without you?"

"Badly. Now you sit back and rest, while I do some thinking."

Fanny really did not give *due fischi* about Ippolito. He got paid enough. And taking the mistress out on these afternoon gondola meetings would provide him with the perfect excuse to sit around doing what he loved best, smoking and sleeping.

No, she was more concerned for her *own* payment, her own big tip for sitting around waiting for hours, when she *could* be back in the house, hard at her work, sewing and mending and ironing. This chaperone business was something that was required of her only in Venice – so Venice should pay.

Tomorrow, before her mistress was taken into the other gondola, she must find a way of giving a secret whisper to Mylord's gondolier about payment to Ippolito and the chaperone.

The next day at noon, when Tita had stepped into the gondola and while Teresa was giving her long fair hair one last comb, Fanny whispered to Tita about payment for the gondolier and chaperone.

In response Tita looked highly offended; telling her that recompense for their time was already understood by his master, so there was no reason for her to ask.

Fanny was delighted, and then seeing Teresa emerge from the felze, raised her voice louder. "And you will tell Mylord to take good care of my mistress?"

Tita did not deign to answer such a stupid command, lifting the young lady into his gondola, and then rowing away without looking back.

And once the gondola was far out on the large expanse of the blue lagoon, far from watching eyes, Byron and Teresa came out of the felze to sit near the prow of the boat in the sunshine and warm breeze, and continued getting to know each other.

Every afternoon they met on the water, their time together stretching longer and longer, falling more in love each day – until Fanny spoiled it all by telling Teresa some gossip she had learned from Ippolito, which he had picked up on the streets and canals of Venice.

"You must be careful, my Terasina, and safeguard your heart. I think Mylord Byron might be a dangerous man to become too involved with, for you will have many rivals."

"Rivals? Are there others? How can that be? He spends the afternoons with me on the water, and then sees me at the theatre, and later at Contessa Benzoni's sala."

"While you are here in Venice, but what then? They say many beautiful women are excited by him and attracted to him in a strong way – stronger than iron is drawn to a magnet!"

Teresa was speechless; but Fanny was genuinely concerned; warning her solely for her own good.

"When we leave here, I will not have you pining for him in Ravenna, while he is forgetting you with other women here in Venice. I could not endure it."

Neither could Teresa endure it; not even the thought of it.

The following day, which was their fifth day of meeting in the gondola, she was very reserved and cool with him, leaving him utterly baffled, until she told him what Fanny had said.

Byron was silent for a time, but when he spoke, it was in a very serious tone. "It's true," he said. "Before I knew you, I felt an interest in many women, but never in one only. Now I love *you,* and there is no other woman in the world for me."

The soft sounds of the lagoon floated around her. She put her hand on his arm, and he lifted her hand and kissed it. It was the first intimate thing he had done, keeping his pledge to respect her honour. Her eyes filled with tears and her heart felt as if it was bursting. She had never known love for a man before, but she knew it now.

He bent and kissed her lips for the first time. Her arms slowly moved around his neck. Their fate together was sealed, and both knew it.

The following day they met even earlier, at eleven, and sailed over to Fusina; leaving Fanny and Ippolito in the care of Tita, while they travelled on together in a carriage to Byron's country house at La Mira.

All three servants were happy enough to chat and exchange news with the other gondoliers who had their boats parked at Fusina.

Fanny could not keep her adoring eyes off Tita Falcieri, thinking him the handsomest big Italian she had ever seen. His eyes were a vivid blue, and their look could occasionally be kind and gentle; but the rest of him – *mascolino!*

Chapter Twenty

~ ~ ~

Not until sometime in the following week did the Contessa, Marina Benzoni, notice the change in Count Guiccioli's young wife when she came to her salon. The girl was coming out of herself, not as nervous and shy, and she seemed to have *matured* by a few years or so.

Byron had noticed it too, the change in Teresa, more confident in herself now, and visibly happier. He had been making love to her every afternoon for the past five days at La Mira, and it seemed to be doing her the world of good.

Although now that she *was* at last coming out of herself, he could see her minor flaws; writing with his usual honesty and amusement to Hobhouse:

'She has no idea of tact; talking of age to old ladies who want to pass for young; and this blessed night horrified a correct company at M. Benzoni's by calling out to me –"Mio Byron"– in an audible voice, causing a dead silence of pause among the other prattlers, who stared and whispered.'

Yet, despite her social inexperience, her lack of tact, in every other way she was a *'perfect angel'* in his eyes, and he loved her, madly, crazily, and truly.

Teresa was not totally devoid of tact. She had seen all the fans fluttering, and she had not cared. If it was true that Byron was her lover, then it was true, and all those other ladies should know it. She was a girl in her first love, and she wanted the whole world to know her happiness ... all except her husband.

"He, Alessandro, he is not my husband," she said to

Fanny as she lay on the bed in a cool silk nightgown. "He is only my ... business master."

"In law, he is your husband," Fanny reminded her. "And he could prove it, because he could truthfully swear on a Bible that he has conjugled you."

"What is that?" Teresa said with contempt. "Five or six times he has jumped on me, and I closed my eyes and endured until it was over. He has never made *love* to me, not like my Byron makes love to me."

"How? How does he make love to you?" Fanny slipped a secret slice of still-warm *polenta* from out of her apron pocket and nibbled on it excitedly. "Tell Fanny how?"

"No, it is too private and too sacred to be shared in gossip," said Teresa, oblivious to her own hand moving slowly over her body. "It is bad for you to even ask."

Fanny was undeterred. "So tell me only little things; does he –"

"Quell'odore - aglio!" Teresa had suddenly caught the smell of garlic and jumped up, slapping the half-slice of *polenta* out of Fanny's hand. *"Non qui!"* she cried furiously, ordering Fanny out of the room. *"Esci! Esci!"*

"Terasina ..." Fanny woefully pointed to the half-slice on the floor. Teresa picked it up and slapped it into her hand. *"Non qui!* I told you – not here in my bedroom!"

Fanny stared at the remains of the polenta which had been on the floor; she could not eat food that had been on any floor, no matter how clean.

"Now I will have to throw it away," she said sullenly, looking bale-eyed at Teresa as if she had committed the most egregious sin against her and her lovely polenta.

"Santa Madre – what a fuss! What is food without garlic, eh? What is land without rain? What is –"

"Buonanotte," Teresa said, and closed the door, shoving home the bolt and smiling at her own cleverness as she slipped back into bed.

"Now *that* was a good excuse to get rid of Fanny and her impolite questions. A good excuse. Now I can lay here in silence and enjoy my dreams in peace."

~~~

The next night was a party-night at the Contessa Benzoni's sala. All her favourite guests had been sent an invitation card that afternoon. Delicious food was laid out in the supper room, champagne was flowing, and a special announcement was about to be made.

When all were assembled, Count Rangone held up his glass and delivered the declaration – after more than thirty years of being her lover and *cavalier servente,* Marina Benzoni had finally agreed to marry him.

Amidst the applause someone called out to Marina – "Why did you make him wait for so long?"

Marina laughed. "I waited until I knew he was too old to find another mistress."

A small group of violinists had been hired for the night, playing soft Italian love songs that would not be too loud to prevent conversation.

Byron spent a decent amount of time in conversation with his friends, and then at an opportune moment, wandered off alone through the crowded salon.

He and Teresa were standing together in their favourite corner when Count Rangone approached him.

"Mylord Byron, here is Count Alessandro Guiccioli, who has asked if he may have an introduction to you."

"Of course." Byron did not appear at all nonplussed by the sudden arrival of his *amica's* husband. He had spent years being introduced to people he did not wish to be introduced to, and his manners on such occasions were always perfect.

Staring at Byron, Count Guiccioli appeared puzzled. He was first and foremost a man of business and he had never been inclined to waste his time by coming in here to mix with the socialites.

He looked around the salon and pointed to Alexander Scott. "I thought he was the one – is he not Inglese?"

"He is," Byron answered, "but he prefers to be known as *scozzese.* "

Guiccioli looked at him, still puzzled, and Byron smiled, "From Scotland. It is a country in Northern
~~~

Britain."

Teresa stood with her head bowed, but Count Guiccioli was now appraising Byron, assessing him, involuntarily admiring him. The Inglese seemed to have it all, looks, manners, money – a fine young gladiator to pit his wits against.

Count Rangone diplomatically drew Teresa aside and engaged her in quiet conversation, saying in a low voice, "Does he know Mylord is your *amante?*"

Teresa shook her head nervously. "I don't know."

"No gentleman here would tell him," Rangone assured her. "That would be very bad form. Although I cannot vow for the ladies."

Rangone and Teresa continued their conversation, while both kept discreet and watchful eyes on the two men who seemed to be getting along pleasantly, and Count Guiccioli was doing a lot of smiling.

Byron responded in kind, but he was not fooled. Guiccioli was a man of polished manners, a smooth talker with an easy smile, and possessed all the fake charm of a Borgia Pope. He spoke of his appreciation for the Arts, but he also had an immense amount of respect for the Church and its traditions.

"The Roman Church. Are you Catholic?"

"No."

Guiccioli frowned. "*Protestante?*"

Byron smiled. "No, my Bible is Plato."

"*Plato?* Ah, the Greeks! You must beware of them. What do they say – 'Beware of Greeks bringing gifts'?"

"And said by a fool," Byron replied. "It was the ancient Greeks who *gave* to the world all of its richest gifts."

Guiccioli was amused. "Name these Greek gifts?"

"Medicine, science, politics, philosophy, architecture and sculpture. And you, who say you have an appreciation of the Arts, must know that even the origins of the *theatre* and stories told in performance were first given to us by the Greeks."

"Of course, that is all true, now you say it."

"Yes, so pray let me go on," Byron insisted, "because people speak too glibly about the Greeks without appreciating their essential and outstanding contributions to this world."

Guiccioli suddenly realised he was dealing with an intellectual. A novelty to be sure.

"Go on."

"I will, sir, because few people, if any, speak up for the Greeks these days. Yet it was the ancient Greeks and Herodotus who taught us how important it was to keep written records of History, so those who became behind us could learn from it. And *where* would this world be without the theorem of mathematics? – which all stem from the work of Thales of Miletus. How would people count their money?"

"Count their money? They would not know how." Guiccioli had never learned any of this about the Greeks at school, nor had such a teacher.

"Greece was also the place of the first trial by jury of its citizens. And the first competitive sports of Olympia. And most valuable of all, Greece gave us the understanding and aspirations for Democracy."

Guiccioli stiffened slightly. "Democracy?"

"Yes. *Demokratia,* which is Greek for 'power of the people'."

Guiccioli lowered his tone to almost a whisper, "That is not a subject you should speak of here in Italy, not while we are ruled by the Austrians."

Count Rangone had taken Teresa off to join the ladies, but still he kept a watchful eye on the two men. Marina came to join him and whispered in his ear, "Has Guiccioli rebuked him?"

"No, by God," Rangone was completely baffled. "Guiccioli seems more attracted to *him,* than he ever was to her."

~~~

The following night Teresa arrived at *La Fenice* opera house at almost at the same time as Byron. She rushed
~~~

after him into his box in a state of distress.

He was surprised by her sudden appearance, for the boxes on this side of the theatre were solely for men, and the sight of a young lady entering one of these boxes would cause every fan to flutter.

"Where is Guiccioli?" he asked her.

"He is down in the cloakroom, so I must tell you quickly – today he said we must leave Venice."

"Leave? But you are not due to leave for another week."

"I know, but he says Count Rangone is showing no interest in his business proposition and so now there is no reason to stay here. Our luggage is already packed. We go early in the morning."

Byron had not expected this, and paused to think.

"And Byron, it is worse – he says Fanny must stay here and supervise his Venice house. She will not be coming back with me to Ravenna."

"I will think of something," he said, his mind blank with the shock of it.

Teresa had already thought of something. "You cannot write to me, and I cannot write to you. He may open the letters. But he will think nothing if Fanny writes to me, and I write to Fanny. He will pay no attention to those letters, no more than he does to the letters from my brother or sisters."

"You are suggesting I send letters under Fanny's cover?"

"Yes, and I can write to you in a cover addressed to Fanny."

She shoved a piece of paper into his hand. "Here is the address of the Venice house where Fanny will be living, and here is the address of a friend of mine in Ravenna. If you write to me under cover to him, your letters will be kept safe. He is a priest. And if you do not write to me soon, I will die."

The orchestra was tuning up to full flute, and Teresa knew she must leave the box now, her eyes filling with tears. "*Addio, mio Byron. Ti amo.*"

He loved her too, his heart wrenching as she hastily left the box. He rushed after her, catching her in the dim corridor and kissing her in a passionate embrace.

"I will write, and I will come to see you in Ravenna."

"No, no, he will kill you! He has used paid assassins against his enemies in the past."

Byron did not believe it. "He showed no animosity towards me last night."

"Because he is an actor, a good actor! Do not trust him, even when he smiles."

"Is that why you are so frightened of him?"

"Not only me, *everyone* in Ravenna is frightened of him. He has friendship and great power with the Austrians."

And then she was gone, leaving Byron staring after her without a clue as to what do next.

He left the theatre, and then went nowhere but to his own house, diving into the Grand Canal and swimming in the cold clean waters outside his Palazzo Mocenigo.

On that same night, in Venice, one of the many spies of the Papal police, which was merely a branch of the Austrian force, demonstrated how stupid some of their spies were, and how little they understood the English and Italian languages, by writing a report, which was very similar to other reports written about Lord Byron when he was in Milan.

Mistaking the English word 'Romantic' for the Italian words *Roma Antica,* meaning *'Ancient Rome'* – the code-word used by those revolutionaries seeking to defeat the Austrians, and return Italy to a *Republic* ruled by Italians.

He has a name as a poet in his native country, and he is suspected of being linked to the secret society of 'Roma Antica', at least his style of writing has been described to me as belonging to the "Romantic School" which I presume means "Carbonaro".

Chapter Twenty-One

~~~

Fanny Sylvestrini was devastated by the separation from her mistress; while Teresa, who was on the road to Ravenna, already missed Fanny terribly. Now she would have no *confidante* to share her thoughts and deeds. No one to laugh with, not in the same way that Fanny made her laugh.

Yet perhaps it was Providence that kept Fanny in Venice, for now she could provide an even more valuable service to her by taking or sending her letters on to Byron.

In Venice, Fanny was feeling somewhat reluctant about these letters she was supposed to write to Mylord Byron. What would he think of her when he saw her handwriting, which was big and often the spelling was not too good.

No, she must perform this duty for her mistress; and now that she was to be a *messaggero* to an Inglese Noble, she had a reputation to preserve.

The solution, she decided, was to be found in one of her old friends here in Venice – Lega Zambelli. A scholar and an ex-priest in his late thirties, whom she had helped a lot during her earlier days in Venice when he had left his Holy Order.

So, with the help of Lega, who wrote while she dictated – and automatically correcting her grammar as he did so – Lega wrote Fanny's first letter to Mylord Byron.

"No," he told her, "in England the correct address for his title is simply 'Lord', said Lega, and commenced to write as Fanny spoke:

My Lord: The most afflicted Terasina, on leaving

here, begged only one thing of me – that I should try
~~~

to see My Lord and speak to him of her, always of her – in order to bring her back more vividly to his memory. This, My Lord, is why I sought the honour of seeing you, and am seeking it again today, if I may do so without being impertinent.

Permit me also to remind you that the aforesaid Terasina is counting on a letter from you on Thursday, when she will arrive in Ravenna, and that the post leaves tomorrow at midday. I hope you will not render her expectations vain.

Awaiting your commands., pray honour me with your kindness and accept my humble duty.

Fanny.

Byron found himself in the same situation as Fanny Sylvestrini. Although he could speak Italian fluently, he was not certain that his *writing* of the language was always grammatically correct or pure in form. And not wanting to give a bad impression to Teresa, he, too, sought the services of Lega Zambelli, recommended to him by Fanny.

Lega was enjoying this new and intriguing employment of his services, not least because the Inglese lord was not only paying him for his time in writing his own letters, but also those letters written for Fanny Sylvestrini.

Only one condition did his lordship firmly require – that the letters remain confidential between the two men; and Lega should come to the Palazzo Mocenigo where the letters could be spoken and written in the privacy of his library

Lega swore confidentiality, and in the library of Mocenigo, wrote Byron's first letter to Teresa as it was dictated:

My Love: Your letter came today and gave me my first moment of happiness since your departure. My feelings correspond only too closely to those expressed in your letter, but it will be very difficult for me to reply in your beautiful language to your sweet expressions. You vowed to be true to me and I will make no vows to you; but let us see which of us will be the more faithful. This however I promise you: You told me that I am your first love – and I assure you that you shall be my last.

The letter was sent under cover to: *Al Signore Gaspare Perelli. Ravenna.*

Byron was uneasy. "How do we know he can be trusted, this priest in Ravenna?"

"He can be trusted." Lega had known him when they younger, and now he smiled. "He is a great believer in *Ancient Rome.*"

Which left Byron none the wiser; but he instinctively trusted Lega , and took his word for it.

The secret letters went back and forth for weeks, and Fanny was enjoying her daily visits to see Lega Zambelli in his lodgings, bringing him slices of her home-made *polenta* to eat at his desk, which was usually smoking-hot when she arrived with it, reeking of her favourite garlic.

Lega accepted his slices politely, and then ate them ravenously, for he too was a lover of polenta.

"Lega, do you know the story of *Romeo e Giulietta?*"

Lega turned up his eyes. *Every* Italian knew the story of Romeo and Juliet, and he said so to Fanny.

"The two lovers who lived up the road in Verona?"

Lega nodded. *"Sì."*

"Am I not like the nurse in that, eh? In that story? The nurse carrying letters to and fro and worrying about her *la femmina*. Like me, eh?"

Lega laughed. "And who am I – Friar Lawrence?"

"You were once a priest."

Lega turned up his eyes again, wondering why women liked to turn all situations into some *storia d'amour*.

"Now we must write," Fanny said, returning to business. "A letter from Fanny to her Terasina."

Lega picked up his quill and dipped it into the ink.

If by a man's words one may judge his heart; if it adds to your happiness to be certain of the love, the tenderness of My Lord, I will tell you that he loves you with the greatest ardour.

He has sworn and declared to me, in the short time that we have seen each other, that this is not a mere flash or whim, but a true love, and that you have made on him an impression that can 'never' be erased.

Lega paused ... this did not sound like Mylord Byron, not the man he now knew, who always appeared embarrassed in saying the words in his presence; and had revealed he had only been persuaded to do so, upon hearing that Lega had once been a priest.

Lega looked at Fanny dubiously. "Did Lord Byron *really* say those words to you?"

Fanny waved a hand dismissively. "You are being paid to write my letters, so write!" And then she was off again, in full flight, as the nurse in *Romeo e Giulietta*.

He loves you! He vows that he is completely

estranged from anything that could distract him from you, and says he is impatiently awaiting your next letter, which will cheer him on his awakening.

But I exhort you, I advise you, I beg you, to be prudent, lest the intensity of your love betrays you. I will not write about the chatter of the idle gossips, for the affair of you going into his Opera Box gave them full scope. Now they have ceased talking about it, and the unconventional – male and female – are all on your side.

"God forgive me," Lega prayed as he dipped his quill into the ink. "But even You, dear God, knows that an honest man must earn his bread somehow."

~~~

Teresa was finding life unbearable, in Ravenna, marooned here in this wilderness with no Fanny to talk with; only silly maids, some of whom she knew slept with her husband, and so could not be trusted.

She found some comfort in playing with the smallest of the Count's six children, but the eldest, being only two years younger than herself, still remembered his own mama, and clearly resented her.

She spent hours during the day wandering around the gardens, thinking of her pleasure in Venice, her delight, her happiness; and then in the evenings writing long love-letters to her beloved.

Regularly every morning, she slipped out from the gardens and walked to the nearest village of Loreo to post her letter, kissing it with her heart as she did so, then sending it on its way to the name written on the cover, Fanny Sylvestrini.
~~~

Suddenly, it all became too much, the waiting each day and the wondering each night, and knowing more with each day that passed how it was all so impossible. She was married and there was no escape.

She longed for Byron to come to Ravenna to see her, even for day, an hour, a minute; but Alessandro would never allow it, even if she was foolish enough to ask.

So she must lie alone, crying each night for her Byron, while Alessandro was up to naughty tricks with the maids – *oh cattivo e cattivo!*

Suddenly, it all stopped, the pain and the misery, and she wrote no more letters to Venice. All her food and drink remained untouched and her face paled as white as the sheet she lay on.

Alarmed, the Count called in a doctor who diagnosed a mysterious illness that he could not define, yet he too was alarmed.

"Her pulse is very slow, and if it continues, she may go into a coma. Yet her head is hot with a fever. It is most strange."

After the doctor had left the bedroom, leaving behind him a concoction of medicines, Alessandro stood gazing down at Teresa, and then shook her awake.

"Teresa? Teresa, what is wrong with you?"

She opened her eyes and looked at him, barely able to speak due to the dryness of her mouth.

"If I cannot have my friend, Alessandro, I will die."

"Fanny?"

"No, my other friend ... Byron."

"The Inglese lord? No, that is impossible! Do you want to disgrace me?"

"No, I want to leave you ... and if you won't let me see Byron ... or let him come to see me ... then –" she slowly lifted her heavy hand and ran a finger across her throat."

Her gesture was one that did not need words, done as it was in the old Italian way. Yet he knew she would not slit her own throat, if only out of respect and reverence to her father. So what was she doing?

After a long silence when she had drifted back into a sleep, Alessandro finally understood the meaning of her finger across the throat – the foolish girl was *willing* herself to die. No food, no drink, a slow starvation. He had never dreamed that Teresa Gamba could be capable of such strength to do this.

To do this – and people would blame *him!* They would say he had poisoned her – *killed* another wife. Yet what had he to gain from Teresa's death? Nothing but a stiletto in the heart from her father.

He paced around the room, beginning to sweat at the thought of a Gamba stiletto piercing into his flesh. *Mio Dio* – he desperately needed a strong drink to help him think about this!

Chapter Twenty-Two

~ ~ ~

My Teresa, where are you? Everything here reminds me of you – everything is the same, but you are not here, and I still am. When I go to the Conversazione, I give myself up to Tedium, preferring to suffer boredom than grief. I see the same faces – hear the same voices – but no longer dare to look towards the sofa where I shall not see 'you' anymore. I hear, without the slightest emotion, the opening of that door which I used to watch with such anxiety when I was there before you, hoping to see you come in.

You who are my only and last love, the delight of my life, has gone away, and I remain here alone and desolate. There, in a few words, is our story! It is a common experience, which we must bear like so many others, but we two must suffer more, because your circumstances and mine are equally extraordinary.

As the weeks passed and few replies came to his letters, and those that did were highly emotional and erratic, saying one thing and then the opposite, Byron began to wonder if Teresa was merely playing with him, and was not as serious in her feelings as he was in his.

"So many of the Italian women are like that, all high-flung emotion, and then nothing when another *amore* catches their eye," Alexander Scott advised him. "It's best not to trust them."

Count Rangone and Marina were not happy either, for now Mylord was staying away from their salon more and more often, due to his need to occupy himself with his *"writing"*. And now some of the other guests were drifting away to Madame Albrizzi's salon.

"Silly girl," said Marina. "Venice turned her head and Byron's admiration made her vain, and now she has become a coquette, happy to make him suffer. Did I ever treat *you* like that, Beppe?"

"In our younger days, yes," said Rangone. "You were always flirting with others."

Byron wrote to Hobhouse, explaining the situation with Teresa, and how it lay now; wondering if he should go to Ravenna? After all, distance was the main problem. Two people could not speak so easily in letters as they could face to face. – "The *eyes* always reveal what the lips will not say."

She is of the Ravenna noblesse, educated in a Convent, sacrificed to wealth, filial duty, and all that. She is as fair as sunrise and warm as noon. I am damnably in love – and nothing but hope keeps me alive – seriously.

Realising it could take weeks to receive a reply from Hobby; he spoke in the same vein to Richard Hoppner, in private, asking his advice.

"Go to Ravenna? Rent a house there? Why, I have never heard such a ridiculous suggestion in my life."

"Why so? All I do is write poetry, and I can do that anywhere."

"But to go to Ravenna – to the *Romagna!* The people of that area are not like those in Venice, you know? They are less sophisticated. And, well, all in all, I would strongly advise you against it."

Byron left him then, giving no reaction one way or the other; nothing more than a polite "Thank you," and then he was gone.

Richard Hoppner was truly horrified at the idea. Lord Byron had become an absolute *boon* to Venice and its economy. All the British knew he lived here. How could they *not* know when he was constantly writing about the place; – "*I stood in Venice, on the Bridge of Sighs.*"

More and more British were coming to Venice to try and meet Lord Byron or even catch a glimpse of him. More hotel rooms booked up, more meals in the restaurants, more earnings for the gondoliers. More of the French were coming too. And more Germans.

Why, there was even a rumour that the famous German writer, *Johann von Wolfgang Goethe*, intended to visit Venice solely to meet Byron.

But it was the *British* that Hoppner was the most interested in. British people who always sought out their Consul – himself – and made his own life in this outpost island more bearable and more enjoyable in being able to speak English to the English, instead of all that gabbling in Italian.

Byron's decision was finally made when a reply came back very quickly from Hobhouse – the man he trusted most in this world; a man who, in discussions, could be counted upon to be calm, pragmatic, and honest.

If you are making love to a Romanguola, and she only nineteen, you will have some job on your hands. Don't you go after that terra firma lady; they are vixens, in those parts especially, and I recollect when I was at Ferrara seeing or hearing of two women in the hospital who had stabbed one another – and all for jealousy. Take a fool's advice and be content with your amphibious fry in Venice; you will make a

*pretty splashing with them in the lagoon, and I
recommend constancy to the neighbourhood. Go to
Romagna indeed! Go to old Nick, because you will
never be heard of again.*

Byron's response was to go to the desk in his library and
write for long hours; losing himself in the continuation
of his new epic poem – *Don Juan*.

~~~

In London, some weeks later, Hobhouse received a
reply from Byron, still in Venice; and he was very
relieved to see that no mention was made of Ravenna
nor anyone living there. This letter was much more
satisfactory, and more in the usual tone of the Byron he
knew so well.

*We have had here in Venice the devil's own row
with an elephant. He broke loose, ate up a fruit
shop, killed his keeper, broke into a church. I saw
him the day he broke open his own house; he was
standing in the Riva, and his keepers trying to
persuade him with loaves of bread to go on board a
sort of ark they had got. I went close up to him that
afternoon in my gondola, and he amused himself by
flinging great beams of water over me.*

*He was then not too angry, but by midnight he
became furious, and displayed the most
extraordinary strength, pulling down everything
before him. All musketry proved in vain; and when*
~~~

he charged, all the Austrians threw down their muskets and ran. Finally they brought a field piece from their arsenal; the first shot missed, the second entered behind and came out at his shoulder. Sadly, I saw him dead the next day. A stupendous fellow.

A few nights ago I had agreed to meet a beautiful girl named Angelina She had asked me to meet her on her balcony at midnight. I decided to go, but for some reason I stepped into the canal instead, flopping into the water like a carp. I made the best of it by going for a swim fully clothed, and now all who saw me think I am mad, but you know that's not true.

Yours ever, B.

~~~

Just before noon, after completing all her morning chores in the Guiccioli's Venetian house, Fanny Sylvestrini arrived at Lega Zambelli's lodgings carrying her box of red-hot polenta.

As soon as he saw her, Lega smiled, *"Buongiorno."*

Fanny smiled coyly and blushed a little, for now her romantic admiration had transferred from Tita Falcieri to Lega Zambelli.

Tita Falcieri was too young for her anyway, so why make a fool of herself like those silly old women who ran after men so much younger than themselves. Lega was no more than five years younger than she, so – a perfect match!

"I have brought you your favourite polenta, Lega."

"Grazie." Lega was about to speak on, but Fanny interrupted him.
~~~

"Are you ready to eat now? While it is still hot?"

"No, not today, Fanny. I have an appointment at the Palazzo Mocenigo in one hour and I still have much to do."

"What are you doing?" Fanny could see that Lega had packed a large trunk full of books, on which he was now closing the lid and tying it with a leather strap.

"Are you going away somewhere?"

"*Si,* I am leaving here." Lega then commenced to pack another smaller trunk with some of his folded clothes. "I am now going to live at the Palazzo Mocenigo as Mylord Byron's official *segretario.*"

Fanny was dumbstruck, her eyes popping out of her head.

"It is sensible," said Lega. "And that is why Mylord said what is the sense of my going in and out every day, when I could live there. The palazzo has many rooms."

Fanny finally found her voice, husky with disappointment. "So we shall not meet here every day now, eh?"

Lega smiled good-humouredly. "We will not be strangers. I will see you around."

"Not around the Palazzo Mocenigo. All his letters to my mistress have stopped, and she no longer writes to him."

She looked down at her box of polenta. "They have cooks at the Palazzo Mocenigo. Soon you will like their polenta more than mine."

Lega nodded. "I am very fortunate, God has smiled down on me. I will have my own personal apartment, also a small office next to Mylord's library."

"And your apartment and food, all will be provided for you *gratis.*"

Lega nodded. "I am told so by Signor Fletcher. Also I will be paid a wage every month, so no more hunger or living meanly on the small handful of *soldi the* peasants pay me for writing and reading their letters, thank God."

Fanny nodded, unable to disagree. She looked down at the box of polenta in her hands, lifted the lid, took out a slice, and bit into it bitterly.

Chapter Twenty-Three

~ ~ ~

A part of Byron's day was devoted to letters. There were always letters to read and reply to – from his many staunch friends in England; from his Genovese acquaintances in Switzerland; from strangers who addressed their letters simply to – *Lord Byron, Venice* – and those he would now leave for Lega Zambelli to deal with.

Most important of all, apart from the letters from his friends, were the letters from his publisher, John Murray.

Today, though, a letter had arrived with the *Ravenna* postmark on the cover – sent directly to him at the Palazzo Mocenigo and not through Fanny.

He ripped it open – surprised to see from the signature at the end that it was *not* from Teresa – but from her husband, Count Alessandro Guiccioli.

The Count wished to inform his "noble friend" that his young wife was very ill, and as Mylord had also been a dear friend to her in Venice, would he now be so very kind as to come to Ravenna to try and cheer her?

Byron could scarcely believe it, but he did not hesitate; replying that he would leave Venice as soon as possible.

Hoppner, Mengaldo, and Alexander Scott did their best to dissuade him, warning him it could be a plot to trap him. The Count Guiccioli may appear to be a respected man in Ravenna, but he was also suspected by some of being a murderer.

"Not only of two wives, but also two *men*, at least," said Angelo Mengaldo. "One man, a business acquaintance named Manzoni, knifed from behind in a dark alley. The other, a *priest,* who they say Guiccioli murdered in his own house – poisoned his wine."

"And yet," said Hoppner – who, as a diplomat, made it his business to know everything about everybody who entered Venice – "Count Guiccioli remains on excellent terms with the prelates of the Cardinal's Court."

"Because the prelates and Cardinals are all lackeys of the Austrians," said Mengaldo. "They may *pretend* to like Guiccioli, but they don't trust him either."

Byron was prepared to risk it; taking with him Fletcher and Tita Falcieri – those two were good old friends now, and both would probably consider a trip over to the mainland and travelling through the Italian country as a kind of holiday.

He also decided to take Mutz along for company as well as some new sights for the dog to see and new roads to run. Poor Mutz, in Venice the only place he had for any decent exercise was galloping along the landings or up and down the main staircase of the Palazzo Mocenigo.

During the following days Fletcher busied himself making sure his lordship's clothes were fit for a prince; while Tita, in his role of bodyguard, cleaned out his pistols, sharpened his dagger and sword, along with a collection of lethal knives.

"No harm will come to my lord," Tita told Fletcher. "If a man tries, he will be the one who dies."

"That's good to know," Fletcher said cheerfully. "I presume you mean harm from robbers and banditti?"

Tita looked at him patiently. "Who else would be a danger to a rich man, Fletcho? Sure I mean robbers and banditti."

Byron carried Allegra off in his gondola and placed her in the trusted care of Mrs Hoppner.

"A week at the most, and then I will be back," he told Allegra, who did not want him to go. He hugged her for a long time, until Mrs Hoppner brought in her own little boy, and Allegra lost all interest in her Papa, eager to get down and play with the boy, happily waving Papa bye-bye.

The next morning, on June 3rd, Byron set off for the mainland. That same afternoon a short report was sent by a spy to the Austrian Directorate in Ravenna.

Lord Byron, a Peer of the Realm in England and a 'Romantica', has left Venice for Ravenna.

~~~

Ravenna, in the *Emilia-Romagna* region of Northern Italy, was once the capital city of the Western Roman Empire until the 5th century, and then of Byzantium Italy until the 8th century, and still housed a vast and beautiful collection of early Christian mosaics.

Now it had lost much of its importance and, although it was a cultured city, it was small in size with a small population, surrounded by large tracts of countryside and pine forests.

As his coach reached the streets of the town, gazing through the window, Byron saw that something strange was going on. Every street was festooned with colourful decorations and holy pictures of Jesus and the Madonna, and all the pavements were littered with colourful flower-petals.

"Why is it?" he asked Tita.

"In Italy, today is the feast of *Corpus Domini,*" Tita told him. "A Holy Day."

"Ah, the same as *Corpus Christi* in the English churches. Well, how do we get past this procession of people, and where do we go?"

Tita did not know. The driver did not know. So Byron stepped out of the coach and walked into the jostling crowd, his eyes picking out a pretty girl to ask where might he find the Palazzo Guiccioli?

She stared at him with curiosity, and then her hands went to both of her cheeks and her eyes glowed with delight as she answered in rapid and excited Italian, not one word of which he understood
~~~

"Scusi!"

Instead of answering more slowly, she turned and ran off through the crowd.

"I think we should wait," Tita advised. "Today is not a good day to distract the people from Corpus Domini, and I too should be going to the church to say my prayers."

Byron took his advice and checked into the *Albergo Imperiale*, at the Via di Porta Sisi. Despite its grand name, the hotel was not large, with only seven rooms, but apparently the best Ravenna had. Fortunately it was empty, so he had a choice of as many rooms as he wished.

Tita took off to say his prayers in the Church; Fletcher decided to lie down in the cool of his room for a while; and Byron wondered what *he* should do now?

The British Consul, Richard Hoppner, had given to him a letter of introduction to Conte Guiseppe Alborghetti, a nobleman of Ravenna, and an occasional writer of poetry.

He decided to make a call on Alborghetti, and found him in residence – a man in his forties who came out to the hall smiling widely and greeting him with open arms and a kiss on both cheeks – *"Byron?* Mylord *Byron?* I did not believe it until they showed me your card with your English crest! You have come from Venice?"

"Yes, from Venice."

"To see *me?"*

"No, well, yes, but also to see Dante's Tomb."

"Ah, our great Dante. Yes, he would be happy to know you have come to see his Tomb. I will be most honoured to take you there tomorrow. Today is not good. Now, come inside and we will talk. I have much to ask you, my dear famous Lord Byron, oh, very much to ask!"

Inside the drawing-room, while coffee was being served, Count Alborghetti asked if Mylord had any acquaintances here in Ravenna?

"Yes, I am friendly with the Count and Countess Guiccioli. I hope to visit them while I am here."

Alborghetti shook his head sadly. "Alas, you will not be able to see the young lady. They say she is at death's door."

The rest of the hour spent with the talkative Count was a torment to Byron, escaping politely and as quickly as he could, determined to find his own way to the Palazzo Guiccioli before nightfall.

A determination that proved unnecessary. Upon his return to the hotel, Count Guiccioli was already there, waiting for him. He had come personally to collect him in his coach and take him to Teresa.

"How did you know I had arrived in Ravenna?" Byron asked curiously as the coach rumbled away from the hotel.

Guiccioli said: "You spoke to a girl and asked her for directions?"

"Yes, a girl who ran away?"

"To tell us that you had arrived. That girl, she is a friend of Teresa. She has been very worried for her."

"And Teresa's illness?"

The Count shrugged. "We do not know. Possibly some fever she picked up in Venice. The doctor bleeds her from her ankles every day, but she remains very frail."

Byron turned up his eyes and looked through the window. Depriving people of their own natural blood was a medical form of vampirism in his opinion. What good could it do, but leave the patient even weaker. Blood was the source of life, so why remove it?

"Does he use leeches?"

"To bleed her?" Guiccioli shook his head. "No, he prefers to make small cuts in the ankles and do it that way."

Byron winced. "Leeches would be less painful."

"Yes, but they are very expensive. Most are bred in the leech-farms in Rome, which is too far away."

"If she does not improve, would you mind if I sent

for my own doctor, Professor Aglietti? He keeps his own stock of leeches, and Venice is much nearer than Rome. He could be here in a few days."

Guiccioli ran his fingers through his facial whiskers, smoothing them down, as if contemplating the suggestion. Finally, he shrugged: "We will see."

When Byron was led into her bedroom, Teresa looked as pale as death, her eyes closed. An older man was sitting anxiously by her bed. Guiccioli introduced him as Count Ruggero Gamba – Teresa's father.

Byron saw instantly that Count Gamba was surprised, and also that his eyes were full of hatred for Count Guiccioli. "Why do you bring this young man into my daughter's bedroom?"

"He was her friend in Venice, at the *Conversaziones*, and she has asked many times to see him."

"And you thought fit to bring him into her bedroom!"

"My friend, she is too ill to be brought out to the salon to see him. I merely sought to satisfy her request."

Under other circumstances, Byron would have turned and left the room, but then even *he* had not expected to be taken directly into her bedroom by her husband.

Count Gamba looked suspiciously at Byron, and Byron saw that he was not a man to have as an enemy.

"So, you are an *Inglese* lord? And what can you do for my daughter that I cannot do?"

Byron was at a loss. "I can read to her?"

"I can also read to her. What would you read to her?"

Byron thought quickly. "Her favourite. Dante's story of Paolo and Francesca."

Count Gamba made a face. He had never read Dante's 'Inferno' and had no patience to do so now.

"Very well, but this is most unusual." He shot a look at Guiccioli. "If the priest calls, do not allow him to enter this room."

And then to Byron. "I will stay and listen to you reading to my daughter."

He pointed to a chair at the other side of the bed, directing Byron to sit; and then resumed his own seat opposite.

Count Guiccioli left the room for the library, and returned with Teresa's copy of Dante's *Divina Comedia;* made his apologies, and quickly quit the room.

Byron had no choice now, but to sit by the bed reading quietly in Italian – while realising he had landed himself into the midst of a ridiculous farce. The husband frightened of the father, and he frightened of both of them – *Mio Dio!* as Tita would say.

As the reading went on, and Count Gamba listened, he began nodding his head ... Yes, the Inglese could read Italian quite well ... He had no idea that Lord Byron was a famous poet nor that others would think he was bestowing a great honour on Teresa by doing this.

Byron had been reading for no more than fifteen minutes when Teresa slowly opened her eyes and looked at him hazily, a slight smile coming to the corners of her lips.

Her father jumped forward and grabbed her hand. "Terasina, you are awake!"

Teresa did not respond to him, her face turned to Byron, who bent and kissed her cheek.

"Mio Byron," she said softly, and her father sat back in the fullness of realisation. This man was not her *friend,* he was her lover.

Did Guiccioli know? ... No, Guiccioli could not know. A proud and vain man like that hypocrite and *bastardo* Guiccioli would not openly bring her lover into his wife's bedroom. So ... Guiccioli was being cuckolded, was he? By this handsome young man and his own Teresa?

Count Gamba sat with an involuntarily smile

moving on his face as the Inglese lord resumed his reading of Dante's story of Paolo and Francesca.

When the time came for him to leave, and return to the hotel, Byron addressed his request to Teresa's father, not her husband.

"May I come again tomorrow?"

Count Gamba was thoughtful. "If you are in Ravenna, Signor, and if it helps her, then why not?"

"Thank you. May I also make a suggestion. The doctor should stop bleeding her with cuts. That will keep her weak and prevent her from improving."

"You say so? Or you know so?"

"I know so."

Count Gamba frowned. "You are certain."

Byron nodded. "*Indubbio*"

"Then he must be stopped. I will instruct Count Guiccioli to stop him making the cuts."

~~~

Teresa was still physically very weak. During the following days the doctor insisted that she must not leave her bed. Byron told her the opposite.

"You need air, and some gentle exercise. It is the best thing for you now. Will I take you for a walk in the gardens? A very *slow* walk?"

"It would be better not," said the doctor. "All she has suffered ... has taken its toll." He smoothed out her pillows and straightened her coverlet. "Now she must have some rest."

Byron wondered if he was more concerned about the cessation of his services and his expensive fee, than the recovery of his patient.

"I am tired," Teresa said quietly to the doctor. "Tired of being told what to do. And I *would* like to take a short walk in the garden."

An hour later Teresa's father stood by a window watching the young Inglese lord escorting Teresa around the garden while she leaned on his arm. She
~~~

was gradually recovering now, and even that was astonishing. The doctor had been certain that she would die. Such a fear had been unbearable – to lose Teresa only months after losing his daughter Faustina and also his wife, would have been too much sorrow for his heart.

Now he could stop worrying. Now Teresina was getting well again. Now he was liking the Inglese lord more and more each day.

Professor Aglietti arrived, reporting first to Byron at the hotel; then carrying on in his carriage over to the Palazzo Guiccioli. At the door he presented his card; and then was escorted upstairs, where he spent a long time in private with Teresa.

Aglietti reported back to Byron in his usual precise way. "I spent a long time with the young lady. You were right to complain about the bleeding. She had already lost too much blood."

"From the cuts?"

"Yes, from the cuts; but also from a miscarriage."

Byron stared.

"From what I have learned," said Aglietti, "when she returned from Venice, a doctor told her she was three month's pregnant. This she did not know in Venice. She says the last time her husband visited her bedroom was two months before she went to Venice. Upon her return, discovering she was pregnant by her husband, her depression deepened, and so began her descent. Her miscarriage took place only three weeks ago."

"And that idiot was bleeding her?"

"In fairness, he did not know. The so-called 'doctor' she went to see was a woman in the village of Loreo, an experienced woman in these matters, and the woman told her she was approximately three months' pregnant; which, according to her, represented the tightening of her chains to her husband. That is when she knew she wanted to die."

Byron was silent, and then looked at Aglietti. "Does she know you will be reporting all this to me?"

"Yes, she knows. She said from you she keeps no secrets. It is very sad, to be in love with one, and married to another ... and he so much *older* than she ... two generations older."

After a silence, Byron sighed with some relief. "Well, at least now I know the truth of what was wrong with her. On my journey here, I feared she might be suffering from something like this Roman fever that is going around. They say it is deadly."

Dr Aglietti nodded. "It is, Roman fever, quite deadly, especially for the young."

PART SEVEN

ROME and RAVENNA

"It is my opinion, that the presence of a third person interrupts or destroys domestic happiness."

Mary Wollstonecraft
(mother of Mary Shelley)

Chapter Twenty-Four

~ ~ ~

The Shelleys were now in Rome, after spending a disastrous five months in Naples. Strange things had happened there; things that Mary still did not understand.

The house at 250 Riviera di Chiaia had been spacious and airy and lovely, with windows looking out to the blue Bay of Naples; yet Claire had spent much of her time in her room, unwell. She blamed it all on her depression about Byron. Now she hated him, she said, but Mary did not believe her.

It was impossible, on occasions, not to feel sympathetic towards Claire. And, at times, emotions of delight towards her too – especially when Claire chose to stay at home with Elise while she and Shelley went off alone to explore the ruins of Pompeii.

Two glorious days on their own. And not having Claire tagging along was a blessing indeed. A chance for herself and Shelley to have some quiet time on their own. Was ever a wife so deprived of living a private life with her husband as she had always been? Did many other wives have their stepsisters constantly living with them night and day, year after year?

Mary's heartache from the loss of her baby daughter was still there, still hurting; but beginning to subside now as she slowly smothered her sadness in her love for little William, her darling boy, her only child now.

Shelley had refused to believe that he was in any way responsible for their daughter's death; and now Mary had stopped silently blaming him. Closer now, they were drawing closer again, and Mary knew she still loved Shelley.

Love had also been in the air between Elise and the servant Paolo Foggi, who had met each other for the first time in Byron's house at Este in September, and had married in Naples after Christmas.

Then so many strange and sudden things had happened. Shelley had approved and given his permission for the marriage of Elise and Paolo, but within weeks he had dismissed them both. He had refused to say why – other than Paolo had been impertinent to Claire. And within another two weeks after that, in February, Shelley had suddenly insisted upon their packing up and leaving Naples.

Confused, and at a complete loss to understand, Mary had simply asked him, "Why?"

"Rome," Shelley had replied. "We have often spoken of going to Rome, so why not go? Before the weather in Rome gets too hot."

"But surely living in a city like Rome will be too expensive for us?"

"We can afford it," Shelley had insisted. "My yearly allowance from my father, stingy as it is, has come through. And what is it for, but to live on – so why not live on it in Rome?"

"Glorious *Rome?*" Claire said. "Oh, we *must* go, Mary, we must!"

Claire's health had recovered, her melancholy banished, and now she was well and fit and ready for anything – except going back to England.

"But why Rome *now?* When we are so settled here?"

Claire quoted Chateaubriand, *"Whoever has nothing else left in life, should come and live in Rome."*

And so, on 28th February, the four left Naples for Rome; Shelley, Mary, their little son, and Claire.

They travelled slowly, taking in every sight, every place on the way. Their nomadic life together over the past five years had made them expert travellers; and Shelley's love for his wife, if it had ever left him, now seemed to have returned.

Sometimes he would go off, hand in hand with Mary, to walk on the beach, or explore ancient ruins. In the evenings they read books or wrote in their journals or played chess on the balcony of their room at the various inns; and by the time they had reached the outskirts of Rome, in the month of March, Mary knew she was pregnant again.

Entering Rome, and seeing for the first time the dome of St. Peter's rising in the blue skyline above the River Tiber, Shelley immediately thought of Byron's words from Canto 4 of Childe Harold:

"Oh, Rome! City of the Soul! What are our woes and sufferance? Come and see the Cypress, hear the owl, and plod your way o'er steps of broken thrones and temples ..."

They rented rooms in the Palazzo Verospi on the Corso, and with every day that passed, they fell more in love with the Eternal City.

"Rome repays for every thing," Mary wrote. And so here they would live, and love and write, and enjoy happiness again.

~~~

In Ravenna, during her afternoon walks in the gardens with Byron, Teresa was still weak; mostly with happiness.

"What is to take place now?" she asked. "Now I am becoming well again, will you go back to Venice and forget me?"

"As if it was so easy to forget you? To love you and to come here was my crossing of the Rubicon, and it has already decided my fate."

Teresa pondered on his words. She was educated enough in her country's ancient history to understand his meaning ... When Julius Caesar had crossed the Rubicon river, south of Ravenna, it meant he was ready to face anything in the Romagna, even war.

"So what are we to do?"

Byron had no idea. "We could go away together; elope."

"Run off to some far land? No, in Ravenna and
~~~

Filetto that would cause a great scandal to my name and also to my father."

"Then I know not."

Teresa told him of another proposed solution. "Today I received a letter from Fanny, and she has proposed something which she thinks is a very good idea."

"A *good* idea ... from Fanny Sylvestrini? Is it possible?

Teresa laughed. "Dear Fanny. *She* thinks we should do like *Romeo e Giulietta* and I should pass myself off for dead, but my body is stolen and spirited away in the night. Then *you* should pass for dead of heartbreak and people are told your body has been sent back to England, and then we both run away to Rome and live happily ever after."

"And Fanny running away with us too, no doubt?"

"Fanny and her *polenta!*"

Sitting on his balcony, Teresa's father watched as the two young people laughed together. Teresa's laugh was so like her mother's laughter. She also reminded him of his son, Pietro, now at University in Rome.

Santa Madre – he had not sent word to Pietro to tell him how Terasina was awake and walking and getting well again – and the boy so worried about his sister.

Stepping back into the shade of his room, he sat down to write a hasty note to his son:

"Saluti, Pierino ..."

~~~

In Rome, Shelley was busy at work on his new poem, *Prometheus Unbound,* while Mary and little William walked in the Borghese Gardens, where Mary watched with pride as her boy ran up the steps on his small three-year-old legs; and where Claire sat reading Wordsworth.

In that same month, Mary met and became friends with an Irishwoman who was an artist, Amelia Curran, a daughter of the famous Irish lawyer, John Philpot
~~~

Curran, who was now Master of The Rolls in Ireland.

Miss Curran possessed the usual friendliness of the Irish, and kindly agreed to paint William's portrait.

Inside her studio, William was so good, sitting very still, while Mary watched as Miss Curran magically captured every delicate line of his little face, his large blue eyes, and little wisps of fair hair falling over his brow.

So impressed was she with the finished portrait, Mary asked Miss Curran if she would also paint Shelley.

"If you wish." And when Shelley arrived and sat in her studio, staring at her with the same large blue eyes as his son, Amelia Curran smiled. "You have the face of a poet, Mr Shelley."

"He also has the mind and *heart* of a poet," Mary said with proud tenderness; and then, blushing, turned to leave Miss Curran and Shelley to get on with the portrait without any further distractions from herself and William.

As they skipped along the street together hand in hand, Mary could not help reflecting that it was a long time since she had felt so happy. And never before had she loved a city as much as she loved Rome.

"*Rome,*" she wrote in her journal "*has such an effect on me that my past life before I saw Rome appears a blank; and now I begin to live.*"

Later that evening, as they stood on their balcony gazing over the city of Rome, Mary said dreamily to Shelley, "It is a scene of perpetual enchantment to live in this thrice holy city ... no wonder Albé wrote about it so passionately in *Childe Harold.*"

Shelley nodded, and wondered what Byron was doing in Venice now? Romancing another nymph? Or writing another poem?

~

Byron was still in Ravenna, still anxious about Teresa's

health. His time with her, so far, had been limited to a few hours walking or sitting in the garden, before she was taken back to her bed, and he returned to his rooms at the hotel.

The situation was ridiculous, and he knew it. And even more ridiculous and perplexing was the attitude of her husband, who was displaying no jealousy at the arrival of Teresa's *"friend"*. No jealousy at all; quite the opposite – even to the Count constantly inviting him to stay for dinner, or to accompany him to the theatre in the evenings; which was all very disconcerting.

He always refused on some pretext or another, refusing to descend into social familiarity, certain that he was not capable of being quite so *blasé* in the face of Teresa's husband, given the circumstances. And yet – having met him only once in Venice – the Count seemed to be under the illusion that "Mylord" was *his* friend too, and not just Teresa's.

Writing to Richard Hoppner in Venice, Byron declared his confusion:

"<u>She</u> is improving well – but I can't make <u>him</u> out at all – he visits me frequently, and insists on taking me out in his carriage and six horses (like Dick Whittington and the Lord Mayor). The people here don't know what to make of us either, as Guiccioli had the character of jealousy with all his wives – Teresa is his third. However, if I come away with a stiletto in my gizzard some fine afternoon, I shall not be astonished."

The following afternoon as they sauntered around a fountain in the garden, Byron voiced his confusion to Teresa.

"Tell me what I am to do? Remain here? Or return to Venice?"

Teresa looked at him nervously. "Are you now *wishing* to go back to Venice?"

"No, but you must understand, I am a foreigner in Italy, and still more a foreigner in Ravenna, and still so little versed in the customs of this part of the country, so how long am I to stay here? Even now, walking in the garden, we are watched at all times by your father or husband or some other relation. How long can this continue?"

Teresa did not know, but she was not willing to give him up or send him away.

"All I wish is to go back to Venice with you, but it will take time to think of how. Meanwhile, could you not enjoy Ravenna more? It is a nice part of Italy, clean and peaceful, yes? And you have the theatre, and the pine forests to ride your horses."

When Byron did not answer, Teresa nervously clutched his hand. "Promise me you will not go away, my Byron. Promise me that you do not regret your suffering in coming here?"

"No ... but I need instructions on how I am to behave in these circumstances? I am not clear as to what is best to do? Remember that I am here because you *ordered* me to come."

"No, it was not I, it was Alessandro who wrote and asked you to come."

"Yes," Byron frowned, "and how strange was *that*?"

Teresa agreed it was very strange. "I know he likes you. Everyone in Ravenna likes you. Papa says you are all that the townspeople talk about now."

"Me?"

"Yes, the young and foreign Mylord who is famous in all Europe, even Rome. They see it as a great honour for Ravenna."

Byron shrugged. "I see it as just one more reason why it will be difficult for you and I to *slip away* in secret from Ravenna."

274

"But *you* will not slip away in secret from Ravenna? Promise me?"

"Terasina ...?" Count Gamba came down the garden path .... "I have a letter from Pietro, from Rome. He thanks God you are recovering – see?"

Teresa took the letter from his hand, knowing it was her father's way of telling Byron that now was a respectable time for him to leave.

After the usual bows and courtesies, Teresa watched Byron go, and knew he was a man directed by his own mind, and too independent in his ways to stay here for much longer.

But if he truly loved her, that would be the test. How could she risk all for a man who was not prepared to risk also?

As Byron rode away from the Palazzo Guiccioli, some of the local nobility of Ravenna had gathered together in the home of Count Alborghetti, the Secretary General of the Province, to drink wine and pass on all their latest news about their famous foreign visitor.

During the first days of his arrival many of these nobles had hastened to his hotel with offers to take him to see some of the great sights of Ravenna, and all were rather disappointed by his reserved English manner.

They had expected a flamboyant modern-day *Casanova*, or a brooding poetic youth similar to *Childe Harold* in Greece – not this perfectly-dressed, extremely handsome young man who was not talkative or loud, and did not seem to welcome their kind attentions.

"On the first day he came here," said Count Alborghetti, "I know he was at the end of a long journey from Venice, but I could have wished him a little more courteous and not so fidgety. He stayed for less than one hour, was almost silent in conversation, and did not appear to be enjoying my long stories. Then as soon as I told him the young lady was known to be at death's door – he was gone!"

"In any case, his stay is a good thing for the town and for the people who see him," said Count Giulio Rasponi. "Although I agree, his preoccupation with his affections do not often make him accessible. I have offered him my own humble service in various forms, but so far he has made no use of them."

"The next day," said Count Alborghetti as if he had not been interrupted, "I called to take him to see Dante's Tomb and he was like a different man, no fidgets, and so relaxed and good-humoured – he has the most *captivating* smile when he is happy – have you noticed? On that day he brought with him a signed book of his own poetry and reverently placed it on Dante's Tomb, in homage to Italy's greatest poet."

Sitting quietly, and taking no part in the conversation, was Count Francesco Rangone, a brother of Count Guiseppe Rangone in Venice who was the *cavalier servente* of Marina Benzoni.

During the past two years Francesco had received many letters from his brother in Venice, telling him many interesting tales about *l'Anglico Mylord Byron* – so rich, cultured, beautiful, generous, rakish – and sometimes irritable and quick-tempered, depending on his moods. He was liked by the learned, and even moreso by the ladies, and Beppe had said he was not adverse to the enjoyment of women.

But all this was nothing compared to some of his strange adventures – swimming late at night in the Grand Canal, and sometimes swimming fully-clothed. He also had his own family of servants, perhaps twenty or more, nearly all Italian; as well as many animals who lived like well-fed princes – dogs, monkeys, parrots, and all kinds of strays.

Beppe had also said that Mylord kept his animals on the ground floor of his palazzo so he could talk and play with them as he went in and out from his gondola, but his favourite was to occasionally feed the animals himself while he conversed with them as if they were human.

Oh, so many strange tales Guiseppe had told him in his letters, and in reply he had always begged for more; and now he was listening carefully to the conversation in the room, hoping for some new information, because he had already started writing his own book intended for publication at some later date; a collection of stories, entitled, *"Peep at a very cultivated and rich, but strange Mylord."*

Now the conversation was moving on to other subjects, so *now* Francesco spoke, hoping to stir the talk back to the subject of his book:

"The common opinion," Francesco said, "is that the Palazzo Guiccioli has impressed Mylord much more than the Ravenna Rotundo or the Byzantium mosaics."

Count Alborghetti maintained a straight Christian face. "That is because he is a good friend of the Count as well as the Contessa. You have heard how Guiccioli collects him and takes him out in his best open carriage and drives him through the town?"

The guffaws of laughter in the room pleased Francesco. Now the fire was lit. Guiccioli had too many enemies in the room for them to sit in silence.

"He takes him out through the town to save face! To prove the old falcon is not being cuckolded by the English Mylord so much younger than he!"

"No, no," insisted Count Alborghetti, "Count Guiccioli truly likes Mylord Byron. He likes him very much."

"Yes, he likes him so much he would like to *kill* him!"

It was not true. Alessandro Guiccioli truly did like Mylord Byron. He liked his money. The young Mylord was rich, and rich men were good to know. He had no intention of killing his wife's lover – he intended to *use* him.

He needed a large sum of money very quickly, and Mylord Byron was the only man he knew rich enough to provide it. So why should he pick a quarrel with him and send him away? Were they not now good friends?

As in all successful business, a good bargain was needed, a good offer. So what could he offer Mylord Byron in return for a large amount of his money? It would have to be an offer that was made with great delicacy, but how?

And then an idea came to him – an idea that gave him some hope.

He visited his wife in her apartment, glad to find her alone. Thank God her Gamba father was not present.

"In one week, Teresa, I have a business meeting in Bologna. You must accompany me."

Teresa stared. "To Bologna? For how long?"

"A month, maybe longer. I also must go to Ferrera."

Teresa became flustered. "But, Alessandro, what about our friend ... our visitor. We cannot go off and leave him alone here in Ravenna."

"Alone? He brought with him some servants and even his own bodyguard, and now he has many friends in Ravenna. He will be very well looked after."

"No, Alessandro, it is a bad way to treat a guest whom *you* wrote and asked to come here because I was ill."

"And now you are well again. So he is no longer needed. No, you must accompany me, and he must return to Venice."

When Teresa lowered her head and sat in gloomy silence, Alessandro exclaimed with a burst of pretended outrage, "Surely you don't expect me to leave *you* alone here, and *he* coming to visit you every day with no husband near? No, that would cause a scandal!"

Teresa knew that was true; and not knowing what else to say: "Then I must go with you, Alessandro, to Bologna."

~

After leaving Teresa, on a sudden impulse, Byron

steered his horse away from his hotel and took a long cantering ride through the pine woods which lay between the town and the sea; eventually slowing down to walking pace, wandering with a loose rein as he looked around and enjoyed the sights and smells of the woodland, and gloried in the peace of its silence.

The forest had all the charms of nature peculiar to its locality, its fine growths of ageless evergreens washed by the waves of the Adriatic; and as he slowly rode and breathed in the wholesome smells of shepherd's thyme and a thousand scented herbs, he also breathed in the spirit of its poetry –

There is a pleasure in the pathless wood,

There is a rapture on the lonely shore,

There is society where none intrudes,

By the deep Sea, and music in its roar:

I love not Man the less, but Nature more,

From these our interviews, which I steal

From all I may be, or have been before,

To mingle with the universe, and feel

What I can ne'er express, yet cannot all conceal.

As he came out of the forest, the sun was about to set amidst one of those gold and opal haloes which, in Italy, so often crown the evening sky on summer days. Everything on the land was green and cool, thanks to the morning and evenings dews. The nightingales had begun to sing, and the crickets were chirping with delight at the return of the cool.

And now, as the daylight waned, and the church bells ringing out in the town could be heard in the distance ... the spirit of poetry possessed him again and he found himself mentally writing another stanza for his new epic, *Don Juan:*

> *AVE MARIA! blessed be the hour!*
> *The time, the clime, the spot, where I so oft*
> *Have felt that moment in its fuller power*
> *Sink o'er the earth, so beautiful and soft,*
> *While swung the deep bell in the distant tower*
> *Or the faint, dying day-hymn stole aloft,*
> *And not a breath crept through the rosy air,*
> *And yet the forest leaves seemed stirred with prayer.*

Now he could hear bugles playing, and he knew from where the sounds came – from outside the church doors where two page-boys bugled their notes to announce the time of the evening Benediction, calling all the women in their veils to come and be blessed, and the men removing their hats to step inside and be greeted with the glow of a hundred candles and the waving wafts of incense as they offered up their prayers for Heaven's blessings.

It was one of the many reasons why Byron liked Ravenna so much, and felt at peace here – because it had so much of *old Italy* about it. Another reason was that Ravenna was so out of the way, and considered to be so old-fashioned now that few foreign visitors passed through here; in fact, none at all – so none to dog his steps and beg his signature.

And here, there was none of the constant gossip of England and Venice, The people were too down-to-earth and too practical to believe all the colourful and dramatic stories about him that England and Venice so readily believed.

Turning onto the main road he saw a young lady carrying a parasol who smiled at him and waved. He waved back and rode on, unaware that she was Count

Alborghetti's daughter.

On entering her house she found her father still in full conversation with his gentlemen friends.

"*Still* talking, Papa?" she asked. "You have missed the evening's Benediction."

"Have I? Oh, well, unlike you I don't go religiously every evening. We have been talking much about our famous visitor, Lord Byron."

"I've just seen him on horseback," she said. "Dear me, how good-looking he is! The men really ought to exile him for our peace of mind, and for theirs as well! Is he married?"

"Unfortunately, yes."

She stared at the young Italian who was merely visiting Ravenna and new to the company. "Why do you say so in such a tone of disapproval? Do you *know* Mylord Byron?"

"No, but I have been in Milan and Venice and I have heard a lot of talk about that young lord."

"*Have* you indeed?" Francesco Rangone almost jumped out of his chair at the possibility of some new material for his book. "Pray inform us?"

"As long as it is not slander and lies," warned Count Alborghetti. "We know how the Milanese and the Venetians gossip."

"Oh, no, it is all very true," said the young Italian. "All of it has been seen and vouched for by persons of immaculate credentials."

"Then do tell us also," Francesco urged.

Seeing that he now had the attention of all the gentlemen who up until now had paid him little notice, the young Italian visitor told all the stories he had picked up in Milan and Venice.

"Apparently, when he was in Greece and Turkey, Lord Byron spent some time as a corsair."

"A pirate?"

"A devilish pirate too, for in the harem he carried off the Sultan's favourite by force and bribery, and then lived with her for a long time on a desert island. Next he had her taken to England, married her there, and then cast her aside."

All stared as the stories were so faithfully relayed. "A great lady in London committed suicide for love of him. And in Venice, too, a charming girl of gentle blood had passionately loved him, and hoped to wed him, but denied in her expectations, she drowned herself. And yet, when Lord Byron was told of these deaths, he merely shrugged, uncaring."

After a silence, the room was engulfed in hilarious laughter.

"You have not met him and so you do not know him as we do," laughed Count Alborghetti. "Otherwise you would know that is all fictions you have been told. Is that how the Milanese flavour their wine?"

"A *pirate?*" Count Giulio Rasponi was still laughing. "Oh, we must tell Lord Byron these incredulous stories and make him laugh too!"

The young Italian's face had turned a deep red with embarrassment. He had told what he had heard and believed to be true, but these high-ranking gentlemen of Ravenna did not believe one word of it."

Francesco Rangone, on the other hand, was feeling quite pleased. Of course, once a man or woman had met Lord Byron personally, they would know these ridiculous stories were untrue, but – *fortunately* – very few men and women were liable to meet him, for it was well known that he had an almost obsessive tendency to avoid strangers at all cost. And there were so many strangers in Italy and France and all over the world who never had, and never would, meet Lord Byron.

So, yes, he would include this idiot's stories in his book – *Peep at a very rich and cultivated, but strange Mylord* – and it would be the making of his much-needed fortune.

Of course, he would have to be careful with his brother Guiseppe Rangone in Venice, who would not suffer himself to hear a bad word about Byron – but then who was Beppe to prove or deny? Was he with Byron in Greece and Turkey? Or anywhere else except Venice? No! And as the old proverb goes – *If enough mud is thrown, some of it must stick."*

Chapter Twenty-Five

~~~

Arriving back at his hotel, Byron found a very thick letter waiting for him from Richard Hoppner.

The British Consul at Venice was writing to him in Ravenna a lot more frequently than he had expected; and in Hoppner's last letter he had made some vague criticisms about Shelley; to which Byron had refused to agree, writing back flippantly–

"I will not hear a word against my friend, Shiloh. I regret that you have such a bad opinion of him; you used to have a good one. Surely he has talent and honour, but he is crazy against religion and morality. You seem lately to have got some notion against him?

And now, as he opened this latest letter, he saw at once that Hoppner was continuing the criticism:

My dear Lord Byron — You are surprised, and with reason, at the change of my opinion respecting Shiloh; it certainly is not that which I once entertained of him : but if I disclose to you my fearful secret, I trust, for his unfortunate wife's sake, if not out of regard for Mrs Hoppner and me, that you will not let the Shelleys know that we are acquainted with it.

Byron sat back. He *hated* secrets, because he was not
~~~

very good at keeping them. He was all too open about his own life, all his own sins, and yet he had never been judged by the world on *them* – but on the fabrications of sins he had *not* committed.

Was Shelley in for the same scandalous treatment now? If so, he would have to warn him. To be forewarned was to be fore-armed against calumny.

He read on – and yet, even in this, Hoppner could not prevent himself from speaking like a diplomat.

This request you will find so reasonable, that I'm sure you will comply with it, and I therefore proceed to divulge to you, what indeed on Allegra's account it is necessary that you should know, as it will fortify you in the good resolution to never trust her again to her mother's care.

You should know that at the time the Shelleys were here in Venice, Clare was with child by Shelley. You may remember to have heard that she was constantly unwell and under the care of a Physician in Padua, and I am uncharitable enough to believe that the quantity of medicine she then took was not for the mere purpose of restoring her health. I perceive too why she preferred to remain alone at Este, to being here with the Shelleys when their little girl died.

Be this as it may, they proceeded from here to Naples, where one night Shelley was called up to see Clare who was very ill. His wife, naturally, thought it very strange that he should be sent for; but she was not aware of the connection between them. Besides, as Shelley desired her to remain quiet, she did not dare to interfere. A Midwife was sent for, and the worthy pair, who had made no preparation for the reception of the unfortunate being she was bringing into the world, bribed the woman to carry the child to the Pietà, where the child was taken half an hour after its birth, being obliged likewise to purchase the Midwife's silence with a considerable sum. During this time, Mrs Shelley, who expressed concern about Clare's illness, was not allowed to approach her, and since then Clare has been doing everything she can to persuade her husband to abandon her. Poor Mrs Shelley, whatever suspicions she may entertain of the nature of their connection, knows nothing of their adventure at Naples, and as the knowledge of it could only add to her misery, 'tis as well she should not know.

This account we had from Elise, who came here, with an English lady. Elise says that Clare does not scruple to tell Shelley, in Elise's presence, that she wonders how he can live with such a timid creature as Mrs Shelley.

I hope this account will encourage you to persevere in your kind attentions to poor little Allegra, who has no-one else to look up to. I cannot conceive what Clare means by her impertinence in letters to you. She ought to be too happy that the child is so well taken care of. Mrs Hoppner was so angry when she heard the above account, that it was with difficulty she was prevailed upon not to write to the Shelleys and upbraid them for their infamous conduct.

Besides that, in pity for the unfortunate Mrs Shelley, whose situation would only have been rendered worse by the exposure, silence on these matters was still more incumbent on her. I think after this account you will no longer wonder why I have a bad opinion of Shiloh.

I fear my letter is written in a very incoherent style, but as I cannot bring myself to go over this disgusting subject a second time; I hope you will endeavour to comprehend it as it stands.

Believe me,
Ever thy faithful servant. R. B. Hoppner.

Byron did not know what to think? Was it true? Was it not? Hoppner seemed so certain, and so full of rage.

It was all very hard to believe, and very unlike Shelley – a man who would prefer to harm himself before harming a butterfly or a croaking frog. So even harder now to believe that he had callously handed over a newborn child to a stranger to be taken away to a Foundling Hospital.

What Hoppner had written of the account of the child's birth was damnable – true or not – and although *he* would keep the letter, he was determined that no other person should see it.

He placed the letter in a secret compartment of his letter-case and securely locked it. It was not his place to defend or prove any libel or defamation against Shelley, but he had to protect Allegra.

One of the two people mentioned in this sordid account of events, was Allegra's mother.

During the rest of the evening Byron thought of no one else more than his little daughter by Claire. In one of his letters Hoppner had said: "*Allegra is well and very good, but as soon as she is dressed in the mornings, she looks around and calls for papa.*"

There was something about the malevolent and gossipy tone of Hoppner's letter that Byron found objectionable, especially as it was all based on the words of one servant.

Although it would be just like them, Claire and Shelley, in their strange relationship, initiated more by Claire than him. And if Claire truly had taken so much medicine after visiting a *medico* in Padua, then it was more likely to have been a miscarriage that necessitated the need of a midwife being called in Naples, not the birth of a child. Perhaps Elise had only seen the furtive comings and goings and had been kept away and told as little as Mary had been told, and so she had concluded her own incorrect reason for it all.

He remembered how Elise had written all sorts of nonsense about himself to Claire – also passed on to him by Hoppner – and how eager Elise had been to return to the Shelleys, and now she had come away to abuse them also. And the Hoppners had chosen to believe every word of it.

And that alone made him decide to become less friendly with Richard Hoppner in the future.

My dear Hoppner – As I am not sure how long

my stay here will be, may I impose upon you

again, and ask you to send Allegra here to me in Ravenna at the earliest opportunity, with a suitable nursemaid, and accompanied by one of your assistants at the Consulate; in particular, if possible, Mr Richard Edgecumbe, who has previously told me he would be willing to do so if necessary. I send this by express, so that Allegra may set out without loss of time – you can surely find a proper woman to accompany her. And Edgecumbe must come too.

Yours, in haste – B

~~~

</div>

Two days after sending the letter, he received one from Venice, from the Contessa Marina Benzoni.

You have forgotten all your friends in Venice – friends to whom you are so dear, it is almost a crime. I am seeing very little of Scott, too. So Marina has lost her two beloved Englishmen. I have been told that Contessa Guiccioli is not well; I am sorry; pray greet her for me. In short, I have nothing by me to remind me of you but my constant friendship, which will never be altered.

If I did not think it would make someone sad, I would tell you to come back to us. I know that in Ravenna, too, you are much loved and respected. I have been told a great deal about the generosity
~~~

of your heart. I was not surprised. That heart of yours is perfect. All the Englishmen who come here ask me at once about Lord Byron, which Mylord doesn't care a pin about, and they know it. A great many have gone through, in this summer season, but they do not stay long.

All the Venetians are off to the country. I shall go to the country for a few days, but if you have any commands, if I can do anything for you, write to Venice.

Count Rangone – Beppe – who speaks of you always as if you were his spoilt child, clasps your hand, and is so very, very fond of you.
Good day, good day –

I am always your
Marina Querini Benzoni

Chapter Twenty-Six

~~~

Shelley considered the expense of a portrait of himself to be an unnecessary expense and a waste of money – money that could be used for more practical needs.

"You see me night and day, so why do you need a portrait?"

Mary smiled. "Because when we are old and grey, I want to be able to look at the portrait and remember you when you were *not* old and grey, but young and handsome."

Upon entering the studio, Amelia Curran greeted Mary with a miniature painting of William in a small round glass case – a duplicate of the original portrait.

"I shall do a miniature for you of your husband also," said Miss Curran. "So many ladies like to have a miniature of the original, because it is more personal, and they can carry it around with them in their reticule."

Mary's delight was beaming. "Thank you, Miss Curran, thank you – and a miniature of Shelley too! Oh, you are so kind ... as all the people here in Rome seem to be."

"But not the *weather*," Amelia Curran warned; her eyes looking with concern at William, who appeared to her to be a rather delicate little boy.

"You should know that the heat of a Roman summer can be very harsh on small children."

"We will confine William to the shade then," Mary said, and was surprised to see Miss Curran shaking her head in reply.

"I would do more than that. I would advise you to move out of the city immediately, or at the latest, before July arrives, when there is often a spread amongst children of Roman fever. Adults too. That is why so many Italians leave Rome in the summer and go to
~~~

places such as Tuscany until the weather cools.

Mary and Shelley looked at each other with dismay, and then at Miss Curran. "But we are so content here in Rome," Shelley said, "so it would be hard for us to leave here now – and for where?"

Mary could not think of anywhere else she would rather be, and dropped her miniature of William into the knitted reticule hanging from a cord on her wrist, somewhat annoyed with Miss Curran for spoiling her delight in receiving the picture.

"We will be very careful with William," she said quietly, and promptly turned to leave, stepping out to the street and looking up at the bright sunshine, wishing Miss Curran had not placed an imaginary black cloud into her mind.

She was even less pleased when she and William walked through the Borghese Gardens and saw Claire talking to a group of Englishwomen. Mary knew they were English straight away, not only from their heavy dresses in the Italian summer heat, but also from their manner which was hand-wavingly pompous and high-nosed.

They *never* engaged with the English, not under any circumstances, yet here was Claire conversing with them without reserve.

As she drew closer Mary could hear Claire's voice, filled with resentment, telling the women that "Yes, she *did* know Lord Byron. She knew him very well!" And went on to complain of his awful treatment of her in the matter of their child, Allegra. "Even my letters to him simply *inquiring* about my child have to be made through Shelley."

"Why, he sounds like an absolute *brute!*"

Mary angrily pulled Claire away and marched her on. "You *know* we always avoid the English visitors," Mary fumed. "Now you have given them a nice piece of tittle-tattle to take back to England."

Claire, wide-eyed, protested her innocence. "What else was I to do? When they spoke to me and found I was English, the first question they asked me was if I knew Lord Byron, and well ... I got rather carried away."

"And unfairly so – because you know Albé gave you every opportunity to keep Allegra, and even supported her financially, but *you* kept insisting she would be better off with him, and *foisted* Allegra onto him so you could stride out and make a new life on your own – something you have still not yet done."

"Why are you so angry?" Claire demanded. "What does it matter what a few silly Englishwomen say back in England? Even Albé delights in scandalising them for fun."

"*You* were not speaking in fun. You were feeding tasty morsels of vengeful gossip to vultures. And you know what some of the English are like – they assume ridiculous pretensions here abroad which they would never dare to use in their own country."

"Why are you being so *overemotional* in your anger?" Claire demanded again. "All I said –"

"Was not dissimilar to what the English have said about my Shelley. That he's a pagan and a brute and an atheist sinner of all sorts of crimes. You should be ashamed of yourself for joining in their charades, Claire, thoroughly ashamed."

The two stepsisters walked on in sullen silence while William skipped on ahead.

Minutes later, Mary said more calmly, "This place is like Geneva, full of English, rich, self-important and foolish. I am sick of them."

Yet Mary did not wish to leave Rome; and later that evening, when discussing it with Shelley, he did not want to leave Rome either.

"But what of this Roman fever?" Mary asked anxiously. "William is so very delicate, and Miss Curran said –"

"Miss Curran is a spinster in her forties, and what do old spinsters do most of the time? Worry about the awful effects of the *weather*, in rain, sunshine, or snow."

"But still ..."

"But still," Shelley agreed, "when it comes to Will, we should take care and be cautious."

A week later they moved out of their lodgings at the Palazzo Verospi, and took up residence in a house just above Rome's Spanish Steps; which was higher and airier, and which Miss Curran approved of, saying it was a far healthier location than the crowded Corso.

Amelia smiled. "It is also full of artists, painters and poets, so you will have some interesting neighbours."

~~~

Seven days after receiving Lord Byron's request, Richard Edgecumbe, a clerk from the British Consulate, arrived in Ravenna with Allegra and a motherly-type nursemaid in her forties.

Byron had not expected Allegra to arrive so soon, yet as soon as he saw her and she reached out to him, he lifted her and took her off to his own apartment to play.

The owner of the hotel beamed pure sunshine when Byron told him he would need three more rooms – two rooms to accommodate his daughter and her nursemaid, and the third for Mr Edgecumbe.

"I can stay for only a day or so," Edgecumbe said regretfully. "Mr Hoppner has instructed me to go straight back to Venice."

"He *would* say that," Byron replied. "Yet if it was he who had come to Ravenna, he would insist that he needed at least a week to recover from the journey. You stay as long as you need, Mr Edgecumbe, and allow *me* to deal with Hoppner.

Edgecumbe smiled. "Thank you, my lord. I must confess, I *am* rather tired."

The following afternoon Byron took Allegra with him to the Palazzo Guiccioli and introduced her to Teresa who instantly loved the child. But the one who played with her the most was Teresa's father, Count Gamba, who pretended to chase Allegra over the lawns while the
~~~

gardens echoed with the two-year-old's screams of delight.

Byron was astounded to see Count Gamba play with the child in such a fun-loving way, and said so to Teresa.

"Your father surprises me."

Teresa smiled. "He is Italian. All Italians love children ... but my Papa, when you get to know him more, you will learn that he is an adorable man with a very kind and loving heart. His only hatred is for the enemies of Italy."

That evening, when they had returned to the hotel, and Allegra was sprawled in her cot in exhausted sleep, Byron wrote a letter about his daughter to his sister, Augusta:

She is very pretty, amiable, remarkably intelligent, and a great favourite with every body. She has blue eyes, dark hair, and a devil of a spirit, but that last is Papa's. She is a true Byron – and like you, Augusta, she cannot pronounce her 'r's. She is English, but can speak only Italian, and keeps telling me I am "Buon Papà" – although I don't think I am a good Papa, but perhaps I will improve.

~ ~ ~

In Rome, Miss Curran's warning had come too late. If only they had left the crowded Corso earlier, William might not be so ill and feverish. Children were so delicate. One had to be so very careful with them.

Mary spent five agonising days tending to her son, sponging him down with cold water, and calling the doctor out three times in one day. But it was all in vain.

William died in Rome, and there he was buried in the

Protestant Cemetery.

Once again Mary was like a stone statue, but this time she was blaming herself. Was not every bad thing that had happened, her fault? Even her own mother had died giving birth to *her*. Had not Shelley's first wife Harriet committed suicide because Mary Godwin had run away with her husband? Had not her sister Fanny committed suicide because she, her sister, had left her behind and neglected her? *Nemesis* was repaying her in full retribution for all her selfishness –and now she had not one child left to her ... And then she remembered the child growing in her womb. Would that child die too?

Beside the small grave in the cemetery in Rome, Shelley was torn with grief, while Claire stood nearby and watched him.

Unaware of her presence, and although blinded by his tears, Shelley pulled out his notebook and began writing a poem:

My lost William, thou in whom

Some bright spirit lived, and did

That decaying robe consume

Which its lustre faintly hid, –

Here its ashes found a tomb,

But beneath this pyramid

Thou art not – if a thing divine

Like thee can die, thy funeral shrine

Is thy mother's grief and mine.

Now Mary could not bear to stay in Rome, not where her little son lay in a grave. She preferred to see him as he was, alive and well in the miniature portrait of him painted by Miss Curran; a miniature which she now held in her hand, night and day.

Now all she wanted was to see her mother's kind

friend, Maria Gisborne.

Shelley made no protest, wishing only to please and console her; and so they left Rome and travelled up to the Gisbornes home in Livorno.

Chapter Twenty-Seven

~ ~ ~

One evening as Byron was about to leave the Palazzo Guiccioli, the Count appeared from nowhere and sought to detain him, his attitude as suave as always.

"Mylord, before you leave, you will oblige me by joining me in a pre-dinner glass of wine?"

Byron hesitated. "I was hoping to get back to the hotel in time to see my daughter before she is put to bed."

"It is a good wine, from my own vineyards, from last year's harvest of the white grape. I would like you to taste it, if only for you to compare it later with the wine that will come from the new harvest of white grapes in September."

Byron paused for only a few seconds before nodding impassively. "Not that I'm a expert on Italian wine."

"No? So what wine do you usually drink?"

"French."

"Even in Italy?"

Byron shrugged. "I'm a man of habit and tradition. And in wine, my tradition has always been French."

"Well, then, let us see if we can improve your taste? To us, there is no better wine than Italian wine."

Inside the Count's dining room, he gestured for his guest to be seated; brought the wine and two glasses to the table, and slowly filled the glasses.

"Let me say, Mylord, I regard you now as my friend also. It was very kind of you to come here to Ravenna to help my wife."

"How could I not, when it was you, her husband, who wrote and asked me to come."

"Still, it was kind. I believe you are a kind young man."

"Not always. Like everyone, I have two sides to my nature."

"Two sides? Is the other side not so charming?"

Byron lowered his eyes and looked at his glass of white wine. This flattery sounded like an attempt at some kind of seduction ... his memory suddenly recalled Ali Pasha, the ruler of Albania.

He raised his eyes and looked at Guiccioli. "I'm no fool."

Guiccioli's smile was almost a leer. "That is good to know, because who would be interested in conversation with an unintelligent man?"

"Ah yes, conversation – you wish my opinion of your wine?"

Byron took a sip, tasted it, swallowed, and then nodded his approval. "Almost as good as the French."

Guiccioli laughed, and sat down. "Now you are teasing me! Do you believe Italians have been making wine for over a thousand years?"

"I do believe, because you have the natural climate for it – so much sunshine on the grapes."

"And our grapes grow on the vine, not tied to a trellis as you often see in France."

"Have you been to France?"

"No, but I have been told."

Guiccioli took a drink of his own wine, and his face became grave "I have something to ask you. Do you think Teresa is fully recovered?"

Byron was thoughtful: if he said yes, Guiccioli would suggest he could now leave Ravenna. If he said no ...

"No. She is still a little weak."

Guiccioli nodded. "So I have observed, and still so pale, but in another few days or so, she will be fully recovered I think. Do you agree?"

Byron was not sure how to answer. "I am not a doctor, so how can I say?"

"Teresa says not. She says she still gets dizzy spells, but I think they soon will cease."

Guiccioli placed his clasped hands on the table and looked at his guest very seriously. "Sometimes it is hard for me to know how to deal with a very young woman. I am a man who respects the Church, a man of feeling and virtue, but I am so much older than she, and I do not like to be unfair to her."

Surprised, Byron remained silent, wondering what was coming next.

"I am not seeking your advice, just your understanding," Guiccioli said. "So allow me to explain to you my predicament. In a few days time, I must leave for Bologna and Ferrara on business. Very important business, for the health of my bank balance. I will be away for almost a month, maybe longer, and it is essential that Teresa accompanies me."

Byron felt his heart wrench. To be so in love was a terrible thing, especially in this terrible situation.

"But now Teresa tells me that, for the improvement of her health, you have suggested taking her to the lakes of Como and the mountain air, which you think will revive her completely."

Byron was astonished – he had not made any such suggestion – but just the thought of it was wonderful.

"However, that cannot be. One of my meetings in Bologna is with the manager of the Bologna Bank in order to secure a business loan. He has amorous feelings for Teresa, and if she is with me, with her lovely smile, I know he will not refuse."

Byron was shocked that Teresa should be so used. "Nevertheless, to risk her health – "

"But what else can I do? I have just lost a lawsuit with a large concern in Brescia, which requires me to make a payment by a fixed date, and time is pressing. Also, I am going through a fallow period because of this lawsuit, and I have workers to pay. Husbands and fathers who look forward to their payments every week to buy food for their families. I must go to Bologna, and she *must* accompany me ... unless, I can borrow the money from somewhere else."

Byron sat back; his first instinct was right – from the start this had all been an attempt at seduction – for a loan.

"How much would you need to borrow from the bank in Bologna?"

Guiccioli said the amount, but Byron could not calculate it.

"In English," said Guiccioli, "one thousand pounds."

Byron stared at him in amazement. "Such a huge amount?"

"Now you understand why I need to have Teresa with me? Only with her help could I secure such a large loan from the manager at the Bologna Bank, but that is the amount I need."

Byron hesitated, calculating. "And if you did get the loan from somewhere else – I presume you mean from *me* – would that mean you would allow me to take Teresa to the lakes in Como, for the sake of her health?"

"Certainly. But I will not insult you and insult myself by not agreeing to the loan on a firm business basis. I will guarantee you five-per-cent interest until the loan is repaid."

"I would want that in writing."

"Of course. I would not accept it otherwise. But I must impose one other condition ... Teresa must not know about this loan."

Byron nodded his agreement.

Guiccioli nodded his appreciation.

He then refilled the wine glasses. "Now tell me what you truly think of my wine?"

Byron took another sip. "To be honest – bloody awful."

Guiccioli laughed. "You are not being serious, you have a twinkle in your eyes."

"Well, it's fine enough, too sweet for me, but superior to a lot of wines I have tasted."

"As good as the French?"

"No, impossible."

Guiccioli decided to push his luck a little further – business and politics, often intermingled in conversation.

"And *Austrian* wine? What is your opinion of that?"

Byron looked at him with unguarded clarity. "I can have no opinion at all of Austrian wine, as I have never tasted it."

Guiccioli could not resist another bite at the peach. "And the Austrian government that now rules here in Italy. Do you have an opinion on them?"

Byron shrugged. "How could I? They have no relevance to me. I am merely an Englishman in Italy. A stranger in this country. So whoever rules it, is no business of mine."

"That is true." Guiccioli smiled, deciding that Lord Byron was either completely honest and disinterested, or, as he said, no fool ... at least, not when it came to politics.

~~~

The following afternoon, when Byron arrived at the Palazzo Guiccioli to call on Teresa, he was just in time to meet her father, who was leaving.

Count Gamba smiled and embraced him, for they were now good friends.

"Yes, I must return to Filetto and my own family and estate, but I am glad we meet before I go, to say thank you, Mylord Byron, for your friendship to Teresa and bringing your own doctor here to Ravenna to attend to her. That was the turning point in her health, I think."

"Professor Aglietti is an excellent doctor," Byron agreed.

More of the usual pleasantries in farewell, until Byron headed to the gardens where he found Teresa waiting for him.

"*What* is all this about me taking you to Lake Como?"

Teresa grinned. "I was trying to scheme, and that was all the only scheme I could think of. Do you approve?"

Byron smiled. "Fully."

Teresa glanced around her, and then whispered. "Now we have to find a way to make Alessandro agree."
~~~

Chapter Twenty-Eight

~ ~ ~

Many of the people of the town of Ravenna were surprised and disappointed to be told Lord Byron was now leaving.

Count Alborghetti, Macchiavelli, Mezzofanti, all were disappointed, for the young Inglese Mylord had a mind that was quite brilliant in serious conversation, and very droll and amusing when the talk was not so serious.

Some of the poorest people in the town sent a petition to his hotel, begging him not to leave. Not one had ever stopped him in the street or gone to his hotel to plead assistance and come away empty-handed

Count Francesco Rangone, in particular, was devastated to learn that fresh material for his book was rolling away. Now he would have to rely on the odd mention by his brother Beppe in Venice to learn anything more.

Those standing outside his hotel saw him entering his carriage carrying his small child, and all of his luggage was strapped to the roof and the back. Another carriage containing his servants rolled away behind him. His friend, the young Contessa, was well again, so now there was no more reason for him to stay.

But then others, walking on the main road and seeing his carriage with his crest on the side, followed by the one carrying his servants, saw another carriage following behind that one – the carriage of Count Guiccioli, and *he* was inside – the falcon – as well as his young wife. Were they all going away to some other place together?

Inquiries from tradesmen delivering produce to the Palazzo Guiccioli were able to learn that the Count had gone to Bologna, but Mylord Byron was returning to Venice.

At Bologna, Byron checked in and took some rooms

in a palazzo on the Via Galleria, quite near to the Palazzo Savioli, where the Guicciolis had lodged.

Immediately the Austrian police were on the alert and watching the British Lord. To them he was more than a poet and a Nobleman – he was a famous free-thinker, an ambassador of Liberalism, and a possible danger to the Vatican and the Austrian Government of Italy if he was or became associated with the secret and revolutionary *Carbonari*.

A report was duly written to the Director of Police in Rome:

I do not conceal from Your Excellency that this news of Byron's arrival both perplexes and embarrasses me. Byron is a man of letters, and his literary merits will attract to him the most distinguished men of learning in Bologna. This class of men has no love for the Government.

The *Carbonari* were extremely secret, and yet they already had 40,000 members in Naples alone, and many more thousands all over Italy, all hoping to eventually overthrow the Austrian Government and replace it with an Italian republic.

Unaware of the alarm he was causing, Byron was taking a solitary visit to the beautiful cemetery of Bologna, and talking to the old Custodian of the cemetery who reminded him of the grave-digger in *Hamlet*.

The Custodian had a collection of Capuchins' skulls, all labelled on the forehead, and bringing out one of them, he said – "This was Brother Desiderio Berro, one of my best friends, who died at forty, and one of the merriest fellows I ever knew. Wherever he went he brought joy. If you were melancholy, just the sight of him was enough to make you cheerful again. And here he is, still with me, my best friend."

"That must be a great comfort to you," Byron said, and walked on, away from the skull; but the Custodian walked with him, carrying the skull, saying that he himself had planted all the Cypress trees in the cemetery and he had the greatest attachment to all his trees, and to all his dead people who rested under them.

He insisted on showing some of the older monuments; one of a Roman girl of twenty, dead two centuries ago. "She was a princess – Princess Barberini – and some time ago, on opening her grave, we found her hair complete and as yellow as gold."

Byron was amazed. "Like the hair of Lucretia Borgia!"

"I never met her myself, and I'm sure I did not have the burying of her ... Lucrezia *Borgia* did you say ... do you mean the daughter of the bad Pope?"

Byron's eyes were fixed on an epitaph on one of the stones: –

> "Martini Luigi
> Implora pace."

> "Lucrezia Picini
> Implora eterna quiete."

He looked at the Custodian in wonderment: "Can anything be more full of pathos? Those few words say all that can be said or wished. The dead had had enough of life, all they wanted was rest, and this they *'implore'*. I hope whoever may survive me will see those two words, and no more, put over me – *'Implora pace.'*"

The Custodian nodded, and then smiled. "Although looking at you, Signore, I would say you have a long way to go before your own sun sets. Wait until you reach my age, and then you can truly hope for words like those ... *Implora pace.*"

~~~

Returning to the Palazzo Savioli, Byron called on Teresa and was told that she had gone out somewhere, but as this was the hour she had appointed for him to visit her, he was to be assured that she would be returning very soon. The Contessa had left the keys so that her apartments could be opened for Mylord Byron, and had given instructions that the garden also should be open to him.

Byron asked: "And the Count?"

"He too is out, but on business."

In her sitting-room, instead of standing or sitting in a chair to wait, he opened the door to her garden and descended the few steps and wandered on, until he found himself standing by one of those lush fountains so common in the gardens of Italy, gazing at the gently-falling water in an unconscious state of trance, wondering why he had written such a typically Byronic and buffooning letter to Hobhouse the previous night about Teresa, as if she was some amusing *amica* and nothing more ...

I have my saddle-horses here and there is good riding in the forest which stretches in and out all the way along the Adriatic, which suits me, as I am very fond of riding, but I do detest 'knowing' the road one is to go – like in your Hyde Park.

As for my amica, she is an equestrian too, but is tedious in her rides, for she can't guide her horse and he runs after mine, and tries to bite him, and then she begins screaming in her sky-blue riding habit, and the grooms have the devil's own work to stop her from tumbling, or having her clothes torn
~~~

by the trees and thickets of the pine forest ...

Why had he written about her in that casual and mocking way? Especially as the dear girl had obviously and bravely only *pretended* she could ride so that she could accompany him.

If Fletcher had not already posted the letter – in his damned efficient way – he would snatch it back and tear it up.

He continued wandering, deep in thought, certain he had been flippant about her in the letter for his own protection, because although he had never been so in love, where could this strange liaison go? She was married, and he was married, and so it would have to end somewhere.

He also suspected that Count Guiccioli would try to find a trick to end it right here in Bologna – but not until *after* he had secured the loan.

Turning a path he came across a small table and a chair positioned under a tree. A thick book was lying open on the table, and he knew from the feminine purple velvet cover that the book belonged to Teresa.

What was she reading?

He picked up the book which was in Italian, and memorised the page number before looking at the front cover, and his heart missed a beat – *Corinne*, by Germaine de Staël ... Ah, that dear French lady, Madame De Staël, who had driven him mad in London with all her lectures to him about his wayward behaviour, and yet she had been so kind and welcoming to him to in Switzerland. He was sorry she had died, because now he could never repay her kindness.

What would Madame de Staël say now about his relationship with Teresa?

As in this book of hers here, which he had read more than once, she would insist that he be *honest.*

He sat down on the chair and took a black-lead pencil from his pocket and wrote a note to Teresa on the blank flyleaf at the front of the book.

My dearest Teresa – I have read this book in your garden – my Love – you were absent – It is a favourite book of yours – and the author was a friend of mine. – You will not understand these English words – and 'others' will not understand them – which is why I have not scribbled them in Italian – but you will recognise the handwriting of him who passionately loves you – and you will divine that in a book which was yours – he could only speak of love. In that word, beautiful in all languages, but most so in yours – "Amore mio" – is comprised of my existence here and hereafter. I feel that I exist here in Italy – to what purpose – you will decide. My destiny rests with you – & you are a woman of nineteen years of age, and only two years out of a Convent – I wish that you had stayed there with all my heart – or at least that I had never met you in your married state – but all this is too late – I love you, and you love me – and the last is a great consolation in all events. I have tried, but I cannot cease to love you – Think of me sometimes when the Alps and the Ocean divide us – but they never will, unless you wish it – Byron. August 23rd 1819, Bologna.

~ ~ ~

The following day, less than one hour after visiting the Bologna Bank where a large sum of money had been transferred – an Austrian police spy saw the young Contessa Guiccioli entering Lord Byron's carriage and leaving Bologna with him — just the two of them in one luggage-loaded carriage — followed by another carriage containing a child, her nurse, and one manservant.

A strong-looking Italian bodyguard armed with pistols and sabre rode on a black horse close behind the two carriages.

Information was sought, questions were asked; and then a second report was dutifully written to the Director of Police in Rome:

"Lord Byron departed suddenly with Contessa Guiccioli, who was therefore said to have been either carried off by him, or sold to him by her husband."

Chapter Twenty-Nine

~ ~ ~

The journey of seventy-two miles from Bologna to Padua had been broken only by the occasional stops at inns for refreshment and rest for the horses.

Allegra enjoyed the stops at the inns where she was fussed over and fed by Teresa, who affectionately called her *"Allegrina"* in the Italian way. Allegra's petitions to be allowed to travel the rest of the journey sitting on Teresa's lap, was gently disallowed by Papa.

A wise move, because once her carriage started rolling and rocking again, combined with the summer heat, the child spent most of her time fast asleep with her head on her nurse's lap.

Teresa had no appetite at all, too wound up by her inner excitement. She did her best to keep herself calm and controlled for fear of her joy brimming over, like a cup ready to spill at the least movement.

In the dining room of the inn she had declined all food, accepting only a peach because of its beautiful colour and fragrance, taking it with her into the carriage, and then as the carriage rolled on, sitting quietly and tossing the peach from one hand to another as if at play, her thoughts engrossed in the sensations of the present, the uncertainty of the future, and the strangeness of their current situation.

Seated beside him, she looked at Byron, who silently nodded, as if he knew what she was thinking. Both had earlier agreed that worrying or talking about it might only serve to ruin everything and bring bad luck. All they knew for sure was that the Count had allowed them the space of a month to go to Lake Como for the sake of Teresa's health. A month together. On their own.

Byron smiled. *"Carpe diem,"* he said, *"quam minimum credulo postero."*

Teresa nodded, knowing it was the only way – *"Seize*

the day, trusting tomorrow as little as possible."

On their arrival at Padua, Teresa was astonished by the zealous way the owner of the inn greeted Byron, not merely with a smile of welcome, but with genuine emotion and devotion.

He grabbed Byron's hands and kissed them, and looked as if he would have preferred to welcome him on his knees. And yet, to Teresa, the proprietor of the inn did not look like a man who read poetry, so why was his welcome so out of the ordinary?

Within minutes, a private dining room had been made available to the small party where Fletcher and Tita were glad to be able to sit and stretch their legs and refresh themselves with some good wine – yet all were surprised when two musicians entered the room playing beautiful soft music on their violins – which ceased all of Allegra's chatter and rendered her speechless as she stared up at the musicians.

Teresa was baffled by it all. "Why?" she asked Byron. "Why does he treat you so, as if you were a prince?"

Byron shrugged. "I met him when I first came to Venice with Hobhouse. We stayed overnight and stabled our carriage and horses here. I met him again on my return from Rome. He is a worthy man, and at that time I was able to do him a good turn."

"A good turn? Is that all?"

Byron nodded. "That's all." He was more interested in what they should do next. "It is only fifteen more miles to La Mira. I think we should travel on and end our journey there."

Teresa agreed, if only because Byron's house would be more private than lodging here at the inn. She was worried about the fussing proprietor, and staying here together could lead people to talk.

"Will your house at La Mira be empty?"

"No. I sent a letter from Ravenna by express to Lega Zambelli, telling him I would be returning and to ensure the house at La Mira was stocked and staffed."

More fuss was made by the proprietor, who seemed

to wish to put the best of everything at Byron's disposal – platters of the best beef and pork and rice and vegetables were placed on the table for Fletcher, Tita and Allegra's nurse to tuck into. Plates of special cakes and golden grapes were brought for Allegra. More and more platters came, and the sumptuousness of the fare and the selection of the wines was much more than any small party could eat or drink – and yet nothing had been ordered.

And still Teresa wondered why? She knew it would be useless to press Byron further, for being so English in many ways, *good turns* and things like that were not something he cared to talk about, considering it "bad form" to do so. With Byron it was always a matter of – something done – something forgotten.

Later on, before they left the inn, Teresa's curiosity overcame her when she saw an opportunity of speaking to the proprietor alone and in private.

He responded to her question by shrugging up his shoulders, spreading wide his arms and looking all around him, saying – "Because I owe the thriving of this my inn and all my income to him! I would have been *ruined* and left penniless if he had not arrived that day, saw what happened, and came to my aid."

"What happened?"

"That summer, two summers ago, oh, I still sometimes choke to talk about it ..."

Patiently she listened and learned that there had been a terrible fire and a part of his inn had burned, from bottom to top, some of his bedrooms and his kitchens destroyed; his inn had become uninhabitable.

"I saw myself becoming like a beggar on the streets of Venice, for I had no such big money for all the repairs. Then Mylord Byron came, returning from Rome, and saw me sitting on the bench outside crying. He said very little, only listened. Then he seemed to grow tired listening to me crying, and left me to my tears.

"Two days after, I was outside, still sweeping up some of the black dust and the fallen black pieces of the wooden beams, when the workmen came – builders and carpenters with carts full of planks of all the best wood. The bricks were bought from a yard at Mirano, carts and carts of bricks. And day after day all I could do was to stand and watch as my inn was rebuilt. All paid for by Mylord Byron. He had also paid off the bailiffs who, from the fire, had been making my life an even worse misery."

Teresa was wide-eyed but the innkeeper put a warning finger to his lips. "Mylord is strange, he does not like displays of gratitude. It is his *Inglese* blood and because he is a Noble, *molto* noble."

Byron appeared in a state of exasperation – "Allegra wants to bring the two musicians home with her. What am I to do?"

"Take them, take them!" said the innkeeper with a wave of his hand

Teresa could not help laughing, and went straight to the dining-room to coax Allegra to come home with her instead, and the child finally allowing herself to be lifted up and waving bye-bye to the musicians.

"I have promised her she can sit on my lap for the rest of the journey to La Mira," Teresa said. "She can play hand-to-hand ball with my peach."

Byron laughed. "And I have a surprise waiting for you at La Mira."

"A surprise?"

Byron nodded. "It will make you very happy."

Teresa frowned. "I have told you, I will not accept gifts. I am not a courtesan."

"Oh, well, you can send it back if you wish."

It was dark when they arrived at the Villas Foscarini at La Mira, but all the windows were aglow with candlelight.

"Ah, good. Lega has done everything I asked," Byron said. "Now give Allegra to her nurse, otherwise she will be wanting to *sleep* with you."

Stepping down from the carriage Teresa handed

Allegra over to the nurse, then almost jumped with fright when a loud voice thundered through the still night– "*Cara! Mia cara!*"

Turning to the voice Teresa literally *did* jump with delight when she saw who it was – "*Fanny!*"

Fanny Sylvestrini came lumbering down the path waving her hands with excitement. "*Santa Madre!* Oh, my Terasina, *il mia angela*– I did not believe it when Lega said you were coming!"

After much hugging and kisses on cheeks, Teresa turned to look at Byron. "Is this my surprise? Fanny here as my maid?"

Byron shrugged. "Unless you wish to send her back."

PART EIGHT

Outrage

*"You are right – Gifford is right – Hobhouse is right.
You are all right – and I am all wrong – but do pray let
me have that pleasure. Cut me up root and branch.
Quarter me in the Quarterly – Make me, if you will, a
spectacle to men and angels – but don't ask me to alter
– for I can't – I am obstinate – and that's the truth.*

*Circumstances in the past may have placed me at
times in a situation to lead public opinion – but the
public opinion – never led nor never shall lead me."*

Lord Byron to John Murray, 1819

Chapter Thirty

~ ~ ~

The days that followed in the house and fragrant gardens at La Mira were all Italian days – all sunshine and laughter, followed by nights of serenity and splendour.

To Teresa it was all so new – to love and to know that she too was loved – while Byron felt the return of all the romance of his youthful days with something of its first freshness flowing once more. He again knew what it was to truly love and be loved in the same way – too late, it is true, for total happiness, and too wrongly for complete peace.

Fanny Sylvestrini was continually in raptures of happy laughter during the days of sunshine, for not only was she being paid by the Count to look after his house in Venice, she was also being paid by Mylord to attend here at La Mira. Yet her happiness was not all about the money, but the fun she enjoyed with her two young friends who were rarely ever serious together; at least, not in daylight.

"You must stop naming me as Fanny," she instructed Mylord, "and call me in its place – Madame Lega."

"Why?" And then he stared - "What? You and Lega Zambelli?"

Fanny pouted her lips and fluttered her eyes coquettishly, "No, but if the good Saint Jude, he who answers prayers for things the world think *impossibile,* then soon – soon I will be Madame Lega, I will, eh."

Teresa and Byron both kept a straight face until she had wandered off back inside the house, and then they laughed.

"Lega?" Byron said. "Of all people, Lega Zambelli! A former priest. She will never catch him."

Teresa was still amused. "She says her love is divided between Lega and Tita. She is not sure which one she likes best."

"Tita also? Lord preserve us! Tita likes his women young."

"Fanny is not old, only forty."

"Too old for Tita."

They were not laughing the next afternoon when Fanny returned to La Mira, after taking a gondola over to Venice to check on the Count's house.

Breathless and alarmed, Fanny rushed up to them in the garden. "In Venice, I saw Lega. He ordered me to tell you, Mylord ..."

Fanny flopped into a chair, flicked open the fan hanging from her wrist, and began to fan herself rapidly.

"Tell me what?" Byron asked.

Fanny stopped fanning. "The Count. He thinks Lega is still working for him. Lega is most distressed and bids me to tell you that he has received a letter from Count Guiccioli asking him to spy on you and Terasina, and to write back frequently telling all he knows."

Byron frowned. "But Lega knows nothing."

"Nothing? Oh, Mylord, if you knew – " Fanny's fan began waving rapidly again. "I told Lega it was all lies, and Lega said he knew that was so."

"Knew *what* was so?"

Fanny stared at him with her big brown eyes. "It is all over Venice! They say even the British Consul man is very angry with you."

Byron held onto his patience. "Why?"

"I don't know – how can it be – they are all saying you *abducted* Terasina in Bologna and carried her off in your carriage."

"Abducted? What rot. And Hoppner believes that? The British Consul?"

Fanny nodded. "Lega says I must warn you not to trust *him*, the British Consul. Lega says to tell you he is the Devil in disguise, and his sweet Swiss wife is really a snake in the grass. She told all of Venice about Allegrina's mother coming to Venice with Mr Shelley, and so did he, the Consul."

Byron was frowning, puzzled. "Claire came to Venice with Shelley, and went to the Hoppners? No, that is impossible."

"So how can it be – this rumour that you *stole* Terasina?"

Teresa finally spoke, in a firm way. "I have noticed that when people gossip, it is usually only to make themselves appear more interesting. But *we* know that Count Guiccioli gave his permission for me to come here with Lord Byron, so let them talk. We don't care what the people of Venice say."

"They say it was *you* who first stole *him* from Venice, making him go to Ravenna, and they do not like you."

Byron turned up his eyes, and took hold of Teresa's hand. "That is not true, they do like you. But we will keep to ourselves, and stay away from Venice."

Fanny nodded. "And I told Lega the truth, because I know he hates to lie – I told him Terasina lives in one wing of the house with me, and Mylord lives in another wing writing his poetry and ne'er do we see him, apart from in the gardens in the afternoon."

Byron gave her one of his incredulous under-looks. "And Lega believed you?"

Fanny nodded, enjoying her role in this conspiracy with gusto. "I told Lega to write to l'Conte saying the sweet air here at La Mira is doing wonders for Teresina's health, and I recommend she be allowed to stay here for as long as possible."

In the following weeks the days continued happy and hot, the nights mild and cool. Today, though, it was so hot that all Teresa wanted to do was to strip off completely and lie under a cool sheet in her shaded bedroom.

Later, in her bed, covered by a cool sheet, her eyes beginning to droop, she felt so delirious in her love that she had began to believe she was living in a world full of fairy-tale colours. These past weeks, these past days –

these were the days that make us thankful to God for the gift of life ...

Some hours later when she awoke, and dressed, and went to find Byron, she met him coming in the front door, a bemused smile on his face.

"I've just had an odd visit," he told her, "you'll never guess from whom – Marina Benzoni and Count Rangone. When they came in they had an embarrassed and comical look about them. They seemed to be wondering whether I deserved their blame or protection."

"Did they come out of curiosity?"

"No, kindness, I think. They were worried about all the gossip in Venice about you, but I assured them you had come at the behest of the Count, for you to consult Professor Aglietti again regarding your health."

"Did that satisfy them?"

"No, it only half-satisfied them, saying how anxious they were about *me,* because of the Count's character. They said in Venice he was considered to be a vain and jealous man, capable of any deed, and he was so *wily* that Vincenzo Monti the poet had written a few lines about him. Byron repeated the lines –

> "That sly nobleman of Ravenna,
> So expert in tricks that Brunello
> Compared to him would be –"

"In Italian, please? Teresa said.

> "Quel sottile Ravengna patrizio
> Si di frodi perito che Brunello
> Saria con esso un Mummeo od un Fabrizio."

He looked at her curiously. "Have you heard it before?"

"No, but it is all true. I suppose no one in Venice can understand *why* the Count allowed me to come away with you. And, in truth, nor can I."

Byron knew the reason why – the provision of a large

loan – but he could not let Teresa nor anyone else know that.

"Do you still wish to go to the lakes at Como?"

"No, I am happy here." She smiled. "Let us spend no more time in travelling. Let us stay here at La Mira in our own beautiful world and be happy."

But for how long? Byron wondered.

Yet happy they were. When they were not lovemaking or laughing, they strolled along the banks of the River Brenta; and rode their horses – at a frustratingly slow pace for Byron – who eventually persuaded Teresa to take up music instead; sending for a piano to be delivered from Venice; and then surprised to discover she was a very good pianist. Her music tinkled throughout the house as he dismissed his usual rapid scrawl and wrote out in a neat hand, the first stanzas of *Don Juan*.

I want a hero: an uncommon want,

When every year and month sends forth a new one,

Till, after cloying the gazettes with cant,

The age discovers he is not the true one;

Of such as these I should not care to vaunt,

I'll therefore take our ancient friend, Don Juan.

We all have seen him in the pantomime

Sent to the devil, somewhat before his time.

Chapter Thirty-One

~~~

Journeying back and forth across the lagoon to Venice, Fanny Sylvestrini was given the task of carrying letters to and fro; and she did so dutifully, even to opening and reading the Count's letters to Lega and Teresa; and letters from Teresa to the Count; before resealing them again.

Fanny was enjoying her new intimate position at La Mira. She found Mylord Byron so much easier to get along with than the Count – even to arguing with him when he dismissed Ippolito.

"The poor young man, is he then to be ruined? He is so timid, discouraged, and what other work can he do? You, have a good heart, Mylord, a kind heart, so can you refuse to listen to his supplications?"

Rather than listen to Fanny, Byron decided it was easier to just reinstate Ippolito.

Power overwhelms simple minds, and Fanny was so overwhelmed by her new-found power, she chastised Teresa on the confusion of her letters, unwittingly giving away the fact that she had opened and read them – "It will not be easy for the Count to understand your letters – not easy for anyone. Why do you write in such a way that no one can understand what you mean?"

If Teresa had not been so pre-occupied reading another letter – one which Fanny had *not* opened because it was from Teresa's father and therefore of no interest – Teresa might have picked up on the realisation that her maid was reading her private letters. But now she was too shaken by the stern letter from her father who had only now found out that she was no longer in Ravenna but in Venice, at the home of Lord Byron; without the escort of her husband.

"You have only just entered society, and that society
~~~

will not make the least allowance for either your youth, or the innocence of your heart, or the lawfulness of your journey, or any of the circumstances that may justify your present situation. An extremely attractive young man is with you and protecting you, no doubt in a straightforward way. That may be enough to convince me and your husband, as well as your own consciences. But the world at large will not be satisfied with those reasons. The retired life you are leading with Mylord will only provide more weapons still for people to invent things to say about your position.

She quickly hid the letter in a drawer to ensure that Byron would not see it. If he did, and knowing how much he respected her father, he could suggest that it might be wise for her to return to Ravenna. And how could she do that? Return to the dreary Guiccioli household and leave her earthly paradise here at La Mira?

Instead, she hastily wrote a reply to her father, insisting that Count Guiccioli had allowed her to come to Venice with Lord Byron, for the sake of her delicate health, to see Professor Aglietti again, and she was now convalescing under the care and ministrations of her chaperone, Fanny Sylvestrini, who stayed by her side night and day.

She slipped the letter to Fanny and whispered, "I want you to go back to Venice without delay and send this by courier, *post express*."

Returning to her room, the next letter she opened was from her husband, and not so easy to answer. He demanded to know why she had not written to him, and why she was not at the lakes at Como, as arranged with Lord Byron.

She *had* written to him, once, a very short and hasty note; but now, too frightened of him to excite his wrath, she would have to write again to explain why she was not at Como. It was hard to lie, but lie she must if she wanted to prolong her stay here.

My dear Alessandro: — I had written two long letters, meaning to send them by the last two couriers, but I have always been too late in sending them to the post. You will see from the address that I am not at Venice, but at La Mira, where I have come by Professor Aglietti's advice as he does not advise me to do more travelling. Byron, who overwhelms me with kindness, greets you cordially. I will write to you at greater length, but at this moment I am dropping from sleep. — Teresa.

She rushed downstairs to see if Fanny had already left, and found her still dawdling in the garden, attempting to flirt with Tita Falcieri.

"Fanny, I have a second letter for you to take to Venice for post express. Now go, at once, or you will miss the courier."

"Do I go in Mylord's gondola?"

"Yes."

Fanny smiled lustily at Tita. "Then I will need Mylord's gondolier to take me."

"No!" Tita cried in fright. "*I* cannot take you without Mylord's permission. You must ask Ippolito."

"Ippolito? That little worm of a man? Why would I want him to take me, eh?"

"Because I am Mylord's *bodyguard*. I go only where he goes – and I row only for him."

"That is true, so you must go with Ippolito," Teresa said anxiously. "Now go, Fanny – find Ippolito and *go!*"

Fanny shrugged, knowing she had failed again to entice Tita into her loving web; but no matter – there was always tomorrow.

She turned and walked away, causing Tita to glance up to the sky and make the sign of the Cross over himself in gratitude – until Fanny's singing voice rose into the air like an out-of-tune soprano – *"C'è sempre domani...!"*

There's always tomorrow.

A few days later, Teresa received another distressing letter, this time from her brother Pietro, at University in Rome.

My dearest sister, so it is true that a young English poet and lord called Byron has found his way into your heart. What I hear about him here in Rome, leaves me on tenterhooks about the consequences this relationship may have for you. You are young, your experience of life is so limited, and his personal attractions, by all accounts, are so superior to most men, that I shudder for your peace of mind. I think that I can see into your heart, my dear sister, but as your brother I want to be your protector as well, and show you the reefs encircling your magic palace.

Well, that man whom you described in your last letter as an angel on earth, let me tell you that he is married to a young woman full of innocence and with her heart in the right place, just like you, but not content with having thrown her over to indulge in a life of debauchery, he kept her secluded in a castle, and tales fraught with dark secrets are told of the goings-on in that castle. It is even said that notwithstanding his rank, he played the corsair during his voyages in the Levant. It therefore seems to me, my dear sister, that before you grow intimate with a man of such dubious reputation, you must weigh things up very carefully, and that is what I beg you to do.

She showed the letter to Byron, and saw real hurt in his eyes as he read it. "So their slanders have followed me as far as Rome ..."

"Is it true?"

"No, I have never owned a castle, nor been a pirate, nor –" He waved his hand in a gesture of hopelessness, and walked away.

Teresa realised that the men in her family were not giving her enough credit for her growing maturity or her own intelligence. And to pursue Byron further about all this would be wrong. Now was not the time, for there was a limit to what any man could take when the world set their hate against the handsome, the successful. And what had he done so wrong? It was not *he* who had ended his marriage! And yet it was that same ended marriage that had turned all the world against him.

Now her only emotion was anger – anger at the world and anger at her brother – but she kept her composure as she wrote back to Pietro, and with her brother she was not afraid to be honest.

My dear brother – so why shouldn't I love such a

friend? The feelings that I pledged to him are stronger than all reasonings, and, in loving Byron as I do, I do not think I am transgressing against God's holy laws. In marrying me off to the Count without love, to a man forty years older than me, was a transgression of God's holy laws. Not even for Italia was it worth it.

You ask me to give up Byron – but why? Would it be for the Count's sake? But it is by his wish I am here. Would it be because of what the world will say? But as for the world, I fancy that I have already sized it up in its injustice.

Is it for fear that the world may find a chance here of satisfying its malice? But from what little I have known of it, it seems not to even require appearances before breaking out into spitefulness. And what would that world give me in return? To compensate for the sacrifice I would make to it of this friendly hand that guides me – which is to be the beacon of my life. Do you ask it of me in the name of my happiness? But where else could I find happiness in the future without him? If I never saw him again, no sun would be left in the sky for me.

As for the gossip broadcast by his adversaries and jealous people in Rome, I beg you to deem them as nothing but fables. Keeping a guiltless young spouse shut up in a castle – as if in the ancient age of Dante! Is it feasible these days? And where? In England – in the land of laws and freedom? And the same goes for living the life of a pirate – it is preposterous. Yet even if you let these accusations go by with a scornful smile, because they are so ridiculous, and if you mean that all these slanders and scandal-mongering mean that Lord Byron ill-treated or was nasty to his wife – well, I do not believe it – because I have seen proofs all the time of his extreme kindness of heart, because the suffering of people makes him almost ill; because the fear of killing an ant impels him to step aside – and because he never wants to make a show of his compassion, (and I think him at fault) he prefers to feign a kind of cold indifference.

Dear Pietro, it is certain that all you have written to me about him is unfounded. As for the causes of his separation, I will find them out and will notify you of them. In this exchange you must report to me the names of your informants, and in this way we shall instruct each other.

Teresa finished the letter and signed it. In her hand she was still holding the cruel letter from Rome. The turmoil in her heart was now so strong, tears were running down her cheeks.

She lifted her head and saw Byron standing in front of her, gazing at her. "Why are you crying?"

She covered the letter with her hand to screen it

from his view. He noticed and said, "Is it the letter from your brother that has you so upset?"

She nodded. "I have tried to make him wise, and give me the names of his informants."

"Oh, that is pointless, because I know something that neither you nor he knows. Wherever I go in Italy, all these tales about me are spread by the Austrian police."

"The Austrian police? How do you know?"

He shrugged. "Because they report on me, and others report on them. I am told I am being watched, and regular reports about me are sent to Rome."

She stood up in fright, but all the vexing letters, all the struggles within her heart and mind, had exhausted her strength and she almost collapsed. She grabbed his arm and he moved her over to the bed and covered her with the coverlet.

"Enough – just close your eyes and rest now. You are not as fully recovered as you think."

She felt as if she had been banged on the head, and drifted off into a fuzzy exhaustion.

Minutes later she was awake again, and he was still watching her.

"*Mio Byron* ... tell me the truth, are you Carbonaro?"

"The truth? Well, if wishing for Italy to be free of the Austrians, and the Italians united, if that makes me a Carbonaro, then yes."

"No!" she sat up. "That is not enough. Are you one of the *Carbonari?* Did you join and swear their oath of allegiance?"

He looked at her archly. "You seem to know a lot about them."

"Which lodge swore you in? Venice? Or somewhere else?"

"Teresa, I have no idea what you are talking about."

"So why do the Austrian police watch and report on you?"

"Because I am a *foreigner,* why else? They know

their rule of Italy is not legitimate, so they distrust everybody. But all these questions are beyond me. You are working yourself into a state about nothing, so I will leave you to rest."

As Byron opened the door she said: "Do you, too, hate the Austrians?"

He stood with his hand on the latch and looked back at her. "Not as much as they deserve."

~~~

In Rome, the Director of Police was evaluating the situation. So much of the information received from the spies was unreliable, and yet he was forced to make sense of it.

The Austrians had many spies. So did the Carbonari. Each slithered around each other, and some disappeared without warning. If it was an Austrian spy that vanished, Rome knew the Carbonari had killed him. If it was a Carbonari spy that disappeared, he usually ended up in prison to suffer torture.

Some of the Austrian's best spies were in Milan. They had not managed to infiltrate the Carbonari there, but they had gleaned enough information about Lord Byron to suspect he was one of them.

Byron's main contact was Ludovico di Brême, a former almoner to Napoleon, who had met Lord Byron at the château of Madame Germaine de Staël at Coppet in Switzerland. There the first sympathies between Byron and the Carbonari must have been initiated.

As soon as Lord Byron and his friend, a Mr John Cam Hobhouse, had arrived in Milan, they were greeted by Ludovico di Brême and taken to his home, where the two Englishmen met other literary and liberal people such as Vincenzo Monti and Sylvia Pellico, known Carbonaros, as well as the Frenchman, Henri Beyle, who now called himself 'Stendhal'. The last was a man with two sides to his face and none of the Italians trusted him. He sat with them in the Opera box but he
~~~

was rarely allowed into Di Brême's palatial mansion. The Carbonari did not trust him, but they pretended to do so, and used him.

Mr John Cam Hobhouse – another Englishman who had idolised Napoleon, even to writing a book about Napoleon's last *"One Hundred Days"* after his escape from Elba and return to France before his defeat at Waterloo – he, too, had been at Lord Byron's side throughout their full three weeks in Milan. It was reported that *he* – Hobhouse – did not believe that Stendhal could be trusted.

And now the difficulty with spies – Italian spies – who could trust *them*? Some were poor, and gave information solely for the payment of money, and so would tell any lie to mislead and confuse, and claim it to be true.

Some of their own Austrian police spies were even worse, especially those in Venice and Ravenna – men who had proved to be stupid with little initiative of their own; and now these fools were so awed by Byron's fame and because he was an English lord and nobleman, most did not dare to go too close to him.

Only in Milan were the spies worth their pay. In Milan, it was reported, Lord Byron was sworn into allegiance with the Carbonari in a secret ceremony at Ludovico di Brême's mansion, as was his friend, Mr Hobhouse. Both claimed their ultimate political aims and sympathies were for the freedom of all oppressed nations and their people.

Was the report true? Nothing Byron had done in Venice appeared to have anything to do with the Carbonari. But who were the Carbonari in Venice? Not one could be found. If there was a lodge there, it was a tight camp of careful and clever conspirators.

There had been a rumour that a possible lodge existed at the inn at Padua, a meeting-place for the Veneto branch of the Carbonari. The proprietor of the inn was said to be a suspected Carbonaro. The inn had been set on fire to destroy it. Only half of it burned before the fire was extinguished. Lord Byron had immediately paid for the inn to be rebuilt using suspected Carbonari workmen.

Suspected, *suspected* – always that word "*suspected*" – but never proved, never certain. If one was to believe all the reports of the spies, then every man in Venice was a Carbonaro. Some reports even said that Byron had now been raised to the level of a *Capo* of the Veneto region – or did the spies just confuse that with his English rank of being a lord?

So, the questions and the problem of Lord Byron remained unsolved – and difficult. Britain was an ally of the Austrians, and Lord Byron was a Peer of the Realm of the United Kingdom. To harm him or imprison him would cause outrage in England and bring the entire British Opposition Party out in fury. He had been one of them in the Palace of Parliament – one of the British Opposition – he had fought for the rights of the poor, and civil equality for the Catholics, Negroes and Jews. A dangerous man, but also a man protected by half of the politicians and nobles of England.

So nothing more could be done at this stage, but to continue the watch and the reports on him, and to discredit him in every way and as much as possible.

Chapter Thirty-Two

~ ~ ~

In silence they walked along the banks of the Brenta in the afternoon sun. Teresa carried a parasol, while Byron pulled the brim of his straw hat lower over his brow.

No other mortal was about, for it was the time of siesta, and all the Italian nobles and their families in the villas above the river were as religiously devoted to their sleep in the daily siesta hours as they were to their daily morning Mass.

"So," Byron said, breaking the silence, "did you finish your letter to your brother in Rome?"

Teresa nodded.

"Did you give it to Fanny to post?"

"No, I have not sealed it. I thought you should see what I have said to Pietro, so you can know that *I*, at least, do not lie about you."

She held up her free hand and shook the reticule on her wrist. "It is in here, if you wish to read it."

"Only if you wish it also?"

She took out the letter and handed it to him, and as he slowly walked along the grass he read her words, his face lowered under the shade of his hat so she could not see his reaction.

He handed the letter back. "Well, if *you* understand me and trust me, that's enough for me. Although you have judged me in your letter as if you knew my history."

"I think I do, but all the same, if you think you can trust *me*, then why don't you tell me about your marriage."

"Oh, it's a sad page in a woeful book, full of too many lost illusions, on both sides ... but if you wish, I shall tell you what I know."

She smiled quizzically. "What you know?"

"I know only half of it. The other half is not mine to

tell. And the conclusion is still a mystery."

There was a bench under a group of shady Plane trees, looking down on the river, and they sat in silence for a while, until she urged him to speak.

"It started as all marriages start," he said quietly, "full of expectations, but the truth is that we did not know each other very well, hardly at all; and as it turned out, we were totally incompatible. I had wished, when we first married, to have remained living in the country, at least until my financial embarrassments were over. But as Annabella had lived in the country all her life, she insisted on London, and so London it was. In every way we were ill-matched – I loved to laugh, but she had no sense of humour. I loved the company of friends, but she hated all my friends, in particular, my friend from Cambridge, John Hobhouse, whom she always referred to as my 'evil genius' – *Hobby* – who is all good and has nothing evil about him at all."

"Was she jealous of him?"

"She was jealous of *everybody*. Of my friends, of any female I spoke to, and especially of my sister Augusta, whom I loved dearly. I thought she loved Augusta too, because she appeared to absolutely dote on Augusta throughout the marriage and right up the end – and even at the end, when she left with Ada to visit her parents, she *ordered* Augusta to stay with me in the house in Piccadilly to look after me; so I am still in a quandary as to all she said about poor Augusta later."

"Your sister was poor?"

"No, not poor in that way, but harmless and helpful and always trying to do the best for everybody. Timid. and easily picked on, and surely the most *inoffensive* being in the world."

"Why was she living in your married house?"

"Not at my request – at Annabella's bidding. Augusta lived at Newmarket with her husband and children, but during the seasons when Parliament was in session, she was required to come to London to attend at St James's Palace as a Lady-in-Waiting to the Queen. It was a post she had filled since she was as young as sixteen, and she had her own apartment in the palace when in attendance. But, poor thing, during her hours off, she spent as much time in attendance upon Annabella as she did in the other hours looking after the Queen."

Teresa was intrigued. "Does your sister speak German?"

Byron looked at her. "No. Why?"

"Your queen, she is a German."

"No, you're confusing the Queen with the Princess of Wales, who is not *yet* a queen. Augusta attends upon the *old* queen, the wife of King George the Third, and both monarchs are as batty as each other. It takes a *true* saint like Augusta to do that job."

"Did you not have servants in your married house?

"Of course."

"Then why did your wife need to send for your sister?"

"Because she was pregnant – and so was Augusta pregnant, with her fourth or fifth, I've lost count of her increasing brood, yet Guss would not give up her care of the queen. Annabella, on the other hand, decided she was not fit to do anything other than rest and be waited upon hand and foot by her maid, Annie Rood – *and* my sister Augusta.

"Whenever I got annoyed, she would say to Augusta, 'He's annoyed with you too, my dear Sis. When he's annoyed with one, he's annoyed with both of us.' And in this way she sought to build an alliance between herself and Augusta in any disagreement with me.

"I began to dread all contact with her, although I thought I hid it well, but obviously not. The fault was mine. I have too much of my mother about me to be dictated to. I like freedom from constraint. I hate artificial regulations. My conduct has always been dictated by my own feelings, and Lady Byron was quite the creature of rules.

"She was not allowed to walk, or run, or do anything at all, but what her doctor prescribed. She would not suffer herself to go out when I wished to go. And then that big old house became more and more like a mere ghost-house; I even dreamed of ghosts. It was an existence I could not support.

"But being younger, I did not have the same command of myself as I do now, and sometimes I would lose my temper, and whenever I did, she would just sit there in the drawing-room looking at me primly and silently, which always goaded me and increased my frustration and anger; and then I would say hurtful things, such as wishing I had never married, and despite all her letters when single telling me all she wanted was to bring me happiness, all she had done in her married state was to bring me misery.

"She could not accept it, she saw no flaw in herself at all, so I avoided her and her vanity as much as possible. She later complained that I went in and out and kept to my own part of the house and as long as a month could go by without her seeing me, but that was an exaggeration. Every day I went into her bedroom to see how she was. What else could I do with a woman who had made herself practically bedridden because she was pregnant?

"I occasionally allowed myself to fantasise about leaving her and going to live in Switzerland or Italy, or even back to Greece; anything that might crash the marriage against the rocks. And if she had not been expecting a child, I might have done so."

"And then everything changed when the child came. As soon as she was born, I fell in love with her, my little daughter Ada, and even in those first few minutes of seeing her, and loving her, Annabella accused me of caring more for the child than for her. Which was true, because day after day I could not be kept out of the nursery.

"Ada was ... just over four weeks old when Annabella decided to take her on a visit to her parents in Leicester. It had been agreed, due to my debts, that we should pack up the house in London and move to a cheaper place in the country, so I stayed behind to take care of all that, and told her I would follow her and Ada when it was done. During her journey, from the two inns at which she had stopped for refreshment, she sent me two letters full of love and sending love from Ada

"A few days later I received a letter from her father, demanding a legal separation, on the grounds that I had *dismissed* his daughter from my house. By the holy! I had not a clue what he was talking about."

Teresa had sat in silence listening to the story of his disastrous marriage – of his separation – of all the circumstances that had preceded it – even the honest confession of the wrongs he might have done Lady Byron, wrongs consisting of some angry words provoked by a multitude of annoyances; wrongs in neglecting her because she spent all her time in bed like an invalid. How ridiculous would that behaviour be here in Italy where women felt only joy at the thought of becoming a mother, and carried on living a normal life until the time of the birth drew nearer.

She thought she had heard the worst of it, and said: "Here in Italy, a Catholic country, divorce is not allowed, but many married people apply for legal separations, and *she* was the one who decided it. So why – "

"Hobhouse, who knew her well," Byron said, "was convinced that she knew the marriage would not last, that it would end sooner or later, and decided to get in first and leave me, instead of it being her that was left at a later date. Her pride would never have suffered that."

"Was her own pride everything to her?"

"Everything. She is as proud as Lucifer, but she is also very practical, much more so than I. She knew she would need very strong grounds to be legally allowed to keep the child for herself. In England, the man, being the breadwinner, is always given custody of any children, unless it can be shown that he is either morally or mentally unfit."

Teresa was still somewhat confused. "So why do so

many blame only *you* for the separation, and not her also?"

"And therein lies the mystery. She would not speak about it, insinuating that the reasons were too terrible for words; and yet when urged by both myself and John Hobhouse to come into a Court and state these terrible things openly, she refused."

Teresa's Italian anger was rising as she listened to the behaviour of that proud and selfish woman who had finally risen from her bed to start a war and carry out the cruellest injustice of all, by using her subsequent silence to give the impression she was being delicate and magnanimous by sparing him – a deliberate silence creating the most poisonous weapon that could have been used against him, opening the door to all kinds of suppositions and accusations – and all without her saying a word – how clever, how *devilishly* clever.

So now she knew, and she considered the most terrible injury of all had been done against *him* – by that clever woman's silence which had created the mystery of the separation – a mystery which, since it makes all suppositions possible, was *still* being supposed at by scandal-mongers everywhere, and coming up with their own imagined conclusions and deciding them as facts.

She said quietly, "I will pray that one day Heaven will avenge you."

"Or *Nemesis.*"

"Nemesis?"

"She is the Greek Goddess of Retribution, and I have always had faith in her power, because I see it in action all the time. People usually get their just deserts, eventually, good and bad."

It had been a lengthy and upsetting talk, and now all Teresa wanted to do was get him home to their bedroom at the Villa Foscarini and cover him with kisses and love.

Entering the house, Fletcher handed him a letter. "For you, my lord. Tita brought it over from Lega."

Byron sighed. "Letters, letters, always letters ... and from the seal I know this one is from John Murray."

He read it quickly, and looked at Teresa. "Talk of coincidence – here is Nemesis again, dishing out her retribution. Murray says that Thomas Moore's epic poem, *Lallah Rook*, good as it is, has failed abysmally in America."

"Moore? Is he not one of your friends?"

"Indeed, one my best. But Moore came back from America full of complaints and harsh criticisms about the country and the American people in general – and now his latest epic has failed in America. I told you – everything thrown out on the tide, floats back on a future tide, good and bad."

Chapter Thirty-Three

~ ~ ~

In London, John Hobhouse was in a state of furrowed anxiety, rushing to Scrope Davies's lodgings where they had agreed to have lunch.

"Now look," he said to Scrope, "John Murray wants us to read these stanzas of *Don Juan* and tell him if they are publishable."

Scrope frowned. "Why? Byron never writes anything low or ... *unpublishable*."

"He's done it now, though." Hobhouse sat down as if he had the weight of the world on his shoulders. "Murray thinks he has written an absolute masterpiece of comedy, but it's these early stanzas of *Don Juan* that has Murray in a state. Here, *you* read them, Scrope, and you tell me what *you* think?"

"My pleasure." Scrope wiped his fingers on a napkin and took the manuscript and began to read:

I want a hero: an uncommon want,

When every year and month sends forth a new one,

Till, after cloying the gazettes with cant,

The age discovers he is not the true one;

Of such as these I should not care to vaunt,

I'll therefore take our ancient friend, Don Juan,

We all have seen him in the pantomime

Sent to the devil, somewhat before his time.

Hobhouse watched as Scrope smiled here and there ... but then his eyes opened wide, "Oh, my goodness ... *Donna Inez* ... it's Lady Byron!"

"Exactly," said Hobhouse. "And anyone who knows

her will recognise her instantly – so why has he done it?"

"I don't know," Scrope said, "that is, I don't know why he has done it *now*, but I am not as alarmed as you. His wife has been touting herself around England as this wronged, saint-like person, and all Byron has done is to *agree*, that yes, she is so very saintly, and he really was quite unworthy of her."

"Unworthy, my eye! The woman was a nightmare. The only good thing about her is the name she swags around under – *his* name."

"And she won't change that – ever. That's why she won't agree to a divorce."

"And now John Murray is terrified that her father will come down on his publishing business with a ton of lawsuits."

"Oh, I don't think so," Scrope said impassively. "Old man Milbanke truly believes his daughter is a saint in disguise, sent to this earth to convert Byron away from his wicked ways, and anyone else who comes within the circle of her glowing halo."

"I know that, I know *that*! But think, Scrope, and remember – all the gentlemen of the newspapers know her too, and after reading this, will they not attempt to raise another uproar and *destroy* Byron?"

"Again? You mean destroy him *again?* I thought Lady Byron had already done that with her damned dishonesty and silence. Can you believe that vain woman is still of the belief that he will eventually come back to her – on his knees, and more easy to control."

"Oh, I detest her," Hobby said, sighing heavily, "but that is not the issue here, the issue is Byron. We must protect him."

"Does he *need* our protection? In what way?"

"In this way – at the time of the separation, when all the gossip and furore was going on, he said nothing. *He* truly did keep his silence. But now, in this, he is giving the world a glimpse of the woman he was married to, and in doing so, I think he is opening the gates of Hell again. Jealous poets like Robert Southey and Thomas Campbell will grab the opportunity to lacerate him in every newspaper."

"Oh, surely not. What Byron has written is not so bad, it's just ... typically Byron. And don't forget, this will go around the world, and strangers in other nations will take it at face value and think Byron is simply describing Donna Inez, the mother of the young Juan – not his own wife! Only those who know his wife, will know."

"I'm getting nowhere with you, am I?" Hobhouse said huffily, standing up. "But pray do me a favour, Scrope, read it calmly and sensibly, and when I pop in tomorrow, tell me if we should tell John Murray whether it should be published or not."

Scrope stared. "Is it down to us?"

"I think so, at least, Murray is determined to have our joint opinion."

"What if it's a split vote?"

"Oh, don't ask. Just read it and be honest in your vote." Hobby sighed heavily again. "As if I didn't have enough to worry about without Byron adding to my fears – you know there are rumours brewing of an imminent revolution in this country?"

"Well then go and join it – instead of you and Murray brewing up a storm in a teacup about a harmless piece of poetry. At the beginning here, Byron says he wants a hero – so let that hero be *you,* Hobby, let it be *you* fighting in the revolution."

"You're ribbing me now."

Scrope Davies laughed. "Yes, Hobby, I'm afraid I am. So don't be so damned serious in future. A poem is just a poem, nothing more."

"You think so? Then during their separation, why did Lady Byron submit *Childe Harold's Pilgrimage* as proof of Byron's wickedness?"

"Did she? By God! Is she insane? Childe Harold was a *poem,* not a legal deposition."

"Exactly! So now you understand what we are up

against."

"We?"

"Yes, all of us in Byron's camp and on his side. Can any of us bear to go through that kind of malicious whispering campaign again?"

"Definitely not. So I shall have to read this piece of poetry very carefully."

When Hobby had gone, Scrope threw himself down on the sofa and continued to read the early stanzas of *Don Juan:*

Seville was he born, a pleasant city,

Famous for oranges and women – he

Who has not seen it will be much to pity,

So says the proverb – and I quite agree;

Of all the Spanish towns is none more pretty,

Cadiz, perhaps – but that you soon may see –

Don Juan's parents lived beside the river,

A noble stream, and called the Guadalquiver.

His mother was a learned lady, famed

For every branch of every science known –

In every Christian language ever named,

With virtues equalled by her wit alone.

She made the cleverest people quite ashamed,

And even the good with inward envy groan,

Finding themselves so very much exceeded

In their own way by all the things that she did.

She knew the Latin – that is, 'the Lord's prayer',

And Greek – the alphabet – I'm nearly sure;

She read some French romances here and there,

Although her mode of speaking was not pure;

For native Spanish she had no great care,

At least her conversation was obscure;

Her thoughts were theorems, her words a problem,

As if she deemed that mystery would ennoble 'em.

Some women use their tongues – she looked a lecture,

Each eye a sermon, and her brow a homily –

Scrope Davies could not stop giggling, because knowing
Lady Byron as he did, Byron's description of her was
spot-on.

In short, she was a walking calculation,

Miss Edgeworth's novels stepping from their covers,

Or Mr Trimmer's books on education,

Or 'Coeleb's Wife' set out in search of lovers,

Morality's prim personification,

In which not Envy's self a flaw discovers,

To others let 'female errors fall',

For she had not even one – the worst of all.

Oh! she was perfect past all parallel –

Of any modern saint's comparison;

So far beyond the cunning powers of hell,

Her guardian angel had given up his garrison;

As those of the best time-piece made by Harrison:
In virtues nothing earthly could surpass her,
Save thine 'incomparable oil' Macassar!

Perfect she was, but as perfect is
Insipid in this naughty world of ours.
Where our first parents never learned to kiss
Till they were exiled from their earlier bowers,
Where all was peace, innocence, and bliss,
(I wonder how they got through the twelve hours)
Don Jóse, like a lineal son of Eve
Went plucking various fruit without her leave.

He was a mortal of the careless kind,
With no great love for learning, or the learned,
Who chose to go where'er he had a mind,
And never dreamed his lady was concerned.
The world, as usual, wickedly inclined,
To see a kingdom or a house overturned,
Whispered he had a mistress, some said "two",
But for domestic quarrels "one" will do.

Now Donna Inez had, with all her merit,
A great opinion of her own good qualities;
Neglect, indeed, requires a saint to bear it,
And so, indeed, she was in her moralities;
But then she had a devil of a spirit,

And sometimes mixed up fancies with realities,
And let few opportunities escape,
Of getting her liege lord into a scrape.

She kept a journal, where his faults were noted,
And opened certain trunks of books and letters,
All which might, if occasion served, be quoted;
And then she had all Seville for her abettors,
Besides her good old grandmother (who doted);
The hearers of her case became repeaters,
Then advocates, inquisitors, and judges,
Some for amusement, others for old grudges.

And then this best and meekest woman bore
With such serenity her husband's woes,
Just as the Spartan ladies did of yore,
Who saw their spouses killed, and nobly chose
Never to say a word about them more —
Calmly she heard each calumny that rose
And saw his agonies with such sublimity
That all the world exclaimed, 'What magnanimity!'

Don Jóse and his lady quarrelled – why?
Not any of the many could divine,
Though several thousand people chose to try,
'Twas surely no concern of theirs nor mine;
I loathe that low vice curiosity,

But if there's any ring in which I shine

'Tis in arranging all my friends' affairs

Not having any, of my own, domestic cares.

And so I interfered, and with the best

Intentions, but –

Scrope Davies lowered the manuscript, grinning ... Oh, this was Byron firing back with guns blazing bullets of satire! And now that he had done with the perfectly perfect awful wife – it was all the interfering, scandal-mongers he was now aiming at – Excellent!

Scrope read to the very last word of the unfinished manuscript, for Byron had moved on to other topics, even more satirical, and often very, very funny.

"Well?" said Hobhouse, popping in the next day. "Do you agree with me now, Scrope? Do you agree that publishing *Don Juan* will make a lot of people here in England feel very offended?"

"I think it will make a lot of people feel very *embarrassed*, and quite rightly, too."

Hobhouse stared at him wearily. "Scrope, what are you saying?"

"I'm saying I'm with Byron all the way – *publish* and bedamned to them!"

Chapter Thirty-Four

~ ~ ~

Their month together at La Mira was nearing its end. Teresa would be duty-bound to go back to Ravenna; and now that her health was fine, Byron knew he would have no reasonable excuse to go with her.

And what then? A visit to Ravenna once or twice a year, perhaps, as a *friend* – and how could he maintain that fiction? Looking at her, loving her, sitting with her in her garden while her husband watched from a window?

He wondered if he could persuade her to go away with him and try a new life in some other country – perhaps America?

"How?" asked Teresa, "when I speak only Italian?"

"I could teach you English."

"Do they speak only English in America?"

Her question served only to remind him of how limited the scope of her life had been so far, from a Convent to the house of a husband forty years her senior.

"How do you stand it? Married to a man old enough to be your grandfather? Could you not have refused?"

Teresa lowered her head. "I have told you ... I was educated at Santa Chiara's, trained in the practice of obedience."

"Then well done Santa Chiara's – because I train all my *dogs* in the practice of obedience too."

"There was another reason, but I cannot say."

"Why can't you say?"

"Because my first duty is to my father, and my second duty is to my country, Italia. If you don't know why, then it is something you will not understand."

Byron paused, now thinking he understood, or at least suspected, and decided not to push the subject further.

"You should not have compared me to an obedient dog," she said. "That was unkind."

Byron showed no remorse. "I wish *I* was a dog," he said, "then I could *bite* you viciously on the ankle for allowing yourself to be placed in such a situation."

Teresa smiled humorously. "You would not bite *me.*"

"I would not bite anyone – but I *would* if I was a dog and refused to be trained into obedience."

Teresa's smile faded as she gazed around the perfumed garden of her earthly paradise. "Why do you make it even harder for me? It will be very hard for me to go back to Ravenna now ... to know there will be a time when I will never hear your voice again, or see you physically as a human presence in my life. Even the thought of it is .... beyond bearing."

Byron felt the same. "I truly wish I had never met you in your married state."

"You are married too," she reminded him gloomily. "Separated, but still you are married."

That was true, and Byron could not help thinking that although it seemed impossible now, somehow, perhaps, he could make a better fight for her if *he* was not married also. What if her husband died? He would still not be able to marry Teresa.

Later that afternoon he wrote a brief but serious letter to his sister in London:

Dear Augusta – If you see my Spouse – do pray tell her that I wish to marry again; and as probably she may wish the same, is there no way a divorce can be got in Scotland? without compromising her immaculacy – cannot it be done there by the husband solely?

He had hardly finished this letter when Teresa came into the room, flushed and bright-eyed and smiling excitedly, holding a letter. "From Alessandro – he says I must return at once as he has an important business meeting in Ferrara."

Byron stared. "So why are you looking so happy?"

"Because he says he will not need me as his escort, if you could make him a small loan of a few thousand francs. If so, he will go hunting with his cousin instead, and I can stay for another month."

Byron hid his disgust. To use his wife to borrow money from others was a debasement, and not the behaviour of an honourable man. Yet he could see that Teresa was too excited to have given thought to that ... and she had no knowledge of the previous loan. Her own disinterestedness in the money was beyond question. Although how the Count could give her the impression that a few thousand francs was "a small loan" was dishonest and deceitful.

Teresa was reading the letter again. "He says if you send him a cheque he will cash it in Ravenna and repay you later. Oh, my Byron, just think – another full *month* together!"

After some reflection, Byron decided that even the sacrifice of this sum, for Teresa's happiness as well as his own, was not too high a price to pay.

Fanny Sylvestrini was overjoyed to learn that her double-pay from two employers was to continue. She would soon have a small fortune saved for her old age, if she did not become Madame Lega in the meantime.

Still, her curiosity was uppermost – how did Teresa manage to persuade the Count to allow her to stay longer? They called him the "Falcon" but Fanny knew he was more of a vulture. He did not have a soft feeling in his heart for anyone but himself.

So different to Mylord who had the heart of an angel.

At her window overlooking the Brenta, Fanny watched Teresa strolling slowly on the bank of the river under the evening sun, alongside her beloved Byron. Between them, they were each holding a hand of little Allegrina.

She watched as Byron bent to pick up a small piece

of a broken branch of a tree and throw it for Mutz or Leander to catch. Mutz raced forward as if thinking it was a bone for him, while poor old Leander lolloped behind him.

When the two dogs returned, she saw it was the loser, old Leander, whom Byron petted the most, laughing at Mutz who dropped the small branch from his mouth to growl complaints.

She watched the two lovers walking along as slowly as tortoises while they talked to each other. She loved them both, and feared for them both in the time ahead.

This affair of theirs could not last. It was only a dream, and one day they would wake up and find the other gone. Which one would the Count kill first?

Maybe he would kill only one. One of them killed was all that was needed to break the affair. Would he poison Teresa in her cup? Or would he arrange for Mylord to be knifed on a dark night?

Or maybe the Count was getting tired now in his older years, and so would allow them both to live.

Fanny heaved a trembling sigh. "How will it all end, eh?"

She was about to turn away from the window when a dark shadow caught her eye. She swiftly looked back and saw the two lovers playing with the dogs, while a large hawk flew steadily down towards them on a shaft of sunlight.

Ω

To read the beginning of the final book in the BYRON series – *No Moon At Midnight* – turn the page.

BYRON

No Moon At Midnight

A Biographical Novel

Gretta Curran Browne

SPI
Seanelle Publications Inc.

Prologue

~~~

At his home in Filetto in northern Italy, on this October morning in 1819, Count Ruggero Gamba was surprised to be visited by a priest from Ravenna, Don Gaspare Perelli.

"I have come, Conte, because I think you should know what all Ravenna is saying, what all Venice is saying, and what I cannot believe."

Count Gamba respectfully gestured to an armchair, inviting the priest to sit down, but Don Gaspare declined. "I must return to Ravenna to say Mass at noon. I came only to tell you what they are saying."

"About myself? What can they say about an honourable man such as I?"

"No, Conte, they are saying it about Count Guiccioli, and that is why the young Contessa is no longer in Ravenna."

"Teresa? She is not in Ravenna?" Count Gamba frowned prodigiously. "But she was to return from Venice a month ago. Why has she not returned?"

Don Gaspare lowered his voice to almost a whisper. "They are saying she will never return, because Count Guiccioli has sold her to Mylord Byron for a very large sum of money."

"*Sold* her? That cannot be true!"

Don Gaspare nodded. "I agree. It is hard to believe. Mylord Byron seems too cultivated a young man to enter into such a mercenary bargain. Yet a clerk from the Bologna Bank has confirmed that a large amount of money was transferred to Guiccioli's account."

"How large?"

The priest shrugged. "They are saying one million lira."

"One *million* ... paid to Guiccioli?"
~~~

Count Gamba looked like a man on fire. "Go!" he exclaimed furiously, waving his hand in dismissal. "You have said enough! Go and say your Mass. And while you do so – say a prayer for Alessandro Guiccioli that this should not be true."

Don Gaspare Perelli bowed respectfully, but on leaving the palazzo his face wore a slight smile. Only Ruggero Gamba would dare to confront the detestable Count Guiccioli. And if Guiccioli was guilty of the crime, and Count Gamba decided his daughter must be avenged, Don Gaspare was certain that Guiccioli's punishment would be swift.

Ruggero Gamba may be a Count of rank and have the appearance of a genial and respectable gentlemen, which indeed he was, most of the time; but he was also a Carbonaro.

Too vexed and too anxious to ride the fifteen miles to Ravenna, Count Gamba ordered his carriage and directed his driver to go at full speed.

Inside the carriage he fumed. Why had he arranged for Terasina to marry Guiccioli, a man forty years her senior, and twenty years older than himself – why?

Because Guiccioli was suspected of being a traitor to Italy, in league with the Austrian rulers, and he had wanted to place a trusted spy in Guiccioli's house – his daughter, Teresa.

It was something any good Carbonaro would do, but now he realised – bad for a father to do. And what had he got for it in return? Nothing more than confirmation of what he had already suspected.

In the past year or so of their marriage, all that Teresa had been able to pass on to him was that Guiccioli constantly raged against the Austrian rulers, bellowing for all the household to hear how much he hated them and their government in Rome – protests so loud it was a sure sign that he was one of them, one of their paid spies.

During Napoleon's occupation of Italy, Guiccioli was

known to have been friends with the French; and now he was friends with the Austrians – a man who always went where the smell was sweetest and likely to do him the most good.

And now, it seemed, Guiccioli had focused his greed for money on the young Inglese lord, using Lord Byron's friendship with Teresa to fill his own pockets. But if Guiccioli *had* sold Teresa, he would soon fill his own coffin.

In the garden of his palazzo, Count Guiccioli was enjoying his breakfast on the balcony overlooking the gardens. His table was placed at the side of the long balcony, near to a group of lemon trees below. The citrus fragrance of the lemon trees always awakened him fully, and brought his energy back to life.

He was eating with pleasure, knife and fork in hand, tucking into a plate of roasted chicken strips covered in fried onions, when Count Gamba stepped out to the balcony escorted by a servant.

Guiccioli looked furiously at the servant who had disobeyed his rigid rule – no other person was to be allowed onto the balcony while he was eating his breakfast.

Count Gamba held up his palm. "It is not his fault. I insisted he bring me to you at once."

Guiccioli instantly noticed a certain coolness in Count Gamba's manner, so unlike his usual fake pleasantness whenever they met.

"Ruggero ..." Guiccioli gestured to a vacant chair at the table. "Please join me. Would you like some roasted chicken ... or some coffee?"

"No, nothing, but I will sit."

Count Gamba sat on a chair and then spoke very quietly, for it was normal for servants to be moving about in the gardens below, and they must not hear this.

"Alessandro, do you know what the world is saying about you?"

Alessandro shrugged. "I have always been indifferent

to the opinion of the world."

Count Gamba looked at Guiccioli, his cold blue eyes taking in every detail of Guiccioli's face ... the brown fleshy cheeks, the small eyes the colour of black raisins, but worst of all was the colour of his grey-streaked red hair and the whiskers on his face. Why had he not paid more attention to these features in the past? Was Judas Iscariot not reputed to have had red hair? At least he did so in some of the famous Italian paintings of Christ's *Last Supper* ... Judas the traitor.

"They are saying you have *sold* your wife."

"*Sold?*" Alessandro was so shocked he dropped his knife.

"To the Inglese Mylord."

"I have not *sold* Teresa to anyone. Who has fabricated this slander?"

"Do you deny that Lord Byron paid you a large sum of money before he took Teresa away?"

"Yes, but it was a *loan*. A loan to be repaid with five-per-cent interest."

"Of one million lira?"

"Of one thousand English pounds. I forget how many lira it came to. But it was only a *loan*?"

If it was a loan, Count Gamba was certain Guiccioli had no intention of ever paying it back; which was a shame, because he liked Lord Byron. He was young and handsome and kind, and he treated Teresa like a princess.

"Why did you allow Teresa to go away with him?"

"Because she begged me, and I with my soft heart *indulged* her, due to her ill health! She said Byron had offered to take her to the lakes at Como where the air was pure and her recovery would be hastened. How could I deny such a request?"

"And yet they are both still in Veneto, nowhere near the lakes of Como. At least, they *were* in Veneto a month ago, in his palazzo at La Mira."

"La Mira? Not Venice?"

Count Gamba could not bear to look at Guiccioli for

one more minute. The man had either not troubled himself to find out anything about Teresa since she had gone, or he was hedging in his answers.

"I do not approve of you allowing my daughter, an inexperienced young woman, to go off alone, and still less, with a young man such as Lord Byron. If you do not go at once to bring her back, I will go and fetch her myself."

Guiccioli had no doubt that Ruggero Gamba would do that.

"No, I will go. I will write to her at Venice and inform her to prepare for my arrival. If she is not at Venice, then someone must be carrying my letters to her at La Mira."

"And if you find she is not there, at La Mira or in Venice, but on a ship to England with Lord Byron; then you know, Alessandro, that Italy will no longer be a big enough country for both of us."

Guiccioli was dumbstruck. He knew what the threat meant. He was also fairly certain that Count Gamba was one of the secret society of the *Carbonari,* and if for some reason he personally could not carry out his threat, it would be done by another Carbonaro in his place.

He affected innocence and ignorance. "Ruggero, we are both Italians, born and bred, so I don't understand why you say this?"

"I say it to make you understand that if you have *sold* my daughter to another man, you will be left with only two choices ... a fast-sailing ship down to the coast of Africa and safety, or the alternative route down to the devil."

Thank you

Thank you for reading *'Another Kind Of Light'* the sixth book in the Lord Byron Series. I hope you enjoyed it.

Please be nice and leave a review.

*

I occasionally send out newsletters with details of new releases, or discount offers, or any other news I may have, although not so regularly to be intrusive, so if you wish to sign up to for my newsletters – go to my Website and click on the "Subscribe" Tab.

*

If you would like to follow me on **BookBub** go to:- **www.bookbub.com/profile/gretta-curran-browne** and click on the "*Follow*" button.

Many thanks,

Gretta

www.grettacurranbrowne.com

Also by Gretta Curran Browne

LORD BYRON SERIES

A STRANGE BEGINNING

A STRANGE WORLD

MAD, BAD, AND DELIGHTFUL TO KNOW

A RUNAWAY STAR

A MAN OF NO COUNTRY

ANOTHER KIND OF LIGHT

NO MOON AT MIDNIGHT

***

LIBERTY TRILOGY

TREAD SOFTLY ON MY DREAMS

FIRE ON THE HILL

A WORLD APART

***

MACQUARIE SERIES

BY EASTERN WINDOWS

THE FAR HORIZON

JARVISFIELD

THE WAYWARD SON

***

ALL BECAUSE OF HER
A Novel
(Originally published as GHOSTS IN SUNLIGHT)

RELATIVE STRANGERS
(Tie-in Novel to TV series)

ORDINARY DECENT CRIMINAL
(Novel of Film starring Oscar-winner, Kevin Spacey)